The author of fourteen highly acclaimed works of fiction, Philippe Djian lives in Biarritz, France. BETTY BLUE, the first of his books to be translated into English, was the basis for the award-winning film by Jean-Jacques Beineix.

Howard Buten, an American novelist living in Paris, is the author of BURT.

BETTY BLUE

The Story of a Passion

—◦◦◦—

A Novel by

PHILIPPE DJIAN

Translated from the French by Howard Buten

ABACUS

ABACUS

Originally published in France as *37,2° le matin* by Editions Bernard Barrault
First published in Great Britain by Weidenfeld and Nicolson Ltd 1988
Published by Abacus 1989
Reprinted 1989, 1990 (four times), 1991, 1993, 1994, 1995, 1997,
1998, 2000, 2001, 2003, 2006, 2011, 2012, 2014

A CIP catalogue record for this book
is available from the British Library.

ISBN 978-0-349-10110-1

Printed and bound in Great Britain by
Clays Ltd, Elcograf S.p.A.

Papers used by Abacus are from well-managed forests
and other responsible sources.

MIX
Paper from
responsible sources
FSC
www.fsc.org   FSC® C104740

Abacus
An imprint of
Little, Brown Book Group
100 Victoria Embankment
London EC4Y 0DY

An Hachette UK Company
www.hachette.co.uk

www.littlebrown.co.uk

BETTY BLUE

The Story of a Passion

1

They were predicting storms for the end of the day but the sky stayed blue and the wind died down. I went to take a look in the kitchen—make sure things weren't getting clogged up in the bottom of the pot. Everything was just fine. I went out onto the porch armed with a cold beer and stayed there for a while, my face in the sun. It felt good. It had been a week now that I'd been spending my mornings in the sun, squinting like some happy idiot—a week now since I'd met Betty.

I thanked my lucky stars again and reached for my chaise longue, grinning. I lay down comfortably, like somebody with time on his hands and a beer in his fist. I hadn't slept more than twenty hours all week and Betty had slept less—maybe not at all, who knows? She was always shaking me, always thinking there was something better we should be doing: Hey, you're not going to leave me alone here, she'd say. What do you think you're doing? Wake up! I would open my eyes and smile. Smoke a cigarette. Fuck. Talk. I did my best to keep up with her.

Luckily my job wasn't too tiring. When everything was going well I'd finish work around noon and have the rest of the day to myself. All I had to do was stay around the complex till seven—be available if somebody needed me. When it was nice out you could just find me in my chaise longue. I stayed glued to it for hours. I thought I'd struck a good balance between life and death— found the only intelligent thing to do, when you stop to think about it. Life doesn't have much to offer outside of a few things that aren't for sale. I opened my beer and thought about Betty.

"For God's sake, there you are! I've been looking all over for you!"

I opened my eyes. It was the lady from number three, an eighty-pound blonde with a squeaky voice. Her false eyelashes were twinkling like crazy in the light.

"What's the matter?" I asked.

"How should I know, for God's sake? There's this thing over-flowing in the bathroom. You better come stop it right away! I'll never understand how things like this happen. . . ."

I sat up quickly. I was not amused. Look at this woman for three seconds and you can tell she's nuts. I knew she was going to drive me crazy, too. Her bathrobe was sliding all over her dried-out shoulders. I got wasted just looking at her.

"I was about to eat," I said. "Can't this wait five minutes? Be nice and just . . ."

"Are you kidding? This is a disaster! There's water all over the place! Hurry up, come with me. . . ."

"Hold on. First tell me exactly what broke. What's overflow-ing?"

She giggled in the sunlight, her hands shoved in her pockets.

"Well, you know . . . it's the . . . the white thing that's overflowing. For God's sake there are little shreds of paper all over the place!"

I took a swallow of beer and shook my head.

"Look," I said. "Don't you understand? I was just sitting down to eat. Can't you just close your eyes for fifteen minutes? Is that too much to ask?"

"Are you crazy or what? I'm not kidding, you better come right away!"

"Oh, all right. Take it easy," I said.

I went into the house and turned the fire off under the beans. They were just getting done. Then I grabbed my toolbox and started off after the madwoman.

I got back an hour later, soaked from head to foot and half-dead from hunger. I lit a match under the saucepan and jumped into the shower and stopped thinking about her. I felt the water run over my skull and the smell of beans slide under my nose.

Sunlight flooded the house. It was nice out. I knew that my problems were over for the day. I'd never seen a toilet clog up in the afternoon. Most of the time it was calm; half the bunga-lows were empty. I sat down to eat, smiling. My schedule was all fixed: eat, then navigate out onto the porch and wait there till evening. Wait until she came, her hips swaying, to sit on my lap.

I was lifting the lid on the saucepan when the door swung wide open. It was Betty. I put my fork down, smiling, and stood up.

"Betty!" I said. "Jesus . . . you know, I don't think I've ever seen you in broad daylight. . . ."

She sort of struck a pose, one hand in her hair, her curls tumbling down on all sides.

"So what do you think?" she asked.

I sat back down and looked at her, acting detached, one arm slung over the back of the chair.

"Well, the hips aren't bad, and the legs aren't bad either . . . yeah, turn around. . . ."

She turned around. I stood up and pressed myself into her back. I stroked her chest and kissed her neck.

"But this . . ." I whispered. "This is perfect."

I wondered what she was doing here at this time of day. I

stepped aside, then spotted the two canvas suitcases sitting on the doorstep. I didn't say anything.

"It smells good in here," she said.

She leaned over the table to look in the saucepan.

"Oh God, I don't believe it!"

"What are you talking a—"

"It's chili! Don't tell me you were going to eat all this chili by yourself."

While she was dipping two fingers into the pot I got two beers out of the fridge. I thought about all the hours we had ahead of us—it was like swallowing opium.

"Oh Lord, it's fabulous. And you made it yourself! I love it, it's incredible! But in this heat—you must be nuts. . . ."

"I can eat chili in any weather, even with the sweat running onto the plate. Me and chili—we're like two pieces of bread in a sandwich.'

"Me too. Anyway, I'm so hungry I could . . ."

The second she'd walked through the door the house had changed. I couldn't find anything anymore. I walked around in circles looking for silverware, opening up cabinets and smiling. She came and put her arms around my neck. I loved it. I could smell her hair.

"Hey, you happy to see me?" she said.

"Well, let me think it about it. . . ."

"You're all bastards. . . . I'll explain later."

"Betty, is something wrong?"

"Nothing too serious," she said. "Nothing worth letting the chili get cold over. Kiss me."

By the time I'd had two or three spoonfuls of those spicy beans I'd forgotten all about it. Betty's presence had made me euphoric—she laughed all the time, she complimented me on my beans, she made my beer foam, she reached out across the table and caressed my cheek. I didn't know yet how she could go from one mood to another with the speed of light.

We were just finishing lunch—it was delicious—having a nice time gulping it down, winking at each other and joking around. I was looking at her, finding her so wonderful, when all of a sudden she changed before my eyes. She turned completely white and her eyes got incredibly hard. It took my breath away.

"Like I was saying . . ." she began. "They're all bastards. Sooner or later it's always the same—I find myself with my suitcases in my hands. You get the picture?"

"What are you talking about?" I said.

"What do you mean what am I talking about? Are you listening to me? I'm trying to explain something to you! Why aren't you listening to me?"

I didn't answer. I went to touch her arm. She pulled away.

"Let's get something straight," she said. "I'm not looking for a guy who just wants to fuck."

"I see," I said.

She ran a hand through her hair, sighing, and looked out the window. Nothing moved outside—just a few houses sprinkled with sunlight and the road going straight across the countryside into the hills.

"When I think that I stayed a year in that dump . . ." she muttered.

She stared into space, her hands squeezed between her legs, her shoulders hunched over as if she suddenly felt very tired. I'd never seen her like that. All I knew was her laughter. I'd always thought that she could stand up to anything. I asked myself what this was all about.

"A year," she went on. "And every godforsaken day that bastard never stopped ogling me, his wife screaming from morning to night. I worked there for a year. I waited on customers, wiped the tables, swept the floor, and look where it got me. The boss runs his hand up my crotch and everything is back to square one.

Me and my two suitcases. I've got just enough left to last me a few days, or buy myself a train ticket."

She shook her head for a long time, then looked up at me and smiled. I recognized her again.

"That's not even the punch line," she said. "I don't even have anywhere to sleep. I got my things together in a hurry—the other girls stared at me with bug eyes. 'I'm not staying here one more minute!' I told them. 'I can't stand the sight of that bastard's face one more second!' "

I opened a beer on the edge of the table.

"Well, I'll tell you. . . . You're right," I said. "I think you're a hundred percent right."

Her eyes sparkled at me. I felt her coming back to life—felt it grab her around the waist and shake her. Her long hair billowed over the table.

"Yeah, somehow that guy must have got it in his head that I belonged to him. You know the type. . . ."

"Yeah, sure, I know. Believe me, I know. . . ."

"Yeah. I think they all go crazy after a certain age."

We cleared the table and I took the two suitcases inside. She started doing the dishes—I could see the water squirting in front of her. She reminded me of some strange flower equipped with translucent antennas and a violet Naugahyde core. I didn't know many girls who could get away with wearing that color miniskirt so carelessly. I tossed the suitcases on the bed.

"You know, when you think about it," I said, "it's not bad, what's happening to us. . . ."

"Yeah? You think so?"

"Yeah. Usually I can't stand people, but I'm glad you're here."

The next day she was up before me. It had been such a long time since I'd had breakfast with someone, I'd forgotten what it was like. I got up and got dressed without saying a word. I slipped behind her and kissed her neck. I sat down in front of my coffee cup. She was buttering bread wide as water skis, rolling her eyes, and I couldn't keep from smiling. The day was off to a really good start.

"Okay, I'm going to try to get through with work as soon as I can," I said. "I've got to go into town for a minute, you want to come?"

She glanced around the house and shook her head.

"No, I think I better try to straighten up a little around here. It really needs it. . . ."

So I left her there and went to get the truck out of the garage. I parked in front of the entrance, by the guard house. George was half asleep, a newspaper on his stomach. I went in behind him and grabbed the laundry bag.

"Oh, it's you," he said.

He grabbed one too and followed me out, yawning. We threw the bags in the back of the truck and went back for the others.

"I saw that girl again yesterday," he said.

I hauled a bag, not answering.

"It's you she was looking for, right?"

He was dragging his heels. The sun was starting to beat down hard.

"A girl in a little violet skirt and lots of black hair," he added.

Just then Betty came out of the house and ran toward us. We watched her come.

"You mean a girl like that?" I said.

"Jesus H. Christ!" he said.

"Well, you're exactly right. It *was* me she was looking for."

I introduced them, and while the old man was doing his Romeo number, I went back and got the shopping list. I shoved it in my pocket and went back to the car, lighting up my first cigarette of the day. Betty was sitting in the passenger seat, talking to George through the window. I walked around and slid in behind the wheel.

"On second thought," she said, "I decided to come along for the ride."

I slipped my arm around her shoulder and pulled away slowly, trying to make the pleasure last. She handed me a stick of mint chewing gum, throwing the wrappers on the floor. She squeezed herself against me the whole way. I didn't need a fortune-teller to see how terrific it all was.

First we got rid of the laundry and then I went across the street with the shopping list. The guy at the store was busy pasting labels all over the place, so I just slid the paper in his pocket.

"Take your time," I said. "I'll come back later. Don't forget my bottle."

He stood up too fast and smashed his head into a shelf. He made a face—he was ugly enough without it.

"We said a bottle every other week, not every week," he said.

"Right, but it turns out I had to take on an associate. That changes things."

"What are you talking about?"

"Don't worry about it. It doesn't change anything between you and me. I'll keep doing my shopping here as long as you show some smarts."

"Jesus, one every week, though. That's a little—"

"Things are tough all over."

Just then he noticed Betty in her little tank top waiting for me out in the truck, her crazy earrings twinkling in the light. He played around for a second with the lump on his skull, then shook his head.

"I know things are tough all over, but I think some bastards make out better than others."

I didn't think I was in a good position to argue. I left him standing in the middle of his boxes and went back out to the car.

"Okay, well, we have a little time," I said. "How would you feel about some ice cream?"

"Jesus, Mary, and Joseph, I'm with you!"

* * *

I knew the old lady at the ice cream place pretty well. I was one of her best customers in the liquor-topped-sundae department. She usually left the bottle on the counter. I made conversation with her. I waved when we came in. Betty sat at a table and I went up to order.

"I think that'll be two peach sherbets," I said.

I went behind the counter to give her a hand. She stuck her arms down into the steaming freezer and I took out two parfait glasses that held about a quart each. I went down into the cupboard looking for the jar of peaches.

"Hey," she said. "A little excited today, aren't we?"

I straightened up and took a look at Betty sitting there with her legs crossed, a cigarette in her mouth.

"What do you think of her?" I asked.

"A bit vulgar . . ."

I took the bottle of maraschino and sprinkled it on the sherbet.

"That's understandable," I said. "She's an angel, straight from heaven. Can't you see . . . ?"

On the way back we stopped to get the laundry, and I went across the street to pick up the groceries. It must have been about noon—it was starting to get really hot out. We had no time to lose, getting back.

I spotted my bottle right off. He'd left it there in plain sight, in front of the bags. It was not exactly service with a smile—in fact it was hardly service at all. I made off with my bags and bottle.

"You sulking?" I asked him, on the way out.

He didn't even look at me.

"Too bad," I said. "You're the only black spot in my whole day."

I shoved everything in the back of the truck and steered toward the motel. At the edge of town, a hot wind started blasting. The whole area suddenly looked like a desert—wilted plants and long shadows. I liked it. I liked the color of the dirt, and I've always had a thing for large, lonely spaces. We rolled up the windows.

I had my foot to the floor, but the car would do only forty-five, what with the head wind. After a while, Betty turned to look out the back. Her hair must have made her hot—she kept lifting it up all the time.

"You know what?" she said. "With this little truck and all that food, two people could go just about anywhere."

Twenty years earlier, the idea would have set me on fire. Now, it was all I could do to keep from yawning.

"Right, a whirlwind tour," I said.

"Yeah! We could blow this pop stand . . . !"

I lit a cigarette and crossed my hands on the wheel.

"It's funny," I said. "But I don't think the scenery around here is so ugly. . . ."

She threw her head back, laughing.

"Shit, you call this scenery?"

You could hear the dust flying against the chassis, swirling wildly in the wind. Outside things were burning. I started laughing too.

That evening the wind died down all of a sudden and the air got very heavy. We took the bottle out on the porch and waited for the night to cool off a little, but nothing changed, not even after the stars came out—not one little breeze. Still, I have to say it was all just fine with me. My only real complaint had been the immobility, but I was getting used to it. The past five years had given me time to figure out ways of dealing with the heat. It was different now with a girl around—there were other things to do than lie still and wait for it to blow over.

After a few drinks we decided to stuff ourselves into the chaise longue. We were sweating heavy in the dark, but everything seemed perfect. It's always like that in the beginning—you can handle anything. We stayed there for a long time without moving, trying to breathe on a thimbleful of air.

She started squirming. I gave her a drink to calm her down. She let out a sigh that could have blown down a tree.

"I wonder if I'll ever be able to get up," she said.

"Forget about it. Don't be silly, nothing could be important enough—"

"I think I have to pee," she said.

I slid my hand down into her panties and stroked her behind. It was a wonderful behind, a trickle of sweat running down from the small of her back, and skin soft as the Gerber baby's. I didn't want to think about anything. I pulled her to me.

"Jesus," she said. "Don't press on my bladder."

In spite of everything, she crossed one of her legs over mine and started twisting my T-shirt in a funny kind of way.

"I would like to say that I am happy to be here with you, and that if possible I would like us to stay together."

She said this in the most normal voice imaginable, as if she were commenting on the color of her shoes, or the paint chipping off the ceiling. I took it lightly.

"Well, yeah, I think it might be possible to work something out like that. Let's see: I'm not married, no kids. My life isn't too complicated—I have a house and a job that's not too tiring. I'd say that in the end I'm a pretty good deal."

She flattened herself against me a little more and in no time we were drenched from head to foot. Still, it wasn't unpleasant, even in the heat. She bit my ear and growled.

"I have faith," she said. "We're still young, you and me. We'll make out okay."

I didn't understand what she meant. We kissed for a long time. Try to understand everything that goes on in a girl's head and you'll never see the end of it. I didn't want any explanation. All I wanted was to keep kissing her in the dark—stroking her behind as long as her bladder held out.

2

For several days we floated through a sort of Technicolor dream. We were never more than an inch away from each other. Life seemed amazingly simple. I had a few jobs—a kitchen sink, a haywire toilet tank, a stove with multisized burners—but nothing very serious. Betty gave me a hand, picking up the dead branches and litter and emptying the garbage cans in the alleys. We spent our afternoons lounging around under the porch, playing with the buttons on the radio or talking about unimportant things—that is, when we weren't fucking or preparing a few of the complicated dishes we'd picked out of the cookbook the night before. I'd pushed the chaise longue into the shade, she'd spread her mat out in the sunshine. Whenever anybody came by I'd toss her a towel, taking it back once the asshole had gone, then return to my chaise longue to look at her. I noted how all I had to do was lay my eyes on her for a little over ten seconds to completely clear my mind. It was a trick that came in handy.

One morning she jumped on the scale and let out a scream.

"Oh shit, I don't believe it!"

"Betty, what is it?"

"Jesus Christ, I've gained another two pounds. I just knew it . . . !"

"Don't worry about it. Believe me, it doesn't show."

She didn't answer, and I forgot the whole incident. Then at lunch I found myself with a tomato cut in half on my plate—just a tomato, nothing else. I didn't say anything, though—just dug right in as if there was nothing at all unusual. I left the table feeling fit, not weighted down by a bunch of calories, and we took a roll in the sheets—one of our best sessions. Outside the sun was vibrating, crashing down on the crickets.

I got up later and went straight to the icebox. Once in a while life hands you moments of absolute perfection, wraps you up in stardust. I was under the impression that my ears were whistling, as if I'd attained a higher level of consciousness. I gave the eggs a big smile. I grabbed three and scrambled them in a bowl.

"What are you doing?" Betty asked.

I started looking for the flour.

"I never told you, but the only time in my life that I really made money was selling crêpes. I set up this little stand by the seaside and the folks stood in line in the glaring sun with their money in their hands. Yeah, every last one of them. I made the most fabulous crêpes within twenty-five miles and they knew it. I'm going to show you I'm not joking. . . ."

"Oh really, I shouldn't. . . ."

"You kidding me? You're not going to make me eat alone. You wouldn't do a thing like that. . . ."

"Really, I'm not in the mood. Please. I won't eat any."

I saw right away that there was no sense arguing. It would be like beating my head against a brick wall. I watched the eggs slide out of the bowl and make their way one by one toward the drain, while my stomach growled. But I got a hold of myself and washed the bowl out without making a fuss. She smoked a cigarette and looked at the ceiling.

I spent what was left of the afternoon on the porch fixing the motor from the washing machine. At the end of the day, seeing that all was calm—she was just reading a book—I went in and put the water on. I tossed in a handful of rock salt, tore open a package of spaghetti, and went back out on the porch. I crouched down in front of her.

"Betty, is something wrong?"

"No," she said. "Everything's fine."

I stood back up, folded my hands behind my head, and swept my eyes over the horizon. The sky was red and clear, promising winds for the next day. I wondered what kind of crap could have jammed the machine up.

I turned back to her, bent my knees, and leaned over. I ran a worried finger over her cheek.

"I can see that something's not all right. . . ."

She gave me the same hard look that had shaken me up a few days earlier. She lifted herself up on one elbow.

"You know a lot of girls who don't have a job? Who don't have a cent to their name, who are stuck in some retarded one-horse town, and who can still smile about it?"

"Shit, what difference would it make if you *did* have a job, a little cash in the bank? Why are you getting bent out of shape over a stupid thing like that?"

"Plus, I'm getting fat. I'm going to pot in this hole!"

"What the hell are you talking about? What's so horrible about this place? Don't you see that it's the same all over—that only the scenery changes?"

"So? That's better than nothing!"

I glanced at the pink sky and shook my head slowly. I looked back down.

"Look," I said. "How about going into town for a bite and taking in a movie?"

A smile spread over her face like an atomic bomb. I actually felt the heat coming at me.

"Great! Nothing like a little drive to change the mood. Just let me slip into a skirt."

She took off into the house.

"A skirt? That's all?" I said.

"Sometimes I wonder if you ever think of anything else. . . ."

I went inside and turned the fire off under the pot. Betty fixed her hair in the mirror. She winked at me. I had the feeling I'd scored a point.

We took Betty's car, a red VW that burned oil. We parked in the middle of town with one wheel on the curb.

We hadn't been in the pizzeria five minutes when this blonde walks in and Betty starts jumping up and down next to me.

"Hey, that's Sonia. HEY, SONIA! OVER HERE!"

The girl in question suddenly moved toward our table, almost knocking the guy behind her off balance. The girls kissed and the guy plunked himself down in front of me. The girls seemed happy to see each other—they held hands. They introduced everybody. The guy let out a sort of mumble. I lost myself in the menu.

"God, let me look at you! You look like you're in great shape!" said Betty.

"You too, sweetheart! You don't know how happy I am to see you!"

"Pizza for everybody?" I asked.

When the waitress showed up, the guy seemed to wake up. He took her by the arm and slipped a bill in her hand.

"How much time do you need to make champagne appear on this table?" he asked her.

The waitress looked at the bill without saying a word.

"A little under five seconds," she said.

"You got it."

Sonia threw herself at him and bit his lips.

"Oh, baby, you're fantastic!" she said.

After a few bottles I agreed with her completely. The guy was telling me how he'd struck it rich speculating on coffee just when the prices skyrocketed.

"My telephone rang off the hook and money rolled in from all directions at once. See, you had to play it close to the chest. You had to hold off until the last minute, then sell everything at breakneck speed. At any second you could either double your money or go bust. . . ."

I listened attentively. That kind of story fascinates me. Talking about money blocked the effects of the alcohol in this guy. All he did was burp a little loudly from time to time. I sucked on this bad-ass cigar he'd given me and kept the glasses filled. The girls' eyes were shining.

"I'm going to tell you something," he added. "You know that movie where the guys jump out of their cars just at the last minute before they go over the cliff? Can you imagine how they must feel?"

"Hard to imagine," I said.

"Well, that's what it was for me, multiplied by a hundred!"

"You jumped out at the right time?" I asked.

"Yeah, I think I jumped out at the right time. After that I collapsed and slept for three days straight."

Sonia ran her fingers through his hair and squeezed herself against him.

"And in two days we're taking a plane to the islands!" she cooed. "It's my engagement present! Oh, sweetie, maybe that seems silly to you, but I'm crazy about the idea!"

Sonia looked like a ruffled bird with a sensual mouth. She laughed all the time. It kept things nice. The bottles came and went and for a little while Betty took my arm and put her head on my shoulder. I dragged on my Davidoff.

Toward the end I couldn't listen to anybody anymore. I heard only a faint murmur. Everything seemed far away. The world was absurdly simple and I was smiling. I wasn't waiting for anything. I was so plastered that I started laughing to myself.

*   *   *

At the stroke of one in the morning, the guy fell over without warning and broke his plate in half. It was time to go home. Sonia paid the bill by getting some cash out of the pockets of his sport coat, and we dragged him outside. It was hard, given the state we were in, but once outside he got a little life back in him, and that helped. Even so, we had to stop at each streetlight to get our wind back. We were hot. Sonia stood in front of him while we took a breather. He was wobbling on his legs—Oh baby, she said, my poor little baby. I wondered if they hadn't parked on the other side of town.

Finally she opened the door of a hot new sedan with a ten-foot hood and we dumped her little baby inside. Sonia kissed us good night quickly, anxious to get home and put something on his head. We watched them start up. We waved. The thing took off into the night like the Loch Ness monster.

After a while we found our VW. I wanted to drive. To drive like I wanted, I needed something truly responsive—high beams by the row, a hundred miles per hour in no time flat, smooth as butter—I HAD to drive.

"You sure you're going to make it?" Betty asked.

"I assume you're joking. Nothing the matter with me."

I got through town without a hitch. There weren't many people out. It was a real joyride, except that once in a while the engine freaked out and the VW jumped forward.

The night was black. The headlights swept the road ahead and there was nothing—just the pale lights of a dancing road sign. I had to lean into the windshield to see.

"You get a load of this fog?" I said.

"I can't see anything. What are you talking about?"

"Remind me to adjust the headlights. This is the pits."

I followed the white line, putting the left front wheel right on it. After a while something intrigued me. I knew the road well, there wasn't the least turn in it, no curves at all, but now, very gently, almost imperceptibly, the goddamn little white line was going off to the left, bending incomprehensibly. I opened my eyes wider and wider.

Betty screamed when I drove into the ditch. The car sank its nose into a sorry little pond. I tried to turn the motor off—the windshield wipers went on.

Betty opened the door in a rage, without a word. I asked myself what I had done wrong, how this could have happened, exactly. I got out behind her. The VW looked like a big stupid animal in its death throes. The bumpers were all smashed in.

"We've been attacked by martians," I said.

By the time I turned around to look at her, she was gone, marching down the road in her high heels. I galloped after her.

"Jesus, don't worry about the car," I said.

She was walking fast, like she was on springs, looking straight ahead of her. I had a hell of a time keeping up.

"I couldn't care less about that hunk of tin!" she said. "It isn't that. . . ."

"There's no problem. . . . We can't have more than a couple of miles to go. It'll do us good. . . ."

"I'm thinking about Sonia," she went on. "You remember Sonia . . . ?"

"Yeah . . . you mean your girlfriend?"

"Yes, right. Don't you think she's lucky, my girlfriend? Don't you think that SHE can afford to SMILE?"

"Shit, Betty, don't start that again."

"You see," she went on. "Sonia and me were waitresses in the same place before I came here. We did the same job—polish the glasses, serve, sweep. At night we sat around together in our apartments and talked about what life would be like once we got out of there. Tonight I saw how she's done since then. I think she's found herself a nice little place in the sun. . . ."

You could see the motel lights in the distance. We weren't out of the woods yet, and the downward slope was getting slippery.

"You don't agree?" she insisted.

I told myself, Just keep walking, don't pay attention to what she says—in a second she'll forget all about it.

"Explain to me why I'm always in the same rut. Tell me what I do wrong that keeps me from climbing up the ladder a little. . . ."

I stopped to light a cigarette and she waited for me. Her eyes went through me. I sort of shrugged, as if to say, "Search me."

"We'll never get a break if we stick around here," she said.

I looked over her shoulder. She was breathing quickly.

"I don't know . . ." I said.

"What do you mean you don't know? What kind of answer is that?"

"Shit, it means I don't know!"

To put an end to the scene, I took a few steps off the shoulder of the road and pissed. I turned my back to her. I thought I'd gotten her to button her lip. I made a little blue cloud of steam in the night, thinking that, sure, living with a woman always has its inconveniences, but in the end the scale always tips in favor of doing it. Let her bitch all she wants, I thought, it doesn't really bother me. It's a small price to pay for all the good things I get from her. I felt her boiling over behind me. I couldn't remember how long it had been since I really had someone by my side. It had been a long time.

I zipped my pants up, feeling good. That's how it is when you take up with a high-spirited girl—you can't avoid a few hot moments, no way around it. The alcohol made my blood warm. I pivoted around on one leg to face her.

"I don't feel like discussing this anymore," I said. "I'm not up to it. Be a pal. . . ."

She looked at the black sky, sighing:

"But God, don't you ever think that life is passing us by, right under our noses? Doesn't that just get to you sometimes?"

"Listen: Ever since I've been with you I don't feel like life is passing me by. I even feel like I have more than my share, if you really want to know. . . ."

"Oh shit, I'm not talking about that! I mean let's get out of this together! Somewhere opportunity is knocking at the door. We just have to find where. . . ."

"Too simple. A mistake."

"God, you'd think you'd found paradise here in this crummy desert. You must be half nuts."

I had decided not to answer. I stepped toward her, but unfortunately got my foot stuck in a hole and fell flat on my face. I hurt my knee. It was obviously a detail that didn't bother her. She kept at me about her rage to live in the fast lane while I was busy crawling behind her in the dust.

"Take Sonia. Look how she made out. Now she can really live! Imagine what we could do if we just got off our butts and . . ."

"Betty, for Christ sakes . . . !"

"I can't understand why you don't feel suffocated here. There's nothing happening—nothing that's *going* to happen!"

"Come here and help me, goddammit. Come . . ."

But I could see she wasn't listening. She hadn't budged an inch. She was totally locked into her fantasy by then—breath short and eyes shining.

"Don't you ever see yourself taking off for the islands one of these mornings?" She added. "One of these days, just setting sail for paradise?"

"Let's get home and go to bed," I said.

She fixed her eyes on me:

"All we have to do is stir things up a little! All we have to do is *want* to."

"And what do you hope to accomplish, exactly? What do you think is going to—"

"God, can you imagine what it's like on the islands?"

The vision of it had set her brain on fire. She let out a little nervous giggle, then took off without me, juggling her sugar-plum daydreams while I barely managed to get up on my knees.

"SHIT . . ." I yelled after her. "YOU KNOW WHAT YOU CAN DO WITH YOUR ISLANDS!?"

3

For the next few days we didn't talk about it. We were over our heads in work. I'd never seen so much all at one time. A fucking cyclone hit us. So many things were torn up that after a while you gave up counting. Windows broken into a thousand pieces, all kinds of crap scattered in the alleys. Looking at a disaster this size, all we could do was shake our heads and stare at each other. George scratched his head and grimaced. Betty just sort of laughed.

I spent all my days running from one bungalow to another with my toolbox, a pencil behind my ear. Betty made the trip back and forth into town, getting me boxes of nails, cans of putty, lumber, and tanning lotion. I spent most of my time outside—up on a ladder or on someone's roof. From morning till night the sky stayed limpid blue, rained out once and for all. I passed hours and hours in the sunlight, a handful of nails in my mouth, fixing all those little houses that were falling apart.

George was useless—it was even dangerous to work with him.

He was always letting the hammer get away from him or sawing your hand off while you were holding the board. After working with him one morning, I asked him to just take care of the alleys—to stay away from my ladder or I'd dump my toolbox on his head.

Little by little the place started looking habitable again. I was lost in the ozone every night. It was especially tough to fix the TV antennas—bending the wire back while holding onto the cables at the same time. I didn't want Betty climbing on the roofs, I didn't want anything to happen to her. From time to time I'd see her head pop up on top of the ladder with a cool beer. The heat had me totally wasted—I saw lightning in her hair. I would lean over, roll my tongue in her mouth, and grab the bottle. It helped me make it to the end of the day. Then I would put my tools away and go eat, strolling under the caress of the sun till I reached the house and found her there, lying under the porch with my fan. She would always ask me the same questions:

"You doing okay? Not too tired?"

"So-so . . ."

She would get up and follow me inside. I would jump into the shower while she surveyed the stove. I was, in fact, really wiped out, but I also played it up a little—I wanted all her attention. The fatigue gave me all kinds of preposterous ideas. I wanted to be laid out and powdered on my bottom like a baby—things like that; to lay down on her belly and suck on her breasts—that got me excited. I would close my eyes while she sat behind me and rubbed my shoulders and neck. My cute little cyclone, I thought, oh, my cute little cyclone . . .

We would eat, and clear the table fast. Everything was orchestrated like sheet music. I would light a cigarette and go out onto the porch while she did a few dishes. I would take a long look at the chaise longue and lie down in it. I would hear her whistling, and more than once I felt happy, felt so calm that I would always fall asleep with a little idiotic smile turning up the corners of my mouth. Then my cigarette would fall onto my chest and I would wake up screaming.

"Shit, did you fall asleep again?" she said.

"Huh?"

She would come over and lead me to bed, her arm around my waist. She would push me over onto the mattress and start undressing me. Unfortunately I would realize after about ten seconds that I was too beat to fuck. I couldn't keep my eyes open. I passed right out.

So we figured out a new system: we fucked in the morning. The only bad thing was that I had to get up to piss first—her too—and that spoiled the magic a little. We got over it, though, with a few dumb jokes, then got to the heart of the matter. Betty was always in great form in the morning—I wondered if she wasn't reliving some of what she'd dreamed during the night. She was always hot to try some strange new position—things that really knocked me for a loop, left me with my mouth hanging open. I would go back to work with renewed faith in Heaven and Hell, climbing back up on the roofs to fix those little antennas, my legs like butter.

One morning I woke up before Betty. The sun was coming in from all sides. I lifted myself up on one elbow: Somebody was sitting in a chair at the foot of the bed. It was the owner of the motel, watching us attentively—watching Betty, that is. It took me a few seconds to figure out what he was doing, then I saw that we had really sent the sheets flying the night before, and Betty was lying there with her legs wide apart. The guy was greasy, fat. He was dabbing at himself with a handkerchief and his fingers were covered with rings—the kind of guy who can make you throw up first thing in the morning.

I threw the sheet over Betty and got up in a hurry. I dressed without being able to say a word, wondering what in the world he was doing there. He watched me, smiling silently, like a cat who's just found a mouse. Then Betty woke up. She sat up suddenly, breasts bare. She pulled her hair out of her eyes with one hand.

"Hey . . . who the fuck is this guy?" she said.

He made a little gesture with his head and stood up.

"No, really . . . since when does just anybody—"

I dragged the owner outside before things started getting complicated. I closed the door behind us.

I walked back and forth in the sun, clearing my throat. He had his sport jacket over his arm and big sweat rings on his shirt. I couldn't think straight—I didn't feel too well. Normally at that time of morning I should have been peacefully fucking. The guy ran his hanky behind his neck and looked at me with a grimace.

"Tell me," he said. "Is that young woman the reason you're still in bed at ten o'clock in the morning?"

I stuck my hands in my pockets and looked at the ground. This both made me look bothered and kept me from having to look at his face.

"No, no," I said. "She has nothing to do with it."

"You mustn't, you see. . . . You really mustn't let her make you forget why you are here—why I house you and pay you. Do you understand?"

"Sure, yeah, but . . ."

"You know . . ." he went on. "One little ad in tomorrow's paper and there'll be a hundred guys knocking each other over, begging to have your job. I don't want to do anything underhanded—you've been here a long time and I've never had any complaints—but I don't like this. I don't think you can have a girl like that here and do your job at the same time. Do you see what I mean?"

"Have you been talking to George?" I asked.

He nodded. The guy was repulsive and he knew it. He used it like a weapon.

"Well," I went on. "He must have told you what a help she's been to us. I can tell you we wouldn't have gotten along this well without her. You should have seen the damage after that fucking cyclone, there was hardly anything left standing, and she took care of all the shopping while George and I tried to get everything fixed in a hurry. She put the putty on the windows, picked up the dead branches, ran all over the place, never sat still for a minute, she . . ."

"I'm not saying—"

"And let me just add that she never even asked to be paid for it. George can tell you that she saved us a hell of a lot of time."

"In other words, you'd like me to look the other way on this?"

"Listen, maybe it's true that I got up a little late this morning, but these days I'm working ten, twelve hours a day. We've had a hell of a job here, just take a look around. Usually I'm up at dawn, I don't know what happened. It won't happen again."

He was dripping in the sun. He was thinking about something, twisting his face in all directions. He took a glance around.

"Got to give these houses a paint job," he said. "They look like hell."

"Yeah, wouldn't hurt. It'd attract attention from the road too. We've already talked about it, me and George. . . ."

"Okay, then maybe there's a way to work this all out. You can get to work on it with your friend there."

The idea was so outlandish that it made me turn white.

"Hey, are you kidding?" I said. "That's a job for a painting company. . . . We'd never be able to finish."

"The two of you already *are* a little company," he chuckled.

I bit my lip. The guy really had us right where he wanted us, and it was a tough pill to swallow. Why do these things always happen? Why do we always find ourselves in these situations? I hadn't even started the day yet, and I was already exhausted.

"Okay, but I want to know how she'll be paid." I sighed.

His smile widened. He put his chubby little hand on my shoulder.

"My goodness, you make me laugh," he said. "Five minutes ago you were asking me to forget the girl—isn't that right? How am I supposed to do that if I have to pay her? It doesn't make any sense."

He was really one of those classic assholes you meet all over, the kind who leave a bad taste in your mouth. I looked at my feet. It felt like they were nailed to the floor. My jaw hurt. I wiped my mouth slowly, my eyes closed. This meant that I gave in. He must have been used to that—he got the message.

"That's fine. I'll just let you get to work, then. I'll come by later to see how you're getting on with it. I'll see about ordering the paint with George."

He took off, kneading his handerchief. I stood there, dancing from one leg to the other before deciding to go back inside. Betty was in the shower, I saw her through the curtain. I was hemmed in on all sides. I sat down at the table and had a lukewarm cup of coffee. Disgusting.

She came out rolled in a towel and sat right down on my lap.

"Say, who the hell was that guy? Who ever let him in here?"

"He doesn't need anyone to let him in," I said. "He owns the place."

"What difference does that make? You don't just go walking into somebody's house like that. . . ."

"Yes, you're right. That's what I told him."

"What did he want, anyway?"

I stroked her tit without having an idea in my head. I felt sort of empty. The job that was waiting for us—mama mia! . . . my legs were shaking. It was making me sick.

"So what did he want?" she insisted.

"Nothing. Bullshit . . . he wants us to paint a couple of things."

"Oh yeah? Great! I love painting!"

"What luck," I said.

The next morning this guy showed up in a truck with about a hundred gallons of paint and some rollers.

"There you go," he said. "That'll give you something to get

started with. When you need more just give me a buzz and I'll be back lickety-split."

We unloaded the cans into the shed. It made a nice little hill in there. It gave me a stomachache: fireball rage and impotence mixed together. I had forgotten what a horrible feeling it is—it had been a long time since I'd had a taste of it. It's funny, there were really a lot of things I'd forgotten.

The deliveryman split, whistling. It was sort of relentlessly nice out. I took a sad look at the houses and started lugging a fifty-pound can of paint down the road, making sure my fingers got good and crippled. George was waiting for me by the entrance. I didn't stop. He walked across to join me with his crazy-old-man grin.

"Hey, looks heavy what you got there."

"Don't be cute," I groaned. "Leave me alone."

"Well, shit, what did I do to you?"

I changed hands without slowing down. I hit myself in the leg with the can and saw stars for a minute. He wouldn't let me be.

"Jesus, I never saw you like this."

"That's possible," I said. "Did you really have to go tell him that Betty LIVED here?"

"Jesus Christ, you know how he is. He made me spill the beans. I was only half awake when he came in. . . ."

"Yeah, well, you're never completely awake. What you *are* completely is full of shit," I said.

"Hey, is it true you're going to paint all those things? You really going to make yourself do . . ."

I stopped. I put the can down and looked George in the eye.

"Listen," I said. "I'm still not sure what I'm going to do, but I don't want you talking to Betty about it. Do you get me?"

"Yeah, don't get bent out of shape, pal, your secret's safe with . . . but how are you going to not tell her yourself?"

"I don't know. I haven't thought about it yet."

Just as I got to the first bungalow I was hit by a bad case of the runs and had to leave for a little while. The enormity of the job simply had my guts tied in knots. I didn't have the nerve to tell Betty about it. I knew that she would have chucked the whole thing—she'd never have let herself get screwed like that, she'd have burned the whole place down. What would happen if I told her seemed so horrible that I decided to keep it all to myself—a little diarrhea isn't the end of the world, after all, it's just an unpleasant little moment in life.

Betty was talking to the tenants when I got back. I was a little paler than usual.

"There you are. I was just telling these people that we're going to do a little painting. . . ."

They looked at me benignly, a kind of spaced-out couple, taking it easy in retirement. They'd been there for at least six months already and had hung flowerpots in every possible corner. I muttered a few incomprehensible remarks and dragged Betty out behind the building. My mouth was dry. Betty was looking gorgeous—charged with electricity, all smiles. I cleared my throat a few times, my fist jammed in my mouth.

"Well, what are we waiting for? What do we do?" she asked.

"Ah, okay . . . you paint the shutters and I'll paint around them," I said.

She tied her hair up on top of her head, laughing and care-free—it was enough to make you weak in the knees.

"I'm ready!" she said. "First one finished helps the other one!"

When her back was turned I gave her an incredibly sad smile.

From time to time the geezers came out to see how we were doing. They stood at the foot of my ladder, their mouths twisted in glee. Around eleven o'clock the woman brought us cookies. Betty joked around with them, she thought they were both really nice. Personally, I thought they were boring—I didn't feel like making pleasant conversation every inch of the way. When I'd finished painting the top of one side, I climbed down the ladder and walked over to Betty to play my next hand. She was doing a corner.

"Jesus Christ, you're really a pro!" I said. "You can't do better than that . . . but there's a little problem, I didn't think to mention it. . . ."

"What's wrong?"

"Well, it's the corner there. . . . You went a little outside the lines, like . . ."

"Of course I went outside the lines. What do you want me to do . . . a brush this size . . ."

"I know. It's not your fault. It's just that now it looks like the other side is wrong."

"So?"

I felt myself strangling.

"What do you mean 'so'?" I got out.

"I mean, you're not going to paint just one side of their building. What good does that do?"

I wiped my brow with my arm like a seasoned veteran who has lost all illusions.

"Well, I suppose . . ." I said. "I guess it would make them happy anyway. They'll have a whole new building thanks to you."

For the rest of the day we were stuck there, slaving over that shitty little house.

In fact that one little gig took up practically the whole week. The thermometer climbed all of a sudden and it was impossible to work outside in the early afternoon. All you could do was stay inside the house with the shades down, the icebox rumbling like a washing machine, unable even to crank out enough ice. We walked around the room half naked. Usually we wound up grabbing each other. I followed the little rivers of sweat that ran down her skin with my fingers, and we knocked all the furniture over, puffing like locomotives, hair glued together and eyes bright. I had the feeling that the more we fucked the more we wanted to, but that wasn't the problem. What had me worried was that with each passing day Betty was losing her taste for painting—she wasn't into it like she used to be. The cookies didn't work anymore. We hadn't even finished the first bungalow and she was starting to get fed up. I had no idea how I was going to break it to her that we still had twenty-seven just like it to go. I couldn't sleep at night, I smoked in bed while she slept, letting my mind waft off into the silence and the dark. I wondered what was going to happen. Whatever it was, I knew I'd have a ringside seat. It was like I suddenly found myself in the middle of an arena with a blinding sun in my eyes—I could feel the danger without really knowing which direction it was going to come from. It was not exactly a barrel of laughs.

4

We finished the old couple's bungalow one evening around seven, just as the sun was going down. It looked unreal—pink shutters on a white background. The two geriatrics hugged each other in ecstasy. Betty and I were dead. We sat down on paint cans and opened beers, clinking the cans together in a toast. A light wind had come up during the afternoon—it was quite cool out. There's always something nice about finishing a job, whatever it is, and we took pleasure in it. The fatigue and the pain in our limbs became a kind of special liquor. We started giggling at nothing at all.

We were busy winking at each other and squirting beer all over the place when the owner showed up. His car kicked up a cloud of dust. He drove right up to where we were. We had trouble breathing, especially me. There was whistling in my ears.

He got out of the car and walked over to us with his wet handkerchief. He looked at Betty with a big phony smile. The last rays of the sun gave his skin a purplish tint: sometimes it's easy to recognize people sent from Hell.

"Well, well," he said. "Seems like everything's just fine here. Job moving right along . . ."

"You can say that again," Betty answered.

"Yes indeed. Let's hope you can keep up this pace."

I broke out in a cold sweat. I jumped off my paint can. I grabbed his arm and changed the subject:

"Come take a good look . . . check out the workmanship. Great paint, dries in five minutes . . ."

"Hold on a minute," Betty said. "What did he just say?"

"Nothing," I said. "Don't worry about it. Everybody's happy, right? Let's go see the tenants. . . ."

"What did he say? . . . KEEP UP THIS PACE??"

"Figure of speech," I said. "What say we have a drink with the . . ."

But the owner turned toward Betty. I grimaced involuntarily.

"There's nothing to worry about, miss. I'm not as mean as I look. I'm not asking you to do them all without even taking a breather. . . ."

"All what . . . ? What do you mean 'THEM ALL'?"

For about a millionth of a second the guy looked surprised, then he started smiling.

"Well, I'm talking about the other bungalows, obviously. Is there something you don't understand?"

I couldn't move. I was sweating blood. Betty was still sitting on her paint can. She looked up at the owner and I thought she was going to go for his throat—that or spit flames.

"You think I'm going to waste my time painting all those things?" She sizzled. "Are you joking or what?"

"Do I look like I'm joking?" he asked.

"I don't know. . . . I can't make up my mind. . . . I'll tell you in a second. . . ."

She jumped up. She grabbed the can of pink paint. The lid

sailed over our heads like a Frisbee. Everything happened so fast that no one had time to move. I feared the worst.

"Betty . . . no!" I begged.

But it didn't stop her. She ran to the owner's car and emptied the whole can on his roof. Gallons. Indian pink. The guy sort of hiccuped. Betty smiled at him, her teeth showing.

"See . . ." she said. "I don't mind painting your car. It goes pretty fast. But I'm afraid I'll have to say no on the rest of it. I'm afraid I'm not up to it just now."

With that she split. It took a few seconds for us to get our wits back. The paint oozed down to the middle of the doors.

"It's really no big deal . . . no harm done. . . . It washes off with water. . . . It just *looks* bad," I said.

I washed his car. It took me over an hour. It was all I could do to calm him down. I told him everything would take care of itself, that she was having her period, that she was very tired, that the heat made her edgy, that she'd be the first to apologize, that, hey, what say we forget the whole thing ever happened, and why don't I also paint all the garbage cans and lamp posts while I'm at it . . . ?

He climbed back into his car, gritting his teeth. I gave an extra little polish to the windshield before he drove off in a cloud of dust. Then I was alone in the alley. It was almost nightfall and I was wiped out, at the end of my rope. But, I knew that the tough part was still ahead of me—at thirty-five life isn't a joke anymore. You have to look things straight in the face. The tough part was going to be Betty. I gave myself five minutes, then started over. I saw the lights shining in the house. Five little minutes, with my nose in the air, to sniff the winds of disaster. I think that was the moment things started taking a strange turn.

Betty had the bottle out on the table. She was sitting in a chair, head down, legs apart, all her hair falling forward. She waited a few seconds before she looked up at me. I'd never seen her so beautiful. I'm a subtle guy—I saw right away that she wasn't just angry, she was also sad. I couldn't have stood that for too long.

"Jesus Christ, what the hell is this all about?" she said in a muffled voice. "What have you got going with that asshole?"

I walked over to the table and poured myself a drink. I had to breathe a little more heavily, since I was carrying such an enormous weight on my shoulders.

"He wouldn't agree to let you stay here unless we went to work. It's not so hard to figure. . . ."

She giggled nervously and her eyes shone like marbles.

"Right. Let's see if I understand—I have to knock myself out on all those fucked-up buildings in order to have permission to rot in this . . . Jesus, don't you think it's a little like pissing in the wind?"

"In a way."

She poured herself another drink. I did the same. I was sweating a little.

"You just can't get away from those bastards," she went on. "They're all over the street. But you got to kick their ass, you can't talk sense to them. What drives me crazy is how you let yourself get fucked by that guy, how you could go for a thing like that."

"I tried to weigh the good and the bad," I said.

"You shouldn't have. You should have just told him to go fuck himself—it's a matter of pride, for Christ sakes! What does he think—that we're just a couple of degenerates only fit to shine his shoes? I'm the real jerk, I should have just scratched his eyes out!"

"Listen, if I have to paint the buildings to make sure we can stay together, then I'll paint the buildings. I'll do more than that. It seems like nothing next to what I get out of it."

"Oh shit. Why don't you try opening your eyes? My God, you're totally nuts! Look at this hole we live in—and that bastard paying you peanuts to bury yourself in it! Look at yourself! You're halfway through your life! You want to tell me exactly what you've got out of it so far? You want to show me what's worth getting yourself fucked over for?"

"It's okay. We're all still in the same place. There's no big difference."

"Excuse me, but that's bullshit! What do you think I'm doing here with you? What good is it if I can't admire you, be proud of you? We're wasting our time here! This place is only good for learning how to die!"

"Okay, all right. But what do you want to do—leave here with your hands in your pockets, only to go somewhere else and start the same shit all over again? You think you can just go out and pick money off trees? You think it's worth the trouble?"

We had another drink. We had to gather our strength to continue bitching.

"Anyway," she said, "how in the world can we keep living like this—without any hope, with nothing at all, no ambition. Shit, you're still young, healthy—it's like they've already cut your balls off. I just don't get it."

"Yeah, well, there's another way to look at it," I said. "The world is a zoo. At least here we have a little peace, far from the madding assholes, with a porch and a nice place to fuck. I think you're the one who's nuts."

She looked at me and shook her head. She finished her drink.

"Oh shit," she said. "Here I go again, stuck with another jerk! I should have known better. Something always goes haywire with men."

I went to the fridge to get some ice cubes. I had just about had it with this discussion, after the day I'd had. I went and lay down on the bed, my glass on my stomach, one arm behind my head. She turned around to look at me, her chin resting on the back of her chair.

"What's really wrong with you? What is it that doesn't work right?"

I raised my glass to toast her. I took my shoes off. It probably was not the best thing to do. It was like giving the signal to charge.

She jumped to her feet, legs firmly planted, hands on hips.

"Don't you feel suffocated here? Don't you want to breathe? Well, I do! That's right, I need a little air!"

Saying that, her eyes started sweeping around the room with a crazy look in them. I felt she was going to attack something— maybe me. They settled on the cardboard boxes—there was a stack of them piled up in the corner. I didn't have much room, but it never bothered me. I just filled up boxes from time to time and left them there.

She let out a small shriek and grabbed the first box she could lay her hands on. She lifted it up over her head. It didn't have anything too important in it—I can't say that I remembered exactly what was in there. I didn't try to stop her. It went right through the window. I heard the sound of things breaking.

She did the same with two other boxes. I finished my drink. At the rate she was going she'd tire out quickly.

"Yes!" she said. "I need air! I need to BREATHE!"

Then she went for the box that I kept my notebooks in. I stood up.

"Hold on," I said. "Leave that one alone. You can finish off the others if you want. . . ."

She pushed the hair out of her eyes. She seemed intrigued. She was out of breath from her little cleaning spree.

"What's in there?"

"Nothing special. Just some papers . . ."

"You seem pretty concerned all of a sudden. What kind of papers are they?"

I didn't answer. I walked past her and got myself another drink. My mind was starting to get cloudy.

"I want to see . . ." she said, and turned the box upside down over the bed. All my notebooks spilled out, like a display in some used-book store. I didn't like that—it made me feel edgy. I took a long swig. Betty grabbed two or three at random and started leafing through them.

"Gee, what are these?" she said. "Who wrote this? You?"

"Okay, look. They're just some old things that don't matter anymore. Let's go on to something else. I'll put them away. . . ."

"YOU wrote THIS?"

"Yes, I wrote THAT. It was a long time ago."

She seemed to get off on it. In itself this was pretty good, but I would rather have talked about something else.

"You're not going to tell me that you filled up every single page of all these notebooks! I don't believe it!"

"Betty, I think we ought to forget about this for tonight. I think we should just go to bed. I feel totally sapped and . . ."

"Jesus," she interrupted me. "But what is this, exactly? I don't understand."

"It's nothing. Just some things I wrote when I had a few minutes with nothing to do."

She looked at me with eyes big as saucers—an expression of pain and wonder at the same time.

"What's it about?"

"Nothing. About me—about whatever came into my head . . ."

"How come you never talked about it?"

"I forgot it even existed, sort of. . . ."

"Come off it! You don't just forget about something like this."

She slowly assembled the notebooks, running her fingers between each one like a blind person. There was dead silence in the room. I was starting to wonder if we'd ever get to bed. She took the stack over to the table and pulled up a chair.

"The numbers on the covers . . . that's the order?" she asked.

"What are you doing? You're not going to start reading that now!"

"Why not? You have something more interesting in mind?"

I was going to make a snide remark, but I didn't. Better to leave well enough alone. I got undressed and lay down on the bed. She opened up the first notebook. I'd never shown those things to anyone—never even mentioned them. Betty was the first person to see them. It meant something. It made me feel funny. I smoked a long cigarette before falling asleep, staring at the ceiling while the calm came back. By the time you're thirty-five you get the hang of living. You appreciate it when they let you breathe a little.

The next morning when I rolled over in bed, I saw she wasn't there. She was sitting at the table with her chin in her hands, poring over one of the notebooks. It was already daylight but the lamp was still lit. The room was full of smoke. Jesus, I said—Jesus, she's been at it all night. I got dressed in a hurry, watching her, my mind going a mile a minute. I couldn't decide whether I should say something clever to get the day off to a good start or just shut up. She didn't pay any attention to me. Once in a while she'd turn a page and put her forehead in her hands. It made me nervous. I walked around the room aimlessly, then decided to heat up the coffee. The sun had started climbing the walls.

I ran some water over my face and put the coffee on the table with two cups. I poured one for her. I pushed it toward her. She picked it up without looking at me, without saying thank you, her eyes swollen from lack of sleep and her hair going every which way. She tossed the whole cup down before I had time to put the sugar in, turning her head to drink and read at the same time. I waited to see if something was going to happen—if she was going to pay a little attention to me or fall off her chair from exhaustion. Finally I got up. I slapped my thighs.

"Well, guess I'll take off now . . . ." I said.

"Uh-huh . . . ."

I knew she didn't understand what I said.

"How's it going? You like it?" I asked.

This time she didn't hear me at all. She groped around the table for her cigarettes. At least, I thought, the thing is entertaining, and maybe it'll help settle things down a little around here. It shouldn't be too much to ask. I just wanted to keep her.

I turned the light off as I left. She hadn't looked at me once. I walked out into the nice fresh morning. There was a beautiful yellow light with a few lingering shadows. It was early. Nobody was out yet. I found myself alone, with just a slight hangover.

I went to get a can of paint out of the shed. I grabbed one off the top of the pile but it got away from me and I fell over backward into the side mirror of the VW. Right in the kidneys. I saw stars. The guy from the garage had offered to buy the car from her for next to nothing, and we'd turned it down. Now I was sorry. We had a wreck on our hands I didn't know what to do with. I rubbed my side and swore. One more problem to take care of—the list was starting to get long. I closed the door and headed off with my paint can, squinting in the sun like some sort of imbecile.

I got to work on bungalow number two, thinking of Betty poring over my little notebooks. It gave me strength. I rolled on a first coat, feeling better.

I hadn't been at it five minutes when I saw the shutters snap open and a guy's head poke out. He was unshaven in an undershirt, just out of bed—one of those types who's a regional representative for something—eyeglasses, in this case.

"Oh, it's you," he said. "What the hell are you doing?"

"Can't you tell?"

He tipped his head back and laughed.

"Nice to see you working for a change. You gonna come in and do the inside too?"

"Right. Start moving the furniture. . . ."

He yawned—a wide one—and handed me a cup of coffee. We talked for a minute about the weather, then I went back to work. The roller made a loud sucking noise with every stroke. I wished I had something quieter.

The time passed easily. Nothing much happened—I went up and down the ladder a few times and it got hotter. I was in no hurry. I felt a little numb; the white was making me half blind. The only thing that bugged me was the little rivulet of paint that kept running up my arm. It's unpleasant, and no matter what you do you can't get past it—it tickles you, it drives you nuts. To be honest, painting is not one of my pet projects. Paint gets all over everything. It gets stale in a hurry.

But painting was just what the doctor ordered that morning—something mindless. I felt like insulating myself. I made myself breathe slower—closing my eyes halfway. It worked so well that I didn't hear the truck. I just saw it go by, with Betty behind the wheel.

It was like getting punched in the gut. She's gone, I said—she's gone and I'm alone. It was a wound. I felt the panic rising but I kept moving the roller across the wall until nothing more came out of it. Then I just let loose—racing off toward the house, praying that she hadn't left for good—especially with the company car. I tore into the house like a wild animal, out of breath. It took me a few seconds to realize that all her things were still there. I had to sit down. I was weak in the knees. I must have been nuts to react like that. I got up again. I went to touch her clothes—her skirts, her T-shirts. I kicked myself. I noticed that my little notebooks had been carefully put back in the box. I downed a big glass of water and went back to work.

I came back later to eat, but she was still gone. That's always how it is when women go shopping, I thought—it always takes a while. I made myself some eggs, but I wasn't really hungry. The place didn't look right without her. I felt wrong being there. I couldn't sit still for five minutes. I did a few dishes, then went out to bring back the boxes she'd thrown outside. I reinstilled some semblance of order. Still, I had the feeling that something had changed. Objects seemed less familiar to me, the air had a funny taste to it. It was like I was in a stranger's house—an uncomfortable sensation. In spite of the heat I decided I'd rather return to my paintbrushes. I backed out the front door.

No matter how many times I told myself that she'd just gone into town for a few things, I couldn't shake the anxious feeling. I worked with little wild strokes, and the paint spattered all over the place. I looked like I'd caught some skin disease. From time to time a car passed by and I stopped to follow it with my eyes. Except for a few branches that were in the way I could see for miles. I felt like a lookout in the crow's nest of some half-sunk tub floundering in the Sargasso Sea. I wore my eyes out watching the road. For the first time I started to see the town as a sort of desert—a hellhole. I started to understand what she meant. Seen from that angle, it was not a happy sight. My paradise suddenly looked like a lost wilderness, baking out in the sun—a place nobody would want to live in. I saw it that way because she wasn't there. Still, the fact that a girl can take your world and turn it inside out can shake you up.

When I finally saw the truck coming back, I hooked my roller to a rung of the ladder and lit up a cigarette. The countryside became calm again, the leaves rustled lightly in the trees. I relaxed. Little by little everything came back to normal. I struggled against my desire to go see her. When I felt that I was about to give in, I drove my fist into the side of the house. I lost a little skin off my knuckles, but it worked. I didn't come down off my ladder.

The glasses salesman came out to see what was going on. He had a nudie magazine in his hand, I saw the tits.

"Hey, is that you making all the racket?"

"Yeah. I swatted a mosquito."

"You teasing me? There aren't any mosquitoes this time of day."

"Come up and see for yourself. The little feet are still moving in a pool of blood."

He waved it off, then rolled up his magazine and looked at me through it.

"How you doing up there?"

"I was beat a little while ago, but now I feel it coming back, full speed."

"Shit," he said. "I don't know how you can stay out there in the sun like that. Talk about your idiot jobs . . ."

He went back in with his naked girls folded under his arm and

I got back to work, charged with new energy. I started painting like a madman, a smile on my lips and my jaw set.

I stopped working a little earlier than usual. I'd already proved what I wanted to prove—no sense going overboard. The wait had gotten me excited, and it was all I could do to walk back to the house at a normal gait. I felt sparks going through my arms and legs. I was ready.

I had barely opened the door when Betty threw herself into my arms. This got me. I hugged her. Over her shoulder I saw that the table was set with a huge bouquet of flowers in the center. It smelled good.

"What's going on?" I asked. "Is it my birthday?"

"No," she said. "Just a little dinner, for lovers only."

I kissed the nape of her neck and didn't try to understand. I didn't want to ask any questions—it was all too beautiful.

"Come on," she said. "Sit down. I'll pour you a glass of cold wine."

I maneuvered around gently, still under the effects of the surprise. I looked around me, smiling. It was a fabulous little wine, just right for sipping under a setting sun. Women, I thought, they really know how to take you from Hell to Heaven. They know how it's done.

I poured myself another glass while she looked in the oven. She told me about her stroll through town, her back turned toward me, crouched down in front of the stove, her little yellow dress rising to the tops of her thighs, stretched to the max. I wasn't really listening. I was watching a little bird who had just landed on the windowsill.

"In ten minutes we eat!" she said.

She came and sat down on my lap and we drank a toast. I ran my hand up between her legs. It was the good life. I was hoping she'd remembered to buy cigars. I started diddling around in her panties, but she stopped me. She leaned back away from me. Her eyes lit up.

"Gosh," she said. "Let me look at you."

I was in heaven. I let her caress my face without moving a muscle. She seemed to like that. I downed a few glassfuls of wine.

"Now I understand why you came here to bury yourself," she whispered. "It's because you had something to WRITE!"

I didn't answer but just smiled. In truth, it wasn't at all what she thought—I hadn't settled in that town to write. The thought had never crossed my mind. No, I was just looking for a place that was peaceful, sunny, and away from people, because the world had been getting on my nerves and there was nothing I could do about it. Writing had come much later—maybe a year afterward, and for no real reason—as if that sort of thing happens to you automatically after a few months of solitude: a way to get through sleepless nights, the need to feel alive.

"You know . . . I don't know how to say this," she added. "You have no idea what it does to me. I've never read anything like it! I'm so happy that it's you who wrote it! Kiss me. . . ."

I thought she was going a little overboard, but I didn't need to be coaxed. The evening's temperature was just right. I slid into it as into a warm bath of cinnamon perfume. I was totally relaxed, all the way to the tips of my toes.

Betty was radiant, witty, desirable. I felt like I had gone into outer space and was floating in a vacuum. All that was left was to batten down the hatches and land in bed. But all she was interested in was my notebooks, my BOOK—the hows and whys, this and that. I realized I had really shaken her up, broadened her horizons with what had come out of my brain, and the idea simply overjoyed me. Had I been a genie, I might have knocked her off her feet with my stare.

I tried to calm her down but there was nothing doing. She covered me all over with her tender eyes. She caressed my writer's hands. Her eyes shone like those of a little girl who had broken open a stone and found a diamond. I had been given the red carpet. The only slight dark spot in the picture was that I had the feeling she was mistaking me for someone else. But I told myself I might as well take advantage of my attributes—my big writer's dick and the vast depths of my soul. Life resembled an automat—you've got to know how to grab the food before it passes you by right under your nose.

Around eleven o'clock the writer started flapping his wings. Two little bottles of wine and it was all he could do to keep from falling off his chair. He was happy—ogling his girl, smiling—he no longer understood what she was saying to him and did not have the strength to ask her to repeat herself. The wine had made him drunk, the tenderness had made him drunk, well-being itself had made him drunk, but it was mostly the girl with the long black hair who was rolling her chest around in front of him who made him drunk. It wouldn't even have taken much for her to make him want to go reread all those notebooks himself—she had given them a new dimension. In bed, he amused himself, removing her panties with his teeth. She took him in her arms and hugged him. She'd never hugged him like that—it made him feel odd. She clung to him as though they'd come through a storm, her legs hooked across his back. He went into her gently, staring into her eyes. He clutched her behind and licked her breasts, and the night moved on. They smoked a cigarette. They were drenched with sweat. After a while the girl lifted herself up on her elbow.

"When I think that you're out there painting houses . . ." she said.

The writer had a witty comeback all ready—it was his stock-in-trade.

"What the fuck difference does it make?" he said.

"It's not where you should be. . . ."

"Oh yeah? Where *should* I be?"

"At the top," she said.

"You're sweet," he said. "But I don't think the world is exactly tailored to my measurements."

She straddled the writer and took his head in her hands.

"Now, that . . ." she said, "that's what we're going to find out."

He paid no heed to what she had just said. He was a writer, not a fortune-teller.

5

The owner showed up the next day just as we were taking a nap. I went out to meet him on the doorstep. It was obvious that he was looking for trouble. The heat hadn't spared him on his way over—he was livid. Betty was still in bed so I didn't ask him to come in. I even pushed him outside, casually, and maybe that's what got him mad—maybe he wanted to come in and wash his face.

"You must be kidding," he snarled. "What is it, you get up at ten in the morning and at four in the afternoon? Is the job keeping you awake?"

"Excuse me," I said. "But I work till sunset every night. That racks up quite a few hours. . . ."

"I see. You have an answer for everything, right?"

"You're making a mistake," I said.

I had barely finished my sentence when Betty showed up. She'd thrown on one of my T-shirts, pulling it down to cover her behind. She gave the owner a look that could kill.

"What right do you have to talk to him that way?" she asked.

"Betty, please . . ." I said.

"No really," she went on. "Who do you think . . . ?"

The guy stood there with his mouth open. He looked at Betty, tugging at her T-shirt, her nipples pointy and thighs long and naked. His eyes were popping out of his head. He mopped his face with his handkerchief.

"Listen, I'm not talking to you," he said.

"Lucky for you. But just who do you think you *are* talking to?"

"I'm talking to my employee."

She burst out laughing.

"Your employee? You poor old wasted slob . . . you happen to be talking to the greatest writer of his generation. You get it . . . ?"

"Betty, don't you think you're going a bit too . . ."

"I don't want to hear about it," said the owner.

I saw Betty go pale. Furious, she let go of the T-shirt and it snapped up ten inches. You could see her every hair on her crotch. The guy's eyes were glued. It took Betty a few seconds to figure out what was going on.

"What the hell are you looking at?" she growled.

The man was hypnotized, he stood there biting his lip. She gave him a push and he backed down a few steps from the porch.

"What's the matter, you never seen a woman before? You going to have a stroke?"

She ran after him, bare-assed, and gave him another push. The guy stumbled and almost fell, just barely righting himself. He flushed.

"If there's one thing I can't stand, it's a sex maniac," she said.

The scene was so unbelievable and Betty so sexy that I couldn't even move. I stood on the porch with my mouth open. The owner was green with rage—he beat a hasty retreat, set off against a blue sky. I couldn't keep from laughing, especially when he fell on his face.

He got back up quickly and took a last look at me.

"Take my advice—get rid of that girl!" he yelled.

Betty was still threatening to go after him, so he turned tail and ran, slapping at his suit coat, making little dust clouds in the air as he went.

She walked past me and went into the house without a word, still trembling with anger. I knew better than to get close to her—it was obvious. I would wait until the storm blew over by itself. At that moment even the writer wasn't up to the task. The scenery had changed again—once more I found myself in the middle of a crummy little nowhere. I heard her inside kicking the walls. It was time to go back to work.

All afternoon I spied on her from the top of my ladder. If I stood on tiptoe I could see over the roof of number two and into my windows. I rubbernecked without shame, safe at fifty yards. I wondered how much time it would take for a girl in her state to cool down. I saw a few of my boxes sail back out the window, but not the one with the notebooks—not that one. Haha, I thought: HAHA.

Naturally I didn't get too far on the job. I wasn't into it. I worked halfheartedly. The day plodded along. She was sitting at the table again, her head in her hands. I couldn't figure out if this was good or bad. The old fart had gotten what he deserved. Had I?

The owner's threats spun around in my head, but it didn't get me down; I imagined myself taking him to the cleaner's—or the authorities. I just felt a little tired, like when you catch a chill. I also had miles of painting to do. I was finishing off my can of paint when I saw Betty go out onto the porch. I ducked down behind the roof. When I looked again, she was going up the alley and around the corner.

I wondered where she was going. It got me thinking. I went over all possible answers as I whitewashed the wall. It turned out I didn't even have the time to get worried—one minute later she was back. I hadn't even seen her come—I saw her through the windows going back and forth, bustling around inside the house. I couldn't see too well what she was doing—it seemed like she was shaking something in front of her.

What do you know, I said to myself, she's cleaning. Must be tidying up the house to calm her nerves. I knew she'd make it shine like a new penny.

I worked for another little while, my soul at peace. The sun set, and I rinsed out my paintbrushes conscientiously. It had cooled off. Before I went home I had a beer with the eyeglasses salesman. The sky was an unbelievable red. I lit a cigarette and headed for the house, watching my feet as they walked along. Ten yards before I got there I looked up. Betty was standing in front of the porch. I stopped. Next to her were her two suitcases, and she was looking at me with incredible intensity. I couldn't help but wonder what she was doing holding my Coleman lamp, lit. The sunset make her hair burn—she was ferociously beautiful. Something smelled like gas. I knew she was going to throw the lamp into the house. For a tenth of a second the idea appealed to me, then I saw her arm describe a semicircle in the air and the lamp flew into the sky like a shooting star.

The house went up like the *Hindenburg*—a free sample of Hell. She picked up her suitcases. The flames welled up in the windows.

"Well, are you coming?" she asked. "Let's go."

6

I woke up frowning because the road was so bumpy, and because I was cold. The wind whipped around us in the back of the pickup. It must have been six in the morning. The sun was just coming up. Betty was sleeping with her fists clenched. As luck would have it, we had gotten ourselves a ride from a guy who was hauling fertilizer, and the smell of it first thing in the morning was enough to turn my stomach. The seat next to the driver was full of packages, which is why we had to ride outside in the back. I got a sweater out of Betty's suitcase and put it on. I also put something around her shoulders. We were going through a forest and it was cold. The tops of the trees were so high that it made me dizzy. The driver tapped on the rear window—a young guy who'd picked us up at a gas station; I'd bought him a beer. He was on his way back from some kind of county fair or something.

He offered us some coffee—I could have kissed him. I grabbed the Thermos and poured myself a few little cupfuls. I lit up my first cigarette of the day, sitting on one of the sacks, watching the road go by. I couldn't keep from laughing. At my age it was like a new case of acne. Sure, it wasn't anything fatal. In truth I'd left nothing at all behind me—Betty had stuffed a few shirts and my notebooks in one of the suitcases—it was just that I found the whole thing a little ridiculous. All I needed was Henry Fonda's hat. Practical girl, she had also rescued my savings from the fire. I felt rather rich: we had easily enough to last us a month or two. I had told her, Look, why hitchhike like a couple of dopes? Why drive ourselves crazy? Let's take the fucking train. But nothing doing, she was determined that we not spend money unnecessarily. Put out your thumb, she said. But the truth—the real truth—is that she liked it. What she wanted was to leave a pile of ashes behind her and hit the road like in the good old days. Mark the occasion. I didn't put up a fuss. She was there, hanging on my arm, and that was all that counted. I had picked up the suitcase and stuck out my thumb, laughing.

We'd been on the road for two days, and we were covered with dust. I started missing my shower. I yawned loudly and Betty woke up. Two seconds later she jumped into my arms and rolled her tongue into my mouth. No matter how hard I might have tried, I couldn't have thought of anything else to pray for. Looking at her, I knew she was happy. I still didn't share her drive to conquer the world, but it didn't matter. Things were fine. The road's not so bad when you have a beautiful girl with you.

The guy stopped for gas and we went in and bought sandwiches and beer. It was starting to get hot out again. Once in a while the truck made it up to fifty miles per hour, but even then all we could feel was the sun cooking our skin. Betty loved it—the wind, the road, the sun. I popped open the beer, my head nodding. I couldn't help but think that if she'd have let me just buy some train tickets we'd already have been there instead of taking this fabulous detour—all because the guy had to go see his brother before going on into town, and we didn't want to lose that great little pickup truck. He was the only one who'd take us; we weren't about to let him go until he'd driven us all the way to town. True, we were in no hurry. We were hardly on the road to El Dorado.

We stopped in some little one-horse town. We sat in the shade and ordered cool drinks while the guy went off to see his brother. Betty went to the bathroom and I dozed in my chair. I could find absolutely no reason to worry and the world seemed as absurd as always. The town was quiet, nearly deserted.

After a while we took off again, but it wasn't until the end of the day that we saw the lights of the city. Betty was standing up, stamping with impatience.

"Do you realize it's been more than five years since I've seen her? It feels weird. To me she'll always be just my little sister, you see. . . ."

The guy let us off at an intersection, and by the time Betty and I had gotten out and pulled down our suitcases, there was a whole line of cars honking—guys sticking their heads out their windows. I'd forgotten that kind of atmosphere: the smell of gas leaks, the lights, the greasy sidewalks, the car noises you can never get away from. I didn't feel particularly enthused.

We walked for a while, dragging the suitcases. They weren't that heavy but they were awkward—there was always somebody bumping into us. The only good thing was that we could sit on them while waiting for the lights to change. Betty had stopped talking. She was like a fish that someone had just thrown back in the water. I didn't want to spoil her fun. It wasn't so horrible after all—even if cooling your heels waiting for the lights to change did sometimes seem like punishment.

People were in the street at that time of day—job over, heading home. All the signs lit up suddenly; they blinked like waterfalls of light as we passed under them batting our eyes and pulling in our shoulders. I truly hated all of it, but having Betty at my side made it bearable—all the crap hardly bothered me. Most of the people had hideous faces. I saw that nothing had changed.

Betty's sister, Lisa, lived in a calmer part of town, in a little white two-story house with a twenty-by-twenty-foot terrace overlooking a vacant lot. She opened the door with a chicken wing in her hand. It made me hungry. Betty and Lisa kissed each other exuberantly and Betty introduced us. I eyed a piece of baked-to-a-turn chicken skin hanging off the wing. Hi Lisa, I said. A Doberman pinscher came out of the house, whipping the night with its tail. That's Bongo, she said, patting the animal's head. Bongo looked at me, then at his mistress, and finally at the chicken wing, which he ate. I always knew the world was a mean joke.

Although Lisa lived alone with Bongo in the most total mess I'd ever seen, the house itself was somehow very pleasant. Full of colors, with things hanging all over the place as if they'd been forgotten there. Lisa wore a short kimono. She had nice legs, but otherwise Betty had her beat hand over fist, even though she was five or six years older. I drifted onto the couch while the girls talked, taking a drink and a few munchies with me.

I must have been more tired than I thought—the first glass of sherry went right into my bloodstream. My head started spinning—I almost stepped on the dog when I stood up to go to the bathroom. I splashed some water on my face. I had a three-day beard and eyes circled with dust. I felt rubber-legged, sort of a street-angel-blitzed-on-two-fingers-of-rotgut thing.

When I came back Bongo was finishing the chicken and Betty was recounting the end of our trip. Lisa clapped her hands.

"Perfect timing!" she said. "The upstairs has been free for a week!"

Betty seemed staggered. She put her glass down slowly.

"What? You mean there's nobody upstairs and you'd rent us the apartment?"

"Sure. Might as well have *you* take it."

"Oh Lord, I'm dreaming," Betty said. "This is fabulous!"

She bounded over to me and kneeled down in front of my chair. I wondered if she hadn't actually covered herself with spangles.

"See, what did I tell you?" she said. "See what can happen? If this isn't some kind of luck I don't know what is."

"What's going on, exactly?" I asked.

Betty squashed her breasts into my knees.

"What's going on, honey, is that we haven't even been in town one hour and we've already found a sensational apartment that has fallen into our laps straight from heaven!"

"Ask if it has a big bed," I said.

She pinched my thigh and we raised our glasses. I didn't say anything, but I was willing to admit that we were, in fact, off to a good start. After all, maybe she was right—maybe an easier world was really about to open its arms to us. I started feeling good.

The bottle hadn't gone too far. I told them, Don't worry, and I went out—down to the corner with my nose in the air, my hands in my pockets. I'd spotted some stores farther down the street.

I went into the grocer's—Good evening, everyone, I said. The guy was alone behind the cash register, an old man with suspenders. I got some champagne, some cookies, and a can of food for the dog. The old man added it up without looking at me, nearly asleep.

"You know," I said. "We'll likely be seeing a lot of each other. I've just moved into the neighborhood. . . ."

The good news did not stir him. He handed me the bill, yawning. I paid up.

"You're really a lucky guy," I joked. "I'm going to be dropping a bundle in here every month. . . ."

He gave me a smile—visibly forced—and waited for me to split. His face had a pained expression on it, like most of the people on the street. It made me feel like a leper. I thought for a second, then went back and got a second bottle. I threw the money at him and left.

The girls welcomed me back with cries of joy. While the champagne ran I opened the can of dog food: two pounds of bright pink mush bathed in jelly. Bongo looked at me with his head cocked. I knew it was wise to get on the good side of these animals. I saw that I had already scored a point.

Next we went to see the apartment. We climbed the stairway

that led to the second floor, laughed when Lisa took a few minutes to get the key to turn.

"Usually this door is locked, but from now on we can just leave it open. Gosh, I'm so happy about this! Sometimes I get kind of lonely, you know. . . ."

There was a bedroom, a room with a kitchen in the corner, and the little terrace. In short—paradise. There was a closet that had been turned into a shower. While the girls made the bed, I went out onto the terrace and leaned over the balcony. Bongo did likewise. Standing on his hind legs, he was almost as tall as me. The balcony looked out onto some deserted land, closed off by a fence. You could see houses on the other side, some hills farther on, then a blackness, darker than night. I heard them laughing and squealing in the bedroom. I smoked a cigarette and let it go all through me. I winked at Bongo.

Later, between the sheets, Betty squeezed herself against me and immediately went to sleep. I looked at the ceiling. I didn't know where I was anymore, but I didn't rack my brain about it. I did some deep breathing. Little by little I drifted into sleep, all the time feeling like I was slowly waking up.

7

We didn't start looking for a job right away—we were in no hurry. We spent most of our time on the terrace, talking to Lisa and Bongo, playing cards, reading. The afternoons succeeded each other, threaded together by an amazing calm—I'd never known anything that good. Betty was tanned to a golden turn, Lisa somewhat less so, since she worked during the day as a cashier in a department store. From time to time I'd play with Bongo in the vacant lot, chasing the birds away. Betty would watch us from the balcony. We'd wave at each other, then she'd disappear. Soon all I heard was the tapping of the typewriter—the little bell that rings when you come to the end of a line.

Actually, this worried me a little. She'd gotten it into her head to type my whole manuscript and send it out to publishers. She'd run herself ragged finding a typewriter. I'd written the thing for my own pleasure, not to throw myself to the lions—at least that's the way I'd always looked at it—but Betty was preparing my entrance into the arena. I tossed a stick for Bongo to fetch, fretting about it all, but I didn't let it get to me. I had other things on my mind—the evening's menu, for example. It was something I'd happily put myself in charge of. A clever guy who has all day to ponder dinner can make miracles out of nothing. I even whipped up something special for Bongo—we'd become fast friends.

After putting dinner in the oven, I'd take him for a walk to meet Lisa. Betty kept typing with three or four fingers till the last rays of sunset, and this gave us quite a bit of time. She made a lot of mistakes and the corrections doubled her work, but I didn't worry too much about it. Bongo would run ahead of me and people would just get out of the way. It was fabulous—I always found a seat on the bench at the bus stop. We hadn't had an autumn that mild in a long time. Afterward we'd walk back to the house slowly, Lisa and I, me carrying her things, Bongo sprinkling the cars. She'd tell me about herself; I didn't have much to tell. I found out that she'd married very young and that the guy had dumped her after two years. Not much was left of the marriage— just Bongo and the house, and the apartment upstairs that she rented out to make ends meet. We'd come to a nice agreement about that. There were a lot of things in it that needed fixing— plumbing and electrical work—so we'd estimated that the work would come out to about three months' rent. Everybody was happy.

In the evenings, we'd catch a movie on TV. We'd take it in, all the way to the end—the last commercial—then haggle about who was going to get up and turn the set off. You had to be careful not to fall on all the beer cans. If it was really too boring, we'd turn it off in the middle and get out the deck of cards, or just hang out in the apartment, the girls talking to each other while I played with the dials on the radio, trying to get something decent. Sometimes I'd feel like taking a walk. I'd get my jacket without a word and we'd weave our way through street after street, Bongo running between all our legs. The girls loved that. I told them it made me feel like a rat in a maze and they laughed. It's true—we would turn right, then another right, or left . . . the scenery never changed at all. When we got home we were dead on our feet. Still, it was good for the digestion and made us hungry. By the time the door was closed we'd have already emptied the whole refrigerator onto the table. When Lisa felt tired we'd go upstairs, but we never went to bed until three or four in the morning. It's hard to go to bed early when you get up at noon.

When we weren't doing all this and she felt up to it, Betty would go back to her typing. I'd settle down on the terrace with Bongo's snout across my lap, watching her decipher what was in the notebooks with a furrowed brow. I wondered what I'd done right to wind up with a girl like that—still, I knew that even if I'd been holed up at the North Pole, I'd have come across her sooner or later, trudging across the ice floe with the chill wind blowing around her neck. I loved to watch her. It made me forget all the shit we'd left behind. When I thought about it, I imagined a posse of cops hot on our trail, the burning bungalow hanging like a sword over our heads. Luckily I didn't leave my address. I imagined the tenants in the shadows of the flames, making faces and screaming at us as we took off running with our suitcases in our hands like some yellow-bellied bank robbers. Now when I heard a siren in the distance I'd just take a swig of beer and in five minutes all was forgotten—all except this woman sitting a few yards from me who was the most important thing in my life. It didn't bother me that the most important thing in my life was a woman, in fact it felt great—the feeling in the air had turned into something simple and carefree. Once in a while I'd get up and go cop a quick feel—see how she was getting along with it.

"Doing okay? Still into it?" I'd ask.

"Don't worry about it."

"Well, if it turns out that no one publishes it . . . ."

"What, are you kidding?"

"Look, it's quite possible."

"Oh yeah? Explain to me how that could ever happen."

"Betty, it's a tough world out there. . . ."

"No it isn't. All you have to do is know how to handle it."

It was food for thought. I went back to the terrace and she went back to the typing, Bongo went back to my lap, and over my head the stars came out, chattering.

I woke up one morning wanting to get on with the plumbing. I kissed Betty on the forehead, borrowed Lisa's car, and went to town to get supplies. A few of the pipes stuck out of the car on the way back, and when I got home and started unloading it, this woman suddenly showed up next to me. She was wearing a little gold crucifix.

"Excuse me, sir . . . you wouldn't be a plumber, would you?"

"That depends," I said. "Why?"

"Well, it's about my faucet, my faucet in the kitchen. I've been trying to get a plumber for a month now, but nobody wants to come out to fix my faucet. You don't know how bothersome . . ."

"Yeah, I know. I've been there myself."

She stroked her crucifix and looked at the ground.

"You wouldn't consider . . . it's perhaps just a matter of a few minutes' work. . . ."

I thought it over for a second, looking at my watch like I was already overloaded.

"Shit, it would be tight. . . . You live far from here?"

"No, no. Just across the street."

"Okay, but let's get going."

She was around sixty, with a dress that came down to the middle of her calves. I followed her across the street. It was the house of a retiree who lacked for nothing—the tile gleamed and all was silent. She led me into the kitchen and pointed to the faucet. A little stream of clear water trickled gently onto the enamel. I went up and turned it a few times in every possible direction, then stepped back and sighed.

"Just as I thought," I said. "The rotary has gotten caught in the valve and is botching up the equilateral. It happens all the time."

"Oh no. Is it serious?"

"Could be worse," I said. "Got to replace everything."

"Oh my God. And how much will this cost?"

I did a little vague calculating in my head, then multiplied by two.

"Oh sweet Jesus!" she said.

"And that doesn't include the labor," I added.

"And when do you think you can do this . . . ?"

"Right now or never. I don't take checks."

I ran back to the house and got together all the tools I could find. I told Betty what was going on. She just shrugged and dove back into the notebooks. Two seconds later I was back in the car. I double-parked, bought the faucet, and went back to the old lady's house.

"I can't be disturbed," I said. "I'm used to working in silence. I'll call you if I need anything."

I holed up in the kitchen and went to work. One hour later I put my tools away, mopped up the last drop of water, passed Go, and went up to the teller's window. Sister Mary Magdalen and Baby Jesus were in heaven—the kitchen was in perfect working order.

"Now, young man," she said. "Don't leave without giving me your telephone number. Knock on wood, I hope I won't need you again, but . . ."

She walked me out to the doorstep and waved at me until I disappeared into the house. Not a bad day's work, I thought.

That same night I was keeping an eye on dinner when the phone rang. Betty was setting the table. Lisa answered. She listened for a second, said a few words back, then put her hand over the receiver, laughing:

"Hey, get this, it's the guy from the market down the street. He says he wants to talk to the plumber!"

Betty gave me the evil eye.

"I think you're on call," she said. "Must be something clogged somewhere . . ."

Word spread like wildfire. My phone number made the rounds with the speed of light. I wondered where the other plumbers—the real ones—were hiding, what with all those houses leaking all over the place, all those pipes clogging up. I was standing in line to buy a few yards of copper tubing and a right-angle elbow, when I happened to talk to a pro who told me that they didn't want to bother with the little jobs. I'll tell you something, the guy said, lowering his voice to a whisper, when somebody calls me up for a leak, if I don't think I can wind up selling them a new bathroom, I don't mess with it.

So I found my niche: five-second jobs paid for in cash. In a matter of hours I'd become a neighborhood celebrity. Expensive, but efficient. I knew where my power lay: somebody who has the flu can try to fight it, but somebody with a clogged toilet is at your mercy. I made as much money as I could. I overcharged. I had them all in a hammerlock.

For a couple of weeks it was pretty wild, but then it settled down. I stopped running around so much, booking all my jobs for the morning. Betty didn't like me leaving, cap pulled down over my eyes and toolbox under my arm—it made her nervous. We even had a fight about it one night. I had come home totally wiped out.

I'd just done an emergency job for this military guy—uniform, white hair, blue eyes. It was my fifth job of the day and I was wasted. The guy led me down this long dark hall, his boots clacking on the floor, me following him all hunched over. The minute I got to the kitchen I was hit by this smell, like french fries and burned plastic, horrible. It was all I could do to stay there. It was something that happened every time I went into somebody's house—this desire to turn tail and run. I stayed, though.

The guy was carrying a riding crop in his hand—he pointed it at the kitchen sink without saying a word. It didn't matter—by the end of the day I didn't care if people talked to me or not. It was more peaceful if they didn't. I approached the sink, half holding my breath. There were three plastic dolls in it, mostly melted. The drain was clogged and everything floated in about two inches of oil. I opened the cupboard underneath to take out the garbage can and I saw that the drainpipe was completely corkscrewed, even melted in some places. I stood up.

"You did this with boiling oil?"

"Listen, I don't have to answer you," he whined. "Just do whatever needs doing and let's get it over with quickly."

"Hey, take it easy. It's okay with me if you want to pour hot oil on your dolls. I see weirder things than that every day. It's just that I have to know if there might be something else besides grease and melted plastic in your pipe here. You'll have to tell me."

He shook his head fast and said no, then he left me alone. I took a cigarette break. At first glance it didn't seem very complicated—just a drainpipe replacement—but of course things are never as easy as they seem. I went back into the cupboard and saw that in fact the drainpipe ran through two other cupboards before going into the floor. I saw that I was going to have a good time trying to get through all the crap.

I went out to the car to get a piece of drainpipe. I had all the basic sizes—they were strapped onto the roof and hooked to the bumpers at each end. Betty had rolled her eyes when she saw that. I'd found a whole bunch of them at this construction site during one of my nocturnal outings, and my profits had skyrocketed ever since. I grabbed a beer from under the front seat and chugged the whole thing before going back to work.

It took me an hour to remove the old pipe and another hour

to install the new one. It drove me half crazy—down on all fours in the cupboards, smashing my head in every possible corner. I had to stop every once in a while to close my eyes for a minute. But I did the job. I leaned on the sink and got my breath back, smiling at the little disemboweled dolls. Come on, man, just hold on a little longer and your day will be over—think about the girls fixing you a drink. I grabbed the pipe, sawed off a good yard of it, and fitted it into the joint. I was putting my tools away when the guy in the khaki uniform showed up again. He didn't even look at me, just stuck his nose in all the cupboards to check the installation. Guys like that make me laugh. I slipped the strap of my toolbox over my shoulder, grabbed my piece of drainpipe, and waited for him to come out of there.

He stood up, seized with agitation.

"What is this . . . ?" he said. "WHAT IS THE MEANING OF THIS?"

I wondered if maybe he'd burst a blood vessel in his brain while bending down under the sink. I stayed calm.

"Is something wrong?" I asked.

He tried to dig his eyes into my forehead. He must have thought he was still in the colonies, getting ready to chastise one of his slaves.

"Are you trying to pull the wool over my eyes? Your pipes are not regulation!"

"How's that?"

"Yes . . . the length of pipe that you've put in, THERE—it's a piece of telephone tubing!! It's WRITTEN on it!"

It was news to me. It's true I'd never paid much attention. Still, I didn't let it shake me.

"You scared me," I said. "No, seriously, don't worry about it. It's exactly the same pipe as the other kind. All the sinks in town are fitted with it, it's been that way for ten years. It's good stuff."

"No, no, no. No good. It's not REGULATION!!"

"Really, don't worry about it. . . ."

"Don't try to swindle me! I want things done according to regulation."

It always happens to you at the end of the day, just when you're totally beat. Nobody's willing to throw in the towel. I ran my hand through my hair.

"Listen," I said. "I do my job, you do yours. I'm not going to ask you what kind of dynamite you use to take a hill. If I use telephone tubing it's because I know what I'm doing."

"I want a regulation installation, you hear me?"

"Yeah, I hear you. And I suppose that all the weirdness you do in the sink, that's regulation, too. Look, just pay me and let's forget about it. That thing's not going to budge for twenty years, I guaran—"

"Nothing doing! You're not getting one penny until you change it!"

I looked the old fruitcake right in the eye. It was clear I was wasting my time with him, and I wasn't interested in overtime. All I wanted was to get back in my little car, roll down the windows, smoke a cigarette, and go home in peace, that's all. So I walked up to the sink, bent my knee, and kicked the U joint with all my might. I managed to break off half of it. I turned to the guy.

"There you go," I said. "Something's wrong with your sink. You'd better call a plumber."

The old man hit me in the face with his crop—I felt a line of fire from my mouth to my ear. He looked at me, his eyes gleaming. I smashed him in the head with my pipe. He backed up into the wall and put his hand on his heart. I didn't go get him his pills. I just split.

I felt my cheek burning all the way home. I looked in the rearview mirror and saw a red-purple stripe. One corner of my mouth was swollen—it made me look even more exhausted than I was. It seemed to put into motion some process that made all the fatigue from the past few days show up on my face. I wasn't a pretty sight. Caught in a traffic jam, I was able to recognize all my brothers in misery—we all looked alike. Same wounds, or almost. Every face ravaged by a week of meaningless work— fatigue, privation, rage, and boredom. We crept forward a few yards each time the light turned green, without saying a word.

Betty saw the welt the minute I walked in. My cheek was all puffed up, glistening. I didn't have the heart to make up a lie—I told her exactly what had happened. I poured myself a tall drink and she jumped on me:

"That's what you get for clowning around all day long! It had to happen!"

"Shit, Betty. What are you talking about?"

"Spending your days on your knees under a bunch of fucking sinks, rubbing elbows with garbage cans, unplugging all sorts of shit, putting in toilets . . . you think that's smart?"

"Who cares? It's not important."

She came up close to me. In a sugar-coated voice she said, "Tell me, do you know what I've been doing all these days? You don't know? Well, I've been recopying your book! I've been at it day after day, and sometimes at night—it keeps me up nights, for your information!"

Her voice got more and more bitter. I poured myself another one and grabbed a handful of peanuts. She didn't take her eyes off me.

"I am convinced that you are a great writer. Can you get that through your head at least?"

"Listen, don't start up again with that. I'm tired. Being a great writer is not going to put food on the table. I think you're working too hard on that thing. It's giving you delusions of grandeur."

"But God! Don't you see that someone like you shouldn't have to stoop? Don't you understand that you don't have the right to do that?"

"Hey, Betty . . . you gone nuts?"

She grabbed me by the lapels. I almost spilled my scotch.

"No, it's *you* who's nuts! You're not with it at all! It makes me sick to see how you spend your time. What's wrong with you? Why won't you open your eyes?"

I couldn't help sighing. The crummy day just wouldn't end.

"Betty . . . I'm really afraid you think I'm someone I'm not."

"No, stupid! I know who you are! I just didn't know you were so thick! I'd rather see you out just walking around, gawking, anything—that would be normal. But instead you go out and deaden your mind with a bunch of sinks, and you think it's very cool. . . ."

"I'm doing a little fieldwork in human relations," I said. "I'm trying to store up a maximum of infor—"

"Oh, cut the bullshit! I've already said that I want to be proud of you, to admire you, but I think the idea really bugs you! I think you're doing all this to annoy me!"

"No, I'd never do anything to annoy you."

"Well, it seems that way to me, I swear. I mean, Jesus, try to understand. You don't have time to do a hundred different things with your life. Don't think you're going to get out of it with a few witty remarks. You'd be better off facing it once and for all: you're a writer, not a plumber."

"How can you tell the difference?" I asked.

We glared at each other across the table. She looked like she was ready to slit my throat.

"You're going to give me a lot of work," she said. "Yeah, you probably will—but for now there's nothing we can do about it. I'm warning you, I'm not going to give in. I'm telling you it bugs me to live with a guy who comes home at seven o'clock at night, plops his toolbox on the table and sighs: 'THIS REALLY GETS ME DOWN!' How do you think I feel when in the afternoon I'm completely absorbed in your book and the telephone rings and some creep asks where you are because something just went blooey in his toilet bowl? I can almost smell the shit! How do you think I feel when I hang up? Some hero . . . ."

"Look, I think you're going overboard. I think it's a good thing that there are plumbers. I can tell you I'd rather do that than work in an office."

"Lord, don't you understand anything? Don't you see that with one hand you're pulling my head out of the water and with the other you're dunking me in again?"

I was going to tell her that it was a good metaphor for life in general, but I didn't. I just nodded and poured myself a glass of water and went to drink it looking out the window. It was almost dark out. The writer wasn't very sharp, and the plumber was dead.

It was after this conversation that I started slowing down. I tried at least not to work in the afternoon, and things changed right away. Permanent good times came back between Betty and me—we recaptured the flavor of peaceful days, we winked at each other again.

The plumber had trouble getting up in the morning after the writer had gone to bed at three o'clock. He had to be careful not to wake Betty up—to heat the coffee without his face falling in it. He yawned, unhooking his jaw. It was only when he set foot on the street that he started emerging. The strap from his toolbox sawed his shoulder in half.

Betty was sometimes still sleeping when he came home. He would jump in the shower, then wait for her to wake up, smoking a cigarette at her side. He would look at the paper piling up next to the typewriter, listen to the silence, or play with a rolled-up pair of panty hose at the foot of the bed.

By the time Betty woke up the writer was deep in a session of self-introspection, a small dreamy smile on his lips. Usually they fucked, then had breakfast together. It was the good life for the writer. He felt just a bit tired, that was all, and when the sky was clear he liked to take a nap on the terrace, listening to the noise coming up from the street. The writer was cool. He never worried about money. His brain was empty. Sometimes he asked himself how he had ever managed to write a book—it seemed so far away now. Maybe he'd write another one some day, he couldn't really say. He didn't want to think about it. Betty asked him the question once, and he told her that he just might, but it made him uneasy for the rest of the day.

When he got up the next morning, the plumber had a serious hangover. He waited until his client turned around, then threw up in the shower stall. It gave him the willies. Sometimes he hated that fucking writer.

8

❖ ⟶ ◆ ⟵ ❖

Before we knew it the evenings started getting cooler, and the first leaves fell from the trees and filled the gutters. Betty went to work on my last notebook and I continued to putter around here and there to earn enough money to keep us going. Everything was fine except that now I found myself waking up at night, eyes wide in the dark, brain burning, squirming around in bed as if I'd swallowed a snake. All I had to do was reach out my arm—I'd put a new notebook and pencil right next to the bed—but this song-and-dance had been going on for two days, and no matter how I racked my brain I couldn't come up with the slightest new idea. Nothing came out at all—but nothing—so every night the big writer went down for the count. He had lost his muse's phone number, the poor jerk; he'd even lost his desire to call, and he didn't even know why.

I tried to convince myself that it was a case of temporary constipation. To shake things up a little, I started doing some electrical work in the afternoons. I replaced wires, installed junction boxes, put in switches with dimmers for atmosphere—all the way up at night, then down to just a glimmer to fuck in. But even with all the puttering I felt my soul dragging. I had to stop regularly to down a beer. Only when evening came on did I start to feel better—almost normal. Sometimes I was downright joyful, the alcohol helped me through. I'd go up to Betty and bend over the typewriter:

"Hey, Betty, no use wearing yourself out—I got nothing left inside, my balls are gone. . . ."

I thought this was funny as hell. I gave the top of the machine a good punch.

"Let's go," Betty said. "Out. Go sit down, and stop screwing around. You're talking like a jerk."

I sank down in an armchair and watched the flies fly. When it was warm I'd leave the terrace door open and toss my empty beer cans outside. The message I heard inside was always the same: where? when? how?—but I was having trouble finding a buyer for my troubled soul. I wasn't even asking for much, just two or three pages would do the trick, just something to get me started. I was sure that all I had to do was start. I had to laugh, it was all so stupid. Betty shook her head and smiled.

After that, I would start making dinner and my worries would go out the window. I'd do a little shopping with Bongo. The fresh air woke me up. And if I started going a bit off the deep end again while cracking an egg or grilling a leek, it didn't really matter—I would just look forward to sitting down to eat with the two girls, and try to be as lively as they were. I'd look at them talking, sending sparks back and forth in the living room. Usually I would get into sauces—the girls said I was a genius with sauces—they always cleaned their plates. People also said I was a genius as a plumber. And as a fly-fucker—how did I stack up there? After all those years of peace, I was perfectly within my rights to wonder what was happening to me. It was like trying to restart an old locomotive, overgrown with weeds. It was terrifying.

* * *

The day Betty finished typing my book, my stomach was in knots. My legs hurt. I was standing on a chair, tinkering with a lamp, when she told me. It was like taking 200 volts in your hand. I climbed down slowly, holding onto the back of the chair for dear life. I acted moderately impressed.

"Well, it took you long enough. . . . Listen, I got to split. Got to buy some fuses."

I wasn't listening to what she said—I didn't hear anything anymore. I just walked calmly to my jacket. I was like the actor onstage who gets shot in the guts but won't go down. I slipped my jacket on and went down the stairs, not breathing until I hit the door.

Out on the street, I started walking. A little breeze came up with nightfall, but soon I found myself covered with sweat. I slowed down. I noticed that Bongo was following me. He ran ahead of me, then waited for me to catch up. I don't know why he did that. There seemed to be a smell of blind confidence in the air, and it was getting on my nerves—the smell of emptiness, too.

I went into a bar and ordered a tequila, because it works fast and I needed a jolt. It's hard to accept that the good times are gone—I've always thought so. I asked for another tequila and then I started feeling better. There was this guy next to me, totally blasted, staring at me with his glass in both hands. I saw him attempt to open his mouth and I egged him on.

"Come on, that's it. . . . What kind of bullshit are you going to hand me?" I asked him.

Once I had extricated myself from the bar I felt much better. Everybody was crazy and life was woven from absurdity. Luckily there were always a few good moments—everybody knows what I'm talking about—and if only for that it's worth living. The rest is meaningless. In the end nothing changes anything. I was convinced of the ephemeral nature of all things. I had half a bottle of tequila in my belly and was seeing palm trees in the street, swept away in the wind.

There was a surprise waiting for me back at the house. A half-bald blond guy, about forty-five, with a pot belly. He was sitting in my favorite chair, with Lisa on his lap.

Now Lisa was a normal girl with a pussy and tits, and occasionally she used them. Sometimes she would stay out all night and just show up the next morning to change and go to work. I would run into her in the kitchen. You can tell at a glance a girl who's been fucking all night. I was happy for her—I hoped she'd gotten the most out of it. I shared these little moments with her without saying a word; it brightened up my day. I knew then that I was a privileged character, that life had sprinkled a handful of gold dust in my eyes, that I could handle anything. We made a great little trio. I knew I could fix every sewer in town as long as I could stop at five o'clock, take a shower, and meet the two of them there—one handing me a glass and the other one an olive.

As a general rule, Lisa didn't discuss the men she met, or those she fucked. She would just say it wasn't worth going into and laughingly change the subject. Naturally she never brought a guy back to the house. Believe me, she would say, the one I let walk through that door has got to have something the others don't.

So I was floored when I walked in and saw this guy sitting there in his shirtsleeves with his tie loosened, raising his glass to me to say hello. I realized I was standing in front of the rare bird.

Lisa introduced us with bright eyes, and the guy jumped up to grab my hand. His cheeks were red; he reminded me of a bald-headed, blue-eyed baby.

"By the way," Betty asked, "did you find what you were looking for?"

"Yeah, but it took me a while."

Lisa put a drink in my hand. The guy looked at me and smiled. I smiled back. In a flash, I had the situation well in hand. His name was Edward but people called him Eddie. He'd come to open a pizzeria in town, he bought a new car every two months and laughed a lot. He sweated lightly. He seemed happy to be there. An hour later, it was like he'd known us for twenty years. He put his hand on my arm while the girls were talking in the breakfast nook.

"So tell me, man . . . they say that you write . . ." he said.

"You might say that," I said.

He gave me a wrought-iron wink.

"Make money at it . . . ?"

"It depends. It's not steady."

"Anyway," he said. "Sounds pretty good. You write your little story, you take it easy, you go to the bank. . . ."

"You got it."

"What area you write in?" he asked.

"Gothic novels," I said.

How does a girl's brain work? I asked myself all evening long—surely I was missing something. This Eddie guy—I couldn't figure out what she saw in him, besides that he drank like a fish, talked like a fool, and laughed all the time. I'd given up counting the things in life that surprise you, though. I like to keep my eyes open—you never know when you're going to learn a thing or two. Take Eddie—it turned out that my first impression was wrong. Eddie's an angel.

By the time we got to the baba au rhum, he had talked me to death, but all things considered it wasn't so bad. Being loud and dumb once in a while—provided you have a good cigar—is not the end of the world. Eddie had brought champagne. He popped the cork and looked at me, then poured me a big glass.

"Hey, I want you all to know how happy I am that we get along so good together—no really, I swear . . . girls, your glasses . . ."

The next morning, Sunday, he showed up with a big suitcase while we were eating breakfast. He gave me a wink.

"I brought a few things with me. . . . I like to feel at home. . . ."

He took out two or three rather short kimonos, a pair of slippers, and some underwear. Then he went into the bathroom. He came out thirty seconds later wearing one of the kimonos. The girls clapped. Bongo picked his head up to see what was going on. Eddie's legs were short, white, and incredibly hairy. He spread his arms out to be admired.

"Better get used to it," he said. "It's the only thing I like to wear around the house."

He came and sat down with us, poured himself some coffee, and started talking again. I felt a little like going back to bed.

I spent the early afternoon with Betty packaging copies of my manuscript and looking up publishers' addresses in the phone book. By now I was resigned to it. I approached it with a certain detachment, though once I thought I noticed a little spark coming out of my fingertips as I wrote the name of a well-known publisher. I lay down on the bed with a cigarette in my mouth. Betty came over to me. I felt fine. I felt light as a feather—geared down, somehow.

I was starting to give Betty the eye and play with her hair when I heard a noise on the stairway. Two seconds later there was Eddie, dancing around under our noses with a bottle and three glasses.

"Hey, you two, what's with all the whispering? Listen, I got to tell you what happened to me. . . ."

Lisa, Lisa, I thought, what ever drove you to this?

Later he got us all to climb into the car to go to the racetrack. The sky was getting cloudy, but the girls got excited. The radio cranked out miles of commercials, and Eddie laughed his head off.

We got there for the start of the third race. I took the girls to the bar while Eddie bought tickets. I was bored already. It's always the same—the people run to the betting windows . . . the horses run . . . the people go to the fence . . . the horses finish . . . the people run back to the betting windows—about as exciting as a soccer game. At the homestretch, Eddie would punch at the air, and his ears would turn red; two seconds later, he was pulling his hair out. He'd crumple his tickets up and throw them on the ground, whining.

"You didn't win?" I'd ask.

The sky was getting pink when we left the stands. By the time we got out to the car, Eddie was back in high spirits. He even managed to disappear for a minute and come back with his hands full of french fries.

He had gotten on my nerves at the beginning, but if you didn't listen too much to what he said, it was all right—he'd just wander into the house talking out loud to no one in particular. Once in a while I'd give him a smile. He'd sleep late, and come home around midnight, when the pizzeria closed. He always brought food and something to drink, and we'd have dinner together. Money being what it was, these meals were heaven-sent. Eddie was not completely oblivious to the fact—he would sometimes allude to it:

"Hey, you know, I've forgotten. . . . What are your books about again?"

"Science fiction."

"Oh yeah. That stuff sells pretty well, doesn't it? There's money in it. . . ."

"Yeah, but it takes a long time before you see the royalties. Sometimes they even forget to send the check. I can't complain, though. . . ."

"No . . . I'm just saying . . . if you need a little . . ."

"Thanks, but I'm fine. I'm planning a new one now. Writing doesn't cost much. . . ."

Another time we were sitting in the car with the air-conditioning on, watching the girls walk on the beach in the wind.

"Maybe you should change your subject matter," he said. "Some things sell better than others. . . ."

"No, I think it's just a matter of time."

"Hold on a second . . . I forgot again. . . ."

"Detective novels."

"Oh yeah. Gee, there must be books that make thousands."

"Oh yeah. Hundreds of thousands."

"Millions even."

"Yeah. There are. But I'm really into my new one now, no time to think about things like that. . . ."

In truth, I thought of nothing else. All the money I had was what was in my pocket—a few bills and two or three jobs already booked. God forbid something should happen, or if we ever wanted to take off for a weekend. . . . It was a pain in the ass. Betty had finished typing my manuscript over a week ago and now she was just hanging around the house, doing her nails once or twice a day. There was nothing new to see in the neighborhood. We would go out for a walk in the afternoon anyway, just to break up the day—taking old Bongo along through the maze of streets.

We didn't talk much. Betty always seemed to be thinking about something. She walked with her hands in her pockets. We would just wander around under a gentle, shy sun, collars turned up. The weather had been lousy for a few days now, but we didn't notice. We were getting ready to give birth to something. Bongo and I would come back panting, but one look at Betty told you she could do the whole course over again sprinting, no problem. Life was putting me to sleep, but for her it was the opposite. A marriage of water and fire—the perfect combination to make everything go up in smoke.

One evening I ran up the stairs ahead of her and blocked the way, suddenly seized with passion. I slid a couple of fingers into her skirt, getting ready to make my way down to the fire and brimstone, when she just asked me point-blank:

"What do you think of Eddie's offer?"

"Hmmm?"

"NO REALLY, what do you think?"

We'd done in a couple of bottles of Chianti downstairs, and on our way up the stairs her legs had been sending messages directly into my brain. We went into the bedroom. I closed the door and pinned her to the wall. I was going to set her free—rip her panties off in the icy moonlight. I stuck my tongue in her ear.

"I want your honest opinion," she said. "We have to agree on this completely."

I pushed my knee up between her legs, stroking her hips and sucking her breasts.

"No, wait a minute . . . I have to know what you . . ."

"Yes. Yes . . . what is it again?"

"I mean in the end, maybe Eddie's thing is not such a bad idea. What do you think?"

I had no idea what she was talking about. I pulled her skirt up over her hips. I noticed that she wasn't wearing any panties—just panty hose. I had trouble thinking of anything else.

"Stop thinking," I said.

I buttoned her lip with a wild kiss. Then she said, "We could do it while we're waiting to hear on your book. It isn't forever. . . ."

"Yeah, fine," I said. "Wait, look, let's sit down on the bed. . . ."

We fell down onto the bed and I went crazy, sliding my hands over her nylons. Her thighs were as hot and smooth as a V-1.

"And also that way we can put a little money aside, don't you think? . . . It'll give us time to get ourselves together, buy some things—we don't have anything to wear."

I was writhing all over the bed, trying to get my pants off. I felt her soul drifting away from me.

"Don't you think, don't you think?" I said.

"I'm sure of it," she said. "It's an easy job, especially with pizzas. . . ."

I jumped on top of her with 110 volts AC going through my veins. She grabbed me by the hair.

"I hope you trust me," she said.

"Of course," I said.

She shoved my face between her legs and I fell overboard.

9

I slid open the little serving window that went into the kitchen and stuck my head through it, plunging myself for the thousandth time into the overwhelming food odors that reigned inside. It was quieter than the dining room, though. It was Friday night and everyone was out. We'd had to add tables. I looked at Mario bent over the ovens, his face aglow and his eyes half closed.

"Make me another one with mushrooms, and one plain!" I called out.

Though he never answered, you knew he heard you. It was something engraved in his brain. I leaned in a little farther to get one of those tiny bottles of San Pellegrino and downed it in one swallow. I'd taken to doing that lately. I put away about thirty or forty a night—it made me feel just a little bloated by closing time. Eddie looked the other way.

Eddie manned the register. Betty and I worked the dining room. If you ask me, you needed at least four waiters for that dining room, but there were just the two of us. We ran like chickens with our heads cut off, carrying trays where our heads should have been. By eleven o'clock I was dead on my feet, but the San Pellegrino was free and we were getting good money, so I couldn't complain.

I grabbed my steaming pizzas and headed for the two little blondes who'd ordered them. They weren't too bad, but I wasn't up to making snappy chatter—I wasn't there to have fun. People were shouting at me from all sides. It hadn't been that long ago that I had to strain my ears to pierce through the silence of the night—walked out on the porch and felt myself surrounded by space. It seemed only natural. Now here I was squeezing my ass to steer through the noise of clattering plates and bursting voices.

Betty took it better than I did—she knew how to deal with it. Sometimes we'd cross paths, and she'd give me a wink. It gave me my strength back. I tried not to notice her bangs soaked in sweat—I didn't let myself look. Every once in a while I'd light a cigarette for her and leave it in the ashtray by the kitchen window, hoping that she'd find the time to take a few drags and think of me. I don't suppose she always did.

We'd been working there about three weeks, and they'd never been busier. We didn't know which way to turn. I'd been out of it for a while. We were all sort of numb. The only thing I saw clearly were my tips. What really got me was to see all the people standing outside waiting. It was getting on toward midnight, and we apparently wouldn't be closing for a while. The smell of anchovies was starting to make my stomach turn. I was sticking biscuits in a peach melba when Betty came up to me. In spite of the brouhaha and the circus going on all around us, she managed to whisper a few words in my ear.

"Shit," she said. "You better take over number five or I'm going to wind up pushing that cunt right through the window."

"What's her problem?"

"She's got it in for me," she said.

I went to check it out. There were two at the table—this old guy, sort of hunched over, and this woman. She was about forty but already on the edge of the abyss—just out of the beauty shop. The perfect bitch, out on the town with some poor jerk, dry as a saltine.

"Oh, there you are!" she said. "That girl is retarded! I ordered a pizza with anchovies, and she brings me one with ham. Take this away right now. . . ."

"Don't you like ham?" I said.

She didn't answer. She gave me a dirty look and lit a cigarette, exhaling through her nose. I took the pizza with a smile and headed for the kitchen. I passed Betty on the way. I wanted to drop everything and hug her—help her forget the old bag—but I left that for later.

"See what I mean?" she asked.

"Exactly."

"Before all that, she made me bring her new silverware. There was a drop of water on her fork."

"It's because you're prettier than she is," I said.

I got a smile out of her, and made my way back to the kitchen. Mario was scowling, his hands on his hips. Things were sizzling in the oven, and greasy steam was hovering in the air. Every little thing seemed covered with a glowing cloud.

"You back here for a breather?" he asked.

"A little correction," I said.

I went back to where they kept the garbage, three huge cans with handles—repulsive. I got a fork out of a stack of dirty silverware, then scraped the top of the pizza, getting rid of all the ham. Then I took two or three tomatoes that were lying around and started putting the pizza back together again. It was easy to find the tomatoes—that's what people leave behind most—but it took quite an effort to locate four anchovies, not to mention the glistening lacework of grated cheese that I had to run under the faucet because of a cigarette butt. Mario watched me, his eyes wide, pushing back the oily hair that kept falling over his forehead.

"I don't understand what the fuck you're doing there," he said.

I smashed all the ingredients together and held the little jewel out for him to see.

"Stick this in the oven a minute," I said.

"Shit . . ." he said, shaking his head.

He opened the oven door and we stood there, squinting.

"Some people deserve to eat this sort of thing," I said.

"Yeah, you're right. Boy, it's enough to give you a heart attack tonight. . . ."

"I think we still got at least an hour to go, man."

I got my pizza back and took it to the lady. I set it on the table delicately. It was just like new—piping hot and crispy. The lady made like I wasn't even there. I waited until she'd swallowed the first bite, then went away, avenged.

It kept up like a runaway train for another hour or so—even Eddie had to lend a hand—and then the place started clearing out slowly and we could breathe a little—we could light the first cigarette of the evening.

"Shit, that's good," said Betty.

She was leaning against the wall with her eyes closed and her head bent slightly forward. She held the smoke in as long as possible. We stood in this little alcove where no one could see us from the dining room. All at once she seemed totally done in. Fatigue sometimes makes life painful and sad, there's no way around it. I looked up at the ceiling and smiled wanly. In a way it was a victory just to end up on our feet. Every job I've ever had has only served to demonstrate that man has supernatural powers of resistance. It's tough to get him down. I took the cigarette that Betty was holding. It wasn't good—it was divine.

All that was left to do was serve a few desserts—two or three banana flambé–type concoctions—and the game would be won. Then we could go sit in the booth in back and let Eddie take over. I could already see her slipping her shoes off, her head in my lap, my forehead against the windowpane, watching the empty streets, looking for the first sentence of my new novel.

Among the last customers to leave were the lady and her old

boyfriend. The guy had hardly touched his food but the lady had eaten—and drunk—enough for two. Her eyes were glazed. She was on her third coffee.

What happened next was entirely my fault. The day seemed to be over, and I had stopped paying attention. I let Betty take care of the dining room—clean out the last stragglers. I was a fool. I felt a chill down my back a fraction of a second before the storm hit. Then there was an incredible sound of things being smashed.

When I turned around Betty was standing nose to nose with the lady. The table was overturned. She was white as death and the lady was red as a poppy, blazing in the sun.

"Bitch . . ." said the one in red. "I want to see the manager immediately, you hear me?"

Eddie went over, frowning, not knowing what to do with his hands. No one else moved. The few customers left in the dining room were happy to get their money's worth. It's always a delicate situation for an owner when one of his employees is getting ready to tangle with a customer. Eddie was uneasy.

"Okay, let's calm down," he moaned. "Now what's going on here?"

The lady was half choked with rage.

"What's going on is that the service has been abominable all evening long, and if that wasn't enough, this little twit refuses to bring me my coat! What kind of place is this, anyway?"

Her boyfriend looked away sadly. Betty seemed paralyzed. I threw my dish towel on the floor and went over. I turned to Eddie.

"It's all right," I said. "Just put their bill on my account and get them out of here. I'll explain later. . . ."

"Jesus, now I've seen everything," the lady said. "I'd like to know just who's in charge of this greasy spoon!"

"Fine. What color is your coat?" I asked.

"Don't stick your nose in this! Go back to your dish towels!" she said.

"Easy does it . . ." I said.

"That's enough! Get out of my sight!"

At these words Betty let out a horrifying scream—almost animal—the kind that makes your blood run cold. I had barely seen her grab the fork off another table when the room seemed to light up, and she jumped at the lady with the speed of lightning.

She plunged the fork wildly into her arm. The woman let out a shriek. Betty pulled the fork out and plunged it in again, a bit higher up. The woman fell over backward and tumbled over a chair, her arm covered with blood. Everyone seemed petrified, but the lady shrieked even louder when she saw Betty coming at her again brandishing the fork. She tried to climb up on her back.

It was suddenly hot as hell. It woke me up. I had just enough time to grab Betty around the waist to keep her from doing something really stupid. I pulled her backward with all my strength and we rolled under a table. My muscles were so tense that I felt like I'd fallen over with a bronze statue in my arms. When our eyes met, I realized that she didn't even recognize me anymore—then I felt the fork go into my back. The pain went up to my skull. I managed to grab her hand and twist it until she let go of the fork. It rang on the tile like something that had fallen from the sky, shining and covered with blood.

The people immediately gathered around us. All I could see was their legs, but by then my mind wasn't registering anything. I felt Betty trembling under me. I felt sick.

"Betty," I said. "It's all over. Calm down. It's all over. . . ."

I held her hands against the floor and she shook her head, moaning. I didn't understand anything—all I knew was that I couldn't let her go. I felt miserable.

Eddie stuck his head down under the table. I could see other faces crowded together behind his. I moved around so they couldn't see her, and gave Eddie a frantic glance.

"Eddie, please . . . get them out of here. . . ."

"Shit, what the hell happened?" he said.

"She's got to have some space. EDDIE, GET THEM THE FUCK OUT OF HERE, GODDAMMIT!"

He stood up and I heard him talking to people, moving them

toward the door. Brave Eddie, wonderful Eddie. I knew that what I had asked him to do wasn't easy—people turn into mad dogs when you try to take their bones away. Betty was shaking her head like a metronome, while I stammered out stupidities like What's wrong sweetheart, aren't you feeling well? . . .

I heard the door shut. Eddie came back. He crouched down next to the table. He seemed genuinely upset.

"Jesus fucking Christ, what the hell is wrong with her?" he asked.

"Nothing. She's calming down now. I'll stay with her."

"She should rinse her face off."

"Yes, I'll take care of it. Just leave us alone."

"You don't want me to help?"

"No, it's fine. It's fine. . . ."

"All right. I'll wait out in the car."

"No, don't bother. Don't worry, I'll close up. Go on home, Eddie. Fuck, just leave me alone with her."

He waited for a moment, then touched my shoulder and stood up.

"I'll go out through the kitchen. I'll close up behind Mario."

He turned all the lights off before he left—all except a small lamp behind the bar. I heard them talking in the kitchen for a second, then the back door closed. Silence poured into the restaurant like glue.

She wasn't shaking her head anymore, but her body was stiff as stone against me. It was almost frightening. I felt like I was lying across railroad tracks. I let go of her gently, and when I saw that it was okay, I slid over next to her. I saw that we were drenched in sweat. The tile was glazed and sticky, covered with cigarette butts—a dream.

I touched her shoulder—her wonderful small shoulder. I shouldn't have. Her reaction was terrifying. The touch of my hand set something off in her brain. She turned, groaned, and burst into sobs. It was like someone had stabbed me.

I stroked her gently, pressing against her back, but nothing helped. She was crouched down in a fetal position, her hair falling all over her amid the shit—fists held tight against her mouth. Crying and moaning. Her stomach jumped as if there were a beast trapped inside it. We stayed like that for quite a while, the pale light off the street reflecting on the floor. It was as if all the world's misery had convened under that table. I was broken, at the end of my wits. It did no good to talk. I had no magic words. I'd tried them all. It was a bitter pill to swallow for the writer. I wasn't sure she even knew I was there.

When I couldn't take it anymore, I got up and moved the table away. I had a hard time lifting Betty up—she seemed to weigh six hundred pounds. I lost my balance a little going behind the counter, and wreaked havoc with the bottles, but this was the least of my problems. I wedged my ass against the stainless-steel sink and got the cold water running.

God forgive me. I rolled her hair up in my hand—I had a sort of veneration for her hair—and when I was sure I had a good grip on her, I stuck her head under the faucet.

I counted to ten while she struggled. The water sprayed all over the place. I didn't like doing it, but I didn't know what else to do. I didn't know anything anymore. Anything about women . . . anything about anything.

I let her choke just a little, then let her go. She let out a big cough, then threw herself at me.

"You son of a bitch!" she screamed. "You son of a bitch!"

She slapped me across the face. I managed to get out of the way of a second slap, as well as a kick in the shins. She pulled her hair back and looked at me. Then she slid all the way down the bar, covering it with hot tears. I didn't get shaken, though—I'd seen this before—what happens when your nerves start to let go. All there is to do is wait. I used the pause to fill up a glass. I pushed up on the measuring spigot of a bottle hung upside down—one shot, two, three . . . Over the lips, past the gums, look out stomach here it comes. . . . I downed it in one gulp with my head tilted

back, and with the same movement backed up against the wall.
I closed my eyes. I listened to her crying. I needed a breather.

I breathed for a second, but when I accidentally pushed back
on my wound I jumped. I rushed back to the measuring spigot,
gnashing my teeth. Fill 'er up—I poured two more glasses and
then slid up beside her. I put my arm around her shoulder. I
looked at my glass gleaming in the lamplight, then downed it.

By now she was feeling better—just sniffling. She was sitting
with her knees against her chest, her forehead on her knees, and
her face behind her hair, which I separated with my hand to
offer her a drink. She shook her head. I had an extra glass on my
hands, so I stretched my legs out in front of me to relax a little.
I'd gone past the tired stage and now felt myself sort of floating.
It was a nicer feeling than an hour ago—wiped out, but pain-
less. I kissed her neck softly. She'd been cold before, now she
came alive. I swallowed my drink to celebrate—it was the least
I could do.

"Usually people fall off their stools on the other side of the
bar," I said. "I'm glad we've managed to be different."

That night I fucked Betty with new passion. By some miracle
we'd found a taxi just as we came out of the restaurant, and I'd
hugged her tight all the way home—very tight. We went in
through the back door to avoid running into Lisa and Eddie, but
the house was silent and dark—we could have just gone straight
in and up to bed. Though we hardly said two words to each other,
we made up for it in other ways: I said all I had to say—several
times—in the depths of her vagina.

She fell asleep after that, but I didn't feel like sleeping. I lay
there with my eyes wide open, alone in the darkness; I was dead,
but my eyes wouldn't close. I lay there a long time, thinking over
what had happened. I decided that the old woman had gotten
what was coming to her, and the rest didn't matter. Betty was
simply the kind of girl you shouldn't hassle. Besides, Fridays were
always deadly. I got up to piss. The minute I saw the commode

I threw up. My God, I said, no wonder I couldn't sleep. I washed my mouth out and went back to bed. I was in dreamland in no time. I dreamed I was in the jungle, lost in the middle of the jungle. It was raining like I'd never seen.

10

The next morning I woke up relatively early. I got out of bed quietly and let her sleep. I went downstairs. Lisa had already left for work, but Eddie was there, eating breakfast with his newspaper spread out in front of him. He was wearing a red kimono with a white bird on each side. It was very refreshing.

"Jesus Christ," he said. "There you are. How you doing?"

"Hi," I said.

I sat down across from him and poured myself a cup of coffee. Bongo came over and put his head in my lap.

"So?" he asked. "What's she doing? Sleeping?"

"Of course she's sleeping. What do you think?"

He grabbed his paper, folded it in eight, and tossed it in the corner. He leaned over the table a little.

"Um, do you have any idea what was with her last night? You got any thoughts . . . ?"

"Shit, didn't you ever lose your temper? You read the papers—the world's covered with blood and you're making a big deal out

89

of it because she roughed up some fucking crazy woman who I should have strangled myself before the whole thing even started!"

He put his hand over his face. He kept smiling, but it was obvious that something was on his mind. I calmly drank my coffee.

"Yeah, well, let's just say she had me pretty freaked out," he said.

"She was exhausted, for crying out loud! It's not so hard to understand!"

"Yeah, well, I was watching her when she tipped over the table. I'm telling you, you should have seen her. It was scary."

"Sure, she's not the kind of girl who lets people walk all over her. You know how she is. . . ."

"If you want my advice, you ought to take her on a vacation as soon as the money from your books comes in."

"I don't believe— Look, will you lay off that? I haven't written *books*, I have written *a* book, one. It's something I did once in my life and I'm not even sure I'll ever be able to do it again. At this very moment there's possibly some guy sitting in his office thumbing through my manuscript, but that doesn't mean it'll ever get published. So you see, I'm not exactly counting my money yet."

"Shit . . . I thought . . ."

"Yeah, well, you were wrong. It happened that Betty came across it one day by accident, and ever since she's got it into her head that I'm some kind of genius and she won't get off it. Eddie, look at me. Ever since then I haven't been able to write a single line, you hear me? This is where we are, Eddie. We're here, sitting around waiting to hear. I know that's all she thinks about from morning till night. The whole thing makes her edgy, you understand?"

"Well, why don't you write in the afternoon? You have the time. . . ."

"Don't make me laugh. *Time* isn't the problem."

"Then what is it? You're not comfortable here?"

"No, it isn't that," I said.

"Then what is it?"

"How the hell do I know? Maybe I have to wait for divine intervention, how am I supposed to know?"

It took a few days for the last vestiges of the episode to disappear completely. Every night I knocked out most of the work at the pizzeria—handling three-quarters of the customers, running around like a maniac. I made a beeline for every pain in the ass or troublemaker I saw walk in the door. I didn't let Betty get near them. By closing time I was pale as a ghost. Betty would tell me, You're crazy, you haven't even had time to smoke a cigarette and I stand around twiddling my thumbs.

"I just feel like hustling a little, that's all."

"I think you're just scared I'm going to bite another customer. . . ."

"That's nonsense, Betty. You don't believe that."

"Anyway, I'm not tired. Want to walk home?"

"Sure, good idea!"

We waved to Eddie in his posh sedan, and he took off slowly into the night. I felt like I'd fallen victim to an illusion. I felt like my legs had been sawed off, and it was a hefty little hike back to the house. I bucked myself up by thinking how much farther it would be to walk to Heaven. I shoved my hands in my pockets, turned up my collar, and off I went—the genius—brain empty and feet sore, but somehow I made it. It intrigued me how she thought that being a waiter was better than being a plumber. It didn't keep me up nights, though. It seemed like with her you had to learn everything over again. Still, I had nothing better to do.

One morning when I woke up she wasn't there. It was past noon and I'd slept like a log. I drank my coffee standing up, looking out the window onto the street. It was nice out—the sunlight very white—but I felt a cold draft coming through the pane. I went to take a look downstairs, but no one was there except Bongo, asleep by the door. I asked him how he was doing, then went back upstairs. The silence in the house confused me. I went to take a shower. It was only when I came out that I noticed the envelope on the table.

It had been opened. The return address was printed on it with curlicues—the name of a publisher. My name was on it too, typewritten much smaller in the lower right-hand corner. So here we are, I told myself, the first response. I grabbed the piece of paper folded inside.

The response said no. Sorry, no. "I like your ideas," the guy explained. "But your style is unreadable. You deliberately place yourself outside the literary sphere." I stood there for a moment trying to understand what he was saying—what ideas he was talking about—but I couldn't figure it out. I put the letter back in the envelope and decided to shave.

I don't know why, but when I saw myself in the mirror I thought of Betty. I started feeling low. It was obviously she who had opened the letter. I could see her there, ripping it open, her heart pounding, covered with hopeful goose-pimples—then the guy offering his regrets and the world coming down all around her.

"Shit! No . . ." I said.

I leaned on the sink and closed my eyes. Where had she gone this time? . . . Tell me, what could possibly be going through her head now? I could see her running through the streets. I had this image of her, stuck in my head like an ice pick—her bumping into people, cars screeching to a halt, her running blindly into the street, wilder and wilder, her face twisted and terrifying. It was my fault—me and my book, me and that ridiculous whatever-it-was that popped out of my brain. All those nights, forging and sharpening the blade, only to have it come back and stab me in the gut. How did it happen? Why are we always the source of our own misery?

I felt my blood turning to ink—felt myself going off the edge, hung over a roasting pit spitting flames, ten years older. Then she walked in, fresh, pert—a queen with a cold nose.

"Ooooh," she said. "Damn, it's cold out there. Hey, what's the matter with you? What's with the scowling?"

"Nothing . . . I just got up. I didn't hear you come up the stairs."

"You're going deaf in your old age."

"Right. The worst is that it's all downhill. . . ."

I was trying to be witty, but the truth is I was disconcerted. I was so sure the bad news would have her moaning and groaning that I couldn't handle her easygoing attitude, so carefree. I sat down randomly in a chair. I leaned backward to get a beer out of the icebox. Maybe a miracle had occurred—why not?—maybe on the million-to-one chance that she'd take it in good spirits we'd picked the winning number. The beer hit me like a bottle of amphetamines. I felt my mouth start to twist itself into a half-smile, half-snarl.

"You have a nice walk?" I said. "Tell me, did you have a nice walk?"

"Great. I jogged a little to warm up. Hey, feel my ears, they're frozen!"

There was of course another hypothesis: she was playing with me. Jesus, I said to myself, shit, SHIT—she must have read the letter. What the hell was she trying to pull? What's she waiting for? When is she going to dissolve in tears and start throwing the furniture out the window? I just didn't get it.

I felt her ears, but I didn't know why. She smelled like fresh air, cold outdoor air. I stood there holding her ears.

"See? They're frozen, aren't they?"

I let go of them. I grabbed her hips instead. I pressed my forehead into her belly. A ray of light came through the window and landed on my cheek. She stroked my head. I went to kiss her hand. It was then that I saw her fingers were bright red. It was so odd that I jumped back.

"What in the world . . . ?"

She looked at the ceiling and sniffled.

"It's nothing. . . . It's . . . it's red paint."

Something like an alarm went off in my brain. Somewhere a Cheshire cat was grinning. I felt the motor starting to go out of control, but I didn't put on the brakes.

"Paint? You were painting this morning?"

Her eyes lit up with a glow, her face congealing into a little smile.

"Yeah. I was," she said in a clear voice. "I decided to get a little exercise. . . ."

I had a flash, like a hallucination. It half strangled me.

"Fuck, Betty . . . you didn't . . ."

She gave me a huge smile, but it was bitter.

"Yes I did. Sure I did."

I looked at the floor, shaking my head. I saw stars.

"No, I don't believe it," I said. "I don't believe it. . . ."

"What's the problem? Don't you like red?"

"Why would you go and do something like . . ."

"How should I know? I just did. It makes me feel better."

I stood up and walked around the table gesticulating.

"So every time a publisher rejects my book you're going to go bombard his building with red paint, is that it?"

"Yeah, something like that. I wish you'd have been there to see the look on their faces."

"But that's crazy!"

A chill of anger and admiration went up my spine. She tossed her hair and laughed.

"You got to let the good times roll a little. You have no idea how much good it did me."

She took her jacket off and undid the scarf that circled her neck like a multicolored snake.

"I'd love some coffee," she said. "Darn, look at my hands. Got to wash them."

I went to the window and lifted the curtain with my finger.

"Hey, you sure no one's after you? You weren't followed?"

"No, they were pretty stunned. No one even had time to lift his ass off the chair."

"Next time the cops will be out there surrounding the house. I can see it now. . . ."

"Jesus, you always expect the worst."

"Yeah, it's true. I must be sick in the head. You go out and paint half the town crimson and I shouldn't worry. . . ."

"Listen," she sighed. "You've got to get at least a minimum of justice in this world. You know? I'm not going to spend my life getting pissed off and not reacting."

The story made the last page of the next day's newspaper. Witnesses said they'd seen a "madwoman with two paint-bombs suddenly appear." The end of the article said that the act of terrorism had not yet been claimed by any particular activist group. I tore out the article and put it in my wallet. I put the paper back in the pile while the guy at the newsstand had his back turned—there was nothing else interesting in it. I bought some cigarettes and gum, then left.

Betty was waiting for me across the street at a sidewalk café, drinking a cup of hot chocolate. The weather was clear and crisp. She looked into the sun and closed her eyes, her hands in her pockets and her collar turned up. She was so beautiful that I slowed down, walking toward her. This was something that would never leave me. It made me smile in the morning sun as if I'd just somewhere, somehow hit the jackpot.

"Take your time," I told her. "We can go whenever you're ready."

She leaned over to kiss me on the lips, then went back to her hot chocolate. We were in no hurry. We'd decided to do a little window-shopping, buy what we needed to keep our teeth from chattering too much in the winter. The streets were already full of wolf, wildcat, silver fox, and red cheeks—a sure sign that temperatures were going down, and that the fur sellers were making shitloads of money.

We walked arm in arm for about an hour, not finding what we wanted, not really knowing what it was. All the salesgirls heaved sighs of relief when we left, then set about refolding the mountains of clothes we'd taken down off the racks.

The last place we went was this big department store. One step inside the doors and I thought we'd landed in a box of chocolates left out in the sun too long. I gritted my teeth to keep the perfume-music from coming in through my mouth. It's unhealthy to breathe that stuff, something I'm not into. I didn't say anything, though—I cut my losses with some chewing gum and followed Betty to the women's department.

There weren't many people, and I was the only guy there. I hung out for a while in lingerie, looking at a few of the items they had lit up—familiarizing myself with the latest zipping and hooking devices. It might have been a little voyage among the clouds, if it hadn't been for the saleswoman, a sort of troll about fifty years old, with hot flushes and burn marks on her forehead from so many permanents. The kind who's been laid maybe twice in her whole fucking life and does her best to forget it ever happened. Every time I stuck my hand in a basket of panties, or dared to stretch an elastic, she gave me the evil eye, but I never let go of my special industrial-strength smile. By the time she finally came up to me she was as red as the blood of Jesus.

"Tell me," she said. "What is it exactly you're looking for? Perhaps I can help you."

"Perhaps," I said. "I want to buy some underpants for my mother. I want the kind you can see the hairs through. . . ."

She let out a ridiculous moan, but I didn't see what happened next because Betty came and grabbed me by the arm.

"What the hell are you up to?" she asked. "Come on, I want to try on some things."

She was carrying an armload of brightly colored clothes. On

our way to the fitting room I got a glimpse of a price tag dangling from the bunch. I just about fell on my face—a belly-flop, like a tree struck by lightning. Then I just laughed.

"Hey," I said. "You get a load of that? Must be some mistake. That's two weeks' salary. . . ."

"Whose?" she said.

I cooled my heels outside the fitting room like someone left on a desert island—bare head and broken legs. I didn't feel well. I didn't have enough money to pay for half of what she'd taken. The poor dear—she wasn't aware of what she was doing. I wondered how I was going to console her, except with a pale smile. Obviously the world was not yet our oyster. I heard Betty breathing and moving around behind the curtain.

"How's it going?" I said. "You know you really don't have to worry—girls like you, they look great in anything."

She pulled the curtain back sharply, and what I saw made me choke. I put my hand over my mouth. She'd put on all the clothes at once, in layers. She looked like a two-hundred-pound fat-lady, with hollow cheeks and a very determined look.

"Jesus fucking Christ . . . no . . ." I said.

I closed the curtain quickly and looked around to see if anybody had seen us. Now I was breathing through my mouth. The curtain opened again immediately.

"Don't be stupid," she said. "In thirty seconds we're outside."

"Betty, please. I'm really not into this. We're going to get caught, I can feel it. . . ."

"Hahaha," she said. "Us? Caught?"

She gave me a fevered look and grabbed my arm.

"All right, let's go," she said. "Try and look a little less nervous."

Off we went. I felt like we were walking through rice paddies with Viet Cong hidden in the trees all around us. I was sure we were being watched. I wanted to scream: SHOW YOUR-SELVES, YOU BASTARDS! LET'S HAVE IT OUT ONCE AND FOR ALL! It was all I could do to put one foot in front of the other, with some invisible claw tearing at my guts. The closer we got to the exit, the higher the tension mounted. Betty's ears were red, and mine were whistling. Sweet suffering Christ, I said to myself, two or three more yards and we're home free.

Outside, the light seemed supercharged. I was seized by nervous laughter. Betty reached for the door. In the end it was all rather exhilarating. I was close on her heels, ready to take off like a shot, when I felt a hand tap me on the shoulder. That's it, I'm dead, I thought—it's over. I saw myself lying in the gutter in a pool of blood.

"STOP! DON'T MOVE!" the hand said.

Betty was out the door like a jet plane.

"Don't stop! Lose him!" she advised me.

Like an idiot I turned around. I don't know why. A taste for defeat sleeps somewhere in us all. The guy had two arms, two legs, and a badge. He thought I was going to follow Betty's advice. He was wrong. I was actually in a state of shock. For me the war was over—I had half a mind to start citing the Geneva Convention. Still, the bastard took matters into his own hands: he gave me a good one, right in the eye.

My head exploded. I flapped my arms and fell backward against the door. It opened, and I landed on the street on my back, my legs tangled together. I lay there looking at the sky for a second, before the guy's head appeared over me like a mushroom cloud. I could see out of only one eye—the film started turning at high speed. He leaned over and grabbed me by the lapel.

"Get up," he said.

A few people had stopped on the sidewalk. Free show. I hung on to the guy's arm as he lifted me up. I was planning to make a gallant last stand—a surprise kick in the balls, perhaps—but it turned out I didn't have to. This fat girl came at him, with her foot to the floor in a head-on collision while he was still half bent-over. I fell backward again and the guy plastered himself like a pancake against the door of a parked car. A ray of sunlight shone on me. The fat chick put her hand out.

"You're not my type," I said.

"We'll see about that," she said. "Let's get out of here, quick."

I got up and took off behind her, her long black hair waving in the wind like a Jolly Roger.

"Hey, Betty . . . is that you?" I asked. "Is that you? Hey, Betty . . ."

I opened a beer and sat down in a chair while she got the ice pack ready and took all the clothes off. My eye looked like a sea anemone with the flu. I'd had it up to here with her bullshit.

"I've had it up to here with this bullshit," I said.

She came over with the ice pack. She sat down on my lap and put it on my eye.

"I know why you're upset," she said. "It's because you got beat up."

"Don't make me laugh. I didn't get beat up. I let him have a free shot, that's all."

"Well, it's not the end of the world. It hardly shows. It's just a little swollen around the edges."

"Right, just a little swollen around the edges, she says. Barely even red . . ."

I looked at her with the one eye I had left. She smiled. Yes, exactly, she smiled—and against that I was defenseless. The world became insignificant. She disarmed the slightest attack. I could carry on all I wanted for show, but the poison had already reached my brain. What was this little dried-out, shriveled-up world next to her? What was anything worth next to her hair, her lungs, her knees, and all that went with it—could I ever need anything else? Wasn't what I had something enormous, alive? It was only thanks to her that I didn't feel like a total piece of shit. I was willing to pay any price for that. It wasn't that I'd reduced the whole world down to Betty—it was that I just didn't care about the rest. She smiled, and my anger disappeared like a wet footprint in the burning sun. It would always amaze me.

She put on one of the things she'd stolen and circled around me, posing.

"So . . . what do you think? How do I look?"

I finished my beer first. Then I sent her a valentine.

"I just wish I could see you out of both eyes," I whispered.

11

When I received my sixth rejection letter I knew that my book would never be published. Betty didn't. One more time, she spent two days without unclenching her teeth—mood black. Everything I tried to say was worthless. She wouldn't listen to me. Every time it happened she would wrap the manuscript back up and send it off to someone else. Great, I said to myself—it's like subscribing to the torture-of-the-month club, like sipping the poison down to the last drop—but of course I didn't tell her. My nice little novel just kept taking potshots in the wing every time it passed overhead. But it wasn't the novel I was worried about. It was her. Ever since she'd sworn off painting the town red it bothered me to see her with no way to blow off steam.

In moments like these, Eddie did his best to lighten things up. He joked around constantly and filled the place with flowers. He sent me wondering glances, but there was nothing to be done. If I ever really needed a friend it would be him that I'd choose. But you can't have everything in life, and I had little to give.

Lisa was also great—gentle and understanding. We all did our best to help Betty get her spirits up, but it was all in vain. Every time she'd find one of my manuscripts stuffed into the mailbox she'd look up and sigh—and off she'd go again.

As if things weren't bad enough, it got very cold outside—icy winds blew through the streets, Christmas was on its way. In the morning, we'd wake up to a blizzard. In the evening we'd find ourselves hip-deep in slush. The city started to get me down. I started dreaming of faraway places—silent painted deserts, where I could let my eyes wander across the horizon, musing peacefully about my new novel or what to make for supper, lending an ear to the first call of a nightbird, falling through the sunset.

I knew perfectly well what was wrong with Betty. The damn novel had nailed her to the floor—tied her legs together, her hands behind her back. She was like a wild horse who's cut his hocks jumping over a flint wall and is trying to get back on his feet. What she thought to be a sunlit prairie had turned into a sad, dark corral, and she'd never known what it was to be confined; she wasn't built for it. Still, she went at it with all her might—rage in her heart—and with each passing day she worked her fingers further to the bone. It hurt me to see it, but there was nothing I could do. She had gone someplace where nothing and no one could follow. During these times I knew I could grab a beer and do a week's worth of crossword puzzles without her bothering me. But I stayed close by, just in case she needed me. Waiting was the worst thing that could have happened to her. Writing that book was surely the stupidest thing I'd ever done.

Somehow I was able to imagine what she was going through each time one of those godforsaken rejection slips poured in—all that it implied—and the better I got to know her, the more I realized that she was actually taking it rather well. It isn't easy to let them rip your arms and legs off one by one without saying a word, just gritting your teeth. Since I already had what I wanted, it didn't matter much to me one way or the other—it was a little like getting news from Mars. I didn't lose sleep over it. I didn't really make the connection between what I had written and the book that found its way so regularly into people's wastebaskets. I saw myself as the guy who tries to unload a shipment of bathing suits on a band of freezing Eskimos without speaking a word of their language.

My only real hope, in fact, was that Betty would get tired of the whole thing, forget the writer, and go back to the way she was before: gobbling down chili in the sun and glancing at the intensity of things from the veranda, her soul serene. Perhaps it could actually come to pass. Maybe her hope would end up wilting and fall away like a dead branch some morning—it wasn't impossible. Then some poor asshole had to go set things off again. When I think about it, I tell myself that that little nobody never even got a tenth of what he had coming.

And so they turned down my book for the sixth time, and Betty slowly started smiling again after two days of depression. The house came back to life little by little—the parachute eventually opened, and we floated gently back down to earth. The first rays of sunlight dried up our grief. I was busy brewing a pot of killer coffee, when Betty showed up with the mail. There was a letter. For some time now my life had been trampled underfoot by these fuc' 'ng letters. I looked with a sort of disgust at the one Betty held open in her hand.

"Coffee's ready," I said. "What's new, honey?"

"Not much," she said.

She approached without looking at me and stuffed it down the neck of my sweater. She tapped it a few times, then turned to the window and, without a word, pressed her forehead against the pane. The coffee started boiling. I turned it off. I took out the letter. It was written on stationery with some guy's name and address on top. Here's what it said:

Dear Sir,
    I have been an editor at this publishing house for a good twenty years, and believe me, things both good and not so good have

passed through my hands. I have never seen anything, nowever, that compares with what you have had the incredibly bad taste to send us.

I have often written to young authors to tell them of the admiration I hold for them and their work. I have never until now been tempted to do the opposite. But you, sir, have pushed me over the brink.

Your writing for me evokes the preliminary signs of leprosy. It is with deep disgust that I am sending back this nauseating flower that you mistakenly thought was a novel.

Nature sometimes gives birth to mutations. You will agree that it is the duty of an honest man to put an end to such anomalies. Understand that I intend to do some publicity for you. My only regret is that this thing can never be returned to the one place it never should have left—I am speaking of some murky swamplike zone in your brain.

It was followed by a sort of nervous signature that went all the way across the page. I folded the paper back up and tossed it under the sink, as if it were a publicity flier for take-out Chinese. I went back to making the coffee, watching Betty out of the corner of my eye. She hadn't moved. She seemed to be interested in what was happening outside on the street.

"You know, it's all just part of the game," I said. "You're always going to run into jerks, there's just no way around that."

She chased something through the air with a bothered gesture.

"All right, let's not talk about it anymore. By the way, I forgot to tell you."

"What?"

"I made an appointment with the gynecologist."

"Oh yeah? Something wrong . . . ?"

"I want to check my IUD. See if it hasn't moved down."

"Okay, yeah . . ."

"Want to come along? It would be a nice little trip. . . ."

"Sure. I'll wait for you. I love looking through month-old magazines. I find it comforting."

I thought that this time we'd handled it all very well. It made me real happy. That idiot with his letter . . . It had scared me stiff for a minute.

"What time is the appointment?" I asked.

"I'll just powder my nose and we'll go."

Outside it was cold, dry, and sunny. I took a long, deep breath.

A little while later we found ourselves at the gynecologist's. It surprised me that there was no sign on the door, but Betty was already ringing the bell and my brain was running in slow motion. A guy in a housecoat opened up for us. The housecoat looked like something straight out of *A Thousand and One Nights*—the cloth shimmering like a silver lake. Prince Charming had graying temples and a long ivory pipe between his teeth. He raised an eyebrow when he saw us. If this dude is a gynecologist, I thought, then I'm the darling of the literary set.

"Yes? Can I help you . . . ?" he asked.

Betty stared at him without answering.

"My wife has an appointment," I said.

"Excuse me?"

Just then Betty took the letter out of her pocket. She pushed it under the guy's nose.

"You the one who wrote this?" she asked.

I didn't recognize her voice. I thought of a volcano opening its eye. The man took the pipe out of his mouth and held it tight against his heart.

"What's the meaning of this?" he asked.

I told myself not to worry—any second now I'd wake up. What was surprising was how real everything seemed—the wide, silent hallway, the carpet under my feet, the guy biting his lip, and the letter trembling at the end of Betty's arm like an invulnerable will-o'-the-wisp. I stood there stupefied.

"I asked you a question." Betty started again, in a shrill voice. "Are you the one who wrote this, yes or no?"

The guy made like he was looking closer at the letter, then he scratched his neck and glanced at us quickly.

"Well now . . . you see, I write letters all day long. It wouldn't surprise me if . . ."

I saw he was trying to come up with something while he was talking to us—a child of three on a merry-go-round could see that. He backed up tentatively into the apartment, getting ready to make a run for the door. I wondered if he would make it—he didn't seem particularly agile.

He made a sorry face before playing his last card, and honestly, it couldn't have been worse, him trying desperately to get his engine to turn over. It gave Betty time to bump the door open calmly with her shoulder. Our hero stumbled backward into the entryway, holding one arm.

"What's wrong with you? You're crazy!"

There was a large blue vase sitting on a pedestal. Betty whipped her purse around and the thing came off in one fell swoop. I heard the sound of fine china exploding. It woke me up. Under the impact, Betty's purse had opened up, and everything you'd ever find in a girl's purse had scattered on the floor among the pieces of broken vase.

"Wait, I'll help you pick it up," I said.

She was livid. She looked at me ferociously.

"SHIT, DON'T PAY ANY ATTENTION TO THAT!! TELL HIM WHAT YOU THINK OF HIS LETTER!!"

The guy was looking at us with wild eyes. I bent over to pick up the lipstick that was gleaming at my feet.

"I have nothing to say to him," I said.

I continued picking things up with a thousand-pound weight on my shoulders.

"Are you kidding me?" she asked.

"No. What he thinks doesn't interest me. I've got better things to worry about."

The guy couldn't see what a break he was getting. He was obviously not with it. I don't know what possessed him—he must have realized that I wasn't going to jump on him and so he let himself get carried away by the sudden absence of danger. Instead of staying where he was, shutting up, and letting us just get our things together, he started coming toward us.

I'm certain that at that precise moment Betty had forgotten all about him. All her anger had been turned on me. We were raking the rug, trying to put together the puzzle that had spilled out of her purse. I don't know how she did it, because she never took her eyes off me. She was breathing quickly, and her look was a furious and sad variation on a theme of pain. The guy came up behind her and in a demented gesture touched her shoulder with his fingertip.

"Listen here, I'm not accustomed to this sort of animal behavior. I know how to use only one weapon—my mind. . . ."

Betty closed her eyes without turning around.

"Don't touch me," she said.

But the guy was drunk with his own audacity. These crazy bangs were hanging over his forehead, and his eyes were shining.

"Your manners are unacceptable," he said. "It is obvious that there can't be any dialogue between us, since Speech, like Writing, requires a minimum of elegance, which seems to be a particular deficit in your case. . . ."

She let slide a brief period of silence after this remark—the kind of trembling, empty space that separates the thunder from the lightning. She picked her comb up off the floor. She had it in her hand. It was a cheap one, made of clear plastic—sort of red, with fat teeth. She jumped up and turned around. Her arm traced a circle in the air. She slashed his cheek with it.

At first the guy just looked at her in surprise, then walking backward, he put his hand to his wound—it was pissing blood. It was all rather theatrical, but he seemed to have forgotten his lines—all he did was move his lips. Then it started to get annoying: Betty was breathing like a forge—she went toward him, but my arm came down in front of her and grabbed her by the wrist. I pulled as if I was trying to uproot a tree. I saw her feet leave the floor.

"Hold it. Stop the meter," I said.

She tried to pull away but I held her with all my strength. She let out a little cry. I must say I was not pretending—had her arm been a tube of toothpaste, the stuff would have squirted for miles around. I dragged her toward the door with my teeth clenched. On our way out the door, I turned and took a last look at the guy. He was sinking into an armchair, looking numb. I imagined him reading my novel.

We went down the stairs four at a time, stumbling. I slowed down on the second-floor landing so she could get her balance back. She started yelling.

"GOD, YOU FUCKING BASTARD. WHY DO YOU ALWAYS LET THEM WALK ALL OVER YOU?"

I stopped abruptly. I trapped her against the banister and looked into her face.

"That dude didn't do anything to me," I said. "Nothing—you understand?"

Tears of rage started coming out of her eyes. I felt my strength leaving me, as if someone had blowgunned me with a curare dart.

"WELL GOD DAMN IT ALL! YOU'D THINK THAT NOTHING IN THIS WORLD EVER GETS TO YOU!!"

"You're wrong," I said.

"WELL, THEN, WHAT DOES? TELL ME WHAT GETS TO YOU!"

I looked away.

"Are we going to spend the night here?" I asked.

12

Two days later the cops took her away. I wasn't there when they came. I was with Eddie. It was a Sunday afternoon and we were crisscrossing the town looking for olives—almost all the stores were closed. We had noticed only the night before that we were out—it seemed that Mario had committed a slight act of omission when he sent in his order for the kitchen. He's got his gig down, Eddie explained, but you can't ask him for the moon. It was windy that day—not more than thirty-four or thirty-five degrees. The temperature had gone down all at once.

We were taking our time. Eddie drove slowly. It was a nice little joyride under an icy sun. I felt very relaxed for no reason in particular. Maybe going back and forth all over town in pursuit of a handful of olives made for a great time—if only for the peace that came over my soul, like a light blanket of snow over a field of dead men.

We finally found what we were looking for in Chinatown—no joke—and to make it even better they gave us each a glass of sake, to insure a nonfrozen return to the car. On the way back we talked a bit louder. Eddie was wound up. His ears were red.

"You see, buddy boy, a pizza without olives is like a peanut with nobody inside!"

"Watch the road, will you?" I said.

We parked in front of the house. I had barely stepped onto the sidewalk when I saw Lisa running toward us. We literally froze in our tracks. All she had on was a light sweater. She grabbed me.

"My God, I don't know what this is all . . . they took her . . ." she sobbed.

"What's going on? What are you talking about?" I asked.

"Two cops . . . they came and took her away. . . ."

I bit my lip. Eddie was looking at us over the roof of the car. He wasn't laughing. Lisa was turned inside out; her teeth were chattering. The sun faded.

"All right, let's talk about this inside. You'll die of cold if you stay out here like this."

An hour later, after a brief discussion and a few phone calls, I had all the data. I drank a grog and put my jacket back on.

"I'll go with you," Eddie said.

"Thanks, no," I said.

"Okay, well at least take the car."

"No, it'll do me good to walk. Don't worry, it's nothing."

I left. It wasn't very late, but night had already fallen. I walked fast—hands in pockets, head tucked between my shoulders. The streets had turned into a string of ugly lights. I knew the way. I had fixed a toilet tank in the building next door. I remember I hadn't liked having to walk past the police station with my toolbox slung over my shoulder—I'd had the feeling they were watching me.

I hadn't even made it halfway when I got hit with a terrible pain in my side. It made my eyes blink and my mouth drop open—I felt like I was going to keel over. I stopped to breathe for a second. Great, I thought, as if the shit isn't already deep enough. What had me most worried, though, was this business of pressing charges. The cop on the phone had told me that we were in for "some trouble." I went the rest of the way doubled over, my brain burning. I wondered what "some trouble" meant to a cop. Passersby were puffing out little clouds of steam and so was I—at least one small sign that we all were still alive.

Just before I got there, I was lucky enough to find a store open. I went in. It seemed a little silly to buy oranges, but I didn't know what else to get a girl behind bars. I was having trouble concentrating. On the other hand, oranges are full of vitamins. I finally decided on two cartons of juice. There was a girl dancing half naked on the label—a beach and blue water—without a care in the world.

They showed me to an office where a dude was waiting for me. He was playing with a ruler. I was nervous. He pointed to a chair with the ruler and told me to sit down. He was a broad-shouldered guy with a half-smile on his lips, about forty years old. I was very nervous.

"So here we are . . ." I said.

"Save your breath," he interrupted. "I know the story from A to Z. I'm the one who took the complaint, and I've talked a little bit with your friend. . . ."

"Oh . . ." I said.

"Right," he went on. "Just between us: beautiful girl, but a little jumpy . . ."

"That depends. She's not always like that. You know, I don't know how to explain. . . . It happens once a month. It's hard for us to understand what it's like for them. It must be tough. . . ."

"Yeah, okay, let's not exaggerate. . . ."

"No . . . no . . . you're right. . . ."

He looked at me attentively, then smiled. I was still wary, but I started to feel a little more comfortable. He seemed like a decent guy. Maybe for once I'd pulled the lucky number.

"So . . . you write novels?" he said.

"Yes. Yeah . . . I mean, I'm trying to get published."

He nodded his head for a few seconds. He put the ruler down on his desk. He got up and went to make sure no one was standing behind the door. Then he took a chair and pulled it up right in front of me. He straddled it and put his hand on my shoulder.

"Listen," he said. "I know what I'm talking about. Publishers . . . they're all SOBs."

"Oh yeah?"

"Yeah. Don't move. I'm going to show you something."

He took a stack of papers out of his drawer and dropped it on his desk. I'd say three pounds, just eyeballing it, wrapped with a rubber band.

"What do you think this is? . . . Give up?"

"A manuscript, right?"

I thought he was going to kiss me, but he contained himself. He just slapped my thigh, smiling like a goof.

"You got it! You know, I'm starting to like you. . . ."

"Happy to be of service."

He stroked his stack of papers and looked me right in the eye.

"Brace yourself," he said. "They turned this book down twenty-seven times."

"Twenty-seven?"

"Yeah. And I suppose it's not over yet. Word must have gotten around. They're all SOBs."

"Shit. Twenty-seven times. God almighty!"

"I still think it'd sell like hotcakes—it's the kind of thing people like. Man, when I think about it—ten years of my life in there, ten years of research—and I kept only the best episodes, the great ones. It's a real keg of dynamite. So maybe it isn't Al Capone, but believe me, it's powerful stuff, you can take my word for it."

"Okay."

"Now, you'll ask me why they haven't published my book—ask me what the hell they use for brains. I know cops who've sold their memoirs for millions, so what's the deal all of a sudden? Cop stories out of date?"

"You're right. It's not even worth it to try to understand."

He nodded slowly, then glanced at my orange juice.

"May I . . . ? You want a drink?" he asked.

I was in no position to refuse. I gave him one of the cartons, squashing a smile. He pulled a ten-inch knife out of his pocket and cut a hole in the spout. The knife was razor-sharp, but I didn't bristle. Then he put two plastic cups on the desk and took out a bottle of vodka, already well used. While he filled the glasses, I started asking myself where I was.

"To our success!" he said. "We're not going to let 'em get us down."

"Right on!"

"You know, your friend . . . I can't really say that she was in the right . . . but I won't say she was in the wrong either. Those guys just sit there, calmly cutting to shreds somebody's life's-work in five minutes. You can't tell me that cop stories are old hat. No way . . ."

He poured us another round. I was starting to feel quite good. I was still carrying around the sake and the grog. I felt safe in his office. Things were getting to be just fine.

"Christ, when that asshole called in with this story, it warmed the cockles of my heart. He really had it coming. I tossed down a few short ones to celebrate. Finally, I said to myself, finally one of them has got his just deserts."

"Yeah, well it was only a scratch. No need to to make a federal case out of it."

"Listen, if it was me, I'd have knocked him out cold. I mean, who do those guys think they are? . . . Freshen that up for you?"

The vodka went to my head like a horde of burning suns. I held my glass out with a smile. Sometimes life was lovely after all. I put my hand on the cop's manuscript and looked into his eyes. We were both pretty out of it—good thing we were sitting.

"Listen," I said. "I'm hardly ever wrong about these things, and I'll tell you something—your book is going to get published. I feel it in my bones. I hope you'll send me an autographed copy."

"You really think so?"

"There are certain signs. Your book is warm to the touch. It is an airplane about to take off."

The cop made a face like someone crossing the finish line of a marathon. He wiped his forehead with his hand.

"Shit," he said. "I can hardly believe it."

"Well, that's how it is," I said. "Now, what are we going to do about Betty? Maybe after all we've said, we ought to just call it even and . . ."

"Christ, I'll finally be able to get out of this crummy office. . . ."

"Right. Absolutely. So how about it? . . . Can I go get her?"

I had to wait a few minutes for him to stop emoting. I glanced out the window into the dark night. I hoped that soon it would all be over. He scratched his head with one hand and poured us what was left in the bottle with the other. He sat there, watching the last drop fall.

"Now for your friend . . . It's a little tricky," he said, making a face. "There is this fucking complaint, after all. I don't really have a free hand here."

"Shit, don't you remember?" I said. "She did it for guys like you and me. She sacrificed herself so that those fuckers would think twice before burying our books! She fought for us! Now it's our turn to do something for her!"

"My God, I know. I know. But there's this complaint. . . ."

He couldn't even look me in the eye. He sat there scratching an invisible spot on his pants. All the vodka I'd drunk had gotten me hot. I started raising my voice. I'd totally forgotten I was in a police station.

"So what's it gonna be?" I said. "I mean, who makes the laws around here, anyway? Are we going to let that asshole have the last word?! Are we going to keep writing only to be left behind in the dust?!!"

"You don't understand. The complaint has been filed. . . ."

He seemed embarrassed, but in the end he was just yellow, a lily-livered wimp, hogtied from head to foot. I started choking.

"Listen," I said. "Don't tell me there's nothing we can do here. This is a police station, after all. You ought to be able to do something. . . ."

"Yes, but it isn't that simple. A filed complaint . . . there are records. . . ."

"Fine. I get it. Okay . . ."

"I swear, man, I'm really sorry. If there was a solution I would . . ."

We looked each other directly in the eye. I wondered if he thought it was funny—doling out his words one at a time like that; I wondered if it wasn't conditioning that came with the job. I waited until he was good and ripe. . . .

"Tell me what to do," I said.

He looked at his shoes and shuffled his feet.

"It wouldn't take much." He sighed. "All you have to do is get the guy to withdraw his complaint."

No one talked for a while. Then I stood up and grabbed my carton of juice—one hundred percent natural.

"Can I see her? Is that possible?"

"Yeah, I can arrange that."

"I'll keep my fingers crossed for your book," I said.

There was one other woman in there with her, laid out on the bench in back. There wasn't much light—the minimum. It was awful. She seemed in decent shape, though, even relaxed. You might have wondered which one of us was locked up. I gave her the orange juice with a wan smile, and held on to the bars.

"How you doing?" I asked.

"Okay, and you? What's the matter? You don't look so good."

"This whole fucking thing is my fault. But I'm going to get you out of here in a hurry. Just hold on, baby."

The bars were thick. No way to bend them apart after all I'd drunk—I was out of strength. Her hair was trying to tell me something. I put my hand out to touch it.

"I'd feel better if I had a lock of hair to take with me," I blubbered.

She gave it a toss, laughing. Suddenly it wasn't a prison cell—it was the cavern of Ali Baba. I was surely crazy, but I like being crazy—getting shaken by the sappiest of sights, putting my hand out to a girl to be taken away from all the senseless shit that surrounds us, a small flame burning in my belly.

She had such an effect on me. I stumbled, then righted myself with a smile. All that counted was that she was alive. The rest didn't exist.

"Hey . . ." she said. "Man, you can hardly stand up. Come here. . . ."

I didn't. I backed up a little.

"You don't know what I've been through—I haven't stopped thinking about you one second."

"Yeah, but it hasn't killed you, has it? It hasn't been a waste of time. . . ."

I felt like a moving sidewalk was pulling me toward the door. I backed away, against the wall. I absolutely had to leave with a sweet image in my head—something I could carry around like a good-luck charm.

"Everything's going to be all right," I said. "I got to go now, but I swear you're not going to rot in here very long, because I'm going to take care of everything. I'm going to solve all our problems."

"Yeah, I can see that. You can barely stand up. I'm sure you'll do a good job. Hey, don't go away like that. . . ."

But I did. I kept backing up until I found myself in the shadow of the hallway, where I couldn't see her anymore.

"Don't forget, I'm getting you out of here!" I shouted. "Don't be afraid!"

There was a hollow noise, as if she'd kicked the bars with her foot.

"HAHA!" she said. "YOU THINK THIS STUFF SCARES ME??"

I went home slowly, going in through the back to avoid Eddie and Lisa. I went straight to the bedroom without turning on the lights. I heard them talking downstairs. I lay down and smoked an entire cigarette. I breathed slowly, bringing her image up in my head for as long, and as often, as I pleased. I felt better after that. I splashed a little water on my face, then went downstairs.

I felt their eyes on me halfway down the stairs.

"Don't worry," I said. "It's almost all taken care of."

"You been here long?" Eddie asked.

"Now don't get upset. Do you realize that Mario is working without olives? Looked at your watch lately?"

We jumped in the car. I worked like a dog all night, but my heart wasn't in it. Tips, zero.

13

I woke up the next morning. I didn't think twice. I got out of bed and, while the coffee was heating, did twenty push-ups without batting an eye. I don't usually do things like that, but somehow it felt right. I stood up again and walked to the window. A ray of sunshine hit me in the face. It made me smile. I went to turn off the coffee, and broke the knob on the stove in half. I felt fit—incapable of coming up with a single thought, but wound tight as a spring and responsive as a remote-control engine. This was fine with me. From time to time it feels good to unplug your brain. I watched myself get dressed, straighten up the room, and do a few dishes. I smoked a cigarette before I left—the last cigarette of the condemned man. The condemned man wasn't me, but I smoked it for him, to save time.

When he asked me through the door who I was, I said I was producing a television show on Literature. The first thing I saw when he opened up was the bandage across his cheek. His eyes

bulged when I gave him a hard right to the stomach. He folded
in half. I went in, closed the door behind me, and delivered
another one. This time he went down to his knees. It hurt me to
see him like that—eyes popping out and mouth twisted in an
inaudible cry—it hurt me. I sent him rolling into the living room
with my foot.

He landed under a table. He tried to get up, but I was on him
in two steps. I grabbed him by the lapels of his housecoat and
twisted my fist in it to strangle him. I dragged him coughing and
spitting to an armchair, and sat down. I let up a little on the lapels,
so he could catch his breath, but at the same time gave him a
sharp knee in the nose, to maintain the psychological edge. I
moved aside quickly to keep the blood from getting all over me.

"If you think I'm doing this because you shit on my book,
you're wrong," I said. "Has nothing to do with that."

He slowly got his breath back. His face was finger-painted in
blood from his touching his nose. I held him fast.

"If you think that, you're wrong," I repeated. "Real wrong, you
get me?"

I fired my fist into the top of his skull. He let out a moan.

"I don't hold it against you, because it isn't really your fault,
I recognize that. I didn't write the book for someone like you. So
let's consider that a simple misunderstanding—no harm done.
That's all there is to say as far as you and me go. You agree?"

He let me know he agreed. I grabbed him by the hair and
yanked. Our eyes met.

"Still, you don't know shit from shinola," I said.

I punched him in the ear. I took the telephone in my lap.

"I'll make it brief," I said. "That girl is the only thing that
counts in my life. So you take this phone and you withdraw your
complaint, or I'll be forced to do something unpleasant, okay?"

All those swear words echoing in that room furnished in Louis
XVI—it was like sprinkling confetti on the bed of a dying man.
He nodded his head immediately, a small bubble of blood hanging

from his lip. I tied a noose around his neck with the telephone cord and then let him be. I listened in while he told his little story to the cops.

"Good," I said. "Now say it one more time. . . ."

"But . . ."

"I said say it again."

He repeated the magic words in a tired voice and I gave him a sign to hang up the phone. I sat there deciding whether or not to smash a few more things before leaving, but I thought better of it—I was starting to lose my nerve. I pulled the cord just a little, to squeeze his Adam's apple.

"You'd be foolish not to forget this ever happened," I said. "It's up to you if we ever see each other again. Of the two of us, it's me who's got less to lose."

He looked at me, his head nodding, fingers clenched on the telephone cord. The blood was starting to dry on his nose—blood is something that never lasts too long. For a moment I almost asked myself what I was doing there. I'm used to that kind of change, though—I can slip from one level of consciousness to another with the ease of a leaf floating down a river, regaining its gentle pace after falling over a sixty-foot waterfall. The guy was nothing to me. He was just the cheap image of something that had nothing to do with reality.

I left without saying another word. I quietly closed the door behind me. Outside I got a hit off the icy wind.

We made a lot of money at the pizzeria Christmas Eve—a real haul. Eddie couldn't believe his eyes. We went all out. The night before I'd brought in double the usual amount of champagne, without saying anything. Now there was only one bottle left standing, and there was money overflowing from all sides. It was almost daylight by the time the last customer left. We were dead. Lisa put her arms around my neck; she'd worked all night with us and done a hell of a job. I picked her up by the waist and sat her on the counter.

"Tell me what I can get you," I said.

"I want something fabulous," she said.

Betty melted into a chair, sighing.

"Make that two," she said.

I went up to her, raised her chin, and kissed her theatrically. I could hear them laughing behind me, but I didn't care. I took my time. I found that it was even better after the kind of day we'd had—a broiling kiss served up hot. Then I went and started on the drinks. Mario came around to see what was going on, but was too tired to stay—he just kissed the two girls and split. I'd made enough for five, which left us with four very full glasses. It was something I'd come up with on the spur of the moment, something a bit rough around the edges.

It leveled Eddie right off the bat. He didn't notice, but everyone else did. He started regaling us with some wild idea about seeing the sun rise over the snow. He couldn't live without seeing it.

"What the hell are you bothering us with that shit for?" I said.

"Man, can you imagine anything prettier? What's Christmas without a little snow?"

"It's like a peanut with nobody inside."

"Hey, we can go in the car. Try not to spoil my fun, okay?"

I felt the girls going soft. They were not particularly low on the idea.

"Shit, you have any idea what it'll be like out there in the cold? You playing with a full deck, guy?"

"I just want to see your face when the first rays come through the flakes. I want to see you wisecrack then. . . ."

"It's not that. I'm sure it's great—the sun, the snow, and all that stuff—it's certainly awesome, but it's not that. What I'm wondering, Eddie, is just how you think you're going to drive in the condition you're in?"

"Shit," he said. "Shit—I'm going to teach you something. There is no condition that I can't drive a car in."

His eyes were shining like flying saucers. It's the gin, I said to myself. I had to admit that I'd been a little heavy-handed with the gin—I'd let myself go.

"You're going to get us all killed!" I said.

Everyone laughed, except me. Five minutes later we were in the car, waiting for Eddie to find the keys. I sighed softly.

"What's with you?" he said. "Don't you think this is fun? It's Christmas—don't worry about a thing! Everything's going to be hunky-dory. Here they are. . . ."

He jingled his keys under my nose and one of them gave me a spark—blue and cold. Nice little cunt of a key, I thought—go piss up a rope. I hunched down in my seat.

We crossed town in the wee hours. The streets were practically deserted, and that made it nice—we could drive down the middle at low speeds, spotting the lights from far away in the mild dawn fog. I wondered where all the people were, if the sidewalk hadn't swallowed them in the night. The girls were laughing in the backseat. We left the city, headed for the blazing horizon; we had to hurry. We all had drawn-out faces—all so tired. Still, a new energy slowly slid into the car. We rounded the cape and headed for the sun on that December morning, lighting cigarettes and talking nonsense, while a new day was getting ready to be lived.

We drove for a while, until we came to a snow-covered field. There were a few large buildings—factories—in the background, but we didn't have time to find anything better. By then it was a matter of minutes. We parked on the side of the road. The sky was clearing. There was the sensation of abominable temperatures—approaching zero, with icy winds. We got out of the car anyway, slapping our arms.

In two seconds flat, my nose started running, and my eyes teared. Seats were expensive for this early bloodless morning—it was enough to make your hair fall out. After the work we'd put in the night before, the tranquility of this little corner of the world seemed somehow grotesque. I mean it. Eddie had his hat pulled down over his eyes; he was smoking a cigarette and sitting on the hood of the car, his face turned toward the flames.

"Jesus Christ," I said. "Jesus Christ, Eddie, you falling asleep there . . . ?"

"Stop blabbering and look. . . ."

He motioned to me to turn around. Just then a grazing ray of sunlight swept over the field of snow. We witnessed a festival of sparkles—golds and blues. In the end it was nothing to write home about—I had to struggle to keep from yawning. It's all a matter of disposition here on earth. That morning I was rather disposed to shiver, trampling those dear little flakes underfoot. I was not interested in anything too profound. I was interested only in finding someplace warm, where I could do something that wasn't too tiring—blinking for instance—and as little of that as possible. Betty had been out of jail for two days, and I hadn't slept in three nights. It would take more than a ray of sunshine to get me excited; I was still standing only by the grace of God. A whole day talking to Betty, a whole night decorating the dining room, and finally that miserable Christmas Eve running around between tables, body racked with pain. I was not about to let a frigid little wind come crack every tooth in my mouth, and then smile about it.

Even though I was freezing to death, we didn't leave right away. The girls decided that they simply couldn't leave without feeding the little birds. I was starting to feel weak. The sun was coming up but it wasn't giving off much heat. I felt death approaching. The girls miraculously managed to find some crackers in the glove compartment, and off they went, rosy-cheeked and Santa Claus–smiling. It was "Oh this" and "Ah that" and "Let's smash these crackers into a thousand crumbs and throw them in the air by the fistful."

I sat in the car with the door open, my feet outside. I smoked a cigarette while the sparrows came and landed in the snow like rain.

Eddie was out there too. I watched them all laughing, dumping tons of food on the poor birds' heads, imagining that each crumb represented the equivalent of a large steak and french fries, and it occurred to me that you could probably kill them like that: force-feeding them fifteen or twenty main dishes in a row, things they'd never ordered.

"Merry Christmas, fellas!" Eddie yelled. "Come and get it, boys!"

One bird showed up after the others. I saw him come from the end of the sky, then change course suddenly, his two legs sticking forward. He set himself down away from the others, apparently uninterested in what his friends were up to. He looked away while the steaks tumbled onto his back. I thought it must be the village idiot—he needed a few extra minutes to get what was happening.

He started coming toward me—taking little hops, his feet together. He stopped ten inches from my shoes. We looked at each other for a few seconds.

"Right," I said. "Maybe you're not as dumb as you look."

I had the feeling that something was going on between the bird and me. I decided to take matters into my own hands. I asked the others to throw me a cracker, caught it on the fly. It seemed to be less cold out than before. Life is full of small nothings that warm your heart. You can't ask for the moon. I crushed the cracker with my fingers and leaned forward. The bird foraged under his wings, like somebody who has lost his wallet. I started dropping the crumbs under his nose, smiling in advance. I knew I was working a miracle—making a small mountain of food appear at his very feet. He looked at me and cocked his head.

"Don't worry," I said. "You're not dreaming."

I don't know what the little jerk was thinking of—here was this freight car full of merchandise in front of him and he seemed not to even see it. I could hardly believe my eyes, couldn't get over it. I wondered if there was something wrong with the crackers. How could you possibly not notice that sunlit hill of goodies glowing like a gold-leafed temple, unless you were doing it on purpose. Still, he looked away, ignoring what I'd done, and hopped away to a place where there was nobody around and not a bite to eat. He looked like a penguin walking straight for a precipice.

I got out of the car. I swallowed a cracker and went after him, pacing him as he went. I got snow in my shoes. When he stopped I stopped, and when he flew away there was nothing left to do but go back to the car with the weight of a few snowflakes—disguised as the world—on my shoulders. Yes, I had eaten the cracker myself, and it was good. It would have been better with a little cherry jam on it, but who's counting. . . .

Then we went home. I shoved my feet under the radiator while Eddie got out the champagne and the girls took the cellophane off the scallops.

"Can I do anything to help?" I asked.

No, I couldn't do anything—nothing special left to do. I tried to make myself as comfortable as possible, closed my eyes, and grabbed my drink. Had some asshole come along and whispered in my ear that we only die but once, the ear he would have fallen on would have been deaf.

We ate a little while later. It must have been somewhere around ten o'clock. I hadn't eaten a thing since the night before. Still, I wasn't hungry. I turned my attention to the champagne instead. I needed a kick. I never let my glass leave my hand. In the end I was rewarded for my tenacity. I felt myself float gently off my chair—banking right, then gliding into the middle of the general merriment, overtaking several laughs along the way.

"How come you're not eating?" Eddie asked. "You sick?"

"No, I'm saving myself for the yule log."

Eddie had a napkin tied around his neck and was squinting with satisfaction. I liked him. Human beings like that don't grow on trees—when you find them it's like a little miracle. I decided to light up a cigar. Everyone was sitting there with a smile and a cigar. You have to light them at just the right moment. When you know how to go about it, life can disappear into a cloud of blue smoke. I rocked back and forth in my chair with the lightness of someone who lacks for nothing, and knows the sound of a good cigar being rolled next to his ear. The daylight was weak, but I hung tough. My neck was a little stiff was all, but it was no big deal. I said, Now nobody move, stay right where you are, because I am now going to bring us the yule log and I don't want anybody getting in my way. There are some things a man has to do alone.

So I got up, went to the fridge, and was just about to get the log out when the telephone rang. Eddie went to answer it. There were little elves stuck in the frosting, and a Christmas tree—they formed a little troop, the one in front holding a saw in his hand, with the rest close behind, advancing on the poor little tree, cute enough to eat, with the obvious intention of fixing its wagon. Very big deal. I wondered if the guy who had hatched it went out and cut himself a tree every morning with a handsaw like that, and if so, why not with a bread knife? I offed the little buggers with a flick of the finger—the last one screaming in horror as he fell into the void, as if I'd pulled his arm off. The screaming hurt my ears.

I looked up and saw Eddie wavering by the telephone, his mouth wide open and his face ravaged. Lisa moved back from the table, knocking over her glass. I don't know why, but the first thing I thought of was that he'd just been bitten in the leg by a rattlesnake. The receiver was hanging strangely by its cord. The image went through my mind like a hedge-hopping fighter plane that buzzes you, flips you like a pancake till you fall out of your hammock. All this lasted a fraction of a second. Eddie ran his hand through his hair with a dazed look.

"My God, you guys . . ." he moaned. "My God in Heaven . . ."

Lisa got up with a bolt, but something nailed her to the floor.

"Eddie, what is it?" she said. "Eddie!"

I saw he was going to collapse, his hair all disheveled. He gave us a pathetic look.

"It can't be true," he mumbled. "My mom . . . my dear . . . It hurts. . . . How could you do this to me . . . ?"

He tore the napkin from his neck and wrung it in his hands. Something welled up in his chest like a geyser. We waited. He shook his head back and forth, his mouth twisted.

"I'M NOT FOOLING, SHE'S DEAD!!!" he screamed.

On the sidewalk somebody went by with a transistor radio playing a commercial for a laundry detergent that makes everyday chores a breeze. When it was quiet again we ran over to Eddie, grabbing him and sitting him down; his legs couldn't hold him up anymore. Fatigue, alcohol, and a mother who has just died on Christmas night—it was all well beyond the maximum weight for excess baggage.

He was looking straight ahead, his hands folded on the table. No one knew what to say. We stared at each other, wondering what to do next. Lisa kissed him on the forehead and licked away the beginning of a tear.

Betty and I being there, shifting our weight from one foot to the other without saying a word, didn't help matters much. I couldn't just slap him on the shoulder—Be okay, old pal—I never had that sort of ease. Death has always left me speechless. I was going to give Betty the sign that we should leave them alone together, but just then Eddie stood up abruptly, his two fists pushing on the table and his head down.

"I got to go down there," he said. "The funeral's tomorrow. I got to go. . . ."

"Of course you do," said Lisa. "But first you better get some rest. You can't go down there like this."

You only had to look at him to know he wouldn't make it a hundred yards. Lisa was right. Before anything else he needed a few hours of sleep. We all did, in fact—anybody's mother could understand that. But he was on a roll.

"I'm going to change. I got just enough time to change clothes. . . ."

He was going off the deep end; at that point peeling a banana would have been too strenuous for him. I tried to get him back on course.

"Listen, Eddie. Be reasonable. Lie down for a few hours, then I'll call a taxi. You'll see, it'll be better that way."

He gave me a look, then started unbuttoning his shirt awkwardly.

"I don't need a fucking taxi. . . ."

"Really? You going on foot? I don't know, how far is it?"

"If I leave now I think I can be there before nightfall," he said.

This time it was me who collapsed into a chair. I pinched the bridge of my nose, then grabbed him by the arm.

"Are you kidding me, Eddie? You joking? You think you're going to drive seven or eight hours in a row, when you can hardly keep your eyes open? You think we're going to let you? You're nuts, man. . . ."

He started whining like a little boy, leaning on me. It was the worst thing that could have happened. I know my limits. Still, he insisted.

"But you got to understand," he said. "It's my mother, man. My mother died!"

I looked elsewhere—at the table, at the floor, at the white light waiting for me by the window—and I stopped myself there. There's always a brief moment of hypnotic terror that comes when you realize that you're a rat. It's a fairly nauseating sensation.

14

I stopped at the first place we found open on the side of the road. I parked the car by the pumps and got out.

In the bar, I had them line up three espressos in front of me. I burned my lips a little, but by then it didn't make any difference. I was sore all over, not to mention my inflated eyes, at least doubled in volume. The smallest light bulb looked like a supernova to me. Having already gone about ninety hours without sleep, I decided to take a little three-hundred-fifty-mile drive. Was I not brilliant? Did I not have the stuff of which twentieth-century heroes are made? Yes, except that I served pizzas for a living, and I didn't ride with the Hell's Angels. I was just going to an old lady's funeral—the death waiting at the end of the journey was not my own. Times had changed.

I started giggling nervously to myself; it was impossible to stop. The guy behind the counter looked at me, worried. To reassure him, I grabbed the salt shaker and a hard-boiled egg and gave him the thumbs-up. I absentmindedly cracked the shell on the counter a little too hard and smashed the whole thing to a pulp in my hand. The guy jumped. I let the hand with all the egg on it drop to my side, and with the other hand I wiped away the tears that had welled up in my eyes. I couldn't control myself. The guy came and wiped up the mess without saying a word.

I had barely gotten a hold on myself when Betty came and sat down on the stool next to me.

"Hey, you look like you're in great shape!" she said.

"Yeah, I am. Be fine . . ."

"Eddie just fell asleep. Poor guy, he wasn't making it. . . ."

I started giggling again. She looked at me and smiled.

"What's so funny?"

"Nothing. I'm just beat, that's all."

She ordered coffee. I ordered three more. She lit a cigarette.

"I like this," she said. "Here, with you, in this kind of place. Like we'd just set sail somewhere . . ."

I knew what she meant, but I didn't believe in that anymore. I drank my coffee and gave her a wink. I was too weak to resist.

We went back to the car, clinging together like two sardines under the ice cap.

Bongo came running up to us. The damn dog just about knocked me over in the snow. I must have been walking a little stiff-legged. A gust of wind could have blown me away.

I got back behind the wheel. Eddie was sleeping in the backseat, lying halfway over Lisa's lap. I shook my head, then turned the ignition. When I think that that idiot was ready to hop in the car by himself . . . yeah, I could see it all now—facedown, asleep at the wheel; over the little white line, and bye-bye, baby. It irked me. I didn't ungrit my teeth for quite some time.

A few hours later everyone was sleeping. It was surprising. It was nice out, and the farther down we got the less snow there was. The highway was pretty deserted, and I let myself switch lanes with abandon, to break the monotony. I tried to go over the dotted line without touching the dots. The car pitched gently. I didn't know whether to watch the time or the mileage to know when we were getting close—I couldn't decide. The question began to obsess me. I knew there wasn't time for that. I turned up the radio. Some dude started talking to me in a peaceful voice about the life of Christ—insisting that he had not abandoned us. I hoped he was right, that he had his information straight. The sky was hopelessly empty; there was absolutely no sign of Him. Of course I'd understand completely if he turned his back on us once and for all—anyone would, in his shoes.

I smiled at the little spark in my soul, scarfing down a few crackers to pass the time, one eye on the tachometer. I kept the needle on the edge of the red. I amazed myself, I truly amazed myself. I wondered where I was finding the strength to stay conscious. Of course it's true that my body was tense, my neck stiff, my jaws sore, and my eyelids burning—but there I was, eyes wide open, going up and down the hills while the time sped by. I stopped and tossed down some more coffee, then took off again, no one so much as stirring. The trip seemed like a life in miniature—the highs and the lows. The scenery changed a bit. Solitude whistled through the small opening in the window.

Betty rolled over in her sleep. I watched her. I didn't ask myself where I was headed, nor what I was doing with her—it never entered my mind. I'm not the kind of guy who asks himself questions about why he doesn't ask himself questions. I just liked looking at her. The sun was setting when I stopped for gas. I emptied the ashtray into a little paper bag which I tossed in a garbage can. This guy washed the windshield. I started giggling again for no reason. I pushed back into the seat and dug some change out of my pocket. I gave a fistful to the guy, my eyes tearing. He made a face at me. I wiped my eyes for the next two miles.

Just before we got there I woke everybody up. I asked if they'd all had a good night's sleep. It was an inconsequential little town with a nice feel to it. We drove through it slowly. Eddie leaned over to show me where to go, and the girls checked their faces in their little mirrors.

It was dark. The streets were wide and clean. Most of the buildings were less than three stories high; it made you feel like you could breathe a little. Eddie motioned for me to stop. We pulled over in front of a piano store. He touched my shoulder.

"She sold pianos," he said.

I turned around to face him.

"My God," he added.

We went up to the second floor. I pulled up the rear. The stairway never ended, and the flowered wallpaper made my head spin. There were a few people in the room. I couldn't see too well because of the dimness—there was maybe one lamp lit, in the corner. They all stood up when they saw Eddie, took his hands and kissed him, saying things in low voices, looking at us over their shoulders. They seemed to be familiar with death. Eddie introduced everyone but I didn't try to understand who was who, or who I was—I just smiled. The minute I'd parked, I felt how tired I really was. Now I had to try and maneuver a three-hundred-pound body around. I didn't dare lift an arm—I knew it would make me cry.

When everyone went into the room where the wake was, I just followed along without thinking, dragging my heels. I couldn't see anything, because Eddie threw himself at the bed and his shoulders blocked my view. All I saw were two feet sticking out from under the sheets, like stalagmites. He started crying again. I yawned without meaning to, putting my hand over my mouth just in time. A woman turned around. I closed my eyes.

By chance, I happened to be standing behind everybody else. I backed up a few steps to the edge of the room and leaned myself against the wall, my head down and arms crossed. It felt pretty good—I no longer had to struggle to keep my balance. All I had to do was push a little with my legs and everything fell right into place. I heard a slight breathing sound close to me.

I saw myself on the beach in the middle of the night, both feet in the water. I was squinting into the moonlight, when an immense black wave welled up from who knows where, stretching up to the sky with a frothy fringe on top like an army of snakes standing on their tails. It seemed to stand still for a moment, then came crashing down on my head with an icy hiss. I opened my eyes. I'd fallen over a chair on my face. My elbow hurt. The others turned toward me, scowling. I gave Eddie a lost look.

"Sorry," I said. "I didn't mean to do that. . . ."

He motioned to me that he understood. I stood up and walked out, closing the door softly behind me. I went down to the car to get cigarettes. It wasn't too cold out, nothing to compare to what it was like three hundred fifty miles north of there. I lit up and took a little walk with Bongo down the street. There wasn't a soul—no one to see me shuffling along like an old grandma worried about breaking her hipbone.

I went down to the corner. I tossed my cigarette over the sidewalk in front of me, into the void, then came back. I had to admit that Betty had been right for once: a little change of scene can do you good. To me, it seemed like a great idea, mostly because it allowed us to leave our little bundle of woe behind us, if only for a day or two. It amazed me just then to think that. I was surprised at the bitterness I felt looking back on the life that had begun when Betty set fire to the bungalow. It's true that every day hadn't been a bundle of laughs, but there were plenty of good times and no one with half a brain could have asked for more than that. No, it was obviously my book that had given our life this strange taste, colored it this vague shade of purple. And if closing the door behind you and hopping in the car was all it took to start over again? Wouldn't life be better then? A little easier? At that precise moment I was almost ready to try it—to grab Betty by the shoulders and say, Okay, sweetheart, we're going to go on to something else now—no more pizza, no more city, no more book. . . . Are you with me?

These were pleasant thoughts to have, going back up the calm, wide street. If only for these images the trip was worth it. I saw it all so clearly that I didn't even think about the drive home. Had I thought about it, I would have washed out right then and there, but the patron saint of those who dream watched over me—no dark thoughts came to roost. Far from it: Betty and I, settled there in the town, not wanting to hear any more about some stupid manuscript—finally able to wake up in the morning without looking anxiously in the mailbox . . . good times and bad times, nothing more. This was the kind of thing that made me smile like a kid again as I walked back into the building, all of it melting slowly in my mouth.

I climbed back up the stairway to the second floor, finding it even tougher going than the first time. I used the banister—I wasn't proud. The room was empty. They must have all still been in the little bedroom—stuffed in there around the corpse. I didn't see any reason to bother them. I sat down. I poured myself a glass of water. I tipped the pitcher, I didn't lift it. With any luck they'd stay in there all night with her, no one to worry whether I was sleepy or not. I had the vague feeling that they'd already forgotten me. There was a curtain at the end of the living room. I stared at it for at least ten minutes, my eyes squinting, trying to uncover its secret. Finally I stood up and went over to it.

There was a stairway there that went down into the store. I must have been off my rocker that night. I must have fallen victim to some morbid attraction to stairs, going up and down, puffing like the damned. I went down.

I found myself among the pianos. They gleamed in the light that came from the street, like black stones under a waterfall. There was no sound at all—they were silent pianos. I chose one at random and sat down in front of it. I opened the keyboard. Luckily there was a place at the end of the keyboard where you could put your elbow down. I did. I put my chin in my hand. I looked at all the keys lined up. I yawned a little.

It was not the first time I'd found myself at a piano. I knew how to play, and though I'd never attained the heights of greatness, I could pick out a little tune with three fingers, choosing a

slowish tempo and a minimum of light. I began by playing a C.
I listened to it attentively and followed it around the store with
my eyes, not losing it for a second. When the silence returned,
I started again. To me, this was one hell of a piano. It had
understood what kind of piano player I was, and yet had given me
its all, the best of itself. It was nice to come across a piano that
had found The Way.

I shifted into a simple number that allowed me to maintain my
style as well as a relatively comfortable position, slumped over the
side with my head in my hand. I played slowly, doing the best I
could, and little by little I stopped thinking about anything. I just
watched my hand—the tendons rolling around under the skin
when I pushed my fingers down. I stayed there doing that for a
long time, my little tune repeating itself over and over. It was as
if I could no longer do without it, as if I played it better each time,
as if this little nothing of a song had the power to enrich my soul.
But I was in such a state of exhaustion that I would have mistaken
a glowworm for the divine light. I was beginning to have halluci-
nations. From then on things started deteriorating.

I had started humming my delicious little melody and I was
getting a giant-sized kick out of it. It was unreal—so unreal that
I thought I heard the chords that went with it, clearer and clearer.
It made me so happy to be alive that my strength started to come
back. I got excited. Forgetting where I was, I turned up the
volume and sang louder and louder. I was able to do with three
fingers what normal people need two hands for. It was simply
magnificent. I started to feel hot. I had never in my life had such
rapport with a piano. I'd never been able to play anything like that
before. When I heard a girl's voice mingle with my own, I said
to myself, That's it, an angel has come down from Heaven to pull
me up by the hair.

I sat up without stopping. Betty was at the piano next to mine.
She had one hand squeezed between her legs and with the other
was plunking out the chords. She was in good voice. She was
radiant. I have never forgotten the look she gave me then. That's

me, though—I'm made that way, I have a good memory for colors. We went at it with hearts high for several long minutes, brushing with Beatitude and totally unconscious of the noise we were making. There could be no limits put on what we felt. I was fully afloat. I thought it would never end.

Then a guy appeared at the top of the stairs, making wild gestures. We stopped.

"Hey, are you nuts?" he said.

We looked at him, not knowing what to answer. I was still breathless.

"What in the world do you think you're doing?" he added.

Eddie appeared behind him. He glanced at us, then took the guy by the shoulders and turned him around.

"Leave them alone," he said. "It's okay, just leave them alone. They're not hurting anything. They're my friends."

They disappeared behind the curtain. The silence rang in my ears. I turned toward Betty. It was like crossing over to the sunny side of the street.

"Shit, how come you never told me . . ." I asked.

She lifted her hair up, laughing. She was wearing killer earrings—five inches long, shining like neon signs.

"Don't be ridiculous. I can't really play," she said. "I just know two or three things. . . ."

"Right, two or three things . . ."

"No, really. It's easy."

"You kill me. You're a weird girl. . . ."

I put my hand on her thigh. I had to touch her. If I could have I'd have just swallowed her whole.

"You know," I went on, "I've always chased after something that would make my life make sense. Living with you is maybe the most important thing that ever happened to me."

"You're sweet to say that, but it's 'cause you're so tired you can't see straight."

"No, it's the plain truth."

She came over and sat on my lap. I put my arms around her and she whispered in my ear.

"If it was me who wrote that book," she said, "I wouldn't be asking myself if my life had meaning. I wouldn't have to think about what's most important. Me, I'm nothing, but you . . . you can't say that, not you."

She finished her sentence with a kiss on my neck. I couldn't be upset.

"You're driving me crazy with that," I sighed. "That's where all our troubles come from."

"Jesus, that's not the problem!"

"Yes it is."

"So why did you write the book, then? Just to give me a headache?"

"Not really."

"It means nothing to you. . . ."

"Yes it does. I put everything I had into it when I wrote it. But I can't force people to like it. All I did was write it, it was all I could do. And it's all I can do if it stops there."

"And what about me? You think I'm an idiot? You think I fall in love with every book I read? You think it's just because you're the one who wrote it?"

"I hope you wouldn't do that to me."

"Sometimes I think you're playing a game."

"What . . . ?"

"You seem to think it's cool to deny the obvious. It happens that you're a hell of a writer, whether you like it or not."

"Fine. Then maybe you could explain why I haven't written another line?"

"Sure. Because you're a jerk."

I pushed my face into her chest. She played with my hair. I wouldn't have wanted my future fans to see me like that. Tenderness is a hard pill to swallow—there's always a big risk involved. It's like sticking your hand through the bars of a cage.

Betty had no bra on, and my stool had no back. It all felt so good that we nearly wound up on the floor, but at the last minute I called my back muscles into action, squealing in horror. I felt the end was near. My last bit of strength was disappearing like the cherry blossoms in a Japanese garden. So it is said in *The Art of War*: The brave man must know his limits. I yawned into her sweater.

"You look tired," she said.

"No, I'm fine."

She liked my hair—it got along famously with her fingers. I myself was happy to have her weight on my lap; it made things less dreamlike, made me know she was really there, and nowhere else. I could have just picked her up and carried her away. But I didn't try anything fancy—I didn't want to budge. I'd have died first. I felt lead pouring down my spine, and it made me grimace. And yet my soul was light as a feather, carefree and docile, floating up in the slightest of breezes. I couldn't figure it out.

"Anyway, there's no room for us to stay upstairs," she said. "What are we going to do?"

This kind of remark would have destroyed me a few minutes earlier, but I was beyond it all by then. It hurt to talk. It hurt to breathe. Thinking itself was a herculean feat. Still, I did it.

"I'm going to go get in the car," I said.

Luckily she came with me. I was taller than she was, so it was easy to lean on her. As I feared, the door to the street was locked, so we had to go back up and come down the miserable stairs. On the way, I was suddenly struck with terror—I saw myself being swallowed by a boa constrictor. By the time I sagged into the backseat of the car my teeth were almost chattering. Betty gave me a worried glance.

"You don't feel good? My God, you look like you have a fever."

I made my hand into a white flag. I waved it.

"No, no. Everything's fine."

I pulled a blanket up over my legs in one last act of lucidity.

"Betty, where are you? Don't leave me. . . ."

"I'm here! What's gotten into you? You want a cigarette?"
My eyes closed by themselves.
"Everything's fine," I said.
"Hey, did you get a look at all the stars? Look . . ."
"Hmmm . . . yeah, it's nice out . . ." I mumbled.
"Hey, you sleeping?"
"No, no. I'm cool. . . ."
"You think we're going to stay here all night . . . ?"

15

At around eleven o'clock we went to the funeral. The sun was beautiful and the sky was blue. We hadn't seen weather like that in months. The air smelled sweet. I'd slept well; one of the advantages of luxury cars is that you can just about stretch your legs out and the seats are comfortable. I hadn't been cold. There I was in the sunlight, my eyes half closed, while they lowered the coffin, huffing and puffing. I was meditating on the warmth of the sun on my face, realizing that man and the universe are one. I was realizing these things mostly to make the time pass. I wondered when we were going to eat.

No one seemed to care. We went back to the house without saying a word. I lagged behind. It took a few minutes of walking around in circles above the pianos before someone had the bright idea to open the refrigerator. But she had only been an old woman who lived alone—a poor little thing already half dead, who ate like a bird. We had to make do with a little pork chop, half a can of corn, some plain yogurt already past its expiration date, and some crackers. Eddie was feeling better. He was pale and his forehead was still wrinkled, but he'd recovered his cool—he asked me for the salt in a peaceful voice. Luckily the weather's nice, he added.

He spent part of the afternoon going through a drawer full of photographs and papers, talking to himself. We watched him and yawned. We turned the TV on, then had to get up I don't know how many times to change the channel. Finally night fell. I went out to do some shopping with Betty. We took Bongo with us.

It was a terrific little area—trees everywhere, and very few cars in the street. I felt like I hadn't breathed in centuries. I almost smiled as I walked. When we got back I put a huge casserole in the oven. Eddie had shaved, showered, and combed his hair. After the main dish, we downed six pounds of cheese and an apple pie as big as the table. I cleared, then started on the dishes in the kitchen. The girls wanted to watch this western I'd already seen a hundred times, so it didn't bother me. I was back in good shape.

While Bongo was finishing up the casserole, I sat down and smoked a cigarette. Aside from the gunshots in the next room, all I could hear was the silence in the street. It felt good—as if we were in the heart of a summer night. Then I rolled up my sleeves and sudsed up the kitchen sink, my cigarette between my teeth.

I was putting the final touches on a floral plate when Eddie came in. I gave him a wink. He stood behind me, his drink in his hand, looking at his feet. I started scrubbing at some burned-on grease.

"Listen," he began. "I've got a proposition for you—the two of you."

I tensed, my hands under the water, looking straight ahead of me at the tile on the wall—splattering myself.

"Betty and I stay here and take care of the store," I said.

"How'd you know?"

"Beats me."

"Well, I'm going to go ask Betty what she thinks about it. Is it okay with you, though?"

"Yeah, it's okay with me."

He went back into the other room, nodding his head.

I went back to the dishes. I took two or three deep breaths to get my head back together—to finish the dishes without breaking too many—but I had trouble keeping my mind on what I was doing. I found myself staring at the running water, imagining the serenity that awaited us. From time to time I'd wash a plate. I didn't want to get delirious over Eddie's offer. I didn't want my dreams to get too concrete. I chased them out of my brain. I preferred vagueness, letting the soft feelings wash over me without thinking. It's a shame that movie music is so trite—I deserved better than that.

As expected, Betty flipped. She was always up for anything new. She was always sure that something somewhere was waiting for us, and whenever I dared to modify her thesis a little—saying that it was OTHER THINGS, ELSEWHERE that awaited us—she'd laugh in my face and skewer me with her eyes, saying, Why're you always splitting hairs? What difference does it make? I didn't argue. I just lay down and waited for it to blow over.

We spent most of the evening going over everything. We tried to make it as simple as possible. It was easy to see that Eddie was in fact making us a gift of it, even though he made it seem otherwise.

"Anyway, she was all I had left, and for the moment Lisa and I don't need anything. . . . Now wouldn't be a good time to sell, and I'm not about to leave my mother's house to just anybody."

He was looking at the two of us out of the corner of his eye as if we were his children. I opened his beer for him, laughing, while he explained about selling pianos. All in all, it didn't seem too mysterious.

"Listen, I'm not worried," he said.

"Me neither."

"If anything goes wrong, you know where to find me."

"We'll take care of everything, don't worry."

"Yeah, you're at home here."

"Come by anytime, Eddie."

He nodded and hugged Betty.

"You two are okay . . ." he whispered. "This is really helping me. It would have been a thorn in my side."

He had tears in his eyes. There was a short euphoric silence between us, like the cream layer between cookie wafers.

"I only ask one thing of you," said Eddie.

"Anything . . ."

"Would you mind bringing her some flowers from time to time?"

They left during the night. I drank a last beer and Betty walked around the living room, squinting. It made me want to laugh.

"I see the couch in the other corner," she declared. "What do you think . . . ?"

"Sure, why not?"

"Well, let's try it. . . ."

We hadn't been alone in the house for five minutes. I could still hear Eddie wishing us good luck and shutting the car door. I wondered if she was kidding.

"Now? You want to start with that now?"

She looked at me, surprised. She tucked a lock of hair behind her ear.

"Why not? It's not late. . . ."

"No, but I think it could wait till tomorrow. . . ."

"You're no fun. It'll only take a minute."

The thing dated from the war. It weighed at least three tons. We had to roll up the rug and inch our way across the room—the wheels were stuck, and it was late for that sort of work. But you do certain things without putting up a stink when you live with a girl who's worth the trouble. That's what I told myself as I was moving the buffet table, which was then also in the wrong place. I complained, for show, but inside I was having a good time. Even if all I really wanted was to go to bed, I could certainly move a little furniture for her—in truth I'd have moved mountains for her if I'd known how to go about it. Sometimes I wondered if I did enough for her, and sometimes I was afraid I didn't—it's not always easy to be the man you ought to be. You've got to understand that women are a little strange. They can be as annoying as anything when they set their minds to it. Still, I often wondered if I did enough for her. I thought about it mostly at the end of the evening, when I'd gone to bed first, lying there watching as she took her creams and lotions from the bathroom shelf. Anyway, being what you ought to be in life is not something that just happens to you—you have to work at it.

We had both worked up a sweat. When all was said and done, I have to admit, I felt pretty weak in the knees—perhaps I hadn't really gotten all my strength back. I sat on the couch and looked around me with an air of exaggerated smugness.

"Now this is something else again," I said.

She sat down next to me, her knees tucked under her chin, biting her lip.

"Yeah . . . I'm not sure. . . . Maybe we should try a few different—"

"Different, my ass," I said.

She took my hand, yawning.

"I'm beat, too. No, I was just saying . . ."

A little while later we were in the bedroom. I was about to take the covers off the bed, when she stopped me.

"No, I can't do this . . ." she said.

"What are you talking about?"

She was staring at the bed in a very odd way. It's true that from time to time she would go off into the ozone like that. Her attitude intrigued me—I hardly recognized her. I didn't worry about it, though: girls have always intrigued me, generally speaking, and after a while you get used to it. I've decided that you can never completely understand them—you've just got to resign yourself to it. I've observed them out of the corner of my eye.

After a while they all start doing weird things—incomprehensible and dazzling. It leaves you standing there as if you've come upon a fallen bridge; all you can do is throw a few wistful stones into the void and go back where you came from.

Naturally she didn't answer me. I looked at her face and wondered where she'd gone. I decided to push it.

"You can't do what?" I asked.

"Sleep there. I can't sleep there."

"Listen, it's the only bed in the house. It might not be a barrel of laughs, but . . . think about it. It's ridiculous."

She backed up toward the door, shaking her head.

"No, I can't. For the love of God don't force me. . . ."

I sat down on the corner of the bed. She turned and left. Outside the window, I saw two or three stars—it must have cleared up outside. I went back out into the living room. She was jiggling one of the armrests on the couch. She stopped for a minute and smiled at me.

"We'll just unfold this thing here. It'll be fine for now. . . ."

I didn't say anything. I grabbed the other armrest and shook it like a plum tree until it came off in my hand. The couch obviously hadn't been unfolded in twenty years. She seemed to be having trouble with her side, so I went to give her a hand.

"Go try and find some sheets," I said. "I'll take care of this."

The armrest gave me a hell of a time. I had to use the leg of a chair as a lever to get it off. I heard Betty opening the creaky closets. I had no idea how to work the couch. I lay down on the floor to look underneath. There were these huge springs sticking out in all directions like sharp-edged scrap iron. It looked dangerous to me—like some kind of enormous meat-grinder, just waiting to take your hand off. I spotted a large pedal over to one side. I stood up. I cleared a space around the couch. I held on to the backrest and pushed my foot down on the pedal.

Nothing happened. The thing didn't move an inch. I kicked it all over and jumped up and down on it with all my weight, but nothing helped—I couldn't get the goddamn bed to open. I broke out in a sweat. Betty showed up with the sheets.

"What . . . can't do it?" she said.

"No shit. I don't think this thing ever worked in its life. I'd have to really do a job on it. There's not even any tools around here. Listen, just for tonight . . . it won't kill us—it isn't like she died from something contagious, you know. What do you say?"

She acted like she didn't hear me. She made an innocent face and motioned toward the kitchen with her chin.

"I think there's a toolbox under the sink," she said. "I think I remember seeing one. . . ."

I walked to the table. I finished off a can of beer, one hand on my hip. I aimed it at Betty.

"Do you know what you're asking me to do? You know what time it is? Do you really think I'm going to start puttering around with that thing NOW??"

She came over to me with a smile and the sheets. She put her arms around me.

"I know you're tired," she said softly. "Just go sit down somewhere and let me take care of it. I'll handle everything, okay?"

She didn't give me time to tell her that the wise thing to do was to give the couch a rest for the night. I stood there in the middle of the living room with a stack of sheets in my hand, while she poked around under the kitchen sink.

A few moments later I realized I'd have to help. I got up with a sigh and bent down to the floor, picking up a black hammerhead that had just missed my ear by two inches. Then I went and took the handle out of Betty's hand.

"All right. Let me do this. You're going to hurt yourself."

"Hey, it isn't my fault that thing came off. I didn't do anything. . . ."

"I didn't say you did. It's just that I don't want to go looking for a hospital in the middle of the night, without a car, in a strange place, exhausted, because one of us is bleeding to death. Just stand aside, please. . . ."

I started with a chisel in a few places that seemed strategic, but it turned out I didn't completely understand the subtleties of the mechanism—I couldn't quite figure out where certain springs came from, or went to. Betty suggested we turn the couch upside down.

"No," I snarled.

It wouldn't give. A trickle of sweat ran down my back. What I really wanted to do was smash the whole thing to pieces, but Betty was watching. There was no way I was going to let myself be beaten by a damn Hide-A-Bed. I got back on the floor and looked underneath. I followed the iron rods with my fingers. Suddenly I felt something strange. I stood up scowling and threw off the cushions to see what it was.

"Maybe you better go wake the people next door," I said. "I'm going to need a blowtorch."

"Is it really that complicated . . . ?"

"No, it isn't complicated. They've just soldered ten inches of this thing together, that's all. . . ."

In the end we spread a few cushions on the floor. We put together a sort of bed that reminded me of giant ravioli covered with a striped sauce. Betty gave me a sidelong glance to see what I thought. What I thought was that we were going to have trouble sleeping on it, but if it made her happy—if this is what it took—it was okay by me. I was starting to feel at home there, and it was kind of fun to have to spend our first night sleeping on the floor. It was ridiculous, but there was a certain kind of cheap poetry about it, the kind you find in supermarkets. It reminded me of when I was sixteen—hanging out at surprise parties, content with only one pillow and half a girl. I could see how far I'd come: now I had a bunch of pillows, and there was Betty undressing in front of me. All around us the town was asleep. I took a minute to smoke one last cigarette by the window. A few cars passed by without a sound. The sky was perfectly clear.

"It seems like everybody just got their motors tuned up," I said.

"Who do you mean?"

"I like this place. I bet it's going to be nice out tomorrow. You won't believe this, but I'm dead."

The next morning, I woke up before her. I got out of bed without making a sound and went out to buy croissants. The weather was so nice I could hardly believe my eyes. I did some shopping. I came home casually with a bag under my arm and stopped on the way to pick up the mail that they'd slid under the door at the store. Nothing but fliers and coupons. As I leaned over to get it, I noticed the layer of dust on the showroom window—I made a mental note of it.

I walked straight into the kitchen, unloaded the things onto the table, and got down to work. It was the coffee grinder that woke her. She came in, yawning in the doorway.

"The guy who sells milk is an albino," I said.

"Oh yeah?"

"Imagine an albino in a white coat with a bottle of milk in each hand."

"It makes my blood run cold."

"Me too. Exactly."

While the water was heating for the coffee, I got undressed in a hurry. We started off along the wall, then circled over toward the cushions. The water evaporated in the meantime. This is how we burned our first saucepan. I ran into the kitchen, she into the bathroom.

Around ten o'clock we put the cups away and got the crumbs off the table. The house faced south—we had good light. I scratched my head and looked at Betty.

"Okay," I said. "Where do we start?"

It was the end of the afternoon before I sat down in a chair again. A horrible bleach smell hovered in the house, so thick that I wondered if it would be dangerous to light a cigarette. The light ebbed, slowly. It had been a beautiful day, but we hadn't even put our noses outside. We had stalked the smell of death to the farthest corners—through the closets, along the walls, under the plates—with special attention to the toilet seat. Never could I have imagined that kind of cleaning. There was no trace left of the old woman—not a single hair, not one piece of lint, no trace of a glance left hanging amid the curtains, not even the shadow of a breath; everything was wiped away. I felt like we'd killed her a second time.

I heard Betty scrubbing in the bedroom. She hadn't stopped for one second. She'd held her sandwich in one hand and done the windows with the other. The look on her face reminded me of Jane Fonda in *They Shoot Horses, Don't They?*—the part where she's on her third day of Hell. But she—Betty, I mean—had found what she was looking for. I thought so, anyway. The bad part was that while she was scrubbing, ideas poured into her head like a torrential rain. Once in a while she talked to herself. I tiptoed closer to her. It was enough to give you the willies, what she said.

What really got me, though, was what happened after I'd hauled the mattress downstairs. I'd worked up quite a sweat with it in the hall, turning it every which way for a long time before I realized that it was hooked on the light fixture in the ceiling. I had laid it down next to the garbage cans on the street, then gone back up to clean a few more things—whip the old mop around a little more. When I allowed myself to sit down after all that, I did it with no shame. I'd had it up to here by then, frankly. Betty had to know about it right away, it couldn't wait. She'd asked me to call and I told her, What the hell difference does it make, why call now, and she said, Why wait . . . ?

So I took the phone and turned it toward me. The house shined like a new penny. I called Eddie.

"Hi, it's us! . . . Just get back?"

"Yeah. Everything okay down there?"

"We're doing a major cleanup. We've moved the furniture around a little. . . ."

"Fine. Great. Tomorrow I'm going to put all your stuff on a train. . . ."

"Thanks, great. Listen . . . Betty and I were wondering if we could do a little painting in the kitchen . . . one of these days, I mean. . . ."

"Sure, go ahead."

"Great. That's good news. Actually, we'll probably get on it pretty soon. Right away, even . . ."

"I don't mind at all."

"Yeah, well, that's what I thought. Listen, while I'm at it, I wanted to talk to you about the wallpaper in the hall. You know, the sort of flowered . . ."

"Yeah, what about it?"

"Nothing. Just that maybe someday if it turned out that we could sort of replace it with something a little brighter. You don't see something in a blue there? What do you think of blue . . . ?"

"I don't know. What about you? What do you think?"

"It's a lot calmer."

"Look, do whatever you want. I can't see any problem."

"Okay, cool. I'm not going to bug you about all this, you see, I just wanted your okay, you know what I mean. . . ."

"Don't sweat it."

"Yeah, good."

"Okay . . ."

"Wait. I forgot to ask you something else. . . ."

"Hmm?"

"Well, it's Betty. She wants to break through a wall or two."

" . . ."

"You there? You know how it is when she gets an idea into her head. Listen, it's no big deal—just a couple of little walls, not big walls. It's not like a big job or anything, not what you think. Just puttering, you know . . ."

"Right, puttering. That's not puttering anymore. Breaking down walls, that's a notch above puttering. You guys make me laugh. . . ."

"Listen, Eddie, you know me. I wouldn't bother you with all this if it wasn't important. You know how it is, Eddie. You know how a grain of sand can change the whole world. Imagine that this wall is like a barrier between us and a sunny glade. Wouldn't it be like slapping life in the face to let ourselves be beaten by a silly little barrier? Wouldn't that really worry you, to miss out just because of some stupid little bricks? Eddie, don't you see that life is full of terrifying symbols?"

"Okay. Do it. But go easy. . . ."

"Never fear. I'm not crazy."

When I hung up Betty was looking at me with a Buddha smile. I believe I detected in her eye a spark that dated back to prehistoric times—to the days when guys sweated and groaned to prepare a shelter for their mate standing there smiling in the shadows. In some strange way it was nice to think I was obeying an instinct that went back to the dawn of time. I felt I was doing something good—contributing my drop of water to the great river of humanity. Plus, a little puttering never hurt anybody. You'd have a hell of a time these days not running across a sale somewhere in the electric drill and saw department. It allows you to lift your head up a little—feel good about things like shelves. The real secret lies in not blowing every fuse in the house.

"Okay, you happy now?" I asked.

"Yeah."

"Hungry?"

We ate, watching a horror movie—some dudes who came out of their graves and went running around in the night screaming. Toward the end, I started yawning—nodding off for two or three seconds—and each time I opened my eyes the nightmare was still going on. They'd found this old lady in a deserted street and were eating her leg. They had gold-plated eyes. They were watching me peel my banana. We waited until every one of them had been roasted with a flamethrower, then went to bed.

We carried the cushions into the bedroom and I swore that the first thing I'd do tomorrow was go buy a mattress—I swore on my mother's head. We made the bed in silence. We were wiped out. Not one speck of dust showed as the sheets came down like parachutes, stirring the air in the room. We would be able to sleep on our pillows without risk of inhaling a germ.

Early the next morning I heard somebody drumming on the door. I thought I was dreaming. I saw the pale glow of dawn floating timidly behind the window, and the face on the alarm clock was still lit. I had to get up. It gave me a stomachache, but I got used to it. I made sure not to wake Betty and went downstairs.

I opened the door, shivering in the early morning cold. There was this guy standing there, an old guy with a two-day beard, looking at me and smiling. He wore a cap.

"Hey there, I hope I'm not bothering you," he said. "But are you the one who put that mattress there, by the garbage cans?"

I spotted a garbage truck rolling along slowly behind him, a yellow light revolving on top. I made the connection.

"Well, yeah. Something wrong?"

"We don't handle them things. Don't even want to know about them."

"So, what am I supposed to do with it? Cut it into pieces and swallow it? Take one a day . . . ?"

"Don't know. It *is* your mattress, ain't it?"

The street was empty and silent. The day seemed to be stretching like a cat come down from an easy chair. The old man lit a cigarette butt in the golden light.

"I realize it's a pain," he said. "I can put myself in your shoes. Nothing more annoying than getting rid of a mattress. But after what happened to Bobby, we don't mess with them anymore. Plus, it was one just like that, gray with stripes. I can still see old Bobby trying to push it into the compactor. Bang—took his arm straight off. Get the picture . . . ?"

He brought me up short. My eyes were still half glued shut from sleeping. Who was Bobby, anyway? That's what I was going to ask him, when the guy behind the steering wheel started yelling from the other side of the street.

"Hey, what's going on? He giving you a hard time?"

"That's him—Bobby," the old man said.

Bobby kept it up in the truck. He had his head out the window, making little puffs of steam.

"That guy giving us a pain in the ass over the mattress?" he yelled.

"Cool down, Bobby," said the old man.

I was cold. I noticed that I was barefoot. There were even a few layers of fog here and there, floating in the early-morning air. My brain was going in slow motion. Bobby decided to open the door of the truck and get out, whining. I shivered. He wore a bulky sweater with the sleeves rolled up. One of his arms sent off light reflections—it ended in a giant hook. It was one of those cheap artificial limbs made out of chrome—totally reimbursed by health insurance, fitted like a shock absorber. I was startled. The old man was looking at the end of his cigarette. He crossed his legs.

Bobby came toward us, rolling his eyes, his mouth twisted into a frown. For a second I thought I was back in front of the TV, watching a scene from the horror movie, only now it was in 3-D. Bobby looked totally nuts. He stopped when he got to the mattress. I saw him clearly—there was a lamp post just over his head, as if put there on purpose. The tears on his cheeks looked like tattooed lightning bolts. I couldn't hear too well, but I think he was talking to the mattress—whimpering. The old man took a last drag on his cigarette and spit it out, looking into the sky.

"We ain't come across one in a long time," he told me.

The cry that Bobby let out pierced my ear like a javelin. I watched him lift the mattress with his one good hand, as if he were grabbing someone by the neck. He stared into its eyes, as if he were holding in front of him the person who had ruined his whole life. He drove his arm into the thing. The hook came out the other side, sprinkling little pieces of stuffing onto the sidewalk.

The revolving light gave me the feeling of a giant spider weaving its web all around us.

The old man crushed his cigarette butt, Bobby tore the prosthesis out of the mattress, sobbing. The poor guy tottered on his legs but didn't go down. Day was breaking. He let out another shriek. This time he aimed a little lower—around stomach level—and his moving arm went through it like a howitzer. The mattress bent over in half. Without missing a beat, Bobby freed himself, then went for the head. The cloth must have been brittle—it cracked open with the sound of a pig getting its throat slit.

While Bobby continued to let loose on the mattress, reducing it to bits, the old man looked away. The sidewalk was deserted, with one foot in the night and one finger in daylight. I had the feeling we were waiting for something.

"Okay. That ought to do it," said the old man. "You want to give me a hand . . . ?"

Bobby was completely exhausted. His hair was plastered against his forehead, as if he'd dunked his head in a tub of water. He let us guide him back to the truck. We sat him down behind the steering wheel. He asked me for a cigarette. I offered him the pack. They were filtered.

He started shaking his dull head.

"Hey, those are faggot cigarettes!"

"Right."

I could see that he didn't even remember what had happened. Just to be sure, I glanced over at the mattress. These kinds of people sometimes make you doubt what's real and what isn't, and that's hard enough to deal with under normal circumstances—there's no reason to make things difficult on purpose. By now my feet were completely frozen. The old man tossed a full garbage can into the compactor and I went inside quietly to put some shoes on. Betty was still sleeping. I heard them start down the street and asked myself why I had bothered to put my shoes on, when it was only seven o'clock in the morning. I had nothing special to do and was still pretty sleepy.

16

We worked on the house for a good two weeks, Betty astounding me at every turn. It was a pleasure to work with her, especially now that she'd adopted my pace. She left me alone when I didn't feel like talking. We stopped regularly to down a few beers. It was nice out. She restocked my mouth with nails, she never screwed up, and she was finally able to use a paintbrush without the paint running up to her elbow. I noticed a million little things that she took care to do correctly—she was a natural. There are girls like that—you wonder how many more rabbits they have in their hat. In these cases working with a girl is the best, especially if you're clever enough to have scored a new fifteen-inch foam mattress and can make her come down off her ladder with one well-placed beckoning glance.

Since we had to do our shopping on foot, and since we had a little extra money, I started checking out used cars. I read the want ads, Betty peering over my shoulder. Big cars were cheap because people panicked about gasoline. Big cars were the last flicker of a dying civilization, and now was the moment to take advantage of it. What difference does it make—sixteen or twenty miles to the gallon? Is it really worth making a big deal over?

We wound up with a Mercedes 280, fifteen years old and painted lemon yellow. I wasn't wild about the color, but it ran well. At night I'd look at it through the window before going to bed. Sometimes a little ray of moonlight would hit it. It was by far the coolest car on the street. The front fender was a little dented, but it didn't matter much. What bothered me most was that the headlight frame was missing. I tried not to notice. The back three-quarters looked like new, though. That's how it is—everything in life is but an illusion. Every morning I'd look to make sure it was still there. Eventually I got used to it. I got used to it until the day I had a fight with Betty—the day we were coming back from the supermarket.

She had just calmly run a red light—we had missed becoming pancakes by a hair. I offered a subtle reflection: "Keep this up and we'll be walking home with the steering wheel in our hands. Is that the idea?"

We'd gotten up early that day. We were planning to start on the biggest part of the renovation. At seven in the morning, I took the first swing with the sledgehammer into the wall that divided the bedroom from the living room. I went right through it with ease. Betty was standing on the other side. We looked at each other through the hole while the dust settled.

"You get a load of that?" I said.

"Yeah . . . you know what it reminds me of?"

"Yeah. Stallone in *Rocky III*."

"Better than that. You writing your book."

She came up with things like that from time to time. I was starting to get used to it. I knew that she was being sincere, but she also had this need to prick me with a needle, to see if I reacted. I reacted. When I thought about it, it gave me a feeling like having a bullet lodged in my back. It would move without warning. The pain made me groan inside. I looked away. But that wasn't the most important thing. Sometimes life seemed like a forest full of vines—you have to grab hold of one before you let go of the other, or else you wind up on the ground with both legs broken. In the end, it was all amazingly simple—a child of four could understand. I discovered more things living with her than I ever would by sitting in front of a blank page, my brain boiling. The only thing worth anything here on earth is what you learn by doing.

With my finger I dislodged a little brick that was getting ready to fall.

"I don't see really the connection between breaking a wall down and writing a book," I said.

"I'm not surprised. Forget it," she said.

I went back to smashing the wall without a word. I knew it hurt her when I said things like that—spoiled her fun—but I couldn't help it. I had the feeling I was talking to myself. We spent most of the morning piling up boxes of broken plaster on the sidewalk. She didn't unclench her teeth once. I didn't want to annoy her. I even made a little small talk here and there, not needing a response—about how warm it was for January, how one sweep of the vacuum cleaner would make it look like nothing had happened, how she ought to at least stop and drink a beer, how I'll be damned if the house doesn't look completely different now, how won't Eddie be thrilled when he gets a load of this?

I tried a potato omelet to get her mind off it, but it didn't work—the spuds just stuck to the bottom of the frying pan like the lowlife trash they are. There's nothing more depressing than grabbing onto a branch that only breaks in the end.

It was hard to go back to work comfortably after that. I thought we ought to get a little air. We took the car—destination shopping center. I needed more paint, and I knew she had two or three things to buy—it's rare when a girl isn't out of some cream or moisturizing lotion, it's rare when a girl refuses to go shopping. If everything worked out, I'd be able to chase away the dark clouds with a tube of lipstick, two or three new pairs of panties, or an industrial-strength candy bar.

We drove slowly up the main street with the windows half open—the noonday sun like peanut butter slathered on holy wafers. I zipped into the parking lot. She hadn't said a word the whole way, but I wasn't worried—in thirty seconds I'd have her in the cosmetics department, and the game would be won. I pushed the shopping cart myself. She kept her hands in her pockets and her head turned aside. Twenty more seconds, I told myself.

There weren't many people. I stayed behind her, letting her go, watching her toss box after box into the basket. I thought maybe I could get a discount at the checkout line—all I had to do was show them how damaged their packaging was. But I kept my mouth shut. I still had a few good cards left to play.

We went toward the beauty department. We went right by it, not even stopping. I didn't get it. There was a foxtrot coming over the loudspeakers. Maybe she had decided to keep sulking until nightfall—at any rate that's the way it was looking. I'd have to play it close to the chest.

Same story in lingerie. She didn't even slow down. It didn't matter, though—I stopped anyway. I parked in second gear. I picked out two pairs of panties in a hurry—shiny ones—and caught up with her a few seconds later.

"Look," I said. "I got you size twenty-four. Nice, huh?"

She didn't turn around. Fine. I took the panties and threw them into a bin of frozen food as we went by. Worst thing that'll happen, I told myself, is that in a few hours the night will fall, and she will have kept her oath. I saw that I was going to have to bear with it. I slowed down and stopped in front of the paint with a beatific smile. As I was perusing the labels, I heard what sounded like the flapping of birds' wings behind my back, followed by a small collision. I lifted my head up. Betty and I were the only ones in the aisle; she was standing farther down, looking at the books. Everything seemed calm. The books were arranged on five or six revolving stands in single file, just in front of the computer-memory stoves and microwave ovens. Despite the presence of a lovely girl in the area, there were no birds flying around. Still, I could have sworn . . . I lowered my eyes, looking at a can of acrylic one-coat, and the flapping noise started again. There were two noises this time—one following the other in some sort of aerial ballet. Indeed, such a loving mysterious prologue, the shadow of which I might have surprised, had I not first heard them splatter against yon far wall.

I turned toward Betty. She had just picked out a book—a fat one. She flipped through three pages, then threw it angrily over her head. This one didn't go too far. It fell almost at my feet, then went sliding across the center aisle. I decided not to pay attention. I tilted my paint can and started reading the instructions calmly, while books went flying in all directions.

When I'd had enough I stood up. I picked up my paint can and put it into the cart. For a moment our eyes met. It was hot in the store. I would have loved something to drink just then. She shook her hair all around her, then grabbed the revolving stand in front of her and pushed it with all her might. It turned over with a horrendous crash. She overturned the others without breaking stride, then took off running. I stayed there, nailed to the floor. When I got my wits back, I turned the shopping cart around and walked away in the opposite direction.

A guy in a salesman's coat showed up, running after me. He was so upset I thought he had the devil on his heels. He was red as a bloody poppy. He grabbed my arm.

"My God," he said. "What just happened over there?"

First I took his hand off me.

"I don't know," I said. "Why don't you go take a look?"

He didn't know if he should let me go or survey the disaster area—I could see he was really torn between the two. His eyes were wide, and he was biting his lip, incapable of making a decision. I thought he was going to start whimpering. Sometimes things happen in life that are so horrible you have every right to scream your rage to high heaven, to bewail your helplessness. I pitied the guy. Perhaps he had been born there, raised from childhood in the store itself, passed his whole life there. Perhaps it was all he knew of the world. If everything worked out he could stay there another twenty years.

"Listen," I said. "Take it easy. It's not the end of the world. I saw it all—nothing's broken. Some little old lady tipped the book stands over, but there's no real damage. You've had a shock, that's all. . . ."

He managed to give me a pale smile.

"Yeah? Think that's all?"

I gave him a wink.

"Sure. You're fine."

I made my way to the cash registers. I paid the bill to a made-up girl who bit her nails. I smiled at her, waiting for the change. She didn't react. I was the five-thousandth guy who'd smiled at her like that since the beginning of the week. I got my money and split. In spite of everything, the sun was still shining when I came out. It was a good thing, too. If there's one thing I hate it's being abandoned by everybody at the same time.

Betty was waiting for me. She was sitting on the hood of the car like in the fifties. I couldn't remember what shape car hoods must have been in during those years, but it served them right. And I didn't care. I didn't want her crumpling the metal. If we paid a little attention, we could make the car last till the year 2000. Fifties, my ass. I wasn't about to start wearing pleated pants big enough for three people, with suspenders that make them ride up your nuts.

"Been waiting long?" I asked.

"No, just warming my buns."

"Try not to scratch the paint job getting down. The guy at the garage just polished it. . . ."

She said she wanted to drive. I gave her the keys and put the things in the trunk, reveling in the warm air, momentarily transfixed in space by the supernatural stillness of things—their intensity. I grabbed a package of spaghetti and heard it all break in my hand, like glass, but I didn't kid myself—who ever heard of a guy getting touched by grace in a shopping center parking lot, especially with a girl drumming her fingers on the steering wheel and fifty-seven bottles of things left to unload from the shopping cart, beer included?

I sat next to her and smiled. She jammed the motor a little before getting it started. I opened my window. I lit a cigarette. I put my glasses on. I leaned forward to turn on some music. We started down a long street, the sun slamming through the windshield. Betty was like a golden statue with half-closed eyes. Guys were stopping on the sidewalk to watch us go by, cruising at twenty miles per hour. What did they know, the poor fools— where were they at? I let the air run over my arm—it was almost warm. The radio played nontoxic music. It was all so rare that I took it for a sign. I thought that the moment had come at last, that we were going to make up with each other there in the car, and finish the trip laughing. At first I had actually thought there were birds in the shopping center, no fooling.

I took some of her hair from the headrest and played with it. "It'd really be dumb if you kept pouting all day. . . ."

I'd already seen this scene in *The Invasion of the Body Snatchers*—the girl at the wheel was none other than one of those soulless creatures. Betty was wholly unmoved by the hand I was holding out to her, not budging one muscle of her face. I wished that someday some girl would explain it all to me—why women do that, and how they account for all the wasted time. It's a little too easy to criticize people who ask only that they be left where they are—anybody can do that.

"Hey, you hear me?"

No response. I was wrong. I'd been fooled by a ray of sunshine and a light breeze. I'd been a chump. The last words fell from my mouth like stale candy. It must have been around four o'clock. There were no cars in front of us. I was feeling understandably edgy. After the business in the shopping center, was it too much to ask that she give it a rest? There was an intersection with a green light on the other side. It had been green for quite a while—an eternity, I'd say. By the time we went through, it was bright red.

So she went through a red light without batting an eye. So I told her that if she kept that up we could walk home, and so that's where we left off. I waited there resolutely. She got out of the car and held the door open as if it were me who had screwed up.

"I am not getting back in this car," she said.

"No kidding," I said.

I slid over behind the wheel. She crossed the curb to the sidewalk. I put it in gear and took off up the street.

After a few minutes, I realized I was in no hurry. I made a detour over to the garage. The guy was sitting at his desk with his legs crossed, hidden behind a newspaper. I knew him, he owned the place. It was he who had sold me the Mercedes. It was nice out, it smelled like spring. There was an open pack of gum on his desk—a brand I liked.

"Hello," I said. "Could you check the oil, when you have a minute . . . ?"

I was trying to read the headlines upside down, when the newspaper crumpled, and suddenly there was his fat head. His head was much bigger than normal—half again as big, you get the picture. I wondered where he went to buy glasses.

"Jesus Christ . . . WHY???" he said.

"Well, don't want to get low . . ."

"But this is the fifth time you've been here in the last few days, and every time we check it it's full—I'm not joking, you know—it's not down one drop. Now are you going to come here every day and drive me nuts? I told you, the car does not *use* any oil, *none*. . . ."

"Okay, this'll be the last time. But I want to make sure," I said.

"Listen, understand something: selling cars like this at prices like that is not what's going to set me up for life. I have more important things to do. You follow?"

I threw him a bone:

"Okay, I'll come back and get it changed at fifteen hundred," I said.

He sighed, the asshole. What could I do if the world worked like that? You don't lose a drop for a few days, then one morning the car hemorrhages all over the street. He called over to a bright-looking guy with a sprinkling can.

"Hey, you. Drop that and go check the oil in the Mercedes."

"Yeah, okay."

"Don't worry, the level's fine, but the customer isn't. Go look at it carefully. Check it out in full sunlight. Wipe it off and put it in again, and make absolutely sure that the level is up there between the two little marks. Make sure that you both agree before you put the thing back in."

"Thanks. I'll feel better," I said. "Mind if I take a piece of gum?"

I went out to the car with the junior mechanic to open the hood. I showed him where the gauge was.

"This is the car of my dreams," he said. "The boss doesn't understand."

"You're right," I said. "Never trust anybody over forty."

A little way up the road, I stopped for a drink. As I was getting ready to pay, the article about Betty and the paint-bombs fell out of my wallet. I asked the bartender for another drink. Later, I stopped in front of a newsstand. I looked at all the headlines, one by one. I was drunk. I bought some rag that was about cooking, and another one that wasn't.

In my travels I'd gotten far away from the house. I found myself in a part of town I didn't know. I drove slowly. I was almost at the edge of town when I realized that the sun was setting. I started home calmly. Night had one foot on the ground by the time I pulled up in front of the pianos. It had fallen suddenly. It was an eerie night—a night I wasn't going to forget.

It was simple. When I walked in she was there in front of the TV, eating a bowl of cereal, with a cigarette in her hand. It smelled of tobacco. It smelled of sulfur.

There were three obligatory-girls-with-feathers dancing on TV, and a guy braying into a microphone—something exotic and mushy. I noted how it did not at all go with the tension that reigned in the room. I was not, after all, strolling along a deserted beach in the third world, with miles of fine sand on either side of a hotel terrace, and a bartender making me a special cocktail with curaçao in the shade. No, I was merely on the second floor of a house, with a girl who had swallowed fire, and it was night. Things took a turn for the worse right away. All I did was go into the kitchen, lowering the sound on the television on my way. I had barely opened the refrigerator when the thing started booming.

After that it was the usual story—nothing too original this time. I drank my beer and threw the can hard into the wastebasket to set the mood. Who would be crazy enough to think you can live with a girl like that without incident? Who'd want to deny that such things are necessary?

We had already attained an honorable state—a few lingering lightning bolts in our eyes, the kitchen door swinging open and slamming shut—and for my part I would have been happy to stop there. My comebacks were losing their punch, and the temperature was stabilizing. I was ready to settle for a tie game, if it would keep us from having to go into extra innings.

I have never been able to explain certain of the things she did. I have never understood them either, thus making it impossible for me to avoid them. So there I was, panting in the corner, hoping to get saved by the bell, when she looked over at me and made a fist. It startled me. We'd never really hit each other. Since I was at least five yards away from her I didn't panic. I felt like a native in the jungle, wondering what that thing is that the white hunter is aiming at him. This fist of hers—first she raised it up toward her mouth as if she were going to kiss it, then an instant later she put it through the kitchen window. For a split second I thought I heard the window scream.

The blood came spurting out of her arm, as if she'd just crushed a bunch of strawberries in her hand. I don't like to say it, but I suddenly lost my nerve. A cold sweat squeezed my head like a tourniquet. I heard a whistling in my ears. Then she started laughing. She made such an odd face that for a moment I didn't recognize her. She reminded me of an angel of darkness.

I ran to her like an angel of light, grabbing her arm with the same disgust I'd feel grabbing a rattlesnake. Her laughter hurt my ears, and she kept pounding me in the back, but somehow I managed to examine her wounds.

"Jesus Christ. You fucking idiot—you're lucky, you know . . ." I said.

I took her into the bathroom and ran water over her arm. Now I was getting hot. I started to feel the punches she was giving me. I could no longer tell if she was laughing or crying. Whatever it was, she was really letting loose on my back. I had to hold her down with all my strength to wash her hand off. Just as I was getting the bandages out, she grabbed me by the hair and jerked my head back. I screamed. I'm not like some people—it hurts like hell when someone pulls my hair, especially when they go at it full throttle. I almost started crying. I sent my elbow backward. I hit something. She let go.

When I turned around, I saw her nose was bleeding.

"Shit, I don't believe it . . ." I moaned.

Still, all in all it had calmed her down. I was just about able to put her bandages on in peace, except for the bottle of Mercurochrome she spilled all over in a last spasm. I didn't have time to get my foot out of the way. The night before, I had put a coat of white polish on my shoes. Now one of them was bright red, which made the other one look stunningly white—it was quite a startling effect. Her hand was still bleeding, but her nose was better. She whimpered. I didn't feel like comforting her. What I wanted to do was grab her and shake her, and make her apologize for what she'd done to her hand. I was prepared just to let her cry for days on end if it came down to it.

I wrapped the bandage one more time around her hand to finish up and gave her a Kleenex for her nose, without saying a word. Then I went into the kitchen to clean up the broken glass. Or more accurately, I lit a cigarette and stood there looking at the broken glass, twinkling on the tile like a school of flying fish. A cold draft came in through the window. I shivered. I was wondering about the best way to go about it—was it worth the effort to get out the vacuum cleaner or should I just use a broom and dustpan?—when I heard the downstairs door slam. I put everything on hold. One second later a man appeared on the street, foaming at the mouth, with one red shoe on his foot.

She had a good fifty-yard head start. I let out a long howl that propelled me like a jet, and I caught up fast. I could see her little ass dancing in her jeans, her hair flying sideways as she went.

We went across the neighborhood like two shooting stars. I gained ground inch by inch—she took it with ease. Under any other circumstances I'd have taken my hat off to her. We were puffing along like locomotives. The streets were practically deserted—clouds of weed-scented fog coming down here and there—but I wasn't there to admire the scenery. I was engaged in hot pursuit with fire in my soul, wild race-to-the-finish music on the soundtrack. I called out to her a few times, then decided to save my breath. A few pedestrians turned to watch us. Two girls yelled out some bullshit, cheering Betty on. Their voices carried all the way around the corner. I pitied the next defenseless dude who crossed their path.

I got to within three or four yards of her, the sweet smell of victory whistling in my ears. Dig in, I said to myself, just hang in there, champ, it's almost in the bag. . . . There's the finish line. . . . I felt such exhilaration that I must have sent off vibes. She must have gotten them loud and clear too, because—and I don't know how she did this—I suddenly found myself with a garbage can between my legs. I went flying over it and made a crash landing on the other side, in a blaze of glory.

I got back up as soon as I could. She'd gained at least thirty yards on me. My lungs burned when I breathed, I started running again. That's what I was there for—I had to catch that girl no matter what. Had she known my determination, she would have hung it up, cried uncle. She would have known that a little garbage can wasn't enough to stop me. She would have faced the music.

My knee hurt. It had happened when I fell. She was slowing down, though, and I wasn't that far behind. Without knowing it, we'd covered quite a bit of ground. We found ourselves in a sort of industrial park, with a lot of warehouses and railroad tracks running down the middle. It was not, however, one of those abandoned areas full of savage beauty—one of those places covered with rust and overgrown weeds, bathed in the supernatural light of moonbeams. It was the opposite of that. All the buildings were new, and there was fresh asphalt all around. I don't know who paid the electric bill around there, but it was as bright as day.

Betty rounded the corner of a blue-and-pink warehouse. It was a sort of tender pink. She wasn't really running anymore. My knee was as swollen as a little pumpkin. I dragged my leg and gritted my teeth, my breath short and my brain hyperventilated. What gave me courage was to see her finally out of energy. She was only a little ways ahead of me, and the warehouse, which seemed endless, served as a crutch for her—she had to lean on the wall as she went. I was starting to get cold now. All my clothes were drenched with sweat, and I suddenly felt the winter night get me in a stranglehold from head to foot. I looked down at my measly sweater and shivered.

When I looked up, I saw that she'd stopped. I didn't take advantage of the situation by jumping on her, I just started walking normally—you might even say slowly. I preferred to wait till she'd finished vomiting. There's nothing worse than throwing up when you're out of breath—it just about strangles you.

As for me, my blue jeans were blown up like a sausage around my knee. We were getting down to the dregs now, our own little museum of horrors, like two crippled loons thrown out of the last open bar. The light was so harsh that it felt like we were being filmed—a documentary on married life. I waited till after her last heave to speak.

"Hey, we're going to freeze to death," I said.

I could hardly see her—her face was covered by her hair. I wasn't kidding, either—it was all I could do to keep my teeth from chattering. I felt like the guy who takes one last look at the sunset before sinking away forever into a snowdrift.

Before we turned completely blue I decided to grab her by the arm. She pushed me away. I had had it by then, however. The drama had begun early that morning and it was now the middle of the night and winter. I felt that I had already paid top dollar for the day. I was not going to spend one more penny. I grabbed her by the collar. Her arm had not even made it back to her side yet. I slammed her against the side of the warehouse, sniffling through my runny nose.

"Having style means knowing when you're going too far," I said.

The night had made me mean. Instead of listening to me, she started flailing, but I held her flat against the corrugated metal—I no longer felt my strength. I couldn't have let go of her if I'd wanted to. Something in her must have understood this; she started screaming and pounding the wall. The warehouse rang like the bells at the gates of Hell.

It wasted me to see her like that—mouth twisted, staring me down as if I were a perfect stranger. I couldn't take that very long—her rage, her yelling, how she had me trapped there, little girl wild with anger, claws out. I slapped her across the face to bring her back down to earth. I didn't like doing it, but I slapped her with all my might, in a kind of mystic frenzy, as if trying to chase a demon out of her.

Just then a police car pulled up, like a flying saucer. I let go of Betty. She slipped on her heels. They opened their doors. The car sent off blue light-beams, like a child's toy. One cop did a forward roll out onto the ground, ending up on his feet, aiming something at me. An older one got out normally, on the other side. He had a long billy club in his hand.

"All right, what's going on here?" he asked. It was all I could do to swallow my saliva.

"She wasn't feeling well," I said. "I wasn't beating her up—I was afraid she'd have a nervous breakdown. I know it's a little hard to believe. . . ."

The older one laid his billy club on my shoulder and smiled.

"Why should it be hard to believe?" he said.

I sniffled. I looked over at Betty.

"She seems to be better now," I sighed. "I guess we can go now. . . ."

He put his billy club on my other shoulder. I felt myself freezing to death.

"This is a strange place to have a nervous breakdown, isn't it . . . ?"

"I know. It's just that we ran all the way. . . ."

"Yeah, but you're young. It's good for the heart to run a little."

The pressure from the billy club made my collarbone tremble. I knew what was going to happen, but I didn't want to believe it. I felt like someone watching the pressure mount in his water heater, hoping that the valves will close all by themselves. I was paralyzed. I was frozen stiff. I was disgusted by what was happening. The old guy leaned over toward Betty without letting go of me. I felt like I was grounding his billy club—it had slid off my shoulder and stuck across my stomach.

"And the little lady . . . how is the little lady feeling?" he asked.

She didn't reply. She parted the hair in her eyes to get a look at the cop. I saw that she was feeling better. I took this as a small consolation prize, while waiting for the water heater to explode in my face. I let myself bathe in the softness of despair. After a day like that, I was incapable of getting agitated.

"I'd like to get this over with," I mumbled. "You don't have to make me wait. . . ."

He leaned back slowly. My ears were ringing. I hurt all over. The seconds stretched out like the freestyle event of a gum-chewing competition. I waited for the old guy to straighten up. He looked at me, then he looked at the young cop—still standing there, poised for action, one eye closed, legs stiff, stock-still. Those dudes must have tempered-steel thighs. The old one sighed.

"Jesus Christ, Richard. How many times do I have to tell you not to aim that thing at me?"

All the other guy moved was his lips.

"Don't worry. I'm not aiming at you, I'm aiming at him."

"Yeah, but you never know. I wish you'd put that thing down. . . ."

The young cop didn't seem too hot on the idea:

"I'm not too comfortable with this kind of nut," he said. "You seen the color of his shoes? You get a look at that?"

The old one nodded.

"Yeah, but remember, the other day we passed this guy in the street who had green hair. You got to cope with it. . . . That's how the world is these days. You can't get bent out of shape over things like that."

"Especially since it's just a stupid accident," I added.

"There, you see . . . ?" said the old one.

Halfheartedly the cop lowered his gun. He ran his hand through his hair.

"One of these days we're going to be in deep shit if we aren't more careful. You're asking for it. Didn't it occur to you to frisk this guy? No, of course not. All you're interested in is making me put my gun away, right . . . ?"

"Listen, Richard, don't take it personally."

"Yeah. Right. Shit, man, every time it's the same story. . . ."

He leaned over furiously and picked up his hat, then got into the car and slammed the door. He pretended to look elsewhere, chewing on his thumbnail. The old cop looked irked.

"Jesus Christ," he said. "You know, I been in this business forty years. I think I ought to know by now when to start getting suspicious."

"Fine. Knock yourself out. I couldn't care less. . . ."

"Hey . . . look at them, would you? The girl can hardly stand up, and the guy—I'd break his head open before he could make half a move. . . ."

"Leave me alone. . . ."

"You're a real pill, you know that?"

The young one leaned over to roll up the window. Then he turned the siren on and folded his arms. The old one got livid. He ran over to the car, but the other one had locked the doors from the inside.

"OPEN UP! STOP THAT RIGHT NOW!!" he screamed.

Betty put her hands over her ears. Poor thing, she had barely gotten her wits back—she must have been totally confused. It was clearly just another tacky police patrol. The old one was leaning over the hood, looking through the windshield, the veins in his neck sticking out like rope.

"RICHARD, I'M NOT KIDDING NOW. . . . I'M GIVING YOU TWO SECONDS TO TURN THAT OFF, YOU HEAR ME?"

The horror lasted another few seconds, then Richard turned the thing off. The old guy came back, wiping his hand across his forehead. He scratched the end of his nose, his eyes staring nowhere. The silence was refreshing.

"Pffff . . ." he said. "All they send us now are the young, supertrained ones. I think it damages their nerves a little. . . ."

"Sorry. It's my fault," I said.

Betty was wiping her nose off behind me. The old guy pulled his pants up a little. I looked up at the starlit sky.

"You just passing through?" he asked.

"We're taking over the piano store," I said. "We know the owner."

"Yeah? You mean Eddie?"

"Yeah. You know him?"

He gave me a bright smile.

"I know everybody. I haven't left town since the last war."

I shivered.

"You cold?" he asked.

"Huh? Oh yeah, yeah. I'm frozen stiff."

"Okay, why don't you both just get in the car? We'll take you home."

"No bother?"

"No. I just don't like to see folks walking around these warehouses. Nobody's got any business here at night."

Five minutes later they dropped us off in front of the house. The old cop put his head out the window while we got out.

"Hey, I hope your little lover's quarrel is over for tonight, eh?"

"Yes," I said.

Betty opened the door and went up while I watched them go. I waited till they disappeared down the street. If I hadn't been so cold I wouldn't have been able to lift my feet off the sidewalk. I was totally blank just then, like I was opening my eyes after a lobotomy. But it was a winter's night and the sky was clear. The icy air had the street in its grip, and it was torturing me. I took the opportunity to whimper a little bit, then turned back to the house.

I went upstairs as well as I could with a cracked knee and the certainty that I had caught my death that night. Still, I had to smile when I hit the apartment and found it so warm. I felt like I was slipping into an apple turnover.

Betty was lying on the bed. She was still dressed, her back to me. I sat down in a chair, my knee held out straight and my arm slung over the backrest. Goddamn son of a bitch, I said, deep down inside of me, watching her breathe. The silence seemed like a rainfall of sequins on glue-covered toast. We had still not exchanged one word.

But life goes on. I got up and went to examine my leg in the bathroom. I pulled my pants down. My knee was round, almost shiny—not too pretty to look at. When I stood up, I looked at myself in the mirror. The head goes well with the knee, I said, they go hand in hand: if one brings tears to your eyes, the other one just makes you scream out loud. I was joking, but it's true that I had no idea what to put on my knee—we didn't have anything even vaguely resembling salve in our first-aid kit. In the end I just rolled my pant leg down as gently as I could, swallowed two aspirin, and went back into the living room carrying what was left of the Mercurochrome, some cotton compresses, and a large bandage.

"I think we ought to redo your bandage," I said.

I stood there like I was waiting to take her order. She didn't move. She was in exactly the same position she'd been in a while before—it's possible that her knees were a little closer to her chest, or that a lock of hair had fallen off her shoulder in absolute silence, but I wouldn't have sworn to it. I squeezed the back of my neck a while before going over for a closer look. It made me look like I was thinking of something. I wasn't.

She was sleeping. I sat down next to her.

"You awake?" I said.

I leaned over to take her shoes off. They were sort of tennis shoes—ideal for crossing town at a dead run. It made you wonder about the logic of things. Only yesterday, she'd been walking around in stiletto heels, me waiting to catch her at the foot of the stairs. I tossed the little white things off the foot of the bed and unzipped her windbreaker. She was still sleeping.

I went to get some Kleenex to blow my nose. I sucked on a couple of throat lozenges while washing my hands. The night now seemed like a storm over a forest fire. I took some deep breaths and let the water run over my hands for a few minutes. I closed my eyes.

After that I went back to take care of her bandage. I went about it gently, as if I were putting a splint on the foot of a bird. I took the gauze off, millimeter by millimeter, without waking her. I delicately spread her hand out to make sure that the cuts were clean, and put the Mercurochrome on with the little pipette. I rebandaged it—just tight enough—and cleaned the blood out from under her nails. I got as much of it out as I could. I knew I was going to fall in love with her little scars. I could feel it.

I downed a big glass of hot rum in the kitchen. It made me sweat, but I knew I had to medicate myself in one way or another. I picked up the pieces of glass from the window, then went back to her. I smoked a cigarette. I wondered if I hadn't chosen the hardest path—if living with a woman wasn't perhaps the most terrible thing a man can do—if it wasn't like his selling his soul to the devil or growing a third eye. I remained plunged in the abyss of perplexity, until Betty started moving. She was rolling around gently in her sleep. A breath of fresh air crossed my soul, banishing my dark thoughts like mouthwash on bad breath.

You should get her into bed, I told myself, she must be uncomfortable like that. I picked a magazine up off the floor and thumbed through it distractedly. My horoscope told me that I would have a difficult week at the office, though the time was right to ask for a raise. I'd noticed already how the world was starting to shrink. Nothing much surprised me anymore. I got up to eat an orange—brilliant as lightning and chock-full of vitamin C—then went back to her, faster than a speeding bullet.

I put on my magic fingers to undress her. It was like a huge game of pick-up sticks—breathe wrong and you lose. I had a hell of a time with her sweater, trying to get her head through the neck opening. She started twitching her eyelashes when I did. I felt the perspiration pearl up on my forehead—I just made it by a hair. After that, I decided not to worry about taking off her T-shirt or her bra. I wasn't going to fret over a couple of straps—I just unbuckled it.

The pants were less of a problem, and the socks came off by themselves. Her panties were child's play—I passed them under my nose before letting them fall—O dark flower . . . O little striped thing whose trembling petals close in a man's hand . . . I held you to my cheek for but a second in the wee hours of the morning. After such a sensation I no longer wanted to die. I went and got the bottle of rum to treat my bronchial pneumonia.

I sat on the floor, my back against the bed. I took a swig for my leg, which was hurting me, and one for her hand. And one for the night that was finally ending. And one for the whole world. I tried not to forget anyone. I noticed that if I leaned my head back, my skull touched Betty's thigh. I stayed in that position for a moment, my eyes wide open, my body floating in the intergalactic desert like a guillotined doll.

When I felt fit for action, I lifted her up in my arms. I held her fairly high—high enough so all I had to do was bow my head to furrow my face against her belly. Slowly the heat from her body made me glow. I decided to stand as long as I could. My arms were as stiff as monkey wrenches, but it was the best thing I could find as far as resting my soul was concerned. So I hung tough, bending my nose on her soft skin, growling softly. The rum made my skin sweat, emptying out all the poison in me. I didn't ask any questions.

After a while, she opened one of her eyes a little. I must have been trembling like a leaf. My arms were about to break.

"Hey . . . hey, what are you doing . . . ?"

"I'm about to put you to bed," I whispered.

She went right back to sleep. I set her down on the bed and pulled the covers over her. I started walking around the house. I was sorry I'd eaten the orange. I was tired, but I knew I wasn't going to get to sleep. I went and took a shower. By accident I sprayed some cold water on my knee. My heart started pounding inside my chest.

I wound up in the kitchen. I devoured a ham sandwich, standing by the window. I looked at the lights from the other houses—the reflections spilling into the shadows like underwater lights. I chugged a beer down in one gulp. The Mercedes was parked just below. I opened the window and dropped my empty beer can on its head. The noise didn't bother me at all. I closed the window. In the end it was sort of the car's fault that the shit had hit the fan like it did. It was at that moment, in fact, that I stopped going to the window every morning to see if it was still there.

17

The day I took matters into my own hands was the day we sold our first piano. It started early in the morning, with a meticulous cleaning of the showroom window, scratching off every last spot with my fingernail, balancing high atop my stepladder. Betty teased me from the sidewalk, drinking her coffee, her cup a deep crater, silver-plated and steaming. You'll see, I told her, you'll be taking it all back soon.

I made a quick trip to Bob's store—Bob was the albino grocery man. Actually I'm exaggerating—he wasn't really albino, but blond like I'd never seen. There were two or three women in there, standing in front of the shelves, contemplating the void. Bob piled eggs behind the register.

"Hey, Bob, you got a minute?" I asked.

"Sure."

"Bob, could you give me a little of that white stuff—you know, the stuff you wrote 'All Creamed Cheese Must Go' on your window there with?"

177

I went back with a little container and a paintbrush. I climbed up my ladder. Across the whole width of the window on top I wrote "PIANO PRICE SLASH!!" I stepped back to see what it looked like. It was a beautiful morning. The store looked like a glint of sunlight on a burbling stream. Out of the corner of my eye, I noticed that a few passersby were slowing down on the sidewalk to get a better look. Rule number ONE of sales: let them know you're there. Rule number TWO: shout it loud and clear.

I went up to the window. Under it I wrote "NEVER BEFORE OFFERED!!!" Betty seemed to get off on that one. From time to time she'd laugh at anything. She put in her two cents, writing "MUCHO BIG DEALOS" across the door.

"Go ahead and laugh," I said.

I spent the whole morning in the store with a can of spray wax and a cloth, polishing each piano down to its toenails—I might as well have given them all a bath.

By the time Betty called me for lunch, I was done. I took a circular glance around the store—each and every one of them gleamed in the lights. I knew I had a great team. I went halfway up the stairs, then came back down. I held my hand out to all of the pianos.

"I'm counting on you, fellas," I said. "Don't let that girl have the last laugh."

I tried to maintain an enigmatic smile while ingesting the squid croquettes in hot sauce. Girls go crazy for that.

"Listen, that would really be too unbelievable," she said. "Why today, especially . . . ?"

"Why? Because I've set my mind to it, that's why."

She touched my knee under the table.

"You know, I'm not saying that to discourage you. It's just that I don't want you to be disappointed."

"Ha," I said.

As a writer, I had not yet attained glory. As a piano salesman, I wanted to try to even the balance. I was betting on the idea that life cannot break all your momentum at once.

"Anyway, we're not hard up, you know," she added. "We have easily enough to hold us till the end of the month."

"I know, but I'm not doing it for the money. I'm doing it to test a theory."

"Gee! Look how blue the sky is! We'd be better off going for a drive. . . ."

"No," I said. "We've been taking drives for five or six days now, I'm sick of the car. No, today the store is open for business. I'm not budging from the cash register!"

"All right, whatever you say. I don't know, maybe I'll go for a walk or something. We'll see. . . ."

"Go ahead. Don't worry about me. The sun shines only for you, baby. . . ."

She put some sugar in my coffee and stirred it, smiling, her eyes on me. They were incredibly deep sometimes. Sometimes, with her around, I soared among the clouds—just like that, knocked for a loop, blinded by the light.

"Don't we have any cookies or something—some rose-petal jelly maybe?" I asked.

She laughed.

"What, can't I even look at you?"

"Yeah, you can. It just gives me a hell of a sweet tooth, that's all."

At two o'clock sharp I went to open the store. I took a look out on the street—to get the lay of the land. Perfect. If I was going to buy a piano, this would be the day. I went and sat down in a dark corner in the back of the store, still and silent like a hungry tarantula, my eyes fixed on the door.

Time passed. I scribbled something in the receipt book. I broke the pencil in half. I went out on the sidewalk a few times to see what was happening. All I got was discouraged. Nothing. It was dead. My ashtray was full—you sure can smoke a lot of cigarettes in this life, I thought, and you sure can get bored. It's enough to make you run off with the circus. I didn't like the feeling—like being stabbed in the back in broad daylight. Was it really such a wild flight of fancy for a piano salesman to hope to sell a piano? Was it too much to ask? Was it a sin of pride to want to move the merchandise? What is a piano salesman who doesn't sell pianos, after all? Anguish and absurdity are the nipples of the world—I said it out loud, joking.

"How's that?"

I turned around. It was Betty. I hadn't heard her come in.

"Ready to go? You going to take a walk . . . ?" I asked.

"Just a little one. It's still nice out. You talking to yourself, now?"

"No, just screwing around. Listen, would you watch the store five minutes for me? I want to get some cigarettes. It'll get me out a little bit. . . ."

"Sure."

Things being what they were, I didn't deny myself a double shot of whiskey and Coke, while waiting for the lady to shuffle through the cupboard, looking for a carton of filtered cigarettes. She stood back up, her face flushed and her bun crooked. I handed her a bill.

"How's the piano business?" she said.

I didn't have the heart to take a cheap shot.

"Could be better," I said.

"Yes, well, you know, everybody's scrambling these days."

"Yeah?" I said.

"Yes. Times are tough all around. . . ."

"Could I have a piece of pie, to go, please?"

While she went to get it, I picked up the bill which was sitting on the counter and put it back in my pocket. She wrapped some wax paper around my pie and put it down in front of me.

"That be all?" she asked.

"Yes, thanks."

It was worth a try. Sometimes it works. It's sort of a free lottery.

It can get your spirits back up. The lady hesitated for a fraction of a second. I smiled at her like an angel.

"Not too much silver," I said. "My change, I mean. My wife is tired of my complaining about the holes in my pockets. . . ."

She laughed a little, nervously, then opened the drawer of her cash register. She gave me the change.

"Sometimes I think I'm losing my marbles," she said.

"It happens to everyone," I said.

I was in no hurry to get back to the store. A little piece of baked apple was hanging out of the wax paper, like a teardrop. I stopped in the middle of the sidewalk. I zupped it. Paradise comes cheap here on earth, luckily—it keeps things in their proper perspective. What is it really that measures a man? Surely not breaking one's ass to sell a few pianos—that would be sheer folly; it certainly isn't worth ruining one's life over. A tender corner of apple pie, soft as a spring morn—that's something else. I realized that I'd taken this piano thing too seriously—I'd lost my head over it. It's hard to stave off madness, though—you have to watch out every minute.

I started back, thinking of all this. I swore to myself that even if I sold nothing all day, I wouldn't let it get to me. I'd zen it out. Still, a sale or two wouldn't be bad. I told myself this as I walked through the door. Betty was smiling behind the cash register, fanning herself with a piece of paper.

"Taste this apple pie," I said.

Talk about a smile—her face might have been polished with ammonia. It was like I'd just asked for her hand in marriage.

"You know," I went on. "Let's not delude ourselves. They say business is bad all over these days. I wouldn't be surprised if I don't sell anything today. I'm a victim of the global economy."

"Haha," she said.

"I personally don't see anything to laugh about. But then again I'm more pragmatic. . . ."

I was intrigued by the way she was fanning herself with the paper. It was winter after all, and despite the blue sky it was not particularly warm. The air seemed charged. Suddenly I froze—I blanched, as if I'd just stepped on a nail.

"It's impossible!" I said.

"No, it isn't."

"Shit, no. It's impossible—I left you here for ten minutes. . . ."

"Yes, well, it was plenty of time. You want to see the order form?"

She held out the form—the one I couldn't keep my eyes off of. I was floored. I slapped the receipt with the back of my hand.

"My God, why wasn't it me who sold this? You want to tell me why it wasn't . . ."

She came and took my arm, her head on my shoulder.

"It was you who sold it. It was thanks to you. . . ."

"Yeah, right. Still . . ."

I looked around to see if some mischievous spirit wasn't giggling behind a piano. Life tries to rattle you every chance it gets. I gave it my compliments—I saluted it for its skill at dealing out low blows. I breathed in Betty's hair. Yes, I too knew how to cheat. I wasn't going to be beaten so easily. I bit into the apple pie, and the miracle was accomplished—the storm went away, growling far behind me. I found myself standing before a calm sea.

"If you ask me, this calls for a celebration," I said. "What would you like more than anything?"

"To go eat Chinese."

"Chinese it is!"

I closed the store with no regrets. It was still a bit early, but why push your luck? One piano—I'd happily settle for that. We went off walking up the street—the sunny side—while she told me about her sale. I pretended to be interested. To be honest, it bugged me a little. I didn't listen very closely to what she was saying; I was thinking more about the shrimp toasts I was going to scarf down. The girl bouncing around next to me reminded me of a school of glowing little fish.

We were walking past Bob's place when he came running out, his eyes wild.

"*Buenos días*, Bob," I said.

His Adam's apple was sticking out like a gigantic knuckle. It made you want to push him back into the store.

"My God! Archie's locked himself in the bathroom! He can't get out! What a jerk that kid is. I'm going to try to get in through the window! My God, it's high!"

"You saying Archie locked himself in the bathroom?" I said.

"Yeah. Annie's been trying to talk to him through the door for ten minutes, but he doesn't answer—he just blubbers. You can hear the faucet running, too. Shit, there I was, peacefully watching TV—why do people have children . . . ?"

I ran behind him into the yard next to the house. Betty went up into the apartment. There was a big ladder lying in the grass. I helped him prop it up against the side of the house. The sky was bright. After a brief hesitation, Bob grabbed the sides of the ladder and climbed two rungs, then stopped.

"I can't," he whined. "I swear I can't. This makes me sick. . . ."

"What's wrong with you?"

"What do you think? I'm dizzy. What can I do? It's like being up on a scaffold."

I wasn't especially acrobatic, but the second floor of a building didn't scare me much.

"All right, come down," I said.

He wiped his brow while I climbed up to the window. I saw Archie. The faucets were open full blast. I turned to Bob.

"I don't see many alternatives," I said.

He made a discouraged gesture below.

"Yeah, I know. Go ahead, break the goddamn windowpane."

I smashed it with my elbow, opened the latch, and jumped inside. I was proud of myself—I'd compensated for the day, in extremis. I winked at Archie and closed the faucets. Snot was streaming down his chin.

"Have nice playtime?" I asked.

The sink was clogged and overflowing everywhere. I fixed that, then opened the door. There was Annie with the baby in her arms. Annie wasn't bad. Her mouth was a bit floppy and she had a wild glow in her eyes—the type to avoid.

"Hiya," I said. "Watch out for the broken glass."

"Oh, for the love of Mike! Archibald, what's got into you?"

Just then Bob showed up, out of breath. He looked at the puddles of water on the floor, then looked up at me.

"You can't imagine all the stunts a three-year-old pulls. Yesterday he tried to close himself in the refrigerator."

The baby started crying, twisting his little purple face into an abominable grimace.

"Oh darn, it's time already," sighed Annie.

She turned around and started undoing her buttons.

"Great, and now who's going to wipe up this mess? Me, that's who. I spend all day cleaning up after that little monster."

Archie looked at his feet. He tapped them in the water. He couldn't have cared less about what his father was saying. Betty took him by the hand.

"Come on, we're going to read a book, you and me."

She took Archie into his room. Bob told me to go make some drinks—he'd only be a minute. I went into the kitchen. Annie was sitting there, her nipple jammed in the mouth of Number Two. I smiled at her. I got out the glasses and lined them up on the table. We heard the bathtub emptying. I sat down at the table, having nothing else to do. Her breast was incredibly large—I couldn't keep from staring at it.

"Hey," I said. "You're not kidding around there."

She bit her lip, then answered.

"You're telling me. You can't imagine how hard they are. They hurt even. . . ."

Without taking her eyes from mine, she moved her dress aside and got out the other one. It was truly impressive, I must admit. I nodded.

"Feel it," she said. "You'll see what I mean. Feel it. . . ."

I thought it over for a second, then latched onto it from across the table. It was warm and smooth, with transparent blue veins in it—the type of specimen that's a pleasure to get your hands on. She closed her eyes. I let go, then stood up to go look at the goldfish.

The whole house smelled like spoiled milk. I didn't know if this had something to do with the dairy underneath, or if it was because of the little newborn. It was disgusting for guys like me, who don't go in much for milk products. While she was burping him, the little tyke looked at me, dazed, then spit up on his Oshkosh B' Goshes. I wanted to roll over and die. Bob showed up and got out a bottle.

"You will note that he only pulls this shit on my afternoons off," he said. "Oedipus did not only fuck his mother—he also killed his father."

"Bob, this one needs to go to bed." Annie sighed.

"Bob, you got something to munch on?" I asked.

"Sure. Go get whatever you want out of the store."

Annie didn't take her eyes off me. I gave her a look as cold as a tombstone, then went down. I hate it when they think you're easy. Stay away from easy shots—you come out better in the end. It's never bothered me that I have a soul and know how to use it—it's the only thing, in fact, that's ever really interested me.

It was getting dark in the store. It took me a while to find the party-mix section. Roasted almonds have always been my vice. They were on the bottom shelf. I squatted down and loaded up. I must have been daydreaming. I didn't hear her come in—I just felt a light breathing on my cheek. One second later, she grabbed me around the neck. She pushed my face between her legs. I let go of the almonds. I untangled myself in a hurry and stood up.

Annie seemed to be in some sort of delirious trance. She was vibrating from head to foot—bathing me with her burning eyes. Before I could come up with a good line, she popped her tits out of her dress and pressed herself against me.

"Hurry up," she said. "For God's sake, hurry up!"

She wedged one of her legs between mine, her thing jammed into my thigh. I moved aside. She was panting like she'd just run the thousand-yard dash. Her chest seemed even bigger in the darkness. She was obscenely white. Her nipples were aimed right at me. I raised my hand.

"Annie . . ."

But she grabbed my wrist in mid-flight and plastered my hand over her tits. She started rubbing herself on me again. I sent her flying into the shelves.

"I'm sorry . . ." I said.

I felt a wave of fury come out of her belly, like a torpedo, setting the store on fire. Her eyes glazed over.

"What's come over you? What seems to be the problem, mister?" she hissed.

I wondered why she got formal all of a sudden. It was so strange, I couldn't answer.

"What's wrong with me?" she went on. "I'm not pretty enough? You don't desire . . . ?"

"I don't give in to all my desires," I said. "It makes me feel a little freer, that way."

She bit her lip, stroking her belly gently with her hand. She let out a little childlike whine.

"I can't stand it anymore," she said.

While I was picking up the cans of almonds, she lifted up her dress, her back against the canned goods. Her little white underpants flashed through my skull like a bolt of lightning. My hand started traveling toward her—I told myself it was simply too strong to deny. But then I told myself: Do this and you're a scumbag, selling your soul out for a cheap fantasy. I took a good look at the scoreboard before deciding. Man is nothing. But it's his conscience that makes something out of nothing. These thoughts bore me up—they were part of my emergency kit. I gently took her by the arm.

"Forget all this," I said. "What say we go up and have a nice peaceful drink with the others? Okay . . . ?"

She let her dress down. She lowered her head and buttoned her dress.

"I wasn't asking very much," she murmured. "I just wanted to know if I still existed is all. . . ."

"Stop worrying about it," I said. "Everybody needs to let it out, one way or another."

I stroked her cheek. But clumsy gestures can be like hot coals. She looked at me, desperate.

"Bob hasn't touched me in over a month," she sobbed. Ever since I came home from the clinic. It's making me crazy! Don't you think it's normal to want it? Do I have to just wait for him to decide . . . ?"

"I don't know. It'll all work out."

She ran her fingers through her hair, sighing.

"Yeah, it'll all work out. Sure. Probably one of these nights, while I'm sound asleep, he'll decide. Naturally, it'll be a night when I'm totally exhausted—dead as a doornail. He'll come over and slip me his thing from behind. I can see it all now. He won't even bother to see if I'm awake or not."

It always seems like a tiny little dent in the beginning, but bend over a little and get a closer look—you find that you're standing on the edge of a bottomless abyss. That's why they invented goose pimples, to keep your teeth from chattering.

I put a bag of chips in her arms, and we went upstairs. No one was in the kitchen. She had two drinks, waiting for the others to come. I drank a toast to the goldfish.

In the end, Bob and Annie made us stay for dinner. They insisted. We looked at each other. I said, Betty, it's up to you, you're the one who wanted to eat Chinese. Betty said, Let's stay.

"Now that the kids are asleep we can eat in peace," Bob said.

I went down into the store to get some groceries with Bob. It was practical. In time of war, much more reassuring than pianos, I thought. There were even little garlic croutons, to consume preferably before the end of the next five years. Ideal for freeze-dried fish soup.

"I'll buy the wine," I said.

He rang up my bill and gave me my change. We went back upstairs.

We let the girls make dinner. It made them happy. We gave them a few olives while waiting. In the meantime, Bob dragged me into the bedroom to show me his collection of detective novels. It took up a whole wall. He stood in front of it, his fists on his hips.

"If you read one a day, it would still take you at least five years!" he said.

"You don't read anything else?" I asked.

"There's some science fiction on the bottom shelf. . . ."

"You know," I said, "we're really pushovers. They toss us a few bones so we won't try and grab the real meat. I'm not just talking about books—they've worked it out so they can say anything they want. . . ."

"Huh . . . ? Anyway, if you want I can loan you a few, but be careful, no kidding. Especially with the hardcovers."

I glanced at the unmade bed. No one gets out alive. In the end, chances are you're wasting your time. The problem, though, is that it's never really completely wasted.

"Starting to smell good in the kitchen," I said. "Better go have a look . . ."

"Yeah. But you got to admit, I really floored you there."

After dinner we sat down to a nice easy game of poker. We each had a glass of wine, and there were enough ashtrays to go around. From where I sat I could see the moon. It didn't seem like much in itself, but if you're going to rhapsodize, you might as well go all out. All the greats have. The game did not keep me on pins and needles. When I wasn't looking at the moon, I looked at the others. The mystery was just as profound. Roots entangling endlessly—the chances of lifting a corner of the veil growing fainter each time a cloud comes to cover the moon. One thing led to another. I slid into a bath of gentle stupidity. Not uncommon these days.

The baby's crying woke me. Bob slammed his hand down on the table, swearing. Annie stood up. I hardly had any chips left. I couldn't understand it. Archie woke up and started crying too. Screaming like a banshee.

Annie and Bob came back into the kitchen with the two of them shrieking in their arms. I gave myself three seconds to beat it out of there.

"We'll leave you alone now," I said. "Sleep well, you two."

I shoved Betty adroitly in front of me, and we split. When we got to the bottom of the stairs, I heard Bob call:

"Hey, nice having you guys over!"

"Thanks for everything, Bob."

The fresh air did me good. I suggested we take a little walk before heading home. She took my arm and nodded her head. There were already a few tiny leaves on the trees. The air shook them. You could smell the young buds in the street, an aroma that got stronger and stronger.

We went up the street in silence. There comes a moment when the silence between two people can have the purity of a diamond. Such was the case then. That's all you can say about it. The street is no longer a street. The light becomes fragile as a dream. The sidewalks shine. The air crashes in your face. A joy rises in you that has no name—that amazes you. It's being able to stay calm, to light someone's cigarette with your back to the wind, without the slightest tremble in your hand to betray you. It was the kind of walk that can fill a lifetime.

On the corner was a garbage can with a rubber tree in it. Though it'd been thrown out, it was still in good shape, with lots of leaves. It was just thirsty. My heart went out to it. It looked like a sad coconut tree, agonizing on an archipelago of trash.

"Can you tell me why people do things like this?" I asked.

"Hey, look, it's sprouting a new leaf!"

". . . and why this crummy old rubber tree tugs so hard at my heartstrings . . ."

"We could put it downstairs, with the pianos."

I unwedged the poor thing and took it in my arms. We went home. The leaves clicked like amulets, shiny as mica. Dancing like Christmas Eve. It was a grateful rubber tree—I'd given it another chance.

When I rolled into bed, I looked at the ceiling and smiled.

"What a fabulous day!" I said.

"Yeah."

"How do you like that—first day open and we sell a piano. It's a sign. . . ."

"Don't get carried away."

"I'm not getting carried away."

"You talk like it's something that just happened to us."

I felt the pavement get slippery. I steered into the parking lane.

"What, don't you think it's good to have sold a piano?"

She sighed lightly, pulling off her sweater.

"Yes, it's good."

18

"Yes, Eddie, I know I'm not talking very loud, but she isn't very far away. She's taking a shower."

"Yeah, okay. Well, what do you want me to do—send it?"

I moved away from the receiver a little, to make sure I still heard her splashing in the bathroom.

"No," I whispered. "Absolutely not. If it's not too much trouble, Eddie, I've been crossing out the names in the Writer's Guide. Just mail it out to the next name on the list."

"Anyway, it's really too bad. . . ."

"Yeah, well, maybe they've all decided to wait till I'm fifty years old."

"And the pianos? How's that going?"

"Not bad. We sold a third one yesterday morning."

We said good-bye and I hung up. It was incredible that they'd turn my book down again, on this of all days. I had trouble getting this dark coincidence out of my mind—I had to shake my head to make it go away. Luckily spring had come and the sky was blue, and luckily Betty didn't know what was up. I went to see what she was up to—it was already twenty to ten.

She was rubbing some white cream on her behind. I knew what it was—this stuff that takes hours to sink in—every time I get involved with it I have to go wash it off my hands. But girls don't know what it is to hurry—at least I've never known one who did.

"Listen, you do what you want—me, I'm leaving in one minute."

She rubbed faster.

"Well, all right, but why won't you tell me what's going on? What's got into you, anyway?"

I'd let them break my legs before she'd get one word out of me. I told her the same story as before.

"Listen," I sighed. "We live together, you and me, right, and we try to share everything, right? So it should just be enough that I tell you I have something to show you—you should be shifting into high gear."

"All right, I'll get a move on it."

"Shit, I'll just wait for you in the car."

I grabbed my jacket and went down. Light breeze, nice blue sky, big sun. My plan was going perfectly, with the precision of an atomic clock. I had planned on her being late, worked it into my split-second calculations. The guy had promised me that it would keep for at least two hours once out of the fridge. I glanced at my watch. We still had forty-five minutes to kill. I pushed my fist on the horn.

At ten o'clock sharp, I saw her bound out onto the sidewalk and we took off. I was playing the game with a master's touch. I'd washed the car the night before—vacuumed the cushions and emptied the ashtrays. I wanted to assemble the day, piece by piece, nothing left to chance. Had I wanted night to fall just then, or to conjure up a layered sky, I could have done it with ease—I could have done anything I wanted.

I put my shades on to hide my shining eyes. We headed out of town. The area was fairly dry—a desert. I liked that. The earth had a beautiful color to it. It reminded me of the place we'd lived before. The bungalow episode. It seemed like it had been a thousand years since then.

I felt her squirming around next to me. Poor thing. She lit a cigarette, half smiling, half nervous.

"Jesus, this is far. Tell me what it is!"

"Patience," I said. "Let me handle this. . . ."

It took a while, but eventually she let herself be lulled by the monotony of the countryside, her head turned sideways against the seat. I put on some music, not too loud. There was no one on the road. I drove along at fifty-five, sixty.

We drove up a small hill covered with trees. Trees were rare in these parts—it sort of made you wonder what they were doing there. I didn't worry about it. Everything I saw made me feel that the place was wonderful, that I was surfacing out of nowhere into somewhere. The road wound up and around. I branched off onto a small dirt road to the right. Betty sat up in her seat. Her eyes opened wide.

"What in the world are we doing here?" she whispered.

I smiled silently. The car jerked its way up the last hundred yards. I stopped under a tree. The light was perfect. I waited for the silence to return.

"Okay," I said. "Get out."

"So, this is where you're going to strangle and rape me?"

"Yeah, I could."

She opened the door.

"If it's all the same to you, I'd rather you start by raping me."

"Yeah, well, I'll have to think about it."

We found ourselves at the foot of some sloping land, empty, with gradations of color, from pale yellow to dark red. It was lovely—the last time I'd come, I'd just sat and looked. Betty stood next to me. She whistled.

"Hey, this is really beautiful. . . ."

I savored my triumph. I leaned against the fender of the Mercedes, pinching the end of my nose.

"Come over here," I said.

I put my arm around her neck.

"Tell me something—you see that old tree there, all the way up on the left, the one with the broken branch?"

"Yes."

"And there—you see that big rock on the right, the one that looks like a guy curled up in fetal position?"

I felt her starting to get excited, as if I'd lit a wick in her brain.

"Yes, of course I see it. Obviously . . . ."

"And the cabin in the middle, you see that too? Isn't it cute?"

I was making her jump like a piece of popcorn. I'd set a fire under her. She dug her nails into my arm, nodding her head.

"I don't understand what you're getting at. . . ."

"I love this place," I said. "Don't you?"

She ran her hand through her hair. Her bracelets rang out like a cascade of coins. I watched her hair fall back onto her lambskin collar. She smiled.

"Yes, it's like everything's in place here—like nothing's missing. I don't know if that's what you wanted to show me, but you're right—it's great here."

I glanced at my watch. The moment had come.

"Right," I said. "Well . . . it's yours!"

She didn't say anything. I took the papers out of my pocket and held them out to her.

"Your land goes from the old tree to the rock that looks like a guy curled up, and comes down to here. The door of the cabin locks with a key."

When she finally made the connection, she let out a joyful moan. She went to throw herself into my arms. I held her off with one raised finger.

"Just one more minute," I said.

I went and opened the trunk of the car. If the guy hadn't lied to me, it was still in time. I unwrapped the strawberry cream pie. I stuck my finger into it. The son of a bitch was just right. I brought it to Betty. She turned completely red.

"Happy birthday!" I said. "We have to eat it right away. Here's to your thirtieth year."

I didn't wait to see her sway. I set the pie down on the hood of the car and grabbed her in my arms.

"Now come here and see what's in the trunk," I said.

I'd done everything the night before—filled it with provisions from the supermarket. I'd managed to switch a few price tags on the fancy items.

"There's enough here for three days," I said. "That is, if you'd like to invite me to your house."

She leaned against the car and pulled me to her. It lasted five minutes. It would have gone longer, if I hadn't pulled myself away—if I hadn't stayed lucid.

"We're not going to let a strawberry cream pie melt away, are we? That would be stupid!"

It took two trips to get it all up to the cabin. The land was really sloped, and the sun was already hot. Betty ran all over the place, picking up strange pebbles or standing with her hand shielding her eyes, looking at the horizon. "Jesus, I just can't believe it," she kept saying.

As for me, I knew I'd scored big—my all-time-high game. It was a little nothing of a cabin, yet there she was, running her fingers along the windowsills, biting her lip, and turning in circles. I wasn't allowed to drop my ashes on the floor either. Soon, I thought, we'll be playing house, making make-believe dinner. That's exactly what we did. It was real champagne we poured into the paper cups, though.

"When I think . . ." she said. "When I think that I've had to wait thirty years for someone to give me a present like this . . . !"

I winked at her. I was pleased with myself. The guy figured he'd unloaded his little piece of desert for a hefty sum, and I felt I'd bought a little bit of paradise for a song. I'd been working on the whole thing for a week now, figuring out every detail. Bob was the one who'd put me onto it. We took a quick trip one day to look at it, and my mind was made up immediately. I'd told him, You know, Bob, at first I was just going to buy her a plant, but I realized it would be too small for her, I want to buy her a stretch of mountains or something—a branch of the sea. . . . You wouldn't know where I could find something like that, would you?

I put the champagne back in the ice chest to cool, and we went out for a walk. By the time we got back, it was just perfect. While she was laying out the comforter, I went down to the car to get the radio, and a stack of magazines I had piled up on the backseat. Once touched by civilization, it's hard to leave it completely behind. I filled my pockets with packs of cigarettes and went back up, sucking on a stem as I walked.

We spent some time getting settled, then had a drink outside on a rock. It was hot. I half closed my eyes to the setting sun. I cut the pure air of the bourbon with a handful of black olives. They were the kind I liked best, with the pit that comes away clean from the meat with an air of calm. I lay down on one elbow. It was then that I perceived a sparkling in the ground. Under the angled sun, the earth had taken to scintillating like a princess's gown. God Almighty, this is too much, I said, yawning—this is really wild.

Betty had adopted a more classic position—a lotus-type thing, her back straight and her regard turned inward. She's going to split her jeans, I thought. I couldn't remember if I'd brought along another pair for her to change into. We watched a small bird pass by overhead. I was starting to drown in my bourbon. Who could ever hold it against me for getting a little drunk on her thirtieth birthday?

"It's weird to have bought something like this," she said. "It seems impossible."

"The papers are in order, don't worry."

"No, I mean to buy something that comes all together like this, with its land, its smells, its little noises, the light—everything."

I peacefully bit into a piece of smoked chicken.

"Yeah, well, that's the way it is," I said. "Everything here is yours."

"You mean the sunset hanging there in the treetops is mine?"

"Unquestionably."

"You mean the silence, and the little breeze going down the hill—I own it?"

"Yes. You got the keys right there in your hand. . . ."

"Well, he must have been crazy, the guy who sold you all this!"

I didn't answer. I drew a line of mayonnaise across my chicken leg. There were also those who would think it was crazy to have bought a place like that. I bit into the middle of my leg. The world seemed to cut itself tragically in two.

After dinner, she decided to make a fire. I wanted to help, but realized that I was incapable of moving. I excused myself, saying it was better that I not try anything foolish in the dark—crossing the terrain, for example—lest I be found later in the bottom of a ravine. She stood up, smiling.

"You know, men aren't the only ones who know how to make fires."

"No, but in general they're the only ones who know how to put them out."

It was almost totally dark out—I had trouble seeing anything. I stretched out full-length, my cheek against the rock. Through the darkness, I heard the cracking of small pieces of wood in the dark. It was soothing. I also heard mosquitoes. I don't know why, but when she lit the fire, my strength came back. I managed to stand up. My mouth was dry.

"Where are you going?" she asked.

"Thing in the car," I said.

The glow of the fire stayed in my eyes. I couldn't see anything, but I remembered that the terrain was difficult. I did the soldier's step and proceeded through the darkness lifting my feet high off the ground. Though I almost took one or two nosedives, all in all I did pretty well. I stopped for a moment halfway down just to savor the joy of being drunk and still standing. I felt the sweat run down my back. When I had first decided to stand up, I had thought myself a fool—part of me had wanted to stay plastered on the ground. The other part won out. Now I realized that I'd done the right thing. I'd been right to make myself get up on my feet. You never regret going the extra mile. It always lifts your spirits.

I sniffled once, softly, then went off again on my little stroll, my hands out in front and my heart light. I believe it was a small round pebble that made me fall. I believe it sincerely—otherwise, why would my foot have shot out in front of me like an arrow, why would the image of a bag of marbles exploding in all directions suddenly have come into my head? I experienced a moment of horrible lucidity before slamming into the earth. My body ignited. I started rolling down the hill in a sort of secondary state—just this side of comatose.

The journey ended right in front of the car's left front tire, into which I smashed my head. I didn't hurt anything. I stayed there on the ground for a minute, trying to comprehend what had happened. When you're sixty such things are unforgiving—when you're thirty-five they're sort of laughable. Through the darkness, I saw the car door handle sparkling above my head. I grabbed it and pulled myself up. It was a major effort to remember what I had come down there to get—as if a jar of glue had been spilled on my head. Something to do with mosquitoes . . . yes . . . right . . . the Bug Bomb! I knew I'd thought of everything!

I got the can out of the glove compartment. I pretended not to see myself in the rearview mirror—I just passed a hand through my hair. I stayed there for a while, sitting in the front seat with my legs outside, watching the fire burning up top, the cabin dancing behind it as if it were sitting on top of the world. I tried not to think of what I still had to do.

At least I knew I couldn't get lost. All I had to do was head for the light. Still, I felt like I was at the bottom of the Himalayas.

* * *

We woke up the next day around noon. I got up to make coffee. While the water was heating, I went into Betty's purse to look for some aspirin. Inside, I found other bottles.

"What's all this?" I asked. "These pills?"

She lifted her head up, then put it back down.

"Oh, nothing," she said. "Just for when I can't sleep."

"What do you mean, for when you can't sleep?"

"It's nothing, really. I don't take them very often."

I was annoyed with myself for having found them. I didn't feel like talking about it. She wasn't a little girl, after all, she already knew anything I might have told her. I let the bottles fall, one by one, back into her purse. I took two aspirin. I tried to get a little music on the radio. I tried to be easygoing. One of my arms was all scratched, and I had a bump on my head. I didn't feel like fooling around.

That afternoon Betty decided to clear out a little of the land in front of the house—get a little exercise. I think she was planning to plant a few things the next time we came up. She dug out the grass with an old iron bar we'd picked up on one of our walks. It made a lot of dust. Seeing this, I moved off by myself and started reading. It was nice out. I had to struggle to keep from falling asleep on my rock. These days nine out of ten books are boring—I was ashamed of myself for doing nothing while all those others were out there writing like idiots. This shook me up, surprised me. I went to get a beer. On the way I stopped to mop off Betty's forehead.

"Everything okay, honey? Making progress?"

"Hey, get me one, too!"

I got two beers and noticed that the stock was getting dangerously low. It didn't get to me, though. I understood a long time ago that perfection is not of this world—all you can do is make the most of what you have. You realize this when you look in the mirror.

I said, Cheers, and we lifted our beer cans. The dust had settled. We'd been together almost a year now, and I'd learned how to answer the door when opportunity knocked. I didn't want to end up empty-handed at the age of thirty-five, wondering if it was all worth it. I wouldn't have liked that much. It would have been depressing—the kind of thing that makes you walk the streets at night.

"I just got an idea about how to have less garbage to take out," I said.

I threw my empty can down the slope and we watched it fall. It made it almost all the way to the car.

"What do you think?" I asked.

"Not bad. Not great for the landscape, though."

"Noted, my sweet."

I made myself useful by doing the dishes from lunch. We climbed up the hill to see the sun before it went down—stretched the old legs a little. There was a light breeze.

"I dreamed last night that they published your book," she said.

"Don't start."

She took my arm without another word, and we stood there surveying the countryside in silence. I watched a car go down the road in the distance, its headlights on. Suddenly it just disappeared. It took me a minute or two to unlock my jaw.

"What say we eat?"

When we got back, there was a badger furrowing in our garbage can. I'd never seen such a big one. We were about thirty yards from it. I took out my knife.

"Don't move," I said.

"Be careful."

I lifted the blade above my head, then tore up the hill screaming at the top of my lungs. I tried to remember how you go about slaying a bear, but by the time I got there, the badger had slunk off into the night. I was glad it was him and not me. I threw a rock at him for good measure, to see his reaction.

This little episode gave me an appetite—I could have eaten a horse. I made some pasta with cream sauce. The day had completely exhausted me. There was no particular reason for this. It isn't really so incredible that a guy should feel exhausted when he sees all the people who throw themselves out the window—or those who might as well. It's quite normal, in a way. I didn't worry about it.

After we ate, I smoked a cigarette and dozed off while Betty brushed her hair. I passed out cold. In the middle of the night I opened my eyes again. The badger was just outside the window—we stared at each other. His eyes gleamed like black pearls. I closed mine.

When we woke up the next morning the sky was cloudy. It got worse in the afternoon. We watched the clouds come, filling up every inch of sky. It was our last day. We pouted. It seemed like the land had suddenly shrunk. There was no more sound, as if all the birds and insects hopping through the grass had simply evaporated. The wind came up. We heard faraway thunder.

When it started raining we headed back inside the house. Betty made tea. I watched the earth steam outside, as the sky got blacker and blacker. It was one hell of a storm—the heart of it was less than a mile away. Bolts of lightning split the sky. Betty started to get scared.

"Want to play Scrabble?" I suggested.

"No, not really."

Each time there was a clap of thunder, she froze stiff, her head tucked into her shoulders. Torrents of water pounded down on the roof. We had to talk loud to be heard.

"Anyway, the rain isn't so bad, as long as we're safe inside, and the tea's still hot," I said.

"Jesus, you call this rain? It's a deluge!"

Actually, she was right. The storm was getting dangerously close. I suddenly knew that it was coming right for us—was out to get us. We sat down in the corner of the room, on the comforter. It felt like there was some huge creature beating himself against the house, trying to tear it out of the ground. Every so often the lighting from his eyes glared outside the windows. Betty drew her knees up to her chest and put her hands over her ears. Just perfect.

I was giving her a back rub, when a giant drop fell on my hand. I looked up—the ceiling was dripping like a sponge. We looked around us—the walls were wet. There were small puddles under the windows, and a tide of mud was trying to ooze in under the door. The house had turned into hell; surrounded by lightning, shaken by thunder. Instinctively, I put my head down. I knew that anything I might do would be futile. None of that Man-and-God-are-equals crap. I apologized for ever having thought such a thing.

When a drop fell on her head, Betty jumped. She glanced with horror at the ceiling, as if she'd just seen the devil himself. She pulled the comforter up over her knees.

"No . . . please, no . . ." she whimpered.

The storm had moved off by a few hundred yards, but the rain was coming even harder. The noise was infernal. She started crying.

As far as the roof was concerned, all was lost. I quickly estimated the number of leaks at around sixty. It was easy to see the turn things were taking. The floor was shining like a lake. I looked at Betty and stood up. To try to calm her down would be a waste of time. The only thing to do was get her out of there as quickly as possible, soaking or not. I grabbed a few essential items and put them in a bag. I buttoned my jacket up tight, then went to her. I got her on her feet without hesitation—without fear of breaking her. I lifted her chin up to look at me.

"We're going to get a little wet," I said. "But I think we'll live through it."

I gave her a look that could split concrete.

"Right?" I added.

I put the comforter over her head and pushed her toward the door, realizing at the last minute that I'd forgotten my transistor radio. I shoved it into one of the plastic bags from the supermarket and made a hole in the bottom for the handle. Betty hadn't moved an inch. I opened the door.

We could barely see the car at the bottom of the hill through the curtain of rain. It seemed impossible to get to. The thunder galloped over us in waves—we couldn't even see the sky. The noise was deafening. I leaned over to her.

"RUN FOR THE CAR!" I shouted.

I didn't exactly expect her to take off like a rocket. I lifted her up and set her outside. I went to lock the cabin door, and by the time I turned back around she was already a fourth of the way down the hill.

It was like being under a shower, with both faucets going full blast. I stuffed the keys into my pocket, took a deep breath, and off I went. I hoped to avoid making the trip on my back this time—the ground was really slippery, covered by an inch of water.

No longer having a dry hair on my head, nor a dry anything else that might be considered as part of my body, I paid attention not to confuse speed with progress. I threw myself into the waterworks, the dogs of Hell barking at my heels, but I watched carefully where I put my feet.

Betty was way ahead of me—I saw her silver comforter zigzag toward the car like a sheet of aluminum. One more second and she's home free, I said to myself. At that very moment, I slipped. I threw my left hand behind me and cushioned the fall. I threw my right hand out in front of me and managed to keep from falling forward. The transistor radio went sailing into a rock.

A huge hole appeared, with multicolored wires sticking out of it. I screamed. I swore. The thunder smothered my voice. I threw the radio out as far as I could, grimacing in impotent rage. I was disgusted. After that I didn't hurry—nothing else could touch me.

I sat down behind the wheel of the car. I put on the windshield wipers. Betty was sniffling, but she seemed to be doing better. She rubbed her head with a towel.

"I can't say that I've seen many storms like this one," I said.

Which was true—and this one had cost me a pretty penny. Still, I didn't lose sight of the fact that we'd come out of it all right, with limited damage. Instead of answering me, she stared out the window. I leaned over to see what she was looking at. You could just barely make out the cabin on top of the hill, the rivulets of mud running down the slope. Good-bye, little lines of colored soil, and earth that glitters like diamond powder—good-bye to all that. What was left looked more like the mouth of a sewer, spewing out long streams of shit. I didn't say a word. I started the car.

We rolled into town at nightfall. The rain had let up a little. We came to a red light. Betty sneezed.

"How come we never have any luck?" she asked.

"Because we're just a couple of poor unfortunates," I snickered.

19

A few days later I took the morning off to tar-paper the roof. I worked easily and quietly, then went off in the car, a local station spitting songs out on the radio.

When I came home I found Betty busily moving the furniture around.

"You heard the latest?" she said. "Archie's in the hospital!"

I threw my jacket on a chair.

"Shit, what happened?"

I helped her move the couch.

"The damn kid spilled a pot of boiling milk on his lap."

We moved the table across to the other side of the room.

"Bob called right after you left. He was calling from the hospital. He wanted us to open the store for him this afternoon."

We unrolled the rug in a different corner.

"Shit, he doesn't miss a trick, does he. . . ."

"It's not that. He's afraid the old ladies'll block traffic on the sidewalk in front and cause a riot."

She stepped back to take in the new arrangement.

"What do you think? You like it like that?"

"Yes," I said.

"It's a change, isn't it?"

We fucked in the afternoon, after which I grew suddenly languid, lying on the bed with cigarettes and a book. Betty cleaned the windows. What's nice about selling pianos is that there's never a rush. You have time to read *Ulysses* between sales without even having to dog-ear the pages. Yet it made us a nice living—we paid our bills on time and could fill the gas tank whenever we felt like it. Eddie didn't ask us for money. All he asked was that we keep the store afloat and replenish the stock whenever we unloaded a piano. We did. I also handled the deliveries. The cash went directly into my pocket—why complicate the bookkeeping?

Best of all was that we even had some money put aside, enough to last us a month or so. This was reassuring—I had already had the experience of being out of a job, with barely enough in my pockets to buy two meals. Finding myself with money ahead was like finding myself in a fallout shelter. I could hardly ask for more. I hadn't yet started planning my retirement.

So I took it easy. I watched Betty cleaning her nails by the window, laying on a coat of blinding red nail polish while her shadow climbed the wall behind her. It was wonderful. I stretched out on the bed.

"That going to take long to dry?" I asked.

"No, but if I were you I'd keep an eye on the time. . . ."

I had enough time to hop into my pants and plant a kiss on her neck.

"You sure you can handle it alone?" she asked.

"Sure," I said.

There were already four or five ladies on the sidewalk. They were trying to see inside, through the windows, talking loudly. I got the key from the backyard and hurried up to the apartment. I spotted the small pool of milk on the kitchen floor. A stuffed animal was floating in it. I picked it up and put it on the table. The milk was cold by now.

Downstairs, things seemed to be heating up. I went down and turned the lights on. The ladies were shaking their heads. The ugliest one turned her arm toward me so I could see her watch. I opened the door.

"Easy does it," I said.

I plastered myself into a corner while they stampeded through. When the last one was in, I took my position behind the cash register. I thought of Archie and the teddy bear, draining on the kitchen table, losing all its blood.

"Could you give me a slice of headcheese?"

"But of course," I said.

"Where's the owner? Not here anymore . . . ?"

"He'll be back."

"HEY, DON'T TOUCH MY HEADCHEESE WITH YOUR HANDS, YOU MIND!?"

"Jesus," I said. "Sorry . . ."

"All right, just give me two slices of ham instead. The round kind. I don't want the square kind."

I spent the rest of the day slicing this and cutting that, running from one end of the store to the other, with six arms and ten legs churning, biting my lip. Somehow I began to understand Bob. I realized that if I had to do that job every day, I wouldn't be able to get it on with a woman either—all I'd want to do at night is watch television. I'm exaggerating a bit, but what's true is that sometimes life puts on such an abominable show that no matter where you look, all you see is fury and folly. Charming: this is what we have to put up with while waiting for old age, illness, and death—walking right toward the storm, each step bringing us a bit further into the night.

I closed the store on a last pound of tomatoes. Spirits were at their lowest. This sort of thing can really bring you down—turn your heart to stone. You have to know how to say whoa. I did a quick about-face, grabbing three bananas and eating them one after the other. After that I went upstairs for a beer. I felt neither here nor there. Having a little time on my hands, I wiped the milk off the floor and washed the teddy bear, hanging it by the ears to dry over the bathtub. It had a kind of surrealistic grin on its face, perfectly in keeping with the mood of the day. I sat with it for a while, the time to finish my beer. I split before my ears started hurting.

When I got home, I found Betty lying on the couch, with a yard-high elephant at her feet. It was red with white ears, wrapped in clear plastic. She lifted herself up on her elbows.

"I thought it might cheer him up if we went to visit him—look what I bought him. . . ."

After what I'd just been through, I found the house quite calm. I would have loved to just slide right into it, but there was no way, with a red elephant standing in the middle of the living room, its eyes following me everywhere.

"Okay, let's go," I said.

I got a wink as consolation prize.

"You want to eat something before we go . . . a quick bite?"

"No, I'm not hungry."

I let Betty drive. I held the animal in my lap. I had a bad taste in my mouth. I told myself that when one lifts the goblet of hopelessness to his lips, one oughtn't be surprised if one winds up with a hangover. The streetlights were unspeakably cruel. We parked in the hospital lot and walked to the main entrance.

It happened just as we went through the door. I don't know why. It wasn't the first time I'd been in a hospital. I knew about the odor, the people ambling around in pajamas. I even knew about the strange presence of death. I knew it well, and it had never gotten to me before—never. No one was more surprised than I was when my ears started ringing. I felt my legs get stiff and wobbly, all at once. I started to perspire. The elephant tumbled to the floor.

I saw Betty gesticulating in front of me, leaning toward me with her mouth moving, but I could hear nothing except the ringing of blood in my veins. I leaned against a wall. I felt horrible. An icy shot went through my skull. I couldn't keep my balance. My heels slid out from under me.

A few seconds later, the sound started to return a little. Eventually everything came back. Betty was wiping my face with a handkerchief. I was breathing deeply. People kept coming and going, without paying any attention to us.

"Jesus, I can't believe this—what happened to you? You scared me to—"

"It must have been something I ate . . . must have been the bananas. . . ."

While Betty checked at the information desk, I went and got myself a Coke out of a machine. I had no idea what was going on—I didn't know if it was the bananas or a sign from the Beyond.

We went up to the room. There wasn't much light. Archie was sleeping, Bob and Annie sitting on each side of his bed. The baby was asleep too. I put the elephant down in the corner. Bob stood up to tell me that Archie had just dozed off—the poor kid had really been through the mill.

"It could have been worse, though," he added.

We stood there quietly for a moment, watching Archie move around softly in his sleep, his hair stuck to his temples. I felt sorry for him. I also felt something that had nothing to do with him. As hard as I tried, I couldn't rid myself of the sensation that I had been sent a message I could not decipher. It made me nervous. It's always unpleasant when you feel uneasy and don't know why. I bit the inside of my mouth. When I saw that things weren't getting better, I motioned to Betty. I asked Bob if there was anything we could do for them, told him not to worry about a thing. But no, no thanks, so I backed out the door as if there were snakes falling from the ceiling. I took off down the hall. Betty had trouble keeping up with me.

"Hey, what kind of bee's in your bonnet? Not so fast!"

But I continued straight down the hall. I nearly tipped over an old man folded up in a wheelchair, who tried to enter my lane, jackknifing his vehicle. I didn't catch what he called me—I was out the door in two seconds flat.

The fresh air relaxed me, made me feel better immediately. I felt like I'd just come out of a haunted house. Betty put her hands on her hips and gave me a sideways, worried smile.

"What's wrong? What did that stupid hospital do to you?"

"Must be that I haven't eaten—feel a little weakish."

"A little while ago you said it was the bananas."

"I don't know. I think I better eat something. . . ."

I turned around at the bottom of the steps to look back. Betty didn't wait for me. I examined the building carefully, but couldn't see anything abnormal—nothing particularly terrifying. It was rather pretty, in fact—well lit, with palm trees all around and nicely trimmed hedges. I really couldn't fathom what had gotten into me. Maybe they'd been poison bananas after all—enchanted bananas, mysteriously breeding fear in one's stomach. Add to that a small burned child, rocking his head in a dark room, and you have your answer—no more complicated than that.

I would be lying if I said that a slight feeling of uneasiness didn't linger. It was barely perceptible, though—nothing to drive myself crazy over.

I knew this joint uptown where the steak and fries were edible and there was lots of light. The owner knew us—we'd sold him a piano for his wife. We sat down at the counter, and he got out three glasses.

"So . . . things working out all right?" I asked.

"Yeah, great. The scales are driving me out of my gourd . . ." he said.

There were quite a few people in the place—a few single men, a few couples, and a bunch of brush-cut twenty-year-olds without a wrinkle on their brows. Betty was in a good mood. The steaks were good enough to make a vegetarian wobble. My fries simply swam in their catsup. It put the hospital incident completely out of my mind. I was lighthearted. The whole world was swell. Betty smiled. I fired off jokes at the drop of a hat. We ordered up the Super Giant Strombolis—one full pound of whipped cream.

I downed two big glasses of water, then, naturally, had to hightail it to the men's room. The urinals were Indian pink. I chose the one in the middle. Every time I find myself in front of one of those jobs it reminds me of the time I startled a six-foot blonde in the men's room, straddling the urinal, who told me, Don't fret, baby, I'll give you your thingamajig back in just a minute. I'll never forget that girl. It was back in the days when there was a lot of talk about women's liberation—they bombarded you with it. It was that girl, though, who drove the concept home—I had to admit that something had changed.

I was thinking about her, undoing the buttons of my fly with one hand, when one of the brush-cut dudes came in. He sidled up next to me and stared at the big silver button that makes the water flush.

Nothing was coming on my side. His either. The silence between us was deadly. Every few seconds he'd look over at me to see how I was doing, and clear his throat. He was wearing baggy pants and a colored shirt. Me: tight jeans and a white T-shirt. He was about eighteen. Me: thirty-five. I gritted my teeth and contracted my abdominal muscles. I felt him do the same. I tried to concentrate.

The silence was interrupted by the characteristic tinkle that squirmed out in front of me. I smiled.

"Haha," I said.

"I didn't have to go, anyway," he muttered.

When I was his age, Kerouac told me, Be in love with your life. It was only normal that I pissed quicker. Still, I didn't want to rest on my laurels.

"Got to take advantage of things," I said. "Who knows how long they'll last?"

He scratched his head. He made faces in the mirror while I washed my hands.

"By the way," he said. "I was thinking . . . I may have something that might interest you."

I turned my back to him to dry my hands. I tore off the regulation ten inches. I was in a good mood.

"Oh yeah?" I said.

He came over and unfolded a small piece of paper under my nose.

"There's a good gram here," he whispered.

"Is it good stuff?"

"Must be. But don't ask me, I never even tried it. I'm doing this to raise money for my vacation. I want to go surfing."

God, how youth can lead you astray, I thought. Not to mention that he hadn't even washed his hands. There was quite a bit of crystal there, though. I tasted it. I asked him how much it was. He told me. It had been a long time since I'd dealt in such things—the price had doubled since. I stood there with my mouth open.

"You sure you got that right?" I asked.

"Take it or leave it."

I pulled a bill out of my pocket.

"What'll this buy me?"

He didn't seem impressed. I forced his hand a little.

"This'll buy you a pair of Bermudas at least . . ." I said.

He laughed. We locked ourselves in a stall, and he got it ready for me on top of the toilet tank. I blew my nose conscientiously before snorting. After that I was ready to face a brand-new day— my mood was electric. I grabbed his arm before leaving.

"Just remember one thing," I told him. "Places with only sand and surf do not exist. Blood flows everywhere."

He looked at me as if I'd just solved the riddle of the Sphinx for him.

"Why are you telling me that?" he said.

"Just kidding," I said. "At thirty-five you wonder if you can still make people laugh."

It's true that I felt the world getting more and more somber with each passing year, but it never mattered much to me. I always tried to stand tall, to not let my life turn to shit. It was the best I could do, and I did my best to do it. It wasn't easy. One thing I'm proud of in life, though: I've always tried to be a decent guy. Don't ask any more of me—I wouldn't have the strength. I went back to Betty, sniffling. I grabbed her in my arms, almost yanking her off her seat. People looked at us.

"Hey," she said. "Nothing personal, but we're not alone here."

"Fuck 'em," I said.

I believed I could have bent the stool in half.

On the way home, I felt like I was at the helm of a runaway engine that nothing in the world could stop. Betty had drunk a little wine. The whole world had drunk a little wine, and I was the only one still lucid—the only one still faithful at his post, steady at the wheel. Everybody was signaling me to turn on my headlights. Bums. Betty put a lit cigarette in my mouth.

"Maybe you'd see a little better if you had a little light in front of you. . . ."

Before I had time to look, she'd bent over the dashboard and flicked on the high beams. It was better, okay, but so what?

"You don't have to believe me," I said. "But I could see like it was broad daylight."

"I believe you."

"Just because it's dark out doesn't mean we have to act like blind people, you know. . . ."

"I know."

"Damn straight . . ."

I had an itch to do something extraordinary. We were back in town, and all I could do was crawl down the streets, avoiding pedestrians, stopping at red lights like a wimp, while the dynamite coursed through my veins.

I parked in front of the house. The night was soft, calm, and silent, underlined by moonlight; yet the general feeling was one of incredible violence—blue and pearl-gray. I crossed the street, inhaling the cool air, not feeling sleepy at all. Betty had been yawning since the end of the trip. I didn't want to notice.

We went upstairs and she fell on the bed. I tried to shake her. "Hey, you can't do that!" I yelled. "Don't you want another drink? Let me get you something."

She struggled for a little while, smiling, but her eyes kept closing. I wanted to stay up all night talking—I wanted to TALK, goddammit! I helped her get undressed, explaining that to me things were totally clear. She hid her mouth with her hand, so as not to offend me. I gave her a slap on the butt as she slid under the sheets. Her nipples were soft as rags. It wasn't even worth it to try feeling her up—she was sound asleep.

I took the radio and a beer and went to sit in the kitchen. The news came on, but there was nothing important to report— everyone was more or less dead. I turned off the sound when they came to the sports. The moon was nearly full, and veritably perched on the table. I didn't have to turn the lights on. It was quite restful. I got the idea to take a bath. My head was as clear as a sunny winter's day—I could touch things with my eyes, I could have heard a piece of straw snap a hundred yards away. I chugged the rest of the beer down like a waterfall. It was good shit I'd bought, I had to admit, though the price of a gram still made me shiver.

An hour later I was still sitting there, bent slightly forward, staring between my legs to verify—yes or no—if I still had balls. I was holding a knife to my throat. I stood up with a bemused smile, short of breath. I went and got what I needed, then came back and sat down.

A little while later I had scrawled three pages. I stopped. All I had wanted to see was whether I was still capable of writing. Just one page. I didn't ask for an epic. I hadn't done too badly—far from it. No one could have been more surprised than me. I reread the pages slowly. It was one surprise after another. I couldn't remember ever having written like that before, even at my peak. It was reassuring, like getting back on a bicycle after twenty years and not crashing after two turns of the pedal. It gave me a boost. I held my hands out in front of me to see if they were trembling. You would have thought I was waiting for them to put the cuffs on.

Not looking for trouble, I conscientiously burned the pages. I had no regrets, though. Once I write something, I never forget it. It's the sign of a writer who has the touch.

Around two in the morning, a cat started meowing outside the window. I let him in. I opened up a can of sardines in tomato sauce. We were certainly the only two creatures still awake on the whole block. It was a young cat. I petted it and it purred. It climbed onto my lap. I decided to let it stay there for a while and digest its meal before getting up. The night didn't seem to be moving. Taking every precaution possible, I leaned backward to grab a bag of potato chips. It was nearly full. I spread a few out on the table. It made the time pass.

I finished the bag, wondering if the cat was planning to spend the rest of the night sitting on me. I shoved him off. He rubbed up against my legs. I got him a bowl of milk. The least you could say was that the day had passed under the sign of Milk—at once gentle and scalding, mysterious, unpredictable, unfathomably white—and with bears, elephants, and cats, what more could you ask? For a guy who hates milk I'd had quite a bit that day, and I hadn't left a single drop. You have to acknowledge that force that makes you drink to the dregs. I poured the milk slowly for the cat. I didn't spill any. I sensed it was the last such test of the day—I kind of have premonitions about these things.

I put the cat back out on the windowsill. I closed the window behind him, while he stretched in the geraniums. I put on some music. I had another beer before going to bed. I felt like doing something, but I didn't know what. To get my body moving again, I got Betty's things together and folded them.

I emptied the ashtrays.

I chased a mosquito.

I checked out all the channels on the television, but there was nothing that wasn't so boring you'd die twenty times watching it.

I washed my face.

Sitting at the foot of the bed, I read an article reminding us of the fundamental precautions to take in case of nuclear attack, such as staying away from windows.

I filed a fingernail that was coming unhinged, then got into it and did all the others.

According to my calculations, there were still one hundred eighty-seven cubes of sugar left in the box on the kitchen table. I didn't feel like going to bed. The cat meowed outside the window.

I got up to go look at the thermometer. Seventy-three degrees—not bad.

I got out the *I Ching* and pulled *The Obfuscation of Light*— not bad either. Betty rolled over and moaned.

I spotted where the paint had run on the wall.

Time passed. I plunged to the depths and came back up with my brain on fire—burning a cigarette. The most charming thing about this generation is its experience of solitude, and the deep uselessness of all things. Good thing life is swell. I stretched out on the bed, the silence taking on the form of leaden shell. I tried to relax, to calm this stupid energy that ran through me like an electric current. I turned to face the calm and beauty of a wholly redone ceiling. Betty jabbed me in the hip with her knee.

It wouldn't be reasonable to start making chili for the next day. It had now been thirteen thousand days I'd been alive. I saw neither the beginning nor the end. I hoped the tar paper would hold for a while. The small lamp was only twenty-five watts. I put my shirt over it anyway.

I got a new pack of chewing gum out of Betty's purse. I pulled out a stick and folded it in my fingers like an egg roll. No matter how hard I thought about it, I couldn't figure out why they put

ELEVEN sticks in a pack. It was like they just had to throw a monkey wrench into the works. I grabbed a pillow and lay down on my stomach. I tossed and turned. I was determined to fall asleep. I took the eleventh stick—the one that had caused me so much suffering—and poked it with my tongue. I swallowed it.

20

The cops had been nervous for a few days now. They'd been patrolling the area from morning till night, their cars crisscrossing the roads in the sun. Break-ins of small-town banks always cause an uproar. The only way to avoid crossing a checkpoint within a five-mile radius would have been by digging a tunnel. I had to go see this woman about moving a baby grand through her window. I was driving peacefully along a deserted road, when a cop car passed me and signaled me to stop. It was the young cop from the night behind the warehouse—the one with the steel thighs. I was running late, but I parked diligently on the shoulder. A few dandelions were growing along the side of the road. He was out of his car before I was. I couldn't tell if he recognized me or not.

"Hi. Still girded for battle?" I joked.

"Show me your registration," he said.

"Don't you recognize me?"

He just stood there with his hand out, looking around, tired. I got out the registration.

"If you ask me, the guys who did the bank job aren't from around here," I added. "Myself . . . as you can tell by looking at me . . . I'm on my way to work."

I had the feeling that I was getting on his nerves. He tapped a bebop rhythm on the hood of the car. His holster gleamed in the sun like a black panther.

"Let me look in the trunk," he said.

I knew that he knew that I had nothing to do with his goddamn bank. He knew that I knew. He just didn't like me—it was written all over his face—but I hadn't the vaguest idea why. I pulled my keys out of the ignition and dangled them in front of my nose. He practically ripped them out of my hand. It was clear I was going to be late.

He screwed around with the lock for a few seconds, trying to turn the knob in all directions at once. I got out and slammed the door.

"Okay," I said. "Let me do it. It may seem ridiculous to you, but I'd rather not have my car ruined. I use it for my work."

I opened the trunk and moved away so he could look inside. All there was was an old book of matches, all the way in the back. I waited for a minute before closing the trunk.

". . . Take advantage of the situation to air it out a little," I said.

I got back in the car. I went to turn the ignition key, but he leaned over and grabbed the door.

"Hey, hold on there a minute!" he said. "What about this . . . ?"

I stuck my head out the window. He was running his hand on my tire.

"Feels like a banana peel," he said. "I wouldn't even use it to put flowers in."

I cooled down immediately. I sensed trouble.

"Right, I know," I said. "I noticed it this morning before I left. I was going to take care of it right away."

He stood up without taking his eyes off me. I tried to send him love messages.

"I can't let you go like that," he said. "You're a public menace."

"Look, I'm not going very far. I'll go slow. I'll change the tire as soon as I get home. Rest assured. I have no idea how such a thing could have happened."

He stepped away from the car, fatigued.

"All right, I'll let it go. But in the meantime, put on the spare tire."

I felt the hair bristle on my arms and legs. My spare tire was not in any condition to be seen by a police officer. It had about twenty-five thousand miles on it. The tire he wanted me to change looked practically new next to it. I suddenly got a frog in my throat. I offered him a cigarette.

"Rhuh . . . care for a smoke? . . . Rhuh, rhuh . . . hey, that bank thing must really keep you guys hopping . . . rhuh . . . wouldn't want to be in the culprits' shoes, rhuh . . ."

"Right, now let's get moving. I haven't got all day."

I took out a cigarette. The jig was up. I lit it, watching the road unroll through the windshield. The cop squinted.

"Maybe you'd like me to help you . . ." he said.

"No," I sighed. "It's not worth it. It'd be a waste of time. The other tire's also a mess. I'll have to change it, too."

He grabbed my door with his hands. A wild lock of hair fell down on his forehead, but he didn't seem to notice.

"In principle, I'm supposed to immobilize your vehicle. I could even make you go the rest of the way on foot. Now we're going to turn around here, and you're going to stop at the first garage we come to and change that tire. I'll follow you."

The bottom line was that I was going to be late. But a baby grand is not something you sell every day. I felt like telling him that keeping people from working does not sign his paycheck, but the sun seemed to be getting to his brain.

"Look," I said. "I have an appointment two minutes from here. I'm not out for a joyride, I'm on my way to sell a piano, and you know very well that small businessmen can't afford to miss

appointments. It's hard times for everyone these days. I give you
my word that I'll take care of the tires when I get home. I swear
it."

"No," he snapped. "Now."

I grabbed the wheel, trying not to squeeze it too hard in my
fists, but my arms were already stiff as wood.

"Okay," I said. "Since you're determined to give me a ticket,
just go ahead and do it. At least I'll know why I have to work
today—I don't seem to have any choice in the matter. . . ."

"I didn't say anything about a ticket. I said you have to change
your tire! . . . IMMEDIATELY!!"

"Right, I got that. But if it means missing out on a sale, I'd
rather have a ticket."

He stood there silently for ten seconds staring at me. Then he
took one step back and slowly drew his gun. There was no one
around for miles.

"Either we do as I say," he growled. "Or you get a bullet in
your tire, for starters . . . !"

There was no doubt in my mind that he'd do it. Two minutes
later found us rolling back toward town. I checked the morning
off my list.

There was a wreck sitting in the driveway, so I signaled and
pulled around into the courtyard. A dog, black with motor oil, was
barking at the end of his chain. A guy was sorting bolts in a shed.
He watched us pull in. It was one of those lovely spring days, just
warm, no wind. There were piles of car carcasses all over the place.
I got out. The junkman gave the dog a kick as he wiped his hands.
He smiled at the young cop.

"Hey, Richard, what brings you here?" he said.

"My job, man. Always working."

"I came for the tires, myself," I said.

The dude scratched his head. He allowed as how he had three
or four Mercedes in the junkpile, but the problem was to find
them.

"Allow me," I said. "I got nothing else to do today."

They went off together to drink a beer in the shed, and I strolled through the debris. I was almost half an hour late. The carcasses were warm to the touch. The ball was in the enemy's court. I climbed up on two or three hoods before I spotted a Mercedes.

The left front tire was good, but I'd forgotten to bring my jack—I had to go back for it. There was an aroma of old engine grease in the air. I got the tools out of my car. The two of them were sitting on wood cases, talking. I took my sweater off. I gestured to them as I walked by.

It turned out that the Mercedes in question had a camper attached to the roof. I had a real ball with the jack. By the time I finally got the damn wheel off, I was covered with sweat—my T-shirt had changed color. The sun was almost directly overhead. Now I had to do the same thing all over again. It was like rolling a boulder.

Back in the shed, it was party time; the cop was talking and the junkman was slapping his thighs, laughing. I smoked a cigarette, then got back down to work. The bolts were a little stuck. I wiped my brow with my forearm. I kept an ear tuned, in case they called me to come have a beer. Obviously my place was there among the cinders. I listened to them yucking it up as I took off my tire.

I paid the guy. The cash disappeared into his pocket. The young cop looked at me, smugly. I turned to him:

"If you ever need a favor or anything, don't hesitate to call. . . ."

"Maybe I will," he said.

I went back to my car without another word. Words are blank bullets. I pulled up a little, then circled back, then took off forward. In all of three seconds I was back on the road. Three seconds was all it took for me to realize that shit just leads to more shit.

My hands were completely black, not to mention my T-shirt, and I had a veil of oil on my forehead. I knew instinctively that piano salesmen should avoid presenting themselves this way, like the plague. I was an hour late. Still, I had no choice but to stop back at the house. I had to drive with a Kleenex in each hand.

I ripped my T-shirt off going up the stairway and made a beeline for the bathroom. Betty was in her underpants, admiring her profile in the mirror. She jumped.

"Jesus, you scared me!"

"Boy oh boy, am I late!"

By the time I got my pants off, I'd given her the whole story in brief. I jumped into the shower. I started on the dirtiest parts, using paint thinner. The room filled up with steam. Betty was still looking at herself.

"Hey," she said. "Do you think I'm getting fat?"

"You must be kidding. I think you're perfect."

"I think I'm getting a stomach. . . ."

"What are you talking about . . . ?"

I stuck my head through the curtain.

"Hey, be a sweetheart. . . . Call the woman and tell her I'm on my way. Make something up."

She came and pressed herself against the curtain. I backed up into the faucet.

"Come on," I said. "Not now . . . ."

She stuck her tongue out at me, then left. I soaped up for the twentieth time. I heard her pick up the telephone. I told myself that if I blew this sale I'd have shot the whole day.

She was just hanging up when I got out, hair still wet, but clean, and T-shirt immaculately white. I stood behind her and cupped her breasts in my hands, apologetically. I kissed her neck.

"So what did she say?" I asked.

"No problem. She's waiting for you."

"I'll be back in an hour—two at the latest. I'll hurry."

She reached back and grabbed me, laughing.

"Do that," she said. "I have something to show you. You left so fast this morning. . . ."

"Listen, I'll give you thirty seconds. . . ."

She turned around. She had a little glass tube in her hand. She tried to look nonchalant.

"I didn't like the idea of keeping it to myself all day, but it's okay now."

She held the little tube up to my nose, as if it contained the secret of eternal life. It looked like something you'd find in a cereal box. Except for her eyes, her whole face smiled.

"Let me guess," I said. "It's authentic dust from the lost island of Atlantis."

"No, it's a thing that tells you if you're pregnant." My blood pressure suddenly plunged.

"And what does it say?" I said in one breath.

"It says yes."

"What about your fucking IUD?"

"Well, apparently things like this happen. . . ."

I don't know how long I stood there looking at her, rocking from one foot to the other—at least as long as it took for my brain to start working again. The air went out of the room. I found myself panting. Her eyes were fixed on mine. This helped me a little. I gradually unclenched my teeth. Then she started smiling, so I started smiling too. I didn't really know why—my first reaction was that we had committed the Supreme Fuck-up. Maybe she was right, though—maybe it was the right thing to do. I froze all the old demons in their tracks. We burst out laughing. We laughed so hard it hurt. When I laughed with her, you could have made me swallow a bucket of poison. I put my hands on her shoulders. I played on her skin with my fingers.

"Listen," I said. "Let me get this appointment over with, then I'll come right home. Okay?"

"Yeah. Anyway, I have tons of laundry to do. I won't get bored."

I hopped in the car and drove out of town. On the street I counted twenty-five women with strollers. My throat was dry. I had trouble getting my mind around what was happening—it was an eventuality I'd never seriously considered. Images raced through my mind like rockets.

To calm myself down, I concentrated on the drive. It was beautiful. I passed the cop car, I was going eighty. A minute later he stopped me. Richard again. He had nice teeth—healthy and straight. He took out a pad and a pen.

"Every time I see this car I know it means I have a job to do," he whined.

I had no idea what he wanted me for—no idea of what I was even doing on this road. I smiled at him dubiously. Perhaps he had been standing there in the sun all day, ever since dawn. . . .

"Maybe you think that changing your tire gives you the right to drive like a maniac . . . ?"

I shoved my index finger and thumb into the corners of my eyes. I shook my head.

"Jesus, I was somewhere else," I sighed.

"Don't worry. If I find two or three grams of alcohol in your blood, I'll bring you right back down to earth."

"If it was only that," I said. "I just found out I'm going to be a daddy!"

He seemed to hesitate for a moment, then he closed his pad, with his pen stuck inside, and put it back in his shirt pocket. He leaned over to me.

"You wouldn't have a cigarette, would you?" he asked.

I gave him one. Then he leaned against my door, puffing peacefully, and told me all about his eight-month-old son, who had just started crawling across the living room on all fours, and all the various brands of formula, and the thousand-and-one joys of fatherhood. I almost dozed off during his lecture on nipples. Finally he winked at me and said he'd look the other way this time, that I could go. I went.

During the last few miles I tried to put myself in a woman's shoes, to see if I would want to have a baby—if I would feel a deep urge. But I couldn't put myself in a woman's shoes.

It was a beautiful house on a nice piece of land. I parked in front and got out of the car with my little black briefcase. I didn't keep anything in it, but I'd found that it reassured people—I'd already blown a few sales by showing up with my hands in my pockets. A woman came out onto the stoop. I waved hello.

"At your service," I said.

I followed her inside. On the other hand, if this was really what Betty wanted, I had no right to refuse her—maybe it was all part of the order of things, maybe it wasn't death. And what was good for her would probably be good for me. Still, there was an air of terror surrounding the whole thing. It's the kind of situation that's always frightening. Once inside the living room, I glanced at the window and saw that the piano would make it through, no problem. I went into my spiel.

After five minutes, however, my thoughts got foggy, and I lost control of the situation.

"Does a woman really need to have a child to be fulfilled?" I asked.

The woman's eyelashes fluttered a little. I went on to enumerate the conditions of the sale, then proceeded through the details of delivery. I would have liked to be in some deserted place, where I could sit and think everything over peacefully. This was no laughing matter. Looking around me, I wondered if this was any place for a child to be born—and this was only one small part of the problem. The lady was circling the living room, looking for the right place to put the piano.

"In your opinion, ought I set it here, to the south?"

"That depends on whether you intend to play the blues or not," I said.

Anyway, I was a true bastard—it was clear. Then again, does lacking courage make you a bastard? I spotted the bar by accident. I gave it a sad look, in the style of Captain Haddock. Shit, I said to myself, to think that the fucking IUD slipped out of line and I didn't feel a thing. I had an anxiety attack: Was I merely an instrument? In the end, was there only the blooming forth of the female, and nothing for me? Don't guys ever get a break? The attack mysteriously evaporated when the lady got out the glasses.

"Easy," I said. "I'm not used to drinking in the afternoon."

I couldn't stop myself from downing my drink in one gulp, though—the anticipation had been too great. I saw Betty in her panties standing in front of the bathroom mirror. Here I was, driving myself crazy, when all anyone asked of me was to rise to the occasion—it always pays to go all the way. I poured myself another finger of maraschino.

On the way home, I forced myself to not think about it. I drove carefully, keeping to my right. The only thing they could have given me a ticket for was obstructing traffic. But I was the only car on the road. I was alone and apart from the universe—a speck of dust sliding toward an infinite tininess.

I stopped in town and bought a bottle and some passion-fruit ice cream, plus two or three cassettes that had just come out. It was like I was going to visit a sick person. I must admit, I wasn't too chipper.

When I got home she was ecstatic. The TV was on.

"They're going to show a Laurel and Hardy movie," she said.

It was exactly what I needed—I couldn't have imagined anything better. We plunked ourselves down on the couch with the ice cream and the booze, and let the rest of the afternoon slip away happily without bringing up the subject. She seemed in top form, completely relaxed, as if it were just another day of eating ice cream and watching television. I felt like I'd been making a mountain out of a molehill.

At first I was thankful that she didn't talk about it. I was afraid that we'd be forced to go into all the gory details, while what I really needed was time to adjust. Yet as the evening wore on, I started to realize that it was me who was having trouble containing himself. After dinner, as she was busy gulping down a plain yogurt, I found myself cracking my knuckles.

Finally, in bed, I put my foot in it, while stroking her thighs:

"So, tell me . . . how do you feel about being pregnant . . . ?"

"Gee, I don't really know yet. It's not really sure. To be sure I have to go get a test."

She squeezed herself against me and spread her legs.

"Right, but what if it was sure . . . ? Would you like that?"

I felt her fur under my fingers, but I stopped myself. She could try and squirm out of it all she wanted—I needed a straight answer. She got the message.

"Well, I'd really rather not think about it too much," she said. "But my first impression is that it's not so bad. . . ."

That was all I wanted to know. Things being clear, I went down on her in a way that made my head spin. While we were screwing, I imagined that her IUD was an unhinged door, flapping in the wind.

The next day she went to get tested. The day after that, I stopped in front of a certain kind of store for the first time in my life and did some detailed window-shopping. It was horrible, but I knew that sooner or later I'd have to go in. To get my feet wet, I bought two Oshkosh jammies, one red and one black. The saleswoman assured me that I'd be happy with them—there was absolutely no shrinking.

I spent the rest of the day observing Betty. Her feet were six inches off the ground. I got discreetly plastered while she was making an apple pie. I took out the garbage in the spirit of a Greek tragedy.

Outside, the sky was a dizzying red, the sun's last rays casting a sequined light. I found my arms twice as tan as before, the hairs nearly blond. It was dinnertime, and there was no one on the street—no one to see what I was doing. There was me, though. I went and crouched down in front of the store window. I smoked a cigarette, soft and sweet. There were a few sounds off in the distance, but the street itself was silent. I let my ashes fall delicately between my feet. Life was no longer absurdly simple—it was horribly complicated, and sometimes very tiring. I grimaced in the sunlight, like someone with ten inches up his ass. I looked until my eyes filled with tears, then a car passed by and I stood up. There was nothing left to see, anyway. Nothing but some guy who had just taken out his pitiful garbage at day's end.

After two or three days, I'd gotten used to things. My brain went back to its normal functioning rhythm. There was a strange sort of calm in the house—an atmosphere that I didn't recognize. It wasn't bad. I had the feeling that Betty was breathing a bit easier, as if she'd come to the end of a long race. I noticed that the perpetual tension that had always lived in her had somehow gone soft.

One day, for instance, I was in the middle of dealing with this crazy woman—the kind a piano salesman comes across once or twice in a lifetime—a woman with no age and bad breath, weighing in at about one-eighty. She ran from one piano to another, asking all the prices three times, her eyes looking elsewhere, lifting up all the lids, pushing down all the pedals; and at the end of thirty minutes we found ourselves back where we started, and the store stank from sweat and I thought I was going to choke to death. I was talking a little loud, so Betty came down to see what was going on.

"What I just don't understand," the woman was saying, "is the difference between this one and that one."

"One has round legs and the other one has square legs," I sighed. "Look, we're going to close pretty soon. . . ."

"Actually, I can't decide between getting a piano and getting a saxophone," she went on.

"If you can hold on for a few days, we're getting in a shipment of ocarinas . . ." I said.

But she wasn't listening. She'd stuck her head in a piano to see what was inside. I gave Betty a sign that said I'd had it up to here.

"I've got to get out of here," I whispered. "Tell her we're closing."

I went up to the apartment and I didn't come back. I drank a tall glass of cool water. Suddenly I was struck with remorse—I knew that in two minutes Betty would be chucking the woman's ass through the front window. I almost went down, but I held off for a minute. I didn't hear anything—no breaking glass, not even a scream. I was stupefied. The strangest thing of all was that Betty came up forty-five minutes later, relaxed and smiling.

"She was really annoying," she said. "You should take it a little easier with people like that."

That night we played Scrabble. I could have made the word *ovaries* and gotten a triple-word score, but I scrambled it and exchanged the letters instead.

Ordinarily I got up early when I had to make a delivery. This left me the afternoon to get my strength back. I had struck a deal with these guys who hauled furniture for a store a few blocks away. I'd call them the night before and we'd meet at the corner early the next morning. We'd load the piano in a van that I rented, then they'd follow me in their truck. We'd deliver the piano and I'd give them cash. They always gave me the same smile. The morning we were supposed to deliver the baby grand, though, things didn't exactly work out that way.

We had a seven o'clock meeting time, but I found myself alone on the sidewalk, pacing, waiting for them to show. The sky was gray—it was obviously going to rain later in the day. I hadn't wakened Betty, I'd just slid out of bed like a lazy snake.

Ten minutes later, I saw them round the corner slowly, coming toward me, skimming the curb. They were driving so slow I wondered what the hell they were doing. When they got to me, they didn't even stop. The driver was behind the wheel, making gestures and grimacing at me, and the other one held up a sign that said, "THE BOSS IS ON OUR ASS!!" I saw the problem immediately. I pretended to tie my shoe. Five seconds later a dark car drove by: a little man in glasses at the wheel, his jaws set.

I was not amused. When I set a delivery date I keep it. I started thinking wildly, then broke into a sprint toward Bob's store. The lights were on upstairs. I scooped up some gravel and threw it at the window. Bob appeared.

"Shit," I said. "Did I wake you?"

"Not really, I've been up since five o'clock, trying to get you-know-who back to sleep."

"Bob, listen. I got a problem. I'm all alone here with a piano to deliver. Could you get free?"

"Get free? Gee, I don't know. To give you a hand? Sure."

"Terrific. I'll pick you up in an hour."

I thought that with three of us, we could get the piano through the window. The truck driver alone could carry a closet up six flights, but just Bob and me . . . I wasn't sure. I went back to the van and took off for the rental place. I got a young guy with a striped tie and pants with creases like knives.

"Here," I said. "I brought your van back. I need something bigger, with a device for unloading."

The guy thought this was pretty funny.

"Great timing . . . so happens a guy just brought back a twenty-five-ton pickup with a hydraulic arm."

"Exactly what I need."

"Only problem is you got to know how to drive it," he smirked.

"No problem," I said. "I could drive a slalom course in a semi."

The truth is that it was a hell of a machine to maneuver, and it was the first time I'd ever laid hands on one. I made it across town with no damage, though—it wasn't as diabolical as I thought. You have to start with the idea that it's up to everybody else to get out of your way. The day was having trouble dawning—the clouds seemed glued together. I went to get Bob. I brought croissants.

We all sat down at the table, and I had a cup of coffee with them. It was so dark outside they'd had to turn the lights on. The bulb in the kitchen was a bit cruel. Annie and Bob looked like they hadn't slept in weeks. While we were devouring our croissants, the baby decided to throw a little temper tantrum. Archie spilled his bowl of cereal all over the table. Bob got up, teetering slightly.

"Just give me five minutes to get dressed, and we're out of here," he said.

Archie was washing his hands in the little stream of milk that ran over the edge of the table, and the other little one was still screaming. Why do I always have to bear witness to abominable things? Annie pulled a baby bottle out of a saucepan, and we could almost hear each other again.

"So," I said. "You and Bob getting along a little better?"

"Well, let's say we're getting along a LITTLE better, but that's all. Why, you have something in mind?"

"No," I said. "These days I use all my energy to not think about anything."

I looked over at my little tablemate, who was busy making patties out of his cereal, squeezing it in his hands.

"You're an odd duck," she said.

"I'm afraid I'm not really . . . unfortunately. . . ."

When we were finally outside, Bob looked at the sky and made a face.

"I know . . ." I said. "Let's not waste time."

We carried the piano out onto the sidewalk and tied the straps on. I went and got the user's manual out of the glove compartment, then went over to the mechanical arm. There were all kinds of levers to work it—levers to start it, make it go left, make it go right, up, down, withdraw, extend, levers to work the claw. All you had to do was coordinate everything. I turned it on.

On my first try I almost decapitated Bob—he watched me do it from the other side, standing there with a little smile. The controls were supersensitive and it took me a good ten minutes of practice before I could work them well enough. The hardest part was avoiding the sides of the truck bed.

Don't ask me how, but I loaded the piano. I was covered with sweat. We tied it down like madmen, then took off.

I might as well have been transporting nitroglycerin, I was so nervous. The storm was hanging over our heads. I could not morally allow it to rain on a Bösendorfer—I just couldn't. Unfortunately the heavens slowly started descending, and the truck dragged along at thirty-five.

"Bob, I'm a hair away from sinking the ship," I said.

"I know. Why didn't we put a tarp over it?"

"What tarp? Did you see something that looked like a tarp? Fuck, light me a cigarette, will you . . . ?"

He leaned forward and pushed in the cigarette lighter. I glanced at the dashboard.

"What are all these buttons for, I wonder?"

"Beats me. I don't recognize half of them. . . ."

I had my foot to the floor, a cold sweat running down my back. Just another fifteen minutes, I told myself—a wink of the eye, and we're home free. The suspense was killing me. I was biting the inside of my mouth when the first drop fell on the windshield. It hurt so bad I wanted to scream, but nothing came out of my mouth.

"Hey, I found the window-washer button," said Bob.

When we got there I drove around the house and parked next to the window, doing a slalom between the flower beds. The lady was ecstatic, walking around the truck, wringing her handkerchief.

"I decided to handle this myself," I explained. "All my men split on me at the last minute."

"Yes, I certainly know how it is," she complained. "So hard to find good help nowadays . . ."

"You said it," I added. "Someday they'll come murder us in our sleep!"

"Hahaha," she said.

I jumped out of the truck.

"And we're off!" I shouted.

"I'll show you how to get the window open," she said.

There were occasional light gusts of wind, cool and wet. I knew that every second counted. The piano shone like a lake. Inside, I jittered. The atmosphere was a little like in a disaster film—the part where all you hear is the ticking of the bomb.

I untied the piano with abandon. It rocked back and forth heavily. The sky was about to crack—I was holding it at bay with sheer brain power. As soon as the window was open, I aimed carefully, then sent it through. There was a sound of breaking glass. The first drop fell on my hand. I lifted a triumphant face to the heavens. I found each little drop prettier than the one before, now that the piano was safe and dry. It was with a happy heart that I turned off the controls and went to see what in the world I could have broken.

I asked the customer to simply have the bill for the window-pane forwarded to me, then gestured to Bob that it was time to undo the straps. Bob had tied the knots. I took one in my hand and discreetly showed it to him.

"You see, Bob . . ." I said. "A knot like this is not even worth trying to undo. It is impossibly tangled. I suppose you tied all the other ones the same way . . . ?"

I saw in his eyes that the answer was yes. I pulled my Western S.522 out of my pocket and cut the straps, sighing.

"The devil sent you," I told him.

Still, the piano had found a home—had come through without a scratch. I didn't have much reason to complain. Outside it was coming down in buckets. I took an almost animal-like pleasure in watching the raging storm drown out the countryside. I myself had managed to escape it. I waited for the lady to get it together to pay me, then considered the job done.

I dropped Bob off on the way back and returned the truck to the rental office. I took a bus home. The rain had stopped, and there were a few patches of blue. The tension from the morning had exhausted me, but I was coming home with pockets full of money, and one thing compensated for the other. Even better, I managed to get the window seat right behind the driver, and nobody bothered me. I sat there watching the streets go by.

There was no one home at the apartment. I couldn't remember if Betty had told me that she was going somewhere—yesterday seemed centuries away. I went straight to the fridge and got some things out on the table. The beer and the hard-boiled eggs were all frozen. I went to take a shower, and wait for the world to rise to human temperature.

Back in the kitchen, I gave a kick to a piece of crumpled-up paper that was lying on the floor. I find myself in this position more often than is my share, but that's how it goes. Something's always lying around on the floor. I picked it up. I unfolded it. I sat down and read it. It was the laboratory results. They were negative . . . NEGATIVE!

I cut my finger opening my beer bottle, but I didn't notice right away. I drank it in one gulp. It must have been written somewhere that all my disappointments come by mail. It was vulgar—atrociously trite—it was a glimpse of Hell. It took me a while to react, then Betty's absence began to weigh heavily on my shoulders. If I don't move, I thought, I'll burn. I grabbed the back of the chair to get up. My finger started pissing blood. I decided to run some water over it. Maybe this was why I hurt all over. I went up to the kitchen sink. Then I spotted something red in the garbage can. I already knew what it was. I fished it out with my hand. There was a black one, too. It was the Oshkosh jammies. Maybe it's true that they wash well—we'd never really know— but one thing was sure: they didn't stand up well to a pair of scissors. This little touch made me plunge to the murky depths. It gave me an idea of how Betty had taken the news. To all appearances, the blood was coagulating at the end of my finger, but in truth my skin was crawling—in truth, the Earth had fallen off its axis.

I controlled myself. I had to think. I ran the water over it, then wrapped it in gauze. The problem was that I was suffering for two. I had a keen intuition of what Betty must have felt. My brain was half paralyzed and my intestines were gurgling. I knew I ought to go looking for her, but for the moment I didn't have the strength. I almost just slid into bed to wait for a blizzard to come numb me, to sweep my thoughts away. I stood there in the middle of the room, pockets full of money and finger cut. Then I hit the streets.

I searched in vain for her all afternoon. I must have covered every street in town two or three times, my eyes riveted to the sidewalks. I chased after girls who looked like her, slowed down next to porches, combed the places we frequented. I rolled through deserted streets, until very slowly the night came on. I went and filled the gas tank. When it came time to pay, I pulled out my wad of bills. The dude was wearing an Esso cap with grease smudges on it. He gave me a suspicious look.

"I just pillaged a church," I said.

By that time, I knew she could have been two hundred miles away. All I'd gotten for my efforts was a throbbing headache. There was only one place left to look—the cabin—but I couldn't quite decide to go. I thought that if I didn't find her there, then I'd never find her. I hesitated before firing my last shell. There was one chance in a million that she'd be there. Still, there was no other choice. I drove around a while longer under the neon lights, then stopped by the house to get a flashlight and throw on a jacket.

The lights were on upstairs. This didn't surprise me. I was fully capable of leaving something on the stove, or the faucets running. In the shape I was in, I could have found the house in flames and taken it with a grain of salt. I went up.

She was sitting at the kitchen table. She was outrageously made up. Her hair was cut going in all directions. We looked at each other. In one way, I breathed deep relief. In another way, I felt myself suffocating. No words came to mind. She had set the table. She stood up without a word and got the main dish. It was meatballs in tomato sauce. We sat across from each other. She had simply demolished her face—I couldn't stand looking at it for very long. Had I opened my mouth just then, I would have started whimpering. All that was left were her bangs. Eye shadow and lipstick were smeared all over her face. She stared at me. Her stare was the worst of all. I felt that something was going to rip apart inside me.

Without taking my eyes off her, I bent forward and shoved both my hands into the bowl of meatballs. It was hot. I picked up a handful of it. The tomato sauce ran out between my fingers. I smeared it all over my face—in my eyes, up my nose, in my hair. It burned. I stuck it everywhere, blobs of it sliding down the sides of my head and onto my legs.

With the back of my hand I wiped away a tomato-sauce tear. No one had said anything. We sat like that for quite a while.

21

"Jesus Christ, I'll never be able to do this if you don't let me!"

We were standing by the wide-open kitchen window and the sun was in my eyes. Her hair shone so bright that I had trouble getting hold of it.

"Bend forward a little. . . ."

Snip, snip. I evened out two locks. It had taken three days to get her to the point where she'd let me fix her hair. We were waiting for Eddie and Lisa to arrive that afternoon—that's the real reason she let me. Three days to climb out of the hole. Her, that is, not me.

It turned out that short hair looked good on my little green-eyed brunette. Thank God for small favors. I held the locks between my fingers and trimmed them like ripe stalks of black wheat. Her face was not exactly bursting with health, of course, but I was sure that a little pat on the cheeks would put her back in shape. I'd make the punch. I told her not to worry—people who come down from the city are always pale as death themselves.

I was right. Eddie had gotten a new car—a salmon-pink convertible—so they'd eaten quite a bit of dust on the way down. They looked like sixty-year-olds. Lisa jumped out of the car.

"Oh sweetheart, you cut your hair! Looks great!"

In the course of conversation, we made our way gently toward the punchbowl. It was dynamite, if I do say so myself. Lisa wanted to take a shower. The two girls disappeared into the bathroom with their drinks. Eddie slapped me on the thigh.

"Good to see you, you old bastard . . . !" he said.

"Yeah . . ." I said.

He took another look around, nodding.

"Yep, I got to take my hat off to you. . . ."

I went to open a can of food for Bongo. Eddie and Lisa's presence allowed me to loosen up a little. I needed it. For three days I'd wondered if we were going to make it, if I'd ever be able to get her spirits back up—bring her back to the land of the living. I'd given it all I had—all I had in my head, and in my gut. I'd fought like a wildman. It was difficult to fathom how far gone she was. I don't know by what miracle we came through it, what wonderful tide carried us to the shore. I was exhausted. After an exercise like that, opening a can of dog food seemed like drilling through a safe to me. But two glasses of punch later I was walking into a rising sun. I listened to the girls laughing in the bathroom—it seemed too beautiful for words.

When the flames of reunion had turned to embers, Eddie and I swung into action. The girls wanted to spend the first evening at home, necessitating some grocery shopping, not to mention a stop at Bob's house to borrow a mattress and a Chinese-like partition. The punch was beginning to wear off. The day was coming to an end by the time we left the house. There was a light breeze. I would have felt just about fine, if I could have rid myself of one rather idiotic thought: Though I knew there was nothing I could do about it—it's just one of the little differences between men and women—still, I couldn't help thinking how unequally the pain of the recent events had been distributed. For me it remained somewhat abstract. I felt like there was an air pocket in my throat that I couldn't swallow.

We went and got the mattress and the partition from Bob's house, then came back. We unloaded the mattress onto the sidewalk, swearing and huffing and puffing. The shocks of the car groaned. The trouble was that we couldn't let the goddamn thing drag on the cement. We had to carry it. Next to the mattress, the partition felt light as a feather.

We made it upstairs, winded. The girls fussed over us. While I was getting my breath back, I felt the effects of the alcohol starting to multiply. My blood coursed through my veins at full throttle. It wasn't unpleasant. It was the first time in three days that I had the sensation of having a body at all. The girls had made a shopping list for us. We went back downstairs at a sprint.

Once in town, we took care of business in no time flat. The trunk of the convertible was full. We were on our way out of the bakery, cake boxes under our arms, when this guy walked up to Eddie and threw his arms around him. I vaguely recognized him—I'd seen him the day of the funeral. He shook my hand. He was small and kind of old, but he still had a good grip. I moved away a little to let them talk. I smoked a cigarette and looked at the starlit sky. I overheard every other word. From what I could understand, the guy didn't want to let us go so easily. He insisted that Eddie come see his new gym, just around the corner. He wouldn't believe that we didn't have five minutes to spare.

"What do we do?" I asked Eddie.

"Stop asking stupid questions, and follow me!" said the guy.

I put the cakes in the trunk. I can't refuse, Eddie explained, I've known him for over twenty years. We had some good times together, back in the days when I helped him organize little regional bouts. He didn't have gray hair back then. I told Eddie that I understood perfectly—it wasn't very late and it didn't bother me at all, really. We closed the trunk and took off, following the guy around the corner.

It was a small gym, smelling of leather and sweat. Two dudes were working out in the ring. You could hear the sound of gloves on skin, the water running in the showers. The old man led us behind a sort of counter. He brought out three sodas. His eyes were like bubbles.

"So, Eddie, what do you think?" he asked.

Eddie grazed his fist affectionately on the old man's jaw.

"Yeah, I get the feeling you run a pretty tight ship here. . . ."

"The one in the green trunks is Joe Attila," the old man said. "He's my latest. You're going to hear big things about him one of these days. He's got the killer instinct . . . he's got the stuff. . . ."

He gave Eddie a phony right hook to the stomach. I slowly lost the flow of the conversation. I drank my soda pop and watched Joe Attila practice his technique on his sparring partner, an older guy in a red sweatsuit. Joe Attila laid into the old guy like a locomotive. The old guy hid behind his gloves, muttering, "Attaboy, Joe, keep it up, Joe, good boy." Joe just let him have it, as hard as he wanted. For some reason, I was hypnotized by the spectacle—it set my brain on fire. I approached the ropes. I knew nothing about boxing. I'd seen maybe one or two matches in my whole life. I had never been particularly attracted to it. Once I got a spurt of somebody's blood on my pants. Yet I sat there watching the old guy get showered with punches, my tongue hanging out like a junkie. All I saw were gloves shooting back and forth like arrows. I was captivated.

Eddie and his pal came up next to me, just as Joe was finishing the session. I was perspiring. I grabbed Eddie by the lapels.

"Eddie, look at me. You know, all my life I've dreamed of putting the gloves on—getting into the ring—just for one minute to pretend I'm slugging it out like a pro!"

Everybody laughed—Joe hardest of all. I insisted. I told them, "Just among friends, it'll be fun—I just want to do it once before I die." Eddie scratched his head.

"Are you kidding, or what . . . ?"

I bit my lip and shook my head. He turned to his pal.

"Well, I don't know. . . . You think we could arrange something . . . ?"

The old man turned to Joe.

"What do you think, Joe? Think you could hang in there another minute . . . ?"

Joe's laugh reminded me of a tree trunk rolling down a hill. I was so hyped up that I paid no attention. I was blinded by all the lights, short of breath. Joe grabbed the ropes and gave me a wink.

"Okay, why not? One little round, for fun . . ."

At that moment I suddenly got very scared—my whole body started to tremble. The oddest thing of all was that I found myself undressing, propelled by that force that draws you toward the void. My brain tried to play its card—it was becoming delirious in all the hysteria, trying to break my spirit, make things seem menacing. Don't do it, it told me, it happens one time in a million, but it happens—perhaps death awaits you in the ring, perhaps Joe will tear your head off. Spurred on by alcohol and fatigue, I felt myself drift off into morbid delirium: a horrible plunge into a dark and icy lake. I knew it only too well, it was always the same one. All my phobias tore at me. Fear of the dark, fear of madness, fear of death, the whole shebang. It was the moment of total fear that hits you from time to time. It was not new to me—I had already found the remedy. With great effort, I bent down to untie my shoes, saying to myself: Make friends with death, make friends with death, MAKE FRIENDS WITH DEATH!

This did the trick. I came up for air. The others were talking all around me, paying no attention to my problems. The guy in red sweats helped me suit up. I found myself wearing white trunks. My brain stopped carrying on. I climbed into the ring. Joe Attila smiled at me, nicely.

"You know anything about this?" he asked.

"No," I said. "This is the first time I've ever had gloves on."

"Okay, well, don't be afraid. I'll go easy. It's all in good fun, right?"

I didn't answer. I had hot and cold flashes. Though Joe and I were about the same size, the resemblance stopped there. My head was bigger than his, his shoulders were wider than mine, and his arms were like my thighs. He started hopping around.

"Ready?" he said.

I felt myself take off. All the accumulated rage and impotence of the last few days channeled itself into my right fist. I took a swing at Joe—the punch of a lifetime—letting out a little grunt as I did. I hit his gloves. He backed up, furrowing his eyebrows.

"Hey! Easy," I said.

I must have been running a temperature of 100 or 101. He started dancing around again. I seemed to have lead in my shoes. He faked left, then gave me a right cross to the chin. It wouldn't have hurt a fly. I heard laughing behind me. Joe circled me like a butterfly, tapping me lightly, his gloves a blur. At one moment he turned toward the others to give them a wink. I gave him a straight shot to the mouth. I wasn't playing.

The results were immediate. I blocked a one-two punch with my face, hit the canvas, and slid under the ropes. Eddie's face appeared ten inches away from mine.

"What, are you crazy? What the hell's got into you?"

"Never mind that. Tell me, am I bleeding?"

I couldn't feel anything. My ears were ringing. His voice and mine both seemed to be coming from a dream. I couldn't breathe.

"Jesus," I groaned. "Am I bleeding somewhere?"

"No, but keep it up and you will be. Come on, take those gloves off."

I pulled myself up by the ropes. Everything was fine, except that I weighed about four hundred pounds and my face was on fire. Joe was waiting in the middle of the ring, hopping around. He looked like an ephemeral mountain. He wasn't smiling anymore.

"I like to have fun as much as the next guy," he said. "But don't go too far. I wouldn't try that again, if I were you."

Without warning, I let him have it with all my might. He dodged my punch easily.

"Cut that out, little buddy . . ." he said.

I gave him another one. All I hit was air. I wished he'd stop moving around. I had trouble keeping my guard up—I could hardly lift my arms. Still, I laid into him with all I had, sending him a right cross that I was convinced could have killed a steer.

I don't know what happened. I didn't see a thing. My head exploded, as if I'd taken a dead run at a glass door. I hovered in midair for a moment, then landed on the canvas.

I did not pass out. Eddie's face was floating beside me, a bit pale, a bit worried, a bit crumpled.

"Eddie . . . my man . . . you see any blood?"

"Shit," he said. "It looks like you got a faucet under your nose."

I closed my eyes. I could breathe. Not only was I not dead, but the air pocket in my throat had disappeared. It felt good to lie down.

I lost all sense of what was going on around me. I didn't know where I was, or when, or why. I wanted to pull a sheet over me, but my arm wouldn't move. The old guy in the sweatsuit came and took care of me, splashing water on my face and sticking cotton up my nose.

"It's all right," he said. "It's not even broken. Joe wasn't too tough on you, he could have hit you harder."

Eddie helped me into the shower, calling me all sorts of names. The warm water did me good, and the cold water cleared my head a little. I dried myself off, got dressed, and looked at myself in the mirror. I looked like somebody who'd been treated with cortisone. I went and joined the others, walking at a more or less normal gait. I was totally sober. Joe was wearing a suit, his little gym bag slung over his shoulder. He smiled at me as I approached.

"So, how does it feel to make an old dream come true?"

"Great," I said. "I'm at peace now."

I felt even better back in the convertible, cruising down the main drag with the wind in my face and a cigarette in my hand. Eddie gave me a furtive glance.

"Of course . . ." I said. "Not a word of this to the girls."

He half choked. He turned the rearview mirror toward me.

"Really? And what are we going to tell them—that you got bit by a mosquito?"

"No, just that I went headfirst through a bay window."

One morning the alarm went off at four o'clock. I turned it off quickly, then got up without a sound. Eddie was already in the kitchen. He had gotten the bags ready and was drinking his coffee. He winked at me.

"Want some? It's still hot. . . ."

I yawned. I wanted some. It was still dark outside. Eddie had wet his hair and combed it. He seemed to be in good shape. He stood up to rinse out his cup.

"Don't take too long," he said. "We have at least an hour's drive."

Five minutes later we were downstairs. It's not always easy to get up early, but you never regret it. The last hours of night are the eeriest, and nothing can compare to the shivers you get from the first glow of day. Eddie gave me the wheel. Since it was nice out, we left the top down. I buttoned my jacket all the way up. It was a jumpy little car.

Eddie knew the area like the back of his hand. He told me how to go. The roads were strewn with childhood memories. All it took was a road sign, or passing through a sleepy little village, and he was off and running, his stories flowing one after the other, drifting off into the darkness.

The trip ended on a dirt road. We parked the car under the trees. The night was slowly evaporating. We got the gear out of the trunk and started off along the stream. It had a fairly strong current, all babbles and burbles. Eddie walked ahead, talking to himself—something about when he was eighteen. We stopped at a peaceful spot, a place where the thin river got wider. There were flower-covered rocks and trees all around. Grass, leaves, buds, dragonflies—all that sort of thing. We settled in.

It was barely daybreak when Eddie slipped on his boots. His eyes were glowing. It was wonderful to see. I felt calm and relaxed. Being close to water always does that to me. He checked his equipment, then went off, bounding from rock to rock as if he was walking on water.

"You'll see," he said. "It's not so mysterious. Watch me. . . ."

Of course the main reason I'd come was to make him happy. Fishing was never my idea of exaltation. I'd brought along a book of Japanese poetry, in case I got bored.

"Hey, if you don't watch me, you won't know how to do it. . . ."

"Go on, I'm all eyes."

"Check it out, pal—it's all in the wrist."

He twirled the line over his head, then cast it out. It flew through the air, the reel unwinding at breakneck speed. There was a little plop.

"Hey, you see that? Got it?"

"Yeah, but don't worry about me. I'm just going to watch for a while."

A few minutes later a ray of sunlight slithered through the leaves. I unwrapped the sandwiches slowly, trying to make myself useful. I wanted to avoid falling asleep. Eddie had his back to me. He'd been silent for almost ten minutes. He seemed absorbed, contemplating his little nylon string. Without turning around, he suddenly started talking.

"I was wondering what's going on with you two. I was wondering what's wrong. . . ."

They were ham sandwiches. Nothing is sadder than a ham sandwich, when the little edge of fat hangs overboard. I rewrapped them. They were kind of soggy, too. Since I hadn't answered, he forged ahead.

"My God, I'm not saying this to bother you, but have you

taken a good look at Betty lately? She's white as a ghost. She spends most of her time biting her lip and staring into space. Shit, you never say anything, so how am I supposed to know if there's anything we can do to help . . . ?"

I watched his line drift downstream, growing taut. The water rippled over it.

"She thought she was pregnant," I said. "But we were wrong."

There was a fish on the end of his line. It was the first of the day, but there was no comment—his death went practically unnoticed. Eddie stuck the pole under his arm to unhook the fish.

"Yeah, but don't be ridiculous. These things don't work every time. It'll come out better next time."

"There won't be a next time," I said. "She doesn't even want to hear about it, and I'm not really man enough to overpower an IUD."

He turned to me, with the sun in his wild hair.

"You see, Eddie," I said, "she's chasing after something that doesn't exist. She's like a wounded animal, you know? She gets a little weaker all the time. I think the world's too small for her, Eddie. That's where all her problems start."

He cast his line out farther than he had before, his mouth set in a sort of grimace.

"Still, there ought to be something we could do . . ." he said.

"Yeah, sure. Make her understand that happiness doesn't exist, that paradise doesn't exist, that there's nothing to win or lose, and that essentially you can't change anything. And that if you think despair is all that's left after that, well, you're wrong again, because despair is an illusion, too. All you can do is go to bed at night and get up in the morning, with a smile on your lips, if possible. And you can think whatever you want—it only complicates matters and doesn't change a thing."

He looked up at the sky and shook his head.

"Gee, I ask him if there's some way to pull her out of all this, and all he has to say is she'd be better off putting a bullet through her head . . . !"

"No, not at all. What I'm saying is, life's not a carnival. There are no booths or Kewpie dolls to win by knocking over bottles; and if you're crazy enough to place a bet, you'll see that the wheel never stops turning. That's when the suffering starts. To set goals in life is to tie yourself up in chains."

Eddie pulled another fish out of the water. He sighed.

"When I was a kid, there were more fish than there was water," he muttered.

"When I was a kid I thought someone would light my path," I said.

We took off around noon, as planned. I hadn't tried to fish. I just couldn't get into it. In the end, we took our three lousy fish and went back to Bob's house. Everyone was in the yard, the three girls busy spreading things on toast. Bob watched, talking. I hopped over the fence.

"We have a problem," I said. "Barring a miracle, I can't see how we're going to feed thirty or forty people on three fish."

"Oh yeah? What happened?"

"Hard to say. Bad year, maybe . . ."

Though there were no more fish in the river, there were still, luckily, a few cows left on the prairie—or wherever cows hang out—at least a few skewers' worth. Bob and I handled it.

There were so many little things to take care of that I didn't even feel the afternoon go by. I had trouble getting interested in anything—people had to repeat things two or three times to me. I just stood around buttering the bread or folding the napkins, which is what I preferred to do, leaving my mind behind. After the discussion I'd had with Eddie, I wasn't very excited by the upcoming evening. To tell the truth, I knew that the less I saw of people the better off I'd be. The weight of things kept me from leaving, though. Between getting-away-from and putting-up-with, the first solution is not always the best—after a while it, too, gets old. The weather was nice in a stupid kind of way, the sun barely even shining. The only time I felt any warmth was when I got close to Betty, ran my hands through her short hair. The rest of the time I spent sighing and tossing finger sandwiches to Bongo.

Night was falling when the people came. I recognized some of them, and the ones I didn't know looked like the ones I knew, all categories being confused. There were at least sixty people. Bob jumped from one group to another like a flying fish. He came up to me, rubbing his hands together.

"Boy oh boy, is this going to be fun . . ." he said.

Before leaving, he guzzled down my drink. I hadn't touched it. I found myself standing apart, my empty glass in my hand. I didn't move. I wasn't thirsty, I didn't want anything. Betty seemed to be having a good time. So did Lisa, Eddie, Bob, and Annie. Good time—that is to say that I was the only one standing by myself, trying to get my lips to muster a circumstantial smile. It gave me a cramp. Okay, so I was probably the only pale-face in the crowd. Still, when I looked behind the faces of those around me, all I saw was insanity, unrest, and anguish; or suffering, fear, and loneliness; or boredom, or solitude, or rage and impotence—shit, what was there to be happy about? Some fun, right? I saw a few pretty girls, but they seemed ugly to me, and the men seemed stupid—I'm generalizing, but I had no desire to delve any deeper. What I wanted was to fade into the shadows. I wanted a sad world, a cold one—a world without hope, without substance, without light. That's how it was. I wanted to plunge to the bottom. I'd lost the faith. Sometimes you just want to see the whole show fold—the sky fall. Anyway, this was my state of mind, and I hadn't drunk a drop.

Not wanting to call attention to myself, I started walking back and forth, acting very busy. Suddenly Betty tapped me on the shoulder. I jumped.

"What the hell are you doing?" she asked. "I've been watching you for quite a while now."

"I was testing you to see if you still loved me," I joked. "Girls avoid me, because of my black eye."

She smiled at me. I was standing at the gates of Hell and she was smiling at me. God in Heaven, oh Great God in Heaven above . . .

"You're exaggerating," she said. "You can hardly see it anymore. . . ."

"Take my hand," I said. "Take me where I can get my glass refilled."

I had barely gotten it refilled, when Bob stuck himself between us, drank it, and led Betty away by the arm.

"Bob, you're a real motherfucker," I said. "And you're . . ."

But he was already far away, his ears glowing like bicycle reflectors. I found myself alone again. Thanks to Betty I felt a little less depressed. I allowed myself a small convalescent smile, then turned to the bar, in the hopes of getting a drink without being trampled. It was easier said than done. Everyone was talking louder than me, their arms reaching over my head. I finally had to go behind the bar and serve myself. The ambience was improving. Somebody turned the music up a few notches. I took a lawn chair and went to sit under the trees like an old grandma, except I didn't have my knitting with me and I still had a few miles to go before I slept. My soul was tired. My emotional ebb was at its lowest. People were moving around, talking, yet nothing was really going on. The problem of the age seemed to be about how to dress, how to trim one's hair. It didn't seem worth going inside the store to ask for something you hadn't seen in the window. O my poor generation—born of nothing, knowing neither effort nor revolt, eating itself alive, no way out. I decided to toast my good health. I had set my drink down on the grass, and when I went to reach for it, Bob kicked it over with his foot.

"What are you doing?" he said. "Sitting down already?"

"Tell me, Bob. Didn't you feel anything just now? Your foot hitting something . . . ?"

He backed up, tottering. I, who didn't have one drop of alcohol in my veins, saw how wide the distance was between us. No sense explaining—I put the glass in his hand and turned him to face the right direction. I gave him a push.

"Go in peace, my son," I said.

My generation was committing suicide, and I had to sit there waiting for a drunk to come back with my drink. I told myself that, decidedly, we'd be spared nothing tonight. Luckily the night was warm, and I was in a good spot to get a shish kebab. I felt a little better. Bob never came back, but I managed to get a drink by myself. I held onto it for dear life. I walked over to where people were dancing. I spotted this girl—not too pretty but a great bod. She was writhing to the sounds of a saxophone, wearing tight pants. You could see that she had nothing on underneath. Same for her top, a T-shirt, with breasts pushing through. You could watch her dance for a long time without getting bored—she was like a little cyclone. I squinted my eyes and took my first sip. I had taken only one, when the sax started cooking. The girl switched into high gear, flinging her arms and legs every which way. I was not far behind, no sir—I stood right in her trajectory. Her arm swung back. My drink went all over my face, the glass smashing into my teeth.

"Christ!" I groaned.

I felt the liquid slide down my chest, dripping from my hair. I held my empty glass in one hand and wiped my face with the other. The girl put her hand over her mouth:

"Oh gosh, did I do that?"

"No," I said. "I threw my drink in my own face just to see what would happen."

The girl was nice. She sat me down in a corner and ran off to get some napkins. This latest cruel twist of fate laid me low once more. I waited for her to come back, my head hanging. There are no limits, however, to endurable pain—I no longer felt anything. Nobody paid any attention to me.

She showed up with a roll of paper towels and I let her do her thing. When she stood in front of me to dry my hair, my entire field of vision became her pants. Without closing my eyes it was difficult to look anywhere else but between her legs—the bulges, the creases; her pants were at most one millimeter thick. I thought of sun-ripened fruit—a sliced orange, easily separated with one finger. It was quite a show, but I managed to contain myself. One girl was plenty for me. Be content to watch them dance, I told myself. Don't stop in front of store windows where there's a line waiting to get in.

I left the girl and went up to the apartment. I told myself that with a little luck I'd find myself a quiet place where I could finally have a drink in peace. Alcohol is not the answer any more than anything else, but it does let you catch your breath—avoid blowing your fuses. It's life that makes you crazy, not booze. There were so many people upstairs that I almost ran back down, but what good would that have done? There was a large group in front of the television, arguing about whether to tune in the tennis finals or the landing of the first solo transatlantic flight. Just as it was being put to a vote, I spied a bottle. Without thinking, I went and picked it up. The result of the poll was five to five, with some abstentions. In the relative silence I poured myself a drink. Then this guy with an exaggerated smile got up and came over to me. He had one lock of hair over his eye and nothing on the sides. I held my glass behind my back. He grabbed me around the neck as if we'd known each other for a long time. I don't like people touching me. I stiffened.

"Hey, man," he said. "As you can see, we have a little problem here, and I think everyone agrees that you're the one to set things straight."

I put my head down to slide out from under his elbow. He pushed his hair back.

"Okay, man," he said. "Go ahead . . . we're all ears. . . ."

They awaited my words with bated breath, as if what I had to say could save mankind. I didn't have the heart to make them wait too long.

"Personally, I came up here to watch the Jimmy Cagney movie," I said.

I disappeared with my drink before I could see their reaction. One mustn't tarry when rejected from all sides at once—one must look straight ahead and continue one's journey alone. I found myself in the kitchen. There was another big group sitting around the table, deep in conversation. Betty was among them. She saw me and reached out her arm.

"There he is!" she said. "Now that's what I call a writer—one of only a handful alive today. . . ."

I was swift as lightning, sly as a fox, slippery as an eel or a bar of olive-oil soap.

"Don't move," I said. "I'll be right back. . . ."

By the time they had stood to shower me with accolades, I was already back in the yard. I did not bask in the spotlight. I kept away from the windows. I had spilled most of my drink along the way. I had only enough left to wet my whistle. My writer's ass was safe. This wasn't saying much. I thought it was time to throw in the towel. The night was no longer young. I felt like I was stuck in some train station with all the ticket windows closed.

While no one was looking, I backed up to the bow of the ship, straddled the rail, and slid silently into the bottom of a lifeboat. I snipped the rope with one hand and, before the news had spread through the house, melted away into the night.

Back at the apartment, I was greeted with a delicious silence. I sat down in the kitchen and stayed there in the dark. There was a bluish glow coming through the window. I kicked open the refrigerator door, and a square of light spilled onto my lap. I laughed for a second, then got myself a beer. If *I* don't rhapsodize on the beauty of a beer can to him who wonders what anything's worth in the end, then who will? I refused to go to bed until I'd come up with two or three solid answers to the question. I closed the fridge with a sneeze.

22

The little cable car whined as if it were at the limits of its strength, its cabin swinging to and fro in the breeze, two yards off the ground. The only other people in the car were an old couple, so there was lots of room. Still, Betty squeezed herself against me.

"Oh God, oh God . . . . I'm scared . . . ." she said.

I was not exactly at ease myself, but I told her, You must be kidding—this fucking cable car isn't about to snap TODAY! Millions of people have ridden in it safely. Maybe it'll crash in ten years, maybe five even—a week from now, perhaps—but NOT NOW, NOT JUST LIKE THAT!! In the end, reason won out. I gave Betty a wink.

"Don't worry," I said. "It's a lot safer than riding in a car. . . ."

The old man nodded his head and smiled.

"It's true," he said. "There hasn't been an accident here since the end of the Second World War."

"That's what I mean," said Betty. "We're overdue. . . ."

"DON'T SAY THAT!!" I roared. "Why don't you just look at the scenery like everybody else?"

Whi-i-i-ine . . .

I got out my vitamin C and gave her one. She grimaced. On the bottle it said eight tablets a day. I rounded that out to twelve, which meant one every hour. They weren't bad, either . . . orange-flavored. I insisted.

"I can't take it anymore!" she complained. "I've had that taste in my mouth for two days now. . . ."

I didn't give in. I shoved a yellow tablet into her mouth. I had calculated that at bedtime she would swallow the last tablet in the bottle. According to the label, it was just what the doctor ordered. Add to that a few days in the mountains and a balanced diet, and what more could you ask for to put a little color back in her face. I had given my word to Lisa on the day they left. We were saying good-bye. She begged me to see that Betty didn't get sick. She said she was worried about her.

Whine . . . whi-i-i-i-ine . . . If you ask me, they purposely didn't grease the thing. Taking it up, and taking it down, day after day, year after year, over and over—those people probably had cable cars coming out their ears. The maintenance mechanics probably loosened the bolts once in a while to keep from getting bored—a quarter-turn once a month, a whole turn on days when life seemed too hard. I'm all for facing one's death, but let's not go overboard.

"They should relieve those guys every two weeks," I said. "And keep one in the cabin at all times."

"Who are you talking about?" she asked.

"Those guys who hold life and death in their hands."

"Hey, look at all the little sheep down there!"

"Shit, where?"

"Don't you see those little white dots?"

"OH, JESUS!"

* * *

There was a guy waiting to open the door for us when we arrived. He had a cap on his head, and a newspaper folded in his pocket. Despite his gentle air, he had the face of an ax-murderer. A few people were waiting to go back down. Not young people with the rage to live, but oldsters, with hats on their heads and big cars waiting for them down below. It gave the place a feeling of wilting flowers. Who cared, though—we weren't there to have fun.

I took a look at the schedule. The coffin would be back up in an hour. Perfect—just enough time to get some fresh air, before dying of boredom. I turned around, taking advantage of the scenic panorama. It really was beautiful. There were no words for it. I whistled through my teeth. I don't remember anymore what the place's claim to fame was, but one thing was sure—it didn't draw crowds. Except for the sadist who greeted the cable car, there was only the old couple and us.

I set my sack down on a sort of concrete table with compass points on it and pulled up the zipper of my coat. I called Betty over to drink her tomato juice.

"And you . . . ?" she said.

"Listen, Betty, don't be ridiculous. . . ."

She made like she was going to put her glass down, so I poured myself one, too. It was torture for me. I hate it—I always feel like I'm drinking a glass of blood, but Betty would drink hers only if I drank mine. Though it was a cheap shot, I paid the blackmail—it was just one of those little deaths that we live through every day.

My efforts seemed to be reaping results, though—her face was getting some color back into it, her cheeks were less sunken. For the last three days, the weather had been fabulous. We'd criss-crossed the whole area on foot, breathing the fresh air and sleeping twelve hours a night. We were starting to see the light at the end of the tunnel. I was sure that if Lisa had been there to see

her just then, lovely as the day is long, sipping her tomato juice
in the sun, she would have called it a miracle. I myself had to be
content with that. I still had a disquieting feeling when I looked
at her closely. I felt like I had lost something important that I
could never get back, but I didn't know what. I wondered if I was
just imagining things.

"Oh wow! Come here quick—take a look at this . . . !"

She was looking into a viewer—one of those big jobs on a
pedestal that magnifies, the kind you have to keep shoving coins
into every two seconds. It was aimed at a neighboring mountain-
top. I went over to see.

"Incredible!" she said. "I see eagles! Geez, there are two of
them, perched on a nest . . . !"

"Right, it's a daddy and a mommy."

"Shit, it's beautiful. . . ."

"Really?"

She stepped back to let me take a look, but just as I bent over
to see, the thing stopped working—all I saw was black. We
rummaged through our pockets but we didn't have any change
left. I took out my little nail file. I tinkered with the slot. But no
dice. It was hot. I started to get irked. To be so close to Heaven,
and still have to put up with mechanical bullshit—I couldn't
believe it.

The little old lady tapped me gently on the shoulder. Her face
sagged, but her eyes were bright—you could see that she'd pre-
served the essential. She put her hand out to me. There were
three coins in it.

"This is all I have," she said. "Take it. . . ."

"I only need one," I said. "You keep the rest."

Her laughter was a tiny stream of water, flowing through foamy
lace.

"No, I can't use them," she said. "My vision isn't as good as
yours."

I hesitated for a moment, then took the coins. I looked at the
eagles. I told her a little bit about what I saw, then turned the

thing back over to Betty. I thought she could describe it better than I could. Though there wasn't any snow, mountains for me have always been synonymous with avalanches. I had brought a little flask of rum with me. I went over to the sack and took a few swigs. The old man was there, sitting on the table, smiling in the sun, scraping the mud off his shoes, the little white hairs trembling on his neck. I offered him the bottle, but he refused. He motioned to his wife with his chin.

"I promised her when we met that if we lived together more than ten years I'd never touch another drink."

"And I bet she's never forgotten that," I said.

He nodded.

"You know, you might think it's silly, but I've lived with that woman for fifty years now, and I'd do it all over again tomorrow."

"That's not silly. I'm kind of old-fashioned myself. I'd like to be able to do the same someday."

"Yep, it's tough to go it alone. . . ."

There was enough in my bag to feed a whole family, all delicacies—almond paste, marshmallows, dried apricots, health crackers, those little crunchy things made out of roasted sesame seeds, and a bunch of organic bananas. I put it all out on the table and invited the old couple to eat with us. It was beautiful out. The silence was lovely. I watched the old man busily chewing a cracker. It made me feel optimistic. Maybe I'll be like that fifty years from now, I told myself . . . well, let's say thirty-five to be on the safe side—it seemed less far away than I thought.

We talked easily, waiting for the cable car to come. It arrived, whining. I bent forward a bit and looked down the dizzying descent of the cable. I shouldn't have looked. I pushed a finger against my throat, pressing on the point of my anxiety. Two women followed a colony of children out of the cable car. One of them looked scared to death, her pupils dilated. As she walked past me, our eyes met.

"If that miracle of modern technology hasn't come back an

hour from now, you'll know that it was your lucky day and not mine."

Whereas the trip up had proved to be quite frightening, the trip down was fear itself. The brakes were likely to snap any second—you could distinctly hear them grinding. I was sure they were going to burn up. With all that rubbing there was no doubt in my mind; the car was too heavy. I considered throwing all unnecessary objects—the seats and all accessories, for example—overboard. According to my calculations, the car must have weighed one ton. Once the brakes failed, we would eventually reach a cruising speed of 750 miles per hour. Just behind the finish line, there was a huge buffer made of fortified concrete. Result: impossible to identify the bodies.

I started eyeing the emergency brake, as if it were the forbidden fruit. Betty pinched my arm, laughing:

"Hey, you okay? Take it easy!"

"It's not a sin to be prepared," I explained.

One night at the hotel, I woke up suddenly. There was no explainable reason for this—we'd spent the day taking a ten-mile hike, stopping only to drink our tomato juice, and I was beat. It was three o'clock in the morning. The bed was empty beside me. I saw light coming from under the bathroom door. Now it happens that even girls get up during the night to pee—it was something that I'd been able to verify on several occasions—but three o'clock in the morning seemed a bit unusual. Anyway, so what, I yawned. I stayed there stretched out in the dark, waiting for her to come back, or for sleep to overtake me again. But nothing happened. I couldn't hear anything. After a while I rubbed my eyes and got up.

I pushed open the bathroom door. She was sitting on the edge of the bathtub, her hands clasped behind her neck, elbows in the air, staring at the ceiling. There was nothing to see on the ceiling—nothing, just white. She didn't look at me—she just rocked lightly back and forth. I didn't like it.

"You know, sweetheart, if we're going to make it to the much-talked-about glacier tomorrow, we'd better get some sleep. . . ."

She looked right through me. I could see right away that all my work was out the window. She was horrifyingly pale—her lips were gray. I felt the bamboo slivers go under my fingernails as she flung her arms around my neck.

"Oh my God, tell me it's not true!!" she said. "I HEAR VOICES!!"

I held her head against my shoulder, pricked up my ears. I thought I heard something. I breathed easier.

"I know what it is," I said. "It's the radio! The news. There's always some nut in every hotel who has to know what's going on in the world at three o'clock in the morning. . . ."

She burst into tears. I felt her stiffen in my arms—nothing was more fatal to me than this, nothing more killing.

"No, God, no . . . I hear them inside my head. THEY'RE INSIDE MY HEAD!!"

Everything suddenly turned cold—abnormally cold. I cleared my throat, like a jerk.

"Come on, calm down now . . ." I whispered. "Come tell me all about it. . . ."

I picked her up and carried her to the bed. I switched a lamp on. She turned the other way, poised like a hair trigger, her fist shoved in her mouth. I ran and got a washcloth—I was incredibly efficient—and folded it over on her forehead. I kneeled down beside her. I kissed her. I held her fist to my lips.

"And now do you still hear them?"

She shook her head no.

"Don't be afraid, it'll be all right," I said.

But what did I know? Dumb-ass that I was, what was I supposed to tell her? What could I promise her? Did I hear them in *my* head, those goddamn voices? I bit my lips fiercely. Next thing you know, I'd be singing her a lullaby, or offering her a cup of poppy-flower tea. So I stayed close, tense and silent, about as useful as a refrigerator at the North Pole. Long after she'd gone to sleep and I'd turned off the light, I was still there, eyes wide open in the dark, waiting for a tribe of banshees to come screaming out of the night. I'm sure I wouldn't have known what to do.

We came home two days later and I immediately made an appointment for myself with the doctor. I felt tired, and my tongue was covered with bumps. He made me sit down between his legs. He was wearing a karate outfit, with a small light bulb strapped to his forehead. I opened my mouth, death ringing in my soul. It took three seconds.

"Vitamin overdose," he said.

I coughed delicately into my fist while he filled out some forms.

"Uh, doctor, I wanted to tell you . . . there's something else bothering me. . . ."

"Huh?"

"Sometimes I hear voices. . . ."

"It's nothing," he said.

"Are you sure?"

He leaned over his desk and handed me the prescription. His eyes became two tiny black slits, and his mouth twisted into a kind of smile.

"Listen to me, young man," he snickered. "Hearing voices, or punching a clock for forty years of your life, or marching behind a flag, or reading the stock market returns, or tanning yourself under a sunlamp . . . what's the difference, really? Believe me—don't worry about it. We all have our little quirks."

After a few days my bumps went away. Time seemed to have gone haywire. It wasn't yet summer, but the days were already warm, white sunlight sprinkling the streets from dawn till dusk. Delivering pianos in such weather was like pulling teeth, but things had gotten back to normal. The pianos were starting to get to me, though—it sometimes felt like I was selling coffins.

Naturally I avoided saying this out loud, especially when Betty was around. I didn't want to rock the boat. I wanted to keep swimming, making sure her head stayed above water. I kept all daily problems to myself, never saying a word to her about them. I had acquired a certain look in my eye which I used to stare down people who threatened to bother me. Folks are quick to recognize someone who would just as soon kill them as say hello.

I did a good job of keeping trouble away from her. Things went fairly well. What I didn't like were the times I'd find her sitting in a chair, staring into space. Or when I had to call to her two or three times, or go and shake her. It caused certain physical problems too. Saucepans burning, bathtubs overflowing, and washing machines turning with nothing in them. But all in all it wasn't horrible. I'd learned that you can't live under the sky without seeing a few clouds. Most of the time I was happy with the way things were. I wouldn't have traded places with anyone.

Along the way, I noticed something strange happening to me. Though I had not, in the end, become the writer she dreamed of, and though I could never put the world at her feet—no use looking back—still, I was able to give her all that was inside me, all that I had to give. It wasn't easy, though. I found myself producing these spoonfuls of honey each day, but not knowing what to do with them. They accumulated into a stone that swelled in my stomach—a small rock. I felt like I had an armload of presents and no one to give them to. As if I'd grown a new, useless muscle, or had arrived with a pile of gold bullion on Mars. It did no good to cart pianos around until my veins were ready to pop, or to run around the house puttering—I simply could not exhaust myself. I could not sap the ball of energy that was inside me. On the contrary—fatigue seemed to feed it. And even if Betty herself didn't use it, it was hers, I'd given it to her. I couldn't do anything else with it. I felt sympathy for the general who has hundreds of bombs on his hands, and no war.

I had to watch myself closely—holding onto such a treasure made me nervous. I almost lost Bob as a friend because of it. I'd gone to give him a hand with his inventory. We were on our knees among the boxes, and for some reason we got to talking about women. He was the one who started it—it was not exactly my favorite topic of discussion. The gist of what he said was that he was dissatisfied.

"You don't have to look too far," he said. "Mine has hot pants, and yours is half crazy. . . ."

Without thinking, I grabbed him by the neck and plastered him against the wall, between the instant mashed potatoes and the Cheez Whiz. I nearly strangled him.

"Never say that again about Betty!" I growled.

I let him go. I was shaking with anger, he was coughing. I left without saying a word. Back at the house, I calmed down. I regretted what had happened. Betty was fixing something in the kitchen, so I took advantage of the situation. I took the phone into the bedroom. I sat down.

"Bob . . . it's me. . . ."

"What, you forget something? Wanted to know if I was still alive?"

"I don't take back what I said, Bob, but . . . I don't know . . . I didn't mean to do it. Let's forget it ever happened. . . ."

"It feels like I got a scarf around my throat, made out of fire. . . ."

"I know. I'm sorry."

"Shit, don't you think you went a little overboard?"

"I don't know. Only real Love and real Hate can make you do great things."

"Yeah? Well, then you want to tell me what you used to write your book?"

"I loved it, Bob. I really loved it!"

Bob was one of the privileged few who had read my manuscript. He'd made such a big deal out of it that I finally gave in. I went and got my only copy out of the bottom of a bag. I snuck out of the house with it while Betty was singing in the shower. I really love the way you write, he told me later—but why isn't there any story?

"I don't know what you mean, Bob—no story . . ."

"You know what I mean. . . ."

"No, honestly. Bobby, don't you get enough stories every morning in the newspaper? Aren't you a little sick of reading police novels, or science fiction, or the funnies? Haven't you had it UP TO HERE with all that crap? Don't you want a breath of fresh air for a change . . . ?"

"Nah, all that other stuff bores me stiff. All those things that they've been publishing for the last ten years—I can't get past the first twenty pages. . . ."

"Of course. Most of the people who write nowadays have lost the faith. You've got to feel the energy in a book, the faith. Writing a book should be like knee-jerking four hundred pounds—you should see the author's veins pop."

This conversation had taken place a month earlier. I realized now that my readership was too small to go around strangling them, especially the readers I needed to help me finish my roof. There were certain things I couldn't do alone. It had been Betty's idea to do it, but it was me who did it.

The idea was to remove about six square yards of roofing and replace it with glass.

"Do you think it's possible?" she'd asked.

"I'd be lying if I said it wasn't."

"Then why not do it?"

"Listen, if you say you really want it, then I'll give it a try."

She gave me a hug. I went up into the attic to see what I was in for. I was in for trouble. I came back down and hugged her.

"I think I deserve a second helping," I whispered.

The job was almost finished. All that was left was to waterproof the joints and install the panes. Bob was supposed to come over in the afternoon to help me carry the glass up, but after the little incident that morning, I was afraid he would manage to forget. I was wrong.

It was extremely hot up on the roof. Betty handed us some beers. She was very excited about spending our first night under the stars—she even laughed once or twice. God knows I would have turned the house into Swiss cheese if she'd have asked me to.

We put our tools away in the last rays of sunset. Betty climbed up to join us with a few Carlsbergs. We spent a while up there together, shooting the breeze, squinting into the light. Things seemed absolutely clear.

After Bob left, we emptied the attic and swept it out. Then we brought the mattress up, along with some munchies and the minimum necessary to avoid dying of thirst. We put the mattress right under the window. She fell backward onto it, her hands clasped behind her head. The night was upon us. We could already see two stars, up to the left. A whole week's work. The sky was a bargain at twice the price. I asked myself whether we should eat a little or fuck first.

"Hey, do you think we'll see the moon go by?" she asked.

I started unbuttoning my pants.

"I don't know . . . maybe. . . ."

My own tastes were simpler. I didn't have to go searching the sky for what was in my own backyard. Her underpants knew me so well, I could pet them without getting bitten. I looked under her skirt and found that I had only three fingers left. It didn't bother me at all.

"Wow, I see shooting stars . . . !" she said.

"I know what I'm wishing for. Try not to add anything else to the order."

"No, I mean REAL ONES!!"

I knew that it was either me or the sky. I didn't chicken out. I decided to fight to the finish. I shoved my head down between her legs. I more or less ate her panties whole. Where were all our problems now? Where was all the shit of the last few weeks? Where was Paradise? Where was Hell? Where had it gone to, the invisible machine that had been grinding away at us? I spread her crack and put my face in it. You're on the beach, Daddy-o, I said to myself, you're on a deserted beach, with waves rolling in, lapping at your lips. Daddy-o, I understand why you don't ever want to stand up again.

When I picked my head up, I was glowing like a nebula. My eye was totally glued shut.

"It's a little annoying—I've lost my sense of depth perception," I said.

She smiled. She pulled me to her and cleaned my eye with her tongue. I went inside her then, and for quite a while I heard nothing more about the sky—I simply felt the stars behind me, gliding gently past.

Betty was especially into it that night. I didn't have to outdo myself to ring her chimes. It thrilled me to see her enjoying it. I even slowed down to make it last longer. She got lathered up before I did. I felt it coming. I thought about the Big Bang theory. We lay there stuck to each other for a good ten minutes afterward, then dug into the chicken. I'd brought up a bottle of wine, too. By the end of dinner her cheeks were light pink and her eyes shone. It was rare that I saw her so calm and relaxed, so—how can I say it—almost happy . . . yes . . . almost happy. It made me forget to sweeten my yogurt.

"How come you're not like this more often?" I asked.

She looked at me in such a way that I didn't want to repeat the question. Why insist? We'd already discussed it a hundred times. Why always come back to it? Was it that I still believed in the magic of words? I remembered perfectly our last conversation on the subject. It hadn't been very long ago. I knew it by heart. Jesus Christ, she'd said, shivering, can't you see that life is against me—that all I have to do is want something to know that I can't have it? I can't even have a baby. . . .

When she said that, I could see the doors slamming shut all

around her, and there was nothing I could do to open them. There was no use arguing, no use trying to show her how wrong she was, how easily things could be worked out. There'll always be some joker around who shows up to treat a third-degree burn with a glass of water. Me, for instance.

23

It was a little white building near the outskirts of town, in a fairly deserted neighborhood. I could see people walking past the window of the office on the ground floor, just above the garage. It was early summer, about eighty in the shade. At around two o'clock, I crossed the street and stood by the garage door, pretending to tie my shoes.

I'd been there for only a minute when I saw a pair of pants legs stop in front of me. I looked up slowly. Even as a man I can't stomach that kind of asshole: a jerk, kind of flushed, flabby around the middle, a lecherous look on his face—the kind you see all over.

"So, having trouble with your shoelaces . . . ?" he murmured.

I stood up fast. I got my knife out. I held it discreetly under his nose.

"Buzz off, fuzznuts," I growled.

The dude turned white, then jumped back, his eyes wide. His lips were like the petals of a rotten flower. I made like I was going to lunge at him, and he took off at a run. He stopped at the corner, called me a bitch, then disappeared.

I bent back down over my shoelaces. It was past two o'clock. I'd noticed that they were never exactly on time. All I could do was be patient, and hope that no more perverts came along. In spite of everything, I was calm. It seemed too unreal to be completely true. When I saw the steel door go up, I flattened myself against the wall. I heard the van start up inside. I hugged my bag against my chest. I held my breath. The sun started vibrating. There was no one in sight. I bit my lip. I had a bad taste in my mouth—sort of chemical.

The van pulled out slowly. My only fear was that the guy would see me in the rearview mirror. I took my chances anyway, hoping that anyone pulling into the street out of a garage would look STRAIGHT AHEAD. I was counting on it, anyway. As soon as the delivery truck had pulled out, I slipped inside the garage. I backed into a shadow till the door closed. I swallowed my saliva—it was like swallowing peanut butter.

I stayed there without moving for five minutes. Nothing happened. I breathed. I grabbed my tits, which had fallen down, and put them back where they belonged. I must have measured fifty-five inches around the bosom, little points sticking out through my shirt. It kept me warm. I'd put my jacket on so I wouldn't be noticed too much on the street, but it wouldn't close all the way. I'd put on little white gloves to cover the hair on my hands. For my legs, I'd just worn pants. I'd settled on a short blond wig—a tad trendy for my taste. It was either that or a twenty-inch bun—they were out of stock till next week. I took my sunglasses off and got a little mirror out of my purse to see if my makeup had smeared.

No, everything was in order. I'd done a good job—shaved three times in a row, put on a little cream, some foundation, and finally some rather violent red lipstick. All in all, I looked pretty good. Burning body and icy face—just the kind of girl who would make me nervous. I slid my glasses down to the end of my nose. I hadn't done my eyes. I waited another minute until I felt perfectly calm, then I got on with it.

On the side, there was an open door that led to a little hallway. To my left, the exit—an unbelievable collection of bars and deadbolts. To my right, a stairway going up to the offices. I was struck by the surprising simplicity of it all—I viewed it as a sign from destiny. I took the Barracuda out of my bag. It was an imitation, a perfect imitation—it even scared me. I started up the stairs like a hungry panther.

On the second floor I spotted my man. He was sitting at a desk with his back to me—a young guy of about twenty-five, with pimples on his neck, trying to make it big in life. He was devouring one of those magazines that tells you about the sex lives of famous actors. I shoved the barrel of the Barracuda a good half-inch into his ear, holding one finger up to my lips. He understood—he wasn't as stupid as he looked. Still warming his ear, I took his hands and put them behind his back. I got a roll of adhesive tape out of my bag—extra-strong and three inches wide. When you get a package plastered together with that stuff it's enough to drive you crazy. I pulled a piece off with my teeth and with one hand wrapped five yards of it around his wrists. It took a while, but I had all afternoon. I took his gun off him and taped him to the chair.

"I swear, I'm not going to try anything," he said. "I don't want to get hurt. Don't worry. . . ."

I leaned down to tie his legs. I caught him looking at my chest. I straightened up. It was as if he'd touched me—it was all I could do not to slap his face. I slapped it anyway. He yelped. I put my finger back up to my lips.

Now all I had to do was wait. Think and wait. I glanced at the electronic door-security system. It was easy to figure out. I crossed my legs and sat down in a corner of the office. I smoked a cigarette. The little jack-off gave me the once-over with velvety eyes.

"Golly . . . I mean, golly—you can't imagine how much I admire you," he gushed. "You got to have some kind of nerve to do this. . . ."

He was wrong. Courage had nothing to do with it. Watching Betty sink deeper every day would make knocking over a bank—or blowing up half the world—seem like child's play. Actually, it was not exactly a bank. It was a company that handled surveillance equipment and armored cars. They transported the daily receipts of certain department stores and toll booths. I'd followed them for a few days. I realized that it would be ridiculous to try anything while they were out on their rounds. Those guys were so jumpy—one sneeze and they'd turn you into a screen door. That's why I decided to wait for them in a more relaxed atmosphere—at their home base.

"If you'd like some coffee, there's a Thermos in the bottom drawer," said my admirer.

He devoured me with his eyes. I pretended to ignore him. I poured myself a cup of coffee.

"What's your name?" he asked. "I just want to be able to remember your first name. I swear I won't tell anybody. . . ."

He got on my nerves. There was a good side, though—him talking later, about what a helluva gal I was, would help me cover my tracks. For good measure, I rubbed my chest a little, just to see him change color.

"Jesus, could we open a window?" he said.

From time to time I got up to look out the window. The street was quiet. I never imagined it would all go so well. You could hear birds singing in the trees. The telephone hadn't rung once, and no one came to the door. It seemed like a gag. Once or twice I caught myself yawning It was hot. From the moment the guy saw me run my tongue over my lips, he got delirious.

"Untie me," he said. "I can help you. I can cover you when the others come back—the bastards. Anyway, I'm sick of this job. I'll go away with you—we can ransack the countryside. . . . Why won't you talk to me . . . ? Why don't you trust me . . . ?"

To finish him off, I ran my hand through my hair. It was greasy. Good thing I was wearing gloves. He stuck his neck out toward me and let out a little whimper.

"Oh please," he cried. "Be extra careful of the fat one, the fattest of the three. . . . Don't trust him. . . . He'll shoot you without a second thought. . . . It's already happened several times. . . . He's wounded pedestrians. . . . Oh that bastard, Henry . . . You better let me handle him, ma'am, I won't let him harm a hair on your head. . . ."

I was bored but calm. I'd stopped letting things get to me. Except for Betty, I cared about nothing. I was happy to have something specific to do—it eased my soul. Unless something really went haywire, they wouldn't knock themselves out over a simple crime of passion. To get a little peace, I sat down behind him. I played with his gun. His was a real one—somehow you could tell by touching it. I imagined what it would be like to give myself a bullet in the mouth. It made me smile. I was as capable of doing it as I was incapable of saying why life was worth living. I just felt it. The young dude craned his neck, trying to see me behind him.

"Why are you staying back there?" he complained. "What did I do? Just let me look at you. . . ."

The restrooms were at the bottom of the stairway. I went down to take a piss. I took my wig off and fanned myself with it. I had no real plan. I didn't have a stopwatch or a can of tear gas. I worked by feel, as they say. The truth is that I had other things on my mind; I had enough problems without having to worry about the details. I could understand how you'd want to cover every angle of a bank robbery when money is your prime goal—but what did money mean to me? What difference could piles of money possibly make in my life? Given where we'd come to, I was willing to try anything, though. Anything I could for her. That's what it was all about.

The guy nearly cried tears of joy when I came back.

"Oh Lord . . . I was afraid you'd gone. I was just beside myself. . . ."

I blew him a kiss. He closed his eyes with a sigh. I glanced at
the clock on the wall. The others would be back any minute now.
I grabbed Romeo's chair and tilted it back on two legs. I dragged
him into the corner of the room, where the open door would hide
him. He tried to kiss my hand on the way, but I was too quick
for him. I poured myself another cup of coffee. I looked out onto
the street, keeping my distance from the windows.

It seemed like forty years since they'd left in the van. Since
then, things in the street had changed. Not much excitement.
The way the world looked to me, I preferred to slide through it
rather than ram up against it. At thirty-five you don't want to be
bothered anymore. This requires a certain amount of cash. Seeing
all those faraway lands can run up a bill. Sliding through costs you
your weight in gold. Still, I was willing to go away with her if it
would give her a break. In a way, I was already packing the bags.

The guy's voice made me jump.

"I have an idea—why don't you take me hostage? I could be
your insurance. . . ."

This reminded me that I'd forgotten something. I taped his
mouth shut—three layers of adhesive tape around his head. Without warning, he leaned forward and rubbed his forehead on my
chest. I jumped back.

"Oh Jesus, Mary, and Joseph!" he said with his eyes.

Five minutes later the other three arrived. I watched the delivery van come down the street. When it stopped in front of the
garage door, I pushed the button OPENGAR, then counted to
ten before pushing CLOGAR. I knew that I was starting the
second crap-shoot. I wasn't worried.

I flattened myself behind the door. This time it wasn't the
Barracuda in my hand—it was the real thing. I heard the door
close downstairs, and the sound of conversation. Their voices
carried well.

"Listen, man," one of them said. "When your old lady tells you she has a headache on the night you feel like fucking, just tell her, Don't worry, I won't touch your head."

"Shit, that's a laugh. You think that's all there is to it? You know Maria. . . ."

"Hey, man, she's no different from the rest. They all get headaches sooner or later. Have you ever noticed how when you come home with the paycheck at the end of the month, they never ask for an aspirin?"

I heard them yukking it up in the staircase.

"Yeah, Henry—that's fine for you. . . ."

"Shit, man, do what you want. You want to bust your balls for nothing your whole life? That's exactly what they want. . . ."

They came in, single file, carrying small canvas sacks. I spotted the fat one right off, the one named Henry. He was wearing sandals. As for the other two—how they had escaped retirement was beyond me. Before they could say boo, I had kicked the door closed. They turned toward me. For a millionth of a second, Henry's eyes met mine. I didn't give his brain the time to react. I looked at his feet and fired a bullet into his big toe. He collapsed, screaming. The other two dropped their sacks and put their hands up. I had the situation well under control.

While Henry was writhing on the floor, I tossed them the roll of adhesive tape. I motioned to them to tie up their friend. They snapped to. He put up a struggle, but they had him wound up tight in three seconds flat, telling him over and over not to be a jerk. Then I made a sign for them to tie their own feet. They would have made some kind of storekeepers, those two—just aim something between their eyes and they do whatever you say. I looked at the shabbier of the two and signaled him with my white glove—translation: Tie your pal's hands together, you old fart. When he'd finished, I pointed my finger at him. He smiled sadly.

"Listen, miss, I don't think I can do myself myself."

I shoved my barrel up his nose.

"No, no . . . wait . . . I'll give it a try!!"

He did the best he could—he used his forehead, his teeth, his knees—but he made it. Now that all three of them were tied up, I relieved them of their guns, then I straightened up and looked over at lover-boy, bound tight to his chair. He had circles of joy under his eyes.

Henry was whining, growling, and swearing. A stream of drool ran down his face to the linoleum. Since I didn't want any fuss, I grabbed the roll of tape and crouched down next to him. His foot was still pouring blood. His sandal was ruined. I congratulated myself on having bought the large size—there were still at least ten yards left, ideal for guys like me who are bad at tying knots. He looked up at me and turned red.

"You dirty fucking whore," he said. "If I ever get ahold of you, you'll start by sucking my dick!"

I knocked his front teeth out when I shoved the barrel in his mouth. Even a dirty fucking whore has feelings. I did it for all women who have headaches, for Maria and the others, all my sisters-in-misery: the ones that get razzed in the streets, hit on in the subways, all the women who have ever met a Henry. If I hadn't left mine at home, I swear I would have made him eat a box of Tampax. Sometimes when I see how men are, it makes me want to send a blessing to all the world's women—I don't know why I don't. He spit up a little blood. In his anger, a few small blood vessels in his eyes had burst. I had to pull my gun out of his mouth to gag him. This gave him a chance to say one last word:

"You just signed your death warrant."

I refrained from crying on the office equipment. I wanted silence. I wound the tape a few extra times over his eyes. He was starting to look like the Invisible Man, only shinier and a little more crumpled. The other two were quieter—I merely stuck a symbolic piece of tape over their crummy mouths. I stood up, thinking that the hard part was over. The idea made me smile. I didn't want to contradict myself—I pretended that I didn't know that the hard part always lies ahead.

Though I still felt completely calm, I didn't want to drag my ass. I picked up the money bags. I broke open the clasps and emptied them onto the desk—six sacks full of bills, with rolls of coins at the bottom. I put the bills in my bag. I left the change, afraid that it would be too heavy. I was on my way out the door when the young guy yelled, to get my attention. He motioned with his chin to the wall safe. What a nice boy—he had foresight. But I had a nice wad of bills already. I wasn't looking to become independently wealthy. I mimed that, really, this would do nicely, thanks. He looked like he was going to cry. Since the others couldn't see me, I took a ballpoint pen from the desk and came up behind him. I opened one of his hands and wrote JOSE-PHINE in it. He closed his fingers with the tenderness of some-one holding a butterfly with a broken leg. Just before going out the window I turned and noticed a big tear roll down his cheek.

The yard was overgrown and deserted. I ran through the weeds and jumped over the wall on the other side. My throat was dry, probably from not having said a word all afternoon. I turned right, holding onto my tits for dear life, and ran past the backyards at a sprint without seeing anyone, then crossed a big vacant lot which went right up to the railroad tracks. I climbed the embankment without slowing down, crossed over the tracks, and went down the other side. My lungs were on fire. Luckily, the supermarket parking lot was close by. It was the best I could do to keep my car from standing out—my LEMON YELLOW sedan.

Nobody noticed me as I slipped into the front seat. Nobody ever notices anything in a supermarket parking lot—it's the kind of place that drives you half crazy. I was dripping sweat all over. I put the bag down next to me and looked around while I caught my breath. Nearby, a fat lady was trying to stuff an ironing board into a Fiat 500. We stared at each other for a few seconds. I waited. She finally drove off with her door open, leaving me alone. I opened the glove compartment. I took out some Kleenex and makeup remover—hypoallergenic. Twenty percent of its ingredients were inert, and the other eighty percent weren't too exciting either.

I unfolded the Kleenex between my legs, keeping an eye on the parking lot. I soaked it with the makeup remover. No one was around. I held my breath, then shoved my face into it. For the first time that afternoon, I felt a little sick. I flung the used tissue out the window. The plastic bottle let out obscene noises and spurts of white gunk. I scrubbed as if I wanted to take my skin off. I ripped off my glasses, I ripped off my wig, I ripped off my falsies, and stuffed everything in my bag. Out of breath, I turned the rearview mirror toward me. All that was left was a little tan spot. I wiped it off in one swipe. Josephine was all gone now, wiped away onto small pieces of tissue. I wadded them up into a ball and threw them under my tires as I pulled away.

I drove home slowly. I got there just in time to turn off the front burner on the stove. I watched the black contents twist and sizzle in the bottom of the saucepan. I opened the windows, then went up into the attic. She was smoking a cigarette, playing pick-up sticks on the mattress. A gold light poured in through the roof, making the dust particles dance. I threw the bag on the bed. She jumped.

"Shit, you made me move," she said.

I slid in next to her.

"Boy, baby, am I ever wasted. . . ."

I ran my fingers through her hair. She smiled.

"So, how'd it go with your customer?" she asked. "You hungry? I heated up the ravioli downstairs."

"I'm fine. Don't worry about me. . . ."

I finished off a stale beer that was sitting there. Then I opened the bag.

"Look what I found during my travels . . ." I said.

She raised herself up on one elbow.

"My God, what's all this money?! Jesus, there's piles of it!!"

"Yeah, there's quite a bit. . . ."

"What's it for?"

"For whatever you want."

She reached in to see. When her hand touched the falsies she let out a scream. She pulled the rest of my disguise out of the bag. It seemed to interest her more than the money. Her eyes were like Christmas Eve.

"Ooooo, what *is* all this?"

I had decided not to go into it. I shrugged my shoulders.

"I don't know," I said.

She lifted the bra up by a strap. The boobs spun gently, in the infinitely tender light that enveloped us. Like a merry-go-round. It seemed to hypnotize her.

"Holy shit, you absolutely have to put this on—it's incredible!!"

But I didn't feel much like clowning around. Suddenly the day's caper had wiped me out.

"You're kidding," I said.

"Shit no, hurry up. . . ."

I pulled up my shirt and put it on. Betty got up on her knees to applaud. I struck a few poses, batting my eyes. As one might have expected, I wound up putting on the wig and gloves too. I hadn't wanted to, but seeing her have so much fun was like witnessing a miracle.

"Hey, you know what's missing?" she said.

"Yeah, a plastic vagina . . ."

"A makeup session!"

"Oh no . . ." I whined.

She sprang to her feet, all excited.

"Don't move—I'll get my makeup kit. . . ."

"All right . . ." I sighed. "But don't fall down the stairs, honeybunch. . . ."

Around one o'clock in the morning, I whispered one last word in her ear, as she dozed in my arms:

"By the way, while I'm thinking of it . . . if anyone ever asks where I was today—we spent the whole day together."

"Right. Even though I spent the afternoon fucking a gorgeous blonde. . . ."

"You don't have to bother telling them that. . . ."

I waited until she was sound asleep, then I got up. I went to shower and take off my makeup. I had a snack in the kitchen. Whatever may happen, I said to myself, what I did today was not in vain. I came home with what I went out to get—something to make her happy, to make her smile. In the end it wasn't the money that did it—she'd more or less ignored the money—but I'd gotten what I wanted. Yes, my efforts had been rewarded a hundredfold. I could have cried tears of joy right there in the kitchen at the drop of a hat—just a few discreet ones that I could hide under my foot.

I reminded myself that just two days earlier I'd found her naked, stiff as a board, in the corner of the bedroom. It wasn't the first time, either. She still heard the voices. Things were still overflowing and burning all over the place. I didn't need glasses to see the writing on the wall.

I managed to find a slice of ham in the fridge. I rolled it up like a crêpe and bit into it. It was totally flavorless. I was still alive. Things were exactly as they should be.

24

There was one Sunday that was no fun at all. The weather, however, was beautiful. We got up fairly early. At the stroke of nine, there was loud knocking on the door downstairs. I slipped on some shorts and went down to see. It was a guy in a suit—perfect hair, little black hanky, perfectly folded, and a BIG SMILE.

"Good day, sir. Do you believe in God?"

"No."

"Well, then I'd like to talk to you. . . ."

"Wait," I said. "I was just joking. Of course I believe."

Big smile. VERY BIG SMILE.

"Even better. We put out a small booklet. . . ."

"How much?"

"All monies go directly for . . ."

"Naturally. How much?"

"Sir, for the price of five packs of cigarettes . . ."

I took a bill out of my pocket I gave it to him and closed the door. Knock, knock. I opened the door.

"You forgot your booklet . . ." he said.

"No I didn't," I said. "I don't need it. I've just bought a little piece of Heaven, haven't I . . . ?"

While I was closing the door again, a ray of sunshine smacked me right in the eye. If it had been my mouth I might have said, "While I was closing the door a sourball slid onto my tongue." A vision of sea and waves came over me. I ran up the stairs. I sent the sheets flying all over the room.

"Hey, I feel like seeing the sea!" I shouted. "Don't you?"

"It's sort of far, but if you want to . . ."

"In two hours you'll be roasting on the beach."

"I'm as good as ready," she said.

I watched her stand up in the middle of the bed, nude, as if hatching from some striped egg. I put my naughty thoughts off for later, though—the sun wouldn't wait.

It was a very chic spot—very trendy—but then there are assholes everywhere. They stay around all year, so the stores and restaurants stay open. Finding a beach that isn't too dirty means paying for it. We paid for it. There was almost no one there. We swam and swam, then swam some more. Then we got hungry. You had to pay to take a shower, too . . . and to get your car out of the lot. And for this, and for that. In the end, I just kept my hands loaded with change, ready to toss it away on the slightest pretext. The place seemed like a huge money machine—nothing was free.

We ate at a sidewalk café, under a fake straw umbrella. On the other side of the street were about twenty young women, every one with a four- or five-year-old child—fair-haired boys with fathers in business and mothers who either sat home getting bored or went out to get bored. The waiter explained that the little darlings were there to audition for a commercial—to bring us to tears in a spot for an insurance company: BUILD THEM A FUTURE. I thought it was pretty funny. One look at those kids, full of joy, good health, and money, and you really didn't worry much about their future—depending on how you looked at it, of course.

By the time we dug into our peach melba, they'd already been there for an hour, getting restless in the sun. The kids were running all over the place. The mothers were getting nervous. From time to time they'd call one over to fix his hair or brush away some invisible speck of dust. The sun was turning into an amphetamine rain—a crazy 110-volt shower.

"Jesus, they really got to want that stupid check," said Betty.

I glanced over my sunglasses at the ladies, swallowing a scoopful of whipped cream and candy sprinkles.

"It's not just the check. They want to build a lasting monument to their beauty."

"They got to be crazy, leaving those kids out in the sun like that. . . ."

The ladies' jewels glinted in the sun. We could hear them sighing and bitching from across the street. I looked down, trying to concentrate on my peach melba. Madness is everywhere. Not one day goes by without human misery pouring forth before your very eyes. It doesn't take much. Small details: some guy who catches your eye at the local market, just getting into your car or buying a newspaper, closing your eyes in the afternoon and listening to the sounds of the street—or having to deal with a pack of chewing gum that has eleven sticks in it. It doesn't take much to see that the world is always laughing behind your back. I rid my mind of all those women, because I knew them too well—I didn't need any more examples. I didn't plan on hanging around. They could stay there burning to a crisp on the sidewalk if they wanted—*we* were going back to the beach. Nothing but sea and sky, a giant umbrella, the reassuring clink of ice cubes on glass. I drew a line through the sidewalk and the women—crossed them out—then stood up confidently and went straight to the bathroom. I realized later that it's a mistake to underestimate the enemy. Still, we don't have eyes in the back of our heads.

I was gone for quite a while. There were pay toilets and I was out of change. I had to break a bill at the cash register. The thing kept flushing by itself, and the stall door was on a timer. . . . All in all I wasted a lot of time. When I got back to the table, Betty was gone. I sat down. A thin veil of worry came over me. It suddenly seemed to be much warmer out. I noticed that she hadn't finished her dessert—the vanilla ice cream glistened. I was hypnotized by it.

I came to, thanks to the women yelling across the street. I hadn't paid attention to what was going on—just some flock of seagulls squawking in the sun for no reason—then I saw that they were genuinely upset. They were looking in my direction. One of them in particular seemed especially shook up.

"Tommy! Oh, my little Tommy!" she screamed.

I figured that little Tommy had gotten sunstroke, or melted, like snow. It didn't tell me where Betty was.

I was going to yell to them that I wasn't a doctor, when I saw a dozen of them start across the street. I was going to yell that there was nothing I could do, but something stopped me. They stepped over the little wall that separated the café from the sidewalk, and surrounded me. I tried to smile. Tommy's mother seemed totally out of her mind—she ogled me as if I were Quasimodo, and her friends weren't much better. I was getting bad vibrations. Before I could figure out what was happening, the woman threw herself at me, demanding that I give her her child back. I fell over backward in my chair, baffled. I scraped my elbow. I stood up. Thoughts were going through my mind at the speed of light, but I couldn't manage to grab hold of one. The woman burst into tears, shrieking as if she wanted to burn me at the stake. They had formed a semicircle around me. They weren't bad looking, but at that precise moment I was probably not their type. One second more and they would jump me, I knew it. I knew, too, that I was going to have to pay for the heat, the wait, their boredom, and a hundred other things that weren't my fault. This got me so mad I couldn't even open my mouth. One of them had sky-blue fingernails—this in itself would have made me sick under normal circumstances.

"That girl you were with . . ." she hissed, "I saw her take off with my son . . . !"

"What girl?" I said.

By the time my words hit their ears, I had already jumped over three tables and was halfway inside the restaurant. I left them in the dust. Pack of witches. I heard them roaring, hot on my heels. I managed to close the door of the men's room before they got me. They didn't have the key. I held the door, looking around frantically. The waiter was finishing taking a piss. He raised his eyebrows. I pulled out a wad of bills. He agreed to hold the door for me. Behind the thin wooden panel, inlaid with cardboard Masonite, you could hear the women pounding and screaming. It was the kind of door you can go through like a ricecake, with one good kick. I stuffed two more bills in his pocket. Then I climbed out the window.

I found myself in a small courtyard leading to the kitchen. The garbage cans were overflowing, rusted in the sun. A cook came out, wiping the sweat off the back of his neck. I got an idea. Before he could open his mouth, I pulled out a bill and stuck it in his pocket, smiling. He smiled back. I felt like I had a magic wand—like with a little practice I could make doves appear. I took off through the back door, out into the street. I hotfooted it. I ran up the street, turning off at intersections, doing the sorts of things you can still do at thirty-five if you've stayed in shape. Leaping over parked cars, for example, or pulverizing your personal record for the four-hundred-yard dash—all the while looking behind yourself. After a while I thought I'd lost them. I stopped for a minute to catch my breath. There was a chair. I sat down.

I tried to think clearly and calmly. All I had to do, though, was think of her, and it was like a dragon coming and breathing flames on my brain, reducing everything to ashes. It was all I could do to stand back up, but I had the feeling that if I did, the rest would follow. I headed back toward the beach, keeping close to the wall. A warm breeze had come up. I had a mouth full of cotton. I came to the main drag and spotted my car parked in the distance. My first thought was to comb the city behind the wheel, but then I thought: Okay . . . so there you are—walking around with a kid who just spent two hours in the sun because his mother's a jerk, and now Tommy's tongue is hanging three yards out of his mouth—what do you do? Since you are not the kind of girl who goes chopping up little boys in dark alleys . . . what do you do?

Up the block, standing in the shade of a tree, was an ice cream vendor. I crossed the street, looking around. When he saw me coming, he took the cover off his freezer.

"Single? Double? Triple?" he asked.

"Nothing, thanks. You haven't by any chance seen a pretty brunette with a little boy about three or four years old, have you? They didn't come by to get an ice cream . . . ?"

"Yeah. The girl wasn't as pretty as all that, though. . . ."

I have often met people who are insensitive to beauty. I've never been able to figure out what their problem is, but I've always pitied them.

"My poor man, did you see which way they went . . . ?"

"Yes."

I waited for a few seconds. I ripped my guts open and got out my billfold. The regional customs were no longer amusing—I wanted to jam the whole wad down his throat. A small cloud of steam came out of the freezer. I gave him two bills without looking at him, felt them slide out of my hand.

"They went into the toy store over there. The little boy had blue eyes, he was about three feet tall—he got a double-dip strawberry. He wore a medal around his neck. It was about three o'clock. Now, the girl . . ."

"That's enough," I said. "Don't tell me too much, you'll lose money. . . ."

The store had three levels. A wan little salesgirl came over to me, with the look one often sees in the eyes of those who work for minimum wage. I got rid of her. There weren't many people. I combed the ground floor, then went upstairs. I hadn't forgotten that the savage horde was still hot on our heels; I knew that sooner or later they'd catch up with us. I was starting to get used to this sort of atmosphere—it seemed to follow Betty and me wherever we went. But hey, I told myself, we all have our moments. You have to be patient in life. I went through all the departments without finding her. I felt myself getting warmer, though. Burning, in fact. I went up to the top floor like I was climbing Mount Sinai.

Behind the counter stood a guy smiling, his arm resting on a pile of gift-wrapped packages. He had a manager's smile, and a double-breasted blazer with an overly exuberant pocket handkerchief. He was none too young—his skin sagged low under his eyes. His hanky looked like a small fireworks display. The minute he saw me he rushed over, grimacing or smiling—I couldn't figure out which—miming someone washing their hands.

"Excuse me, sir, but this level is closed."

"Closed?" I said.

I swept the place with my eyes. It seemed empty. On this floor they sold dart guns, cowboy suits, bows and arrows, robots, pedal cars—what you'd imagine. I breathed. I knew Betty was there.

"Perhaps you could come back another time . . ." he suggested.

"Listen, all I need is a laser missile-launching rifle—no gift-wrapping. It'll just take a minute. . . ."

"I'm afraid that's impossible. We've rented the entire floor to a customer."

"BETTY!" I called.

The guy tried to stop me, but I got past him. I heard him running, cursing behind me as I raced through the shelves, but he couldn't get near me—my body heat was radiating in all directions. I went all the way to the back of the store. I didn't find her. I stopped dead. The guy almost ran into me.

"Where is she?" I asked.

He didn't answer. I started to strangle him.

"Jesus Christ, she's my wife! I have to know where she is!"

He pointed to a platform with an Indian village on it.

"They're in the Chief's Teepee, but she doesn't want to be disturbed," he sputtered.

"Which one is it?"

"The one on sale. It's a very good buy. . . ."

I let go of his blazer, then climbed up onto the reservation. I went straight to the Chief's Teepee. I lifted the flap. Betty was smoking the peace pipe.

"Come in," she said. "Come in and sit down with us."

Tommy was wearing a headdress. He seemed totally relaxed.

"Hey, Betty, who's he?" he asked.

"He's the man in my life," she joked.

I crawled into the tent.

"It's crease-resistant," said the store manager, behind me.

I looked at Betty and nodded.

"Hey, you know his mother's looking all over for him? You know, we ought to get out of here. . . ."

She sighed, looking put-out.

"Okay. Give us five more minutes," she said.

"No way."

So saying, I leaned over and picked Tommy up under my arm. I almost got a tomahawk in the ear. I blocked it in mid-flight.

"Don't complicate things, Tommy, sweetheart," I said.

I walked over to the store manager. He was standing there, stiff as a tin soldier.

"We're going to leave him with you," I said. "His mother's coming by to get him in five minutes. Tell her we couldn't wait."

He looked like I'd told him he was getting a tax audit.

"What do you mean . . . ?"

I shoved Tommy into his arms, then felt Betty's hand on my shoulder.

"Wait just a second," she said. "I want to pay for all the presents."

We had to move fast. Navigate through reefs, calculate all risks. I got my money out, sensing a serious rise in my fever. Then one of two things happened: either I started getting delirious, or I heard voices coming from downstairs.

"Okay, how much?" I asked.

The aging playboy let go of the kid, concentrating on his calculations. He closed his eyes. In my nightmare, the stairway was trembling under the footsteps of a furious posse. Tommy grabbed a bow and arrow from a shelf. He looked at Betty.

"An' I want this, too."

"Shut up and behave yourself," I snarled.

The manager opened his eyes. He smiled, as if waking from a pleasant dream.

"I don't know. . . . Should I count the bow, too?"

"Absolutely not," I said.

Tommy started crying. I grabbed the bow out of his hand and threw it as far as I could.

"You're beginning to piss me off," I told him.

By now I felt the floor shaking under my feet. I was about to grab the salesman and shake a figure out of him, when a loud clamor swept through the floor like a sinister, fiery wind. I saw the women surge forth at the other end of the store. No one will believe me, but I swear I saw lightning coming out of their eyes—there were sparks all over the place. I gave Betty a sad look.

"Run, baby. Run," I said.

I hoped to be able to hold them off until Betty made it to the emergency exit. Instead of taking off, though, she just let out a sigh and stood there, her feet nailed to the floor.

"It's no use. . . . I'm tired," she murmured.

The women were halfway to us, screaming. They engulfed the shelves like a frothy wave. I threw my money in the air. The tacky old guy ran under the shower, his arms reaching up toward Heaven. I made my move with lightning speed—pivoted on one leg, picked Betty up in my arms, took off for the emergency exit, and sprang out into the light, in under four seconds.

I didn't look back to see if anyone's hand got caught in the door. I slammed it behind me and went out onto the fire escape overlooking a small street. I put Betty down. I held the door closed once again. I was in the same bind as before, only this time luck was on my side—I didn't have to pay anyone to get out of it. There was an old metal bar leaning against the wall. I spotted it just as the pounding began on the other side. An angel must have left me that bar—it was exactly the right length to wedge under the doorknob. Let them scream, I thought. I wiped my forehead. A blinding light pulsated all around us, hissing. Betty stretched herself. She smiled, and it almost put me over the edge. I ran down a whole flight of stairs, howling, then climbed back up on my tiptoes. Things were lightening up a bit behind the door. Betty was almost laughing. I motioned for her to hush.

"We won't go down, we'll climb over the roof," I whispered.

The roof, it turned out, was actually a huge terrace—a sort of sun-filled swimming pool. We hopped over the parapet. One last fist pounded the door, then there was silence. I went straight to the shade. I sat where the sun could hit only my legs. I reached out for Betty to come sit next to me. She seemed astonished to find herself there.

My plan was less than terrific. It involved a big risk, and this made me nervous. All they'd have to do was use their heads a little, and we'd be cornered—tarred, feathered, and burned at the stake. Still, I didn't have much choice. To try to make a run for the car, I'd have needed a girl who was very together.

This was not the case. Mine, it turned out, had lead in her shoes. I waited for a minute, then, taking every possible precaution, I went to scope out the main drag. The herd was running along the sidewalk. Those in the lead had already turned the corner. The sky was perfectly blue. The sea was calm and green. There was no beer in sight—nothing that could have distracted me. I walked across the terrace to see what things were like on the fire-escape side. In passing, I grabbed Betty by the chin and kissed her, thus summing up the situation.

"I want to go home," she murmured.

"Yeah," I said. "We'll be on our way in five minutes."

I flattened myself against a wall and watched the women arrive. In my opinion their relentlessness had something unhealthy about it—as if they were trying to solve some racial problem. I couldn't let them see me. I flattened myself like a pancake against my little piece of wall. It was all I could do to keep from lighting up a cigarette. I heard them babbling down below. Then I heard the sound of galloping. I stuck my head out and saw them heading back up the street, elbows pumping. Who knows? Maybe those little cunts were off, foaming at the mouth, to see contacts in high places.

I went back and sat down next to Betty, thinking that we might get out of this alive after all. I took her hand in mine and played with it. I felt her resist. The sun had calmed down, gotten over its hysteria—stopped forcing itself into every shadow. The light dimmed from high beams to medium. The terrace turned into a rectangular island of tar paper. It was nearly pleasant out. I can tell you in all honesty that I've known worse places than that. No sense exaggerating.

"See? You can see the ocean . . ." I said.

"Um-hm . . ."

"LOOK OVER THERE, SOME GUY'S WATER SKIING ON ONE LEG!"

She didn't look up. I put a lit cigarette in her mouth. I crossed my legs, staring at a spot on the horizon—there was nothing special about it, it just pleased me.

"I don't know why you did this," I said. "I don't want to know, and I don't want to talk about it. Let's just forget it ever happened."

She nodded slowly, without looking at me. I was content with this as a response—a flutter of eyelashes or the squeeze of a finger would also have done the trick. Though I never completely understand what some people say to me, I could roam around in Betty's silences without ever getting lost—it was like walking down the street of my hometown. I knew her better than I knew anything else in the world—at least eighty-five percent of it . . . something like that—so well, in fact, that I was never even sure she was moving her lips when I heard her talk. You've got to admit that sometimes life fills you with wonder, really knows how to get to you. And guys like me are the biggest pushovers.

We stayed there for a while, not saying anything. Strangely enough, I started to feel my oats again. I felt a smile spread across my face. I felt like I had the world by the short hairs. I could have pulled them if I wanted to. I didn't. I just let it all melt, like chocolate in the sun—not in my hand. I felt *there*, truly right *there*. I had no hesitations about taking the helm. It was the least of my worries. I'd never felt better on a terrace than at that moment. I strutted across the tar paper like a pilgrim entering the gates of Jerusalem. I could have given forth with a sweet little poem, but there was no time to waste thinking seriously—I had to get us out of there.

"Okay," I said. "You think you can run?"

"Yes," she answered.

"No, I mean run—I mean REALLY run, you get it—I'm talking like in the Olympics, and no looking back. Not like the last time."

"Right. Run. I know what run means. I'm not a moron."

"Great. I see you're feeling better already. Anyway, we'll find out soon enough. If you can't make it, wait for me here—I'll swing by with the car to pick you up."

She made a face at me, then jumped to her feet.

"You can talk to me that way when I'm eighty-five. . . ."

"I won't have the strength," I muttered.

Before going over the parapet, I went and checked out the street. The women were nowhere to be seen. Betty and I went down the fire escape on the front side of the building, our born-again legs hurrying us along. We hung by our hands from the bottom rung, then dropped to the sidewalk and took off up the street like bats out of hell.

Of all the girls I've known, Betty was by far the fastest runner. Running next to her was purely and simply one of the things I loved best. Usually, however, I preferred doing it in a more serene setting. This time, I didn't glance next to me to see her breasts dancing, nor did I ogle at the flush that rose in her cheeks. No, none of that—just a delirious dead run for the car.

We slammed the doors. I turned the key, and off we went. Pulling out onto the street, I almost burst out laughing. I felt it rising in my belly. Then I saw one of the women running along-side us. The windshield exploded. Glass fell like raindrops onto our legs. By sheer reflex, I managed to spit out a piece that had flown into my mouth. I put my foot to the floor, and tore out of there. Cursing, I zigzagged down the avenue, people honking behind me.

"Jesus fucking Christ, get down!" I yelled.

"Did we blow a tire?"

"No. They must have hired a hit man!"

She bent over to pick up something, by her feet.

"You can slow down now," she said. "It was just a beer can."

"A full one?"

We drove twenty-five miles, with our hair in the wind. Our eyes teared a little, but it was nice out and the sunset was lovely. We chewed the fat. Whoever invented the automobile must have been an illuminated, solitary genius. Betty had her feet stuck in the glove compartment. We stopped at a garage that had a sign: "WINDSHIELDS—IMMEDIATE INSTALLATION" We didn't even get out of the car while the guys did the job. We probably got in their way, but who gives a shit?

25

294 PHILIPPE DIJAN

It wasn't long after this episode that I started writing again. I didn't push it—it came by itself. I went about it very discreetly. I didn't want Betty to know. Usually I'd work at night. I'd shove my pad back under the mattress the moment Betty started moving next to me. I didn't want to get her hopes up. I didn't write like they did fifty years ago. Contrary to what you'd think, this was rather a handicap. It wasn't my fault that the world had changed. I didn't write like I did to upset people. Quite the opposite: I was a sensitive guy. It was they who upset me.

As the summer progressed, the piano sales dropped off. I didn't pull my hair out over it. I would close the store early, and when the mood was right, I would spend my time thinking about what I was going to write, or taking walks with Betty. We still had a wad of money left. Since she had no desire to go anywhere—she cared nothing for that, or for anything else—the money wasn't much good to us, except to pay bills or relieve the pressure of having to sell pianos to live. Haha! . . . To live! Money is one of those things that never keeps a promise.

Since I didn't kill myself working, it was no skin off my nose to get out my notebook at midnight or one in the morning and go at it till the wee hours of dawn. I slept a little in the morning and sometimes a few hours in the afternoon. I made progress, slowly. I felt like an overcharged battery. In the early morning, I'd erase all traces of the previous night's activities, throwing my beer cans in the trash, a cigarette stinging my eyes. I always looked at Betty before going to sleep, wondering if the few pages I'd scribbled were worthy of her. It was a question I liked to ask myself. It made me aim high. It made me humble.

During this whole period my brain seemed to be going at full tilt twenty-four hours a day. I knew that I had to work fast— VERY FAST. But it takes a lot of time to write a book. The very thought of it suffocated me with anxiety. I cursed myself for not having started sooner, for having waited so long to dive into that little navy-blue spiral notebook. Spiral. Shit, I answered myself, I'd like to have seen you try. You think it's easy? Think all you have to do is sit down at a table, and it pours out by itself? And those months of tossing and turning in bed, eyes wide open— crossing that desert, silent and gray, without seeing one little sparrow . . . wandering through the Great Desert of Dried-up Man. You think it was for laughs . . . ?

It's true, I couldn't have done otherwise. Still, I was crazy enough to imagine I could. I cursed Heaven for not having come down to touch me earlier. I had the horrible feeling that it was too late. It was yet another burden to bear. But I held it together. Maybe my chances were one in a million. Still, each night my pages piled up, like bricks to build something to protect her. It was like nailing the shutters closed while watching the hurricane well up on the horizon. After such a bad start, could a writer overcome such shit? Did the Kid have what it took to turn things around?

* * *

For a week it had been unbearably hot—I couldn't remember ever feeling anything like it. There wasn't a green blade of grass for miles around. A torpor had seized the town. The more nervous types took to looking at the sky, worried. It was around seven o'clock at night. The sun had gone down, but the streets, the sidewalks, the roofs, and the walls of the houses were still burning. Everyone was sweating. I went out to do some shopping. I spared Betty this particular chore. I came home, the trunk full to bursting, wet circles under my arms. Just before I got to the house, I passed an ambulance going in the opposite direction—sirens blaring, shiny as a new penny.

I sat up a little in my seat. I passed two cars that were dawdling. I started breathing hard. By the time I had parked in front of the house I was trembling, as if someone had slipped a noose around my neck. I couldn't say exactly when it was that I understood, it isn't important anyway. I ran up the steps, a knife in my stomach. At the top of the stairs I collided with Bob, kneeling on the floor. I sailed over him, falling into the room, toppling over chairs. I felt a warm liquid flowing under my head.

"BOB!" I screamed.

He jumped on me.

"Don't go in there!" he said.

I sent him rolling under the table. I could hardly talk. I lifted myself up on one elbow, then realized that it was water—it was sudsy water I felt in my hair. Someone must have tipped over a basin. I had trouble breathing. We stood up together. I looked around for her. There was only Bob and me in the room. I didn't know what the hell he was doing there. He rolled his eyes in my direction. I felt my face twist.

"Where is she?" I asked.

"Sit down," he said.

I ran into the kitchen. Nothing. I turned around. Bob was

standing in the doorway, one hand held out toward me. I flattened him against the wall with my shoulder, like a bull charging down an alleyway. There was a strange hissing in my ears. I literally flew toward the bathroom. The house seemed completely foreign to me. I grabbed the door and flung it wide open.

The room was empty. The light was on. The sink was full of blood. There were splatters all over the floor. I felt a spear go through my back, nearly knocking me to my knees. I couldn't breathe. There was a sound of breaking glass in my head—crystal. It was all I could do to close the door, what with all the demons pulling at it from the other side.

Bob came in, rubbing his shoulder. It must have been Bob. I was so busy trying to breathe that I couldn't talk.

"My God," he said. "I wanted to clean it all up. You didn't leave me enough time."

I spread my legs a little, for balance. I broke out in a cold sweat. He put his hand on my arm, I only saw him do it—I didn't feel a thing.

"It's messy, but it's not that bad," he said. "Luckily I came by when I did, to return the blender."

He looked at his shoes. "I was wiping up the blood by the door. . . ."

My arm shot out and grabbed him furiously.

"WHAT HAPPENED?" I shouted.

"She tore an eye out," he said. "With . . . with her hand."

I slid down the length of the door onto my heels. I was breathing now, but the air was on fire. He crouched down in front of me.

"Okay, look, it isn't all that serious," he said. "An eye isn't that serious. She'll be okay—hey, you hear me . . . ?"

He went and got a bottle out of the cupboard. He took a long swallow. I didn't want any. I just stood up and went to the window. I pressed my nose against the pane. I stayed there without moving. He went and got his water basin, and charged into the bathroom. I heard the water running. In the street nothing moved.

By the time he came out, I felt better. I was incapable of stringing two thoughts together, but I could breathe again. I went into the kitchen for a beer—my legs were unstable.

"Bob, take me to the hospital. I can't drive," I said.

"It's not worth it—you won't be able to see her right away. Wait a while."

I smashed the end of my beer can into the table. It exploded. "BOB, DRIVE ME TO THE FUCKING HOSPITAL!!"

He sighed. I gave him the keys to the Mercedes, and we went downstairs. Night had fallen.

I gritted my teeth all the way there. Bob talked to me, but I understood nothing. I sat there, leaning slightly forward, my arms folded. She's alive, I said to myself—she's alive. Slowly, I felt my jaws relax. I could swallow my saliva again. I woke up as if the car had just rolled over three times.

Going through the hospital doors, I realized why I had felt so strange when we'd come to visit Archie, why I'd felt so oppressed, what it all meant. I nearly blacked out again, nearly fell down flat, the monstrous odor sliding over my face, nearly put my head down, lost my strength. I got hold of myself at the last minute. But it wasn't me—it was her. I would have walked through walls for her if need be. I could have simply chanted her name like a mantra and, in so doing, passed right through. Once you know that, you can be grateful—you can be proud of having accomplished something. I shivered once, then went into the lobby. Into the planet of the damned.

Bob put his hand on my shoulder.

"Go sit down," he said. "I'll go get the scoop. Go ahead, go sit down. . . ."

There was an empty bench close by. I obeyed. If he'd told me to lie down on the floor, I'd have done it. As much as the urge to act set me on fire like a tuft of dried grass, the paralysis ran through my veins like a handful of blue ice cubes. I went from one state to the other, without transition. When I sat down, it was in my cold period—my brain was nothing but a soft, lifeless mass. I leaned my head back against the wall. I waited. I must have been near the kitchen. I smelled leek soup.

"Everything's all right," he said. "She's sleeping."

"I want to see her."

"Fine. Everything's arranged. You just have to fill out a few papers."

I felt my body start to warm up. I stood up and pushed Bob out of my way. My mind began to function again.

"Yeah, well, all that can wait," I said. "What room is she in?"

I saw a woman sitting in a glass office, looking in my direction, a stack of forms in her hand. She seemed capable of chasing someone up ten flights of stairs.

"Listen," Bob sighed. "You have to do this. Why make it difficult? She's got to sleep now, anyway. You can take five minutes to deal with the papers. Everything's fine. I tell you. There's no reason to worry anymore."

He was right, but there was this fire inside me that wouldn't stop burning. The woman waved her forms, motioning to me to come over. I suddenly felt surrounded by muscular male nurses, tough and mean. One, in fact, passed in front of me—a shark, forearms hairy and jaw square. I saw that it would do no good to play the human torch; I had to deal with the situation. I went to see what the woman wanted. I'd already capitulated to the Infernal Machine—I didn't want to get ground up by it, too.

She needed information. I sat down facing her. The whole time we talked, I wondered if she wasn't really a guy in drag.

"Are you the husband?"

"No," I said.

"A member of the family?"

"No, I'm everything else."

She raised her eyebrows. She seemed to think she was the key to the universe—the type who wouldn't dream of filling out forms haphazardly. She looked at me as if I was vulgar flotsam. I was forced to bow my head, in the hope of saving a few precious seconds.

"I live with her," I said. "I can probably tell you whatever you want to know."

She ran her tongue over her lipstick, seemingly satisfied.

"Fine, let's go on, then. Last name?"

I gave her the name.

"First name?"

"Betty."

"Elizabeth?"

"No, Betty."

" 'Betty' is not a real name."

I cracked my knuckles as discreetly as possible, leaning forward.

"Then what is it, in your opinion? A new brand of toothpaste?"

I saw her eyes spark. She tortured me for the next ten minutes after that: me helpless in my chair, treading water in her office—the longest route to Betty. After a while, I answered her questions with my eyes closed. In the end, I had to promise to come back later with the necessary papers. I'd completely gone south on certain things—numbers of this, and addresses of that, not to mention the things I never knew existed. She sat there twirling her pen between her lips, then came out with: "This woman you live with . . . you don't seem to know her very well. . . ."

But Betty, should I have known your blood type? The name of the one-horse town you came from? All your childhood diseases? Your mother's name? How you react to antibiotics? Was she right? Did I know so little about you? I asked myself this, not caring about the answer; then I stood up and backed out of the room, doubled over from low blows, apologizing for having caused her so much trouble. I even gave her a smile as I closed the door:

"What's the room number, again?"

"Second floor, room seven."

Bob was waiting in the lobby. I thanked him for having driven me there, then sent him home with the Mercedes. I told him not to worry, I'd make my own way home. I waited until he was completely out the door, then went to the bathroom to rinse my face. I felt better. I started to get used to the idea that she had torn her eye out. I remembered she had two of them. I became a little meadow under a blue sky—licking my own blades of grass after the rainstorm.

There was a nurse coming out of number seven when I arrived—a blonde with a flat behind and a pleasant smile. She knew who I was right away.

"Everything's fine. She needs to rest," she said.

"But I want to see her."

She stepped aside to let me in. I put my hands in my pockets and looked at the floor. I stopped at the foot of the bed. There was only a small light on. Betty had a wide bandage across her eye. She was sleeping. I looked at her for three seconds, then lowered my eyes. The nurse was standing behind me. Not knowing what else to do, I sniffled. I looked at the ceiling.

"I'd like a minute alone with her," I said.

"Okay, but no more than that . . ."

I nodded, without turning around. I heard the door close. There were some flowers on the nightstand. I went over and fiddled with them. Out of the corner of my eye I saw that Betty was breathing—yes, she was, no doubt about it. Though I wasn't sure it would do any good, I got out my knife and trimmed the stems of the flowers, so they'd live longer. I sat down on the edge of her bed and put my elbows on my knees, my head in my hands. It relaxed my neck. I felt together enough to caress the back of her hand. What a wonder, that hand, what a wonder—I hoped with all my heart that it was the other hand she'd used to do the dirty work. I hadn't fully digested all that yet.

I stood up and went to look out the window. It was night. Everything seemed to be moving on rollers. You have to recognize that no matter how you look at it, we take turns here on earth:

you take the day with the night; the joy with the sorrow, shake it up, and pour yourself a big glass of it every morning. Thus you become a man—nice to have you aboard, son . . . watch and see how incomparable and sad is the beauty of life.

I was wiping a drop of sweat off my cheek when I felt a finger tap me on the shoulder.

"Come on, let's leave her alone now. She won't wake up before noon tomorrow—we've given her some tranquilizers."

I turned toward the whispering nurse. I couldn't remember what I'd done that day, but I felt totally exhausted. I motioned to her that I'd follow. My general sensation was one of sliding along a river of lava. She closed the door behind us. I found myself standing out in the hallway with no idea of what my next move should be. She took my arm and led me toward the exit.

"Come back tomorrow," she said. "Hey, watch your step . . . !"

I suppose that being back out on the street was what woke me up. The air was soft and hot—a typical equatorial night. I was about a mile from the house. I walked across the street and bought a pizza from the local Italian. I stood in line at the grocery for two cans of beer. I stocked up on cigarettes. It was nice to do simple things. I tried not to think of anything. I got on a bus and went home. The pizza shaped itself to the contours of my knees.

When I got home, I turned the TV on. I threw the pizza on the table and tossed down a beer, standing up. I wanted to take a shower, but I abandoned the idea—I just couldn't bring myself to go in there, not right away. I listened to what was on television. A bunch of half-dead guys were talking about their latest books. I grabbed my pizza and sat down. I looked them right in the eye. They were gabbing over orange juice, their eyes bright with self-satisfaction. They had their finger on the pulse of today's taste. It's true that an era deserves the writers it gets, and it was edifying to watch them. My pizza was barely warm and very greasy. I wondered if they hadn't invited the worst of the lot, just in case anyone had any doubts. Perhaps the theme of the show was "How to Sell a Million Copies with Nothing to Say, No Talent, No Soul, No Love, No Suffering, Nor the Ability to Put Two Words Back to Back Without Making People Yawn." The other channels weren't much better. I turned the sound off and just watched the screen.

After a while I realized that I was just spinning my wheels. Still, I had no desire to go to bed, especially not there, in the heart of such a hideous trap. I took a bottle and went to Bob's. When I walked in, Annie was busy breaking dishes. She looked at me, a salad bowl poised over her head. There was debris all over the floor. Bob was hiding in a corner.

"I'll come back later," I said.

"No, no," they said. "How's Betty?"

I forayed into the fray and set the bottle down on the table.

"She's okay," I said. "It isn't serious. I don't feel like talking about it. I just didn't want to be alone. . . ."

Annie took my arm and sat me down in a chair. She was in her bathrobe; her face was still pink with anger.

"Of course," she said. "We understand."

Bob got out the glasses.

"Am I interrupting something . . . ?" I said.

"Don't be ridiculous . . ." he said.

Annie sat down next to me. She pushed away a lock of hair that had fallen over her face.

"Where are the kids?" I asked.

"At the bastard's mother's," she answered.

"Listen," I said. "Don't mind me—just act like I'm not here."

Bob filled the glasses.

"No, we were having a little tiff—it's nothing. . . ."

" 'Nothing,' he says. The son of a bitch is cheating on me, and it's nothing!"

"Jesus Christ, you're so full of shit . . . !" said Bob.

He moved aside, thus avoiding the salad bowl, which exploded against the wall. We raised our glasses.

"Cheers!" I said.

There was a brief moment of silence while we drank, then they started back at it again, harder. As far as I was concerned, the ambience was perfect. I stretched my legs out under the table and folded my hands over my belly. To tell the truth, I wasn't very interested in what was going on. I felt the turbulence spinning around me—their screams, the sound of things smashing on the floor—but I felt my sadness calm down, and crumble away like a cookie. For once I gave my blessing to the thing I hated most in the world: a cocktail made of light, humanity, heat, and noise. I slid down in my chair, having first taken care to refill my glass. Everywhere in the world there were men and women fighting, loving, tearing each other apart; people pissing novels without love, without madness, without energy, and most of all without style—taking us to Hell in a handbasket. I was at this point in my literary reflections when I spotted the moon through the window. It was full, majestic, and auburn. Somehow, it made me think of my little bird, her eye wounded on a mimosa branch—I barely noticed the colored bowls flying across the room.

At that moment I felt a kind of inner peace. I grabbed on to it. It was quite something after all those dark hours. It put a mindless smile on my face. Things were heating up. Bob had been dodging things pretty well. He saw Annie with a projectile in each hand. She feigned with the mustard jar, then let loose with the sugar bowl. I'd guessed it. Bob took it in the skull and collapsed. I helped him back up.

"You'll excuse me," he said. "I'm going to bed."

"Never mind me," I said. "I feel better already."

I guided him into the bedroom, then came back and sat down in the kitchen. I looked at Annie, who had started sweeping up.

"I know what you're thinking," she told me. "But if I don't do it, who will?"

I helped her pick up some of the bigger pieces. We made a few silent round-trips to the garbage can, then lit cigarettes. I held the match for her.

"Listen, Annie, I know this isn't exactly the best time, but I was wondering if I could sleep here tonight. I feel a little strange, all alone in the apartment. . . ."

She exhaled a little mushroom-cloud of smoke.

"Shit, you don't even have to ask," she said. "As for Bob and me, we don't love each other enough to really fight. What you saw wasn't even serious."

"Only for tonight," I added.

We finished straightening up, talking about the rain and the weather—the abominable heat that had melted over the town like a gallon of maple syrup. Just sweeping up had us sweating. I sat on a chair. She set her behind down on a corner of the table.

"Just take Archie's bed," she said. "You need anything? Something to read . . . ?"

"No thanks," I said.

She had slid the sides of her robe off her thighs. It was easy to see that she wasn't wearing anything underneath. She was probably waiting for me to say something, but I didn't. Thinking that she wasn't making herself clear, she opened the thing up wide. She spread her legs and put her foot up on a chair. Her pussy was a nice size, and her breasts larger than average. I passed an appreciative moment looking, but didn't awkwardly spill my drink. I just drank it, then went into the next room. I grabbed a few magazines, then sank into an armchair.

I was reading a thing on the North-South conflict when she came in. The robe was now closed.

"I think your attitude is truly stupid," she started in. "What do you think is going to happen? You're making a mountain out of—"

"No, not a mountain exactly. A small hill, yes. . . ."

"Shit," she said. "Shit, shit, shit."

I got up and went to look out the window. There was nothing but the night and the branch of a tree, its leaves limp in the heat. I slapped my leg with the magazine.

"Look, what would we gain by sleeping together? You have something special to offer me? Something out of the ordinary?"

I turned my back to her. I felt a slight burning on the back of my neck.

"Listen to me," I went on. "I never was much for fucking around, I never got much out of it. I know that everybody else does it; but it's no fun if you just do like everybody else. To tell you the truth, it bores me. It does you good to live according to your ideas, to not betray yourself, not cop out at the last minute just because some girl has a nice ass, or someone offers you a huge check, or because the path of least resistance runs by your front door. It does you good to hang tough. It's good for the soul."

I turned around to tell her the Big Secret: "Over Dispersal, I choose Concentration. I have one life—the only thing I'm interested in is making it shine."

She pinched the end of her nose wistfully.

"All right," she sighed. "If you need any aspirin before you go to bed, there's a bottle in the medicine chest. If you want, I can go get you some pajamas. I don't know—maybe you don't sleep in the nude."

"Don't bother. I sleep in my underwear, and I always keep my hands above the sheets."

"Jesus, where's Henry Miller when you really need him . . . ?" she muttered.

She turned on her heel, and I was left alone. You don't need much room when you're alone and not expecting anyone—Archie's bed did the job nicely. His rubber sheet squealed as I lay down. I turned on his little ladybug lamp. I listened to the silence fill the night like invisible, paralyzing cream.

26

They started off by telling me that everything was going fine—that her wound didn't worry them in the least. Whenever I tried to find out why she spent so much time sleeping, they always found somebody to come put his hand on my shoulder, to explain how they knew what they were doing.

From the moment I passed through the door of that fucking hospital, I felt like a completely different man. I was seized by a dead anguish that all but knocked me down. I had to struggle against it with all my might. Once in a while, a female nurse would take my arm and guide me through the hallways. The male nurses never lifted a finger. They must have known that any relationship with me would end up stormy. My brain ran in slow motion, as if I were watching a slide show—swallowing up the pictures without comment, the meaning escaping me.

In such a state, it was easy for me to pull a chair up next to her bed and just stay there, immobile and silent, without noticing the time pass—not drinking, not smoking, not eating—like someone marooned at sea, with nothing in view, no other choice but to hang onto the plank. The nurse with the flat behind occasionally poured some honey on my wounds.

"At least when she sleeps, she gets her strength back," she told me.

I kept telling myself that. Over and over—I was becoming a blithering idiot. When she did open her eyes, it was nothing to jump up and down about. It was like there was a steel bar running through my stomach—I had to be careful not to fall off my chair. I looked deep into her one good eye, but I could never see the spark. I carried on one-sided conversations. Her hand would dissolve in mine like a marshmallow. She'd look right through me, my stomach growling so loud it was embarrassing. Every day at visiting hours I would come, hoping that she'd be waiting for me. But every day no one was there. Nothing but the Great White Desert. I was a silent zombie, walking circles in the wasteland.

"You see, what has us worried is her mental health," the good old doctor finally said. But I think he'd have done better to worry about mine; he could have saved wear and tear on his dentures— that's how obvious things were soon to become. He was a bald guy, with a few tufts of hair on the sides—the kind of guy who slaps you on the back and shows you the door. You and your ignorance, your trembling knees. You and the stupid look on your face.

Yes, it would be only a few days before the bubbles finally popped the cork.

As soon as I got out in the fresh air, I felt better. It didn't seem like it was Betty I was leaving in the hospital—rather, something I couldn't get my mind around. As if she'd just left one morning without giving me a forwarding address. I tried to keep the house in order. Luckily, writers aren't dirty. I just vacuumed a little around the table, emptied the ashtrays, and threw away the beer cans. The heat had already killed two or three people in town, precipitating the end of the already weak.

I stopped opening the store. I quickly realized that the only restful moments I had were those I spent with my notebooks, and that's how I passed most of my time. It was ninety-three degrees in the house, even with the shades drawn. Still, it was the only place I still felt alive. Otherwise I was numb, as if I'd contracted sleeping sickness. Being inside the coals, I couldn't feel the fire. All it took was a small breeze to stir the flames, though. A question of time, no more, no less.

One morning in particular things got off to a bad start. I was turning the kitchen upside down, trying to get my hands on some coffee, sighing deeply from the bottom of my soul, when Bob showed up.

"Hey," he said. "You know that your car is parked right in front of my house?"

"Yeah, I guess it is . . ." I said.

"Well, there are people who might think there's a body in the trunk, if you get my drift. . . ."

That's when I remembered the groceries I'd been bringing home the night I passed Betty on her way to the hospital. I had completely forgotten about them. Given the sun, the temperature inside the trunk must have been a hundred fifty degrees. I thought that I'd already had my share of this sort of thing, but no, there were still a few left—it was enough to make you sick to your stomach. I considered just sitting down and never getting up. Instead, I drank a big glass of water and followed Bob out into the street. As I was closing the door behind me I heard the telephone ring. I let it ring.

I hadn't been taking the car to go see Betty. I walked every day. The exercise did me good. I came to see that life had not come to a complete halt. The young girls' dresses were like a rain of flower petals. I forced myself to look at them, avoiding the old and ugly ones. It is ugliness of the soul, however, that really disgusts me. During these walks, I practiced my deep-breathing exercises. The car was the furthest thing from my mind—but things you forget come back to haunt you.

The stink was unbelievable. Bob was curious to see what it looked like, but I told him to forget it. I'd rather not know.

"Just tell me the shortest route to the dump," I said.

I opened all the windows and crossed town with my hellish cargo. In places, the tar was almost melted—long, shiny, black grooves striping the pavement. Perhaps it was Darkness itself, coming up into the world—nothing surprised me anymore. To keep from getting too spooked by such thoughts, I turned the radio on: OOH BABY, HOLD ME BABY, TIGHTER, TIGHTER, JUST ONE MOOORE KISSSS . . . !

I parked in front of the garbage dump. All you could hear was flies, and all you could smell was something that resembled the atomic bomb. I had just gotten out of the car, when here comes the neighborhood troglodyte, a pickax slung over his shoulder. It took me a while to figure out where his mouth was.

"Lookin' for somethin'?" he said.

"No," I said.

The whites of his eyes were almost supernatural—like in detergent commercials.

"Takin' a walk?"

"No, I'm dropping off two or three things in my trunk."

"Oh," he said. "Well, then, forget it."

I leaned in to get the keys out of the ignition.

"If you don't have anything for me, forget it," he said. "Copper, for example. Like yesterday I turned around, and what do you know, this guy unloads a washing-machine motor."

"Yeah, well, I don't go in for that," I said.

I opened the trunk. The food seemed to have doubled in volume. The meat was multicolored, the yogurt was swollen, the cheese was running, and all that was left of the butter was the foil. Generally speaking, everything had fermented, exploded, and oozed—it all formed one rather large compact block, more or less soldered to the carpet on the trunk floor.

I grimaced. The bum's eyes lit up. It's always the same story.

"You gonna throw all that away?" he said.

"Yeah," I said. "I don't have time to explain. I'm not feeling too hot—I'm unhappy."

He spit on the ground and scratched his head.

"Hey, we all do what we can," he said. "Look, fella, you mind if we sort of unload it easy-like? I'd like to take a closer look. . . ."

We each took an end of the carpet and lifted the plaster-like wad out of the trunk. We put it down to one side, at the foot of a garbage-bag wall. Like iron shavings to a magnet, the flies—blue and gold ones—dove into it.

The bum looked at me, smiling. He was obviously waiting for me to split. In his shoes, I'd have done the same thing. I got back in the car without a word. Before taking off I glanced in the rearview mirror. He was still there, standing in the sun next to my small hill of food—he hadn't moved an inch. He was smiling like he was posing for a souvenir snapshot of one helluva picnic. On the way home I stopped at a bar. I ordered a mint cordial. The oil, the coffee, the sugar, and a big box of chocolate powder—those he'd be able to salvage. And the razors with the pivoting heads. And the antimosquito strips. And my box of Fab.

It was about noon when I pulled up in front of the house. The sun was like a hissing cat with its claws out. The telephone was ringing.

"Yes, hello?" I said.

There was static on the other end of the line. I could hardly make out one word.

"Listen, hang up and call back," I said. "I can't hear a thing!"

I threw my shoes into a corner. I ran my head under the shower. I lit a cigarette, then the phone rang again.

The guy on the other end said some name and asked me if it was mine.

"Yeah," I said.

Then he said some other name, and that it was his.

"So . . . ?" I said.

"I have your manuscript in my hands. I'll send you contracts in the next mail."

I sat my butt down on the table.

"All right . . . I want twelve percent," I said.

"Ten percent."

"Fine."

"I loved your book. I'll have it at the typesetter's soon."

"Yeah, do it fast," I said.

"It's nice to speak with you, hope to see you soon."

"Yeah, well, I'm afraid I'll be pretty tied up for the next little while. . . ."

"Don't worry about it. No hurry. We'll take care of the travel arrangements. Things are in the works."

"Fine."

"Well, I have to let you go now. Are you working on something else at the moment?"

"Yes, it's coming along. . . ."

"Terrific. Good luck."

He was about to hang up—I caught him at the last second.

"Hey . . . wait . . . excuse me," I said. "What did you say your name was, again?"

He repeated it. It was a good thing, too. With all that was happening, it had completely gone out of my head.

I took a pack of sausages out of the refrigerator to thaw. I put some water on. I sat down with a beer. While I was waiting, I laughed louder than I ever had in my life—a nervous laugh.

I got to the hospital early, before visiting hours. I couldn't figure out if I'd left too early or walked too fast. But one thing was sure—I couldn't wait to see her. I had brought with me what she'd always wished for. Shouldn't it be enough to make her jump to her feet? To give me a big wink with the one eye she had left?

I made a beeline for the men's room, as if it were an emergency. From there I surveyed the guy at the reception desk. He seemed to be dozing off. The stairway was empty. I slid by.

I entered the room. I stumbled forward and grabbed onto the bed railing—I didn't want to believe what I saw. I shook my head no, hoping that the nightmare would disappear, but it did no good. Betty was lying immobile in bed, staring at the ceiling. She did not move a millimeter, understandably: they had strapped her to the bed—straps at least three inches wide, with aluminum buckles.

"Betty . . . what's this all about . . . ?" I whispered.

I still had my Western S.522 on me, the one that fits in any pocket. The curtains were open. A soft light spilled into the room. There was no sound—I sharpened it regularly. Me and my knife, we were pals.

I grabbed Betty by the shoulders. I shook her a little. I started perspiring again, but by now I was used to it—it practically never had a chance to dry. But this was bad sweat, different from the rest—like glazed, transparent blood. I stacked her pillows and sat her up. I found her as beautiful as ever. I had barely let go of her, when she fell over on her side. I picked her back up. When I saw this, a part of me tumbled over the foot of the bed screaming. With the other part, I took her hand.

"Listen," I said. "I know that it's taken a long time, but it's over now—we've made it!"

Jerk, I thought, this is no time for riddles. Sure, you're scared to death, but you have only one little sentence to say—you don't even have to take a breath.

"Betty . . . my book is going to be published," I said.

I might have added: DON'T YOU SEE THE LITTLE WHITE SAIL ON THE HORIZON? I don't know how to describe this—she might as well have been sealed in a bell jar . . . and all I could do was leave my fingerprints on the glass. I did not detect the slightest change on her face. A little wind, I was—trying my best to ripple a pond long since covered with ice. A little wind . . . .

"I'm not kidding! And, I'm pleased to announce that I'm working on a new one . . . !"

I was playing all my cards. The trouble is, I'd never played alone. Lose all night long, then deal yourself a hand in the morning after everyone's gone home, only to find yourself with a royal flush—who could stand such a thing? Who wouldn't want to throw everything out the window—stab the upholstery with a kitchen knife?

God, she didn't see me. She didn't understand me—didn't even hear me. She no longer knew what it was to speak, or cry, or smile, or throw a temper tantrum, or revel in the sheets, running her tongue over her lips. The sheets didn't move. Nothing moved. She gave me no sign, not even a microscopic one. My book being published affected her about as much as my showing up with a plate of french fries. The wonderful bouquet I'd brought was nothing but a shadow of wilted flowers, an odor of dried grass. For a fraction of a second I sensed the infinite space that separated us, and ever since then I tell whoever cares to listen that I died once . . . at thirty-five years of age, of a summer's day in a hospital room—and it's no bluff: I am among those who have heard the Grim Reaper whistling through the air. It chilled me to my fingertips. I experienced a moment of panic, but just then a nurse walked in. I didn't budge.

She was carrying a tray, with a glass of water and pills of every conceivable color on it. She wasn't the one I knew. She was fat, with yellow hair. She looked at me, then glanced severely at her watch.

"Excuse me," she said. "But I don't believe it's visiting hours yet . . . !"

Her attention drifted to Betty. Her old sagging jaw dropped open:

"Mother Mary, who untied her?"

She frowned at me and started for the door, but I got there first, blocking her way with my arm. She let out a cry—a petty little whine. I scooped up the pills dancing on the tray and shoved them under her nose.

"What is all this shit?" I asked.

I didn't recognize my own voice—it was an octave lower, and very hoarse. It was all I could do to keep from grabbing her by the throat.

"I'm not the doctor!" she wailed. "Let me go!"

I burned my eyes into hers with all my might. She bit her lip. "No . . . *you're* going to stay with her. *I'll* go," I growled.

Before I walked out, I turned and glanced at Betty. She had fallen over on her side.

I shot across the hall like a rocket and went into his office without knocking. He had his back to me, he was looking at an X ray in the daylight. When he heard the door slam, he spun around in his chair. He raised his eyebrows. I let out a laugh. I walked up to his desk and threw down the handful of drugs.

"What is all this?" I asked. "What are you giving her?"

I couldn't tell if I was really trembling from head to foot or just imagining it. The doctor tried to be slick. He grabbed a huge pair of scissors that had been lying on his desk and played with them.

"Ah, young man," he said. "I've been meaning to talk with you. Sit down."

I was strangled by a sort of crazy rage. For me, the guy represented the source of all unhappiness, of all the world's suffering. I'd unmasked the bastard, cornered him in his hole. He was out to ruin the zest for life. He wasn't a doctor, he was a hideous mixture of every asshole on earth. Meeting somebody like that made you cry and laugh at the same time. Still, I controlled myself—I wanted to hear what he had to tell me; and anyway, there was no way out. I sat down. I had trouble bending my legs. Looking at the color of my hands, I knew that I must have been white as death. I must not have been too frightening to look at, though. He tried to intimidate me.

"Let's make one thing clear," he said. "You are neither her husband nor a member of her family. I therefore have no obligation to explain anything to you. I'm going to anyway, but because I choose to—not because I have to. Is this understood?"

You're a millimeter from the goal line—don't flinch, I told myself. Take this one last whipping. I nodded my head.

"Fine," he said.

He opened one of his desk drawers and dropped the scissors into it, smiling. I swear, the clown thought he was completely invulnerable—either that, or God was on my side. He folded his hands in front of him and nodded his head for a good ten seconds before getting on with it.

"I won't hide from you that her case is very worrisome," he started. "Last night we had to strap her down—a horrible attack, really."

I imagined a gang of them jumping on her, pinning her to the bed while they buckled the straps. It was a grade-Z horror film, and I was the only one in the audience. I lowered my head a little. I shoved my hands under my thighs. He started talking again, but someone had turned off the sound. I noted in the silence that everything was going downhill.

". . . and it would be going out on a limb to say that one day she will completely regain her senses. No, we mustn't hold out too much hope."

This sentence, however, I heard loud and clear. It had a particular color to it—bronze, I'd say. It writhed like a rattlesnake. It squirmed right under my skin.

"We'll look after her, though," he went on. "You know, there have been some remarkable advances in chemistry. We still get fairly good results with electroshock treatment. And don't listen to what they tell you about it—it's perfectly safe."

I bent forward to lean all my weight on my hands. I fixed my eyes between my feet, on a spot on the floor.

"I'm going to go get her," I said. "I'm going to go get her and take her away with me."

I heard him laugh.

"Look, young man, don't be ridiculous. Maybe you haven't completely understood. I'm telling you that the girl is insane, my friend. Strait-jacket insane."

At this I coiled like a spring and hopped up onto his desk with both feet. Before he could make a move, I kicked him in the face. That's when I noticed he wore dentures—they flew out of his mouth like flying fish. Thank you, God, I thought. He fell over backward in his chair, spitting up a small geyser of blood. The sound of breaking glass was his feet going through the windows of his bookcase. He started screaming. I jumped on top of him, pulling like a madman on his tie. I lifted him up. I got him in a figure-four grapevine hold, or something in the same family—rolling him over backward with his one hundred sixty pounds on my legs, then letting him loose just at the moment of takeoff. The wall shook.

I was barely back on my feet when three orderlies came in, single-file. The first one got an elbow in the kisser, the second one tackled me, and the third one sat on top of me—he was the fattest. He squeezed all the breath out of me and grabbed me by the hair. I squealed with rage. I saw the doctor getting back up on his feet, holding onto the wall. The first orderly bent over and drove his fist into my ear. I had a hot flash.

"I'm calling the cops," he said. "They'll put him away."

The doctor sat down in a chair, a handkerchief over his mouth. He was missing one of his shoes, among other things.

"No," he said. "Not the police. It's bad for public relations. Throw him outside. And he'd better not try to set foot inside this hospital again!"

They picked me up. The one who wanted to call the cops slapped me across the face.

"You hear that?" he said.

My shoe found his nuts—I actually knocked him off his feet, which surprised everybody. I took advantage of the pause to get loose. I dove again at the doctor—I wanted to strangle him, obliterate him. He fell out of his chair, me on top of him.

The orderlies all came down on me. I heard the nurses screaming. Before I could push my fingers into the doctor's throat, I felt myself being lifted by an incalculable number of hands and thrown out of the office. They bashed me a little going down the hall, but nothing too serious—they were all pretty embarrassed; in the end I suppose they didn't really want to kill me.

We went through the lobby at a sprint. One of them had me in a hammerlock, another one had a handful of my hair, and an ear—this hurt most. They opened the doors and threw me down the steps.

"If we see you around here again, you've had it!" one of them shouted.

Those fuckers. They almost got me to cry. A tear fell onto the steps. It steamed like a drop of hydrochloric acid.

So I'd struck out. Moreover, I'd gotten myself banished from the hospital forever. The next few days were the worst of my life. I couldn't go back and see her again, and my memory of what I'd seen was intolerable. All the zen I knew came to no good—I was overcome with despair. I suffered like the most foolish of fools. Without doubt, it was during this period that I did my best writing. Later I would be referred to as an "unsung stylist." It wasn't my fault that I wrote well and knew it, though. During this period I filled up half a notebook.

I probably would have written even more, but I couldn't sit still during the day. I took many a shower, downed quantities of beer, miles of sausage, and paced hundreds of thousands of miles on the carpet. When I couldn't stand it anymore, I'd take a walk outside. I often found myself near the hospital. I knew better than to get too close—they once hit me with a beer can from fifty yards. Yes, they kept their eyes peeled. I stayed on the far side of the street and contented myself with looking at her window. Once in a while I'd see the curtain move.

When night started falling, I'd go have a drink at Bob's. It was the long slide into sundown at day's end that was the most abominable, for a guy who'd had his baby taken away from him and isn't sure he still knows how to swim. I'd spend about an hour with them. Bob acted like nothing had ever happened, and Annie always found some excuse to show me her pussy—it got me through the evening. Once it was dark, I could handle going home. I'd turn on the lights. I did most of my writing at night. Sometimes I even felt good—it made me feel like she was still there with me. Betty was the one thing that made me realize I was alive. Writing was tantamount to the same thing.

One morning I took the car and drove all day, aimlessly, my arm flung over the door, my eyes squinting in the wind. Toward evening I stopped at the seaside. I had no idea where I was. All I'd seen for the whole trip were the faces of gas station attendants. I bought a couple of sandwiches at a neighborhood bar and went to eat them on the beach.

It was deserted. The sun had gone down below the horizon. It was so beautiful that I dropped a pickle in the sand. The sound of the waves, the same for millions of years, relaxed me—encouraged me, reassured me, stunned me. My little blue planet, O my little blue planet. May God bless you, goddamn it.

I sat there for a while, getting to know solitude again, meditating on my pain. I rose. So did the moon. I took my shoes off and started walking along the shore, thinking of nothing. The sand was still warm—the perfect temperature for an apple pie.

Along my way I came across a big fish, washed up on the sand. All that was left of it was a decomposed carcass, yet enough remained to see what a magnificent fish it must have been once— nothing less than a silver lightning bolt with a pearl belly, a sort of moving diamond. All that was over now. Beauty had taken a hard kick in the teeth. There were scarcely any scales left to glimmer in the moonlight—two or three hopeless little scales. To find yourself rotting away like that, after having once been the equal of the stars—wasn't this the worst thing that could happen to you? Wouldn't you rather just swim away into the darkness with a final flick of your tail to the sun? if it were me, I wouldn't have to think twice.

Since no one was around to see, I buried the fish. I dug the hole with my hands. I felt a little ridiculous, but if I hadn't done it, I couldn't have lived with myself, and now was not the moment for that.

So that's how it came to me. I thought it over and over and over—I tossed and turned all night, trying to get the idea out of my head, but by dawn I knew it was the only thing to do. All right, fine, I told myself. It was a Sunday. There would be too many people on Sunday. I put it off till the next day. All day long I dragged my ass. It looked like it was going to storm. Impossible to write—no use kidding myself. Impossible to do anything. Days like that are shittier than anything.

I woke up rather late the next day, around noon. Without thinking, I'd made a huge mess of the house. I started putting things away. Before I knew it, I was in the middle of a full-scale cleanup. I don't know what came over me, I even dusted the curtains. After that I showered, shaved, and ate. While I was doing the dishes I noticed a few flashes of lightning. The thunder started to rumble. The sky was as dry as powdered milk. Clouds gathered in the burning air.

I spent the rest of the afternoon sitting in front of the TV, my legs stretched out on the couch, a pitcher of water in my hand. I relaxed. The house was so clean it was a pleasure to see; from time to time it does you good to know everything is in its place.

At around five o'clock, I put my makeup on, then charged out onto the street, disguised as Josephine. The storm that had been coming since the night before still hadn't come—the sky was holding its breath. Through my glasses it all looked even darker, nearly apocalyptic. I walked fast. The wise thing to do would have been to take the car, but I turned a deaf ear to it, leaving it behind to sulk by itself. As a finishing touch I'd taken one of Betty's purses. I held it close to me—it kept my boobs from slipping. I walked with my eyes riveted to the sidewalk, paying no attention to the catcalls that the bums throw at every single girl who passes by—I couldn't waste my time. I tried not to think of anything.

When I got to the hospital, I hid behind a tree and exhaled two or three times, like wind howling through the branches. Then I walked toward the entrance with my purse under my arm—no hesitation, head high, with the poise of a gal who's used to ruling an empire. I felt nothing at all as I went through the door—not the tiniest bit of uneasiness. For once I wasn't carrying an electrified fence on my shoulders, no blood poisoning, no spontaneous combustion or lateral paralysis. I almost looked back to see what I was missing, but I was already on the stairway.

On the second floor, I ran into a group of orderlies. Though I'd just touched up my makeup, all they ogled were my breasts. They were too big, I knew it, and now every last one of them was undressing me with his eyes. To escape, I ducked into the first room I came to.

There was a guy in bed, a tube in his arm and a tube up his nose. He was not in great shape. He opened his eyes when I came in, waiting for the orderlies to pass by. We looked at each other—we obviously didn't have a lot to talk about, but we looked at each other. For a fraction of a second, I wanted to unplug him. Though I didn't make a move, the guy started shaking his head no. I gave up on the idea. I cracked the door open to make sure the coast was clear.

Betty. Room number seven. I slid in silently and closed the door behind me. It was dark. Clouds, or simply nightfall, it was hard to tell. There was a tiny light above her bed, so pallid it made my blood run cold. A nightlight when it's not yet night is like a crippled child. I wedged the door closed with a chair. I ripped off my wig and took off my glasses. I sat down on the edge of the bed. She wasn't sleeping.

"Want some gum?" I said.

It did no good to search my memory—I couldn't remember the last time I'd heard her voice. Or the last words we'd exchanged. Probably something like:

"Hey, who do you have to fuck to get some sugar around here?"

"Have you tried looking in the bottom drawer?"

I wrapped my tutti-frutti back up—it turned out I didn't want any either. I grabbed the pitcher of water off the nightstand and downed half of it.

"Want some?" I asked.

They hadn't tied her down. The straps hung on the floor, like chocolate bars left out in the sun. I acted like she wasn't gone, like she was still there. I needed to talk.

"The hardest thing is going to be getting you dressed," I said. "Especially if you don't help . . ."

I took my glove off and ran my hand under her nightgown, caressing her breasts. An elephant's memory is nothing compared to mine. I could remember every square millimeter of her skin. Give me her cells, all jumbled up, and I'll put them back together for you in perfect order. I teased her belly, her arms, her legs. Finally, I closed my hand over her furry patch—nothing had changed. I felt real joy at that precise moment—a simple pleasure, almost animal. I put my glove back on. Of course the pleasure would have been a thousand times greater had she reacted. But then again, where could you ever find the kind of happiness that would have been—in commercials? At the bottom of Santa Claus's sack? On the top floor of the Tower of Babel?

"All right, we'd better hurry. We have to go. . . ."

I took her chin and put my lips to hers. She never unclenched her teeth. It was still wonderful. I managed to get a little of her saliva on my lower lip. Her mouth—I ate it ever so gently. I slid my hand behind her neck and pulled her to me, my nose grazing in her hair. If this goes on, it's me who'll go nuts, I thought, me who'll come apart at the seams. I took out a Kleenex and wiped her lips—I'd gotten lipstick all over them.

"We still have a long way to go," I said.

A doll, docile and silent. They'd filled her to the gills with drugs. They'd already thrown the first shovel of dirt over her. The right thing to do would have been to ambush them all and slit their throats for being what they were—doctors, nurses, pharmacists, the whole clique; not to mention everyone who'd pushed her to that point, slave drivers, people who crush you under their thumbs, those who offend you, lie to you, use you; people who don't give a shit if you're one of a kind, people who glow brighter in the bullshit, stand taller on hills of crap, who weigh you down like a ball and chain. It wouldn't have made me feel any better, though. Wading through the rivers of their blood, I wouldn't be much better off. Like it or not, what's done is done, as they say—and though I'm not the kind of guy who gives up hope at the drop of a hat, I understood that sometimes the world seems like the worst of all possible Hells. It depends on how you look at it. May God strike me dead: sitting on that bed in that room, for the longest minute of my life, I'd never seen anything so odious or black. Above us, the storm broke loose. I shook.

"I need you to make one last effort," I sighed.

The first drops splattered against the window, like insects on a windshield. I bent over her delicately and took hold of one of the straps. I put the tip of it through the buckle and pulled tight. One for her legs. She didn't move.

"You okay? It doesn't hurt, does it?" I asked.

Outside was the deluge. It was like being inside the *Nautilus*. I picked up another strap and put it around her arms and chest, just under her breasts. I pulled it tight. She stared at the ceiling with her one eye. Nothing I did interested her. The moment had come to test my strength.

"I have to tell you something . . ." I started.

I took one of the pillows from beneath her head, one with blue stripes. I wasn't shaking—for her I could do anything without shaking, I'd already proven that—I was just a little warmer was all.

". . . you and me, we're like two fingers of the same hand," I
went on. "And nothing can ever change that."

I probably could have found something more clever to say or,
better still, kept quiet. But at the time it seemed innocent
enough—a little parade of improvised words. She would have
liked that. It was a confection, written in whipped cream, not in
stone.

I counted to seven hundred fifty, then stood up. I took the
pillow off her face. The rain was making a hell of a din. For some
reason I had a pain in my side. I didn't look at her. I undid the
straps. I put the pillow back where it had been.

I turned toward the wall, thinking that something was going
to happen. Nothing happened. It just kept raining and raining.
The light stayed where it was, and so did the walls—and there I
was, with my white gloves and false breasts, waiting for some
message from death. But no message came. Was I going to get
out of this with only a pain in the side?

I put my wig back on. Just before leaving, I turned and glanced
at her for the last time. I expected some horrific sight, but in the
end she just looked like she was sleeping. Yet she came up with
one more thing to make me happy—she knew how to do it. Her
mouth was open slightly. I noticed a pack of Kleenex on the
nightstand. It took me a moment to understand, then I started
crying. Yes, she was still watching over me, showing me which
way to go, even though she was no longer of this world. Her
sending me this last sign flooded me with a river of fire.

I rushed back to the bed and kissed her hair, then grabbed the
Kleenex and shoved all I could into her mouth, all the way down.
I had a spasm—I almost threw up—but it passed. What I want
is to be able to be proud of you, she'd said.

When I left, everybody must have been on coffee break. No
one was in the halls, and almost no one was in the lobby. I went

unnoticed. It was totally dark. The gutters were overflowing down the whole side of the building. It smelled bad—dried-out grass that's been wet again. The rain was a luminous portcullis of electric wire. I turned my collar up, put my purse on top of my head, and dove into it.

I ran. I had the sensation that someone was chasing me with a flamethrower. I had to take my glasses off to see, but I didn't slow down. As one might expect, there was no one on the street, so I didn't worry about my makeup—luckily I hadn't put on any mascara. I got a lot on my fingers trying to wipe my face off—I must have really smeared it good. Fortunately, you couldn't see three yards in front of you.

I ran like a poisoned rat caught in a web of pearls. I didn't slow down for intersections. Plipliplip went the rain; flap flap flap I went; baroombaroom went the thunder. The rain fell straight down. It stung my face—I swallowed some of it. I ran halfway home like a bat out of hell. My whole body was steaming; my breathing filled the street, no joke. I passed under a streetlight, and everything went blue.

At an intersection, I saw the headlights of a car. I had the right of way, but I let him go first. In the pause, I tore my wig off, then plunged ahead. The rain wasn't enough to put out the fire raging in my lungs. I gave it all I could, then forced myself to give even more. It made me moan and cry, it was so hard. I ran because I'd killed Betty. I ran because I wanted to run. I ran because I needed something else. At the same time, it seemed a perfectly natural reflex—it came from the heart, after all, didn't it . . . ?

The cops paid no attention to the story—not one of them showed the slightest interest. A crazy girl who tears her eye out, then ends it all by swallowing a box of Kleenex—they visibly couldn't have cared less. Of course, when I'd stolen the money they'd made a big deal out of it—it was in all the papers, and they threw up roadblocks all over town. But killing her—I could have done it five hundred times and no one would even have gotten up from his desk.

As for me, everything went just fine. How could a real love story end at the police station? A real love story never ends. It's not as easy as it seems in the storybooks—you must expect to have to fly higher, your brain light as a feather. Anyway, to this day no one has ever come looking for me. No one has bothered me. I was able to get it out of my system in peace.

I took care of the worst of it by turning over a small fortune to the people at the funeral parlor. Despite their frightening faces, I couldn't complain—they handled all the details with the hospital, I hardly had to do anything. In the end they cremated her. I have her ashes. I keep them close by. I still don't know what to do with them, but that's another story.

As soon as I had the time, I wrote a long letter to Eddie and Lisa. I explained everything that had happened, without telling them the decisive role I'd played. I apologized for not letting them know earlier. I hoped they'd understand that I wouldn't have been able to stand that. I'll see you soon, I told them, love to you both . . . P.S. I won't be answering my telephone for a while. Kisses. On my way to the mailbox I realized that the weather had turned lovely again. The heat and humidity had gone. It was mild and dry. I came home with an ice cream cone in my hand. One.

It seems stupid, but I still found myself cooking two steaks, or leaving the water in the tub for her, setting two places at the table, asking questions out loud. I slept with the light on. It's the details that are hell—the little things that remain on the branches, like fog, like a gown of tattered lace. Every time it happened, I'd freeze in my tracks, and take my time digesting it. When I accidentally opened the closet and saw all her clothes in it, I almost choked. I tried to tell myself that each time was less painful than the time before. It wasn't easy to tell.

Still, I didn't die. One morning I hopped on the scale and saw that I'd lost only six pounds. What a laugh. Letting yourself go once in a while—chewing your fingers to the bone—is not what saps a man. I was not even too far away from looking good. Some people take it with them when they go, but Betty was the opposite. She left it all. ALL. So it wasn't surprising that sometimes I felt her there, next to me.

I let several days go by without seeing anyone. I had explained things to Bob and Annie—had asked them not to disturb me. Bob wanted to come over with a bottle. I won't answer the door, I told him. I'd decided to climb back up the hill in a hurry. For that I needed peace—telephone off, television on. One morning I got the proofs of my book to correct, and this made for a change of pace. It was her thing, after all. I took my time with it, and it was probably this that got me back on my feet—morally, I mean. When I went back to my notebooks and found that I could still put two or three good sentences together . . . when I smelled the eerie beauty that they breathed . . . when I saw that they were like children playing in the sun, then I realized that, though I'd gotten off to a bad start as a writer, the rest was going to be just fine—it was as good as done.

The next day I was a new man. It started when I stretched out in bed. Getting up, I realized that I was in good shape. I looked at the apartment in a good mood, smiling. I sat down in the kitchen to drink my coffee, something I hadn't done in a dog's age—usually I just drank it standing up or leaning on the sink. I opened the windows. I felt so good that I ran out to buy croissants. It was a lovely day.

To get out a bit, I went to eat in town. The cafeteria was jammed to the ceiling, the waitresses already had sweat circles under their arms. We'd had that job, Betty and I. I knew what it was all about. I sat down at a little table with my chicken, mashed potatoes, and apple pie. I watched the people. Life was like a bubbling torrent. I'd say that this was the image I kept of Betty—a bubbling torrent—and to that I'd add luminous. If I had my choice, I'd wish she were still alive, that's understood—but I have to admit that, to me, she wasn't too far from it. You can't be too picky, after all. I stood up, thinking that sitting down should be left to those who really suffer.

I went for a walk. On my way back, I ran into a pretty girl looking in the store window. She was blocking the reflections with her hands, blond hairs glimmering beneath her arms. I put the key in the lock. She straightened up.

"Oh, I thought it was closed," she said.

"No, why would it be closed? It's just that I never pay attention to time."

She looked at me and laughed. I felt silly. I'd forgotten that—what that's like.

"That must get you in trouble," she joked.

"Yeah, but I'm going to fix it. I made some New Year's resolutions. You want to see something . . . ?"

"Well, I don't have much time now, but I'll come back. . . ."

"Whenever you like. I'm here every day of the week."

It goes without saying that I never saw the girl again—it was just to show how bright things looked to me. That was the day I plugged the telephone back in; the day I shoved my face into a pile of her T-shirts, smiling; the day I finally looked at a box of Kleenex without trembling. It was that day that I learned that you never stop learning—that the stairway goes on forever. What did you think? I asked myself, while slicing a melon before bed. I thought I heard laughter behind my back, coming from the direction of the melon seeds.

My book came out about a month after Betty's death. My associate was a fast worker, to say the least. He was still a small publisher. I must have come along when he had little else to do. One morning I found myself with a book on my lap. I turned it over in my hands. I opened it. I sniffed the paper. I slapped myself on the thigh.

"Oh, baby, look what's finally happened," I whispered.

Bob decided to celebrate. We took a little trip. Grandma watched the kids. Bob and Annie brought me home early in the morning. We couldn't tell if you were laughing or crying, they told me later. How should I know, I answered. It's not always easy to know if you're attending a funeral or a birth. Writers' brains are no more atrophied than anyone else's. Despite what I've become, I'm still in the same boat as everyone else—I have more than my share of things I don't understand. There must be a Saint Christopher for writers who are a little soft in the head.

Some guy from a small regional newspaper wrote that I was a

genius. My publisher sent me the article. I'm not sending you the others, he said—they're bad. Applause in one corner, boos and hisses in the other. Still, the summer went by calmly, and I found my pace once again. I got along fine. The store was open. I installed a bell on the second floor that rang when someone opened the door downstairs. It didn't happen too often. I gave up the idea of moving, though I'd thought it over more than once. Maybe later I wouldn't be against it, once my book was finished. For the time being, though, I wanted to stay put. The light in the house during the day was great—giant splashes of brightness and shadows; who could ask for anything more? The atmosphere was enough to make you drool. The Rolls-Royce of atmospheres for a writer.

Toward evening, I'd take walks, and if the spirit moved me, I'd go sit at a sidewalk café and watch the eyes go by in the twilight. It got me out of the house. I listened to the people talking among themselves. I sipped my drink slowly, swallowing the last drop fifty times before I decided to head home. There was nothing to rush for, and nothing to hold me.

Once I'd plugged the telephone back in, Eddie called me regularly.

"Jesus Christ, we're up to our ears in work just now. Can't come down . . ."

He said this every time. Then Lisa would take the phone and tell me she missed me.

"I miss you," she would say.

"Yeah, Lisa, same here."

"Keep taking good care of her," she'd add. "Don't ever forget her. . . ."

"No, don't worry."

Then she'd hand Eddie back over.

"Hi, it's me. Listen, you know that if anything happens we'll be there in a hurry . . . you know that . . . you're not alone, you know. . . ."

"Of course I know that."

"Maybe in two weeks or so we can come down. . . ."

"Great. Love to see you."

"Anyway, in the meantime take care. . . ."

"Right, man. You too."

"Right . . . Lisa is motioning to me to say she misses you. . . ."

"Tell her same here."

"You'll let me know if anything . . . you sure you're all right . . . ?"

"Yes, the worst is over."

"Right, well, we think of you often. Anyway, I'll call again soon."

"Fine, Eddie, I'll be waiting. . . ."

It was the kind of phone call that made me melancholy. It was like getting a postcard from the other end of the world that says I LOVE YOU, if you get my drift. If there was something not too horrible on TV, I'd just plop myself down in front of it, with a box of candy on my lap. Going to bed would be a little tougher. Don't forget her, she'd said. . . . Are you sure everything's all right, he'd asked. . . . The worst is over, I'd answered. This is how a large bed becomes a bed for two again, and I would lie down on it like it was a bed of coals. Later, people would ask me how I managed during this period—what I did for sex. But I just told them, Nice of you to ask, don't worry about it—why should I bore you with my troubles? Isn't there something else you'd like to talk about? People always want to know how famous people live, otherwise they don't sleep well at night—it's nuts.

All this to say that I began to live normally again—Life, the standard model: highs and lows, part of me believing in Heaven and part of me not. I wrote, I paid my bills, I changed the sheets once a week, I killed time, I took walks, I had drinks with Bob, I stole peeks at Annie's thing, I kept track of sales, I changed the oil in the car regularly, I didn't write back to my fans, or to the others; and I used my more peaceful moments to think of her. It isn't rare that I still find her in my arms. Under such conditions, I never expected anything to happen to me. Especially nothing like what happened. But you should never assume that you've made your last trip to the checkout counter. There will always be something you haven't paid for yet.

It was a day like any other, except that I'd gone to the trouble of making myself a nice pot of chili. I'd gotten up out of my chair several times during the afternoon to taste it. It made me smile. I hadn't lost my touch. I just had to make sure it didn't stick to the bottom. When the writing was going well, I was always in a good mood . . . and with chili as a reward I was practically in paradise. When I had chili I heard her laughing.

When I noticed it getting dark, I closed my notebook. I got up to pour myself two fingers of gin with a few necessary ice cubes. I set the table without letting go of my glass. There were still a few red streaks in the sky, but it was the color of the chili that interested me, and a lovely color it was.

I served myself a big helping. It was a little too hot to eat, so I sat back peacefully with my drink and put on some music. Not just any music, but "This Must Be the Place," which I love so much. I closed my eyes. Everything was copacetic. I rang my ice cubes like little bells.

I was so into it that I didn't hear them come in. I couldn't have been more relaxed. The house was flooded with the smell of chili. The blow to my arm paralyzed it. The pain made me fall over in my chair. I tried to grab onto the table but all I did was tip over half my plate, falling down on the tile. I thought they must have used a crowbar on me. I yelled. A kick in the stomach took my breath away. I rolled over on my back, drooling. Somehow, through the fog, I managed to see them. There were two of them, a big one and a little one. I didn't recognize them right away— they weren't in uniform, and I'd long since forgotten the episode.

"Scream again and I'll cut you into little pieces," the fat one said.

I tried to get my breath back, but it was like someone had

doused me with gasoline. The fat one took his front teeth out of his mouth and held them up in his hand.

"Perhapth you recognithe me better like thith," he thaid.

I curled up slightly on the linoleum. I couldn't take it—not this. The fat one was Henry, the one whose big toe I'd shot off, and the little one was my lover boy, the one I'd enchanted, the one who wanted to go away with me. For a second, a vision of myself running across the fields with a purse full of bills passed before my eyes—only now the scene took place in twilight, filmed through a frozen lake. Henry let out a little whine as he put his teeth back in, then he came at me, all red in the face. I got his foot in my head. Had it been twenty years earlier, when men wore heavier shoes, I would have woken up in a hospital. Today my aggressors wore tennis shoes. The shoes had plastic soles on them—I'd seen them on sale at the supermarket—they were worth about the price of a pound of sugar. All Henry did was give me a slight cut on the side of my mouth. He seemed very agitated.

"Shit, I can't let myself get too worked up," he complained. "I've got to take my time. . . ."

He grabbed the bottle of wine off the table and turned to the kid, who was staring at me.

"Come on, let's have a drink. Don't just stand there like a jerk. I told you he wasn't a woman."

While they were drinking, I sat up a little. I had practically gotten my wind back, but my arm was useless. There was blood running down my clean T-shirt. Henry emptied his glass, smiling at me out of the corner of his eye.

"I'm glad to see you're getting your strength back," he said. "So we can talk a little."

That's when I saw what he had, slipped through his belt—suddenly I couldn't see anything else. With the silencer, it made a hell of a big gun. I knew he had used it to smash my arm. I nearly hiccuped. I felt as if I'd just swallowed a toad. I wished I were invisible. The young man looked like he'd been struck by lightning—he hardly touched his drink. Henry poured himself another. His skin was shiny, like the skin of someone who's just wolfed down three pepperoni sandwiches and half a dozen beers on a stifling summer night, electricity in the air. He came and stood in front of me.

"So . . . aren't you amazed to see me?" he said. "Isn't this a nice surprise?"

I preferred to look at the floor. He grabbed a handful of my hair.

"I told you you'd signed your death warrant, remember? Thought I was kidding? I never kid."

He slammed my head into the wall. I heard bells.

"Now," he went on. "You're probably thinking, what took me so long to find you? I have other things to do, you know—I only worked on this during weekends."

He went back and got another drink. On his way, he stuck his finger in the chili.

"Hmmm . . . delicious," he said.

The other one hadn't moved an inch. All he could do was stare at me. Henry shook him a little:

"What the fuck is wrong with you? What are you waiting for—search the place!"

He didn't seem to be feeling well. He set his half-full glass on the table and turned to Henry.

"God, are you really sure that's him . . . ?"

Henry squinted.

"Look, do what I say and don't get on my nerves—you get me, little pal?"

The little pal nodded and left the kitchen, sighing. He wasn't the only one who felt like sighing. Henry dragged a chair up next to me and sat down. I think he must have had a thing for grabbing people by the hair. He didn't stand on ceremony—it was like he was determined to pull it out by the roots. It wouldn't have surprised me if half of it had stayed in his hand. He leaned toward me. It no longer smelled like chili in the house—it smelled more like hemlock.

"Hey, have you noticed that I walk with a slight limp? You seen that? It's because I don't have a big toe anymore, see, it makes me lose my balance. . . ."

He sent his elbow into my nose, thus adding it to the ranks of my useless arm, my split lip, and the huge bump on the back of my head. It was not very late, and he didn't seem anxious to go home to bed. I wiped at the blood running down my chin. He didn't let me recover. It wasn't that I was suffering so much, it's just that the pain came from all over at once. It was as if I'd been plunged into a bath that was slightly too scalding. I couldn't analyze the situation coolly. I couldn't do much of anything.

"Okay, now I'll let you in on how I found you. Tough luck for you, it was me you were dealing with—I was a cop for six years."

He let go of my hair to light a cigarette. He's going to put it out in my ear, I thought. He blew a few smoke rings at me. He looked like he'd just won the lottery, his eyes in the air.

"First, I asked myself why you went out the back way, and why nobody heard the car start. It bugged me. I said to myself, that bitch couldn't have come here on foot, she must have parked her car far away to keep it from being spotted. You dig how the Wonderboy's mind works . . . ?"

I nodded. I didn't want to piss him off. I wanted him to forget about the cigarette. I bitterly regretted having done that to his foot. I regretted that all this had to happen to me on the night I was about to dig into a bowl of chili—a night when life seemed almost gentle. He was not the kind of person I could have asked to let me finish my novel.

"So I took a stroll out in back," he went on. "Running it through my brain, I climbed up onto the railroad track. And what do you think I saw, buddy boy? THE SUPERMARKET PARK- ING LOT! Yeah, you got it. And I got to tell you something— that was pretty clever. I walked down there tipping my hat to you. My foot hurt, but I had to give you the parking lot!"

He flicked his cigarette butt out the open window, then bent over me, sporting a horrible, sexual grimace. I didn't deserve a death whose face was so hideous. I was a writer, interested only in Beauty. Henry shook his head slowly.

"I can't tell you the feeling I had when I came across your little Kleenex tissues. They were all in a bright little pile, calling out to me. I picked them up, but I'd already figured it out. I said to myself, for a broad, he sure has some balls. . . ."

I wished he would talk about something else, that he wouldn't all of a sudden get obsessed with that part of my anatomy—you never know what goes through the mind of someone like him. I heard the other one pulling drawers out in the apartment. It had taken me a long time to rebuild the pieces of my life—but I'd been sent these two to remind me of the fragility of all things. Did I need to be reminded?

Henry mopped his brow, never taking his eyes off me. The grease came back almost immediately, shining like a quartz field in the moonlight.

"You know what I did next? Well, tough luck again; the supermarket manager is my wife's cousin, and I never let him forget it—he can't refuse me anything. So I got the names and addresses of everyone who'd paid by check that day, then went to see them all, one by one, asking if they hadn't noticed anything fishy in the parking lot the day in question. You bastard, I almost lost you there. . . . Just then we were even-steven. . . . I thrived on it, you know . . . the chase. . . ."

He turned around and took the wine off the table. What I wouldn't have given for a big glass of water and a handful of sleeping pills. I wasn't particularly interested in how he'd found me—I'm not a detective-story freak. But what else could I do, except listen? I breathed out of my mouth—my nose was plugged with blood. He drained the last drop of wine, then stood up. One of his hands plunged into my hair.

"Come over here," he said. "I can't see you where you are."

He dragged me over to the table and sat me down on a chair under the lamp. Three drops of blood plopped into my bowl of chili. He walked around the table and sat down in front of me—

he pulled out his gun. He aimed it at my head, leaning both hands on the table for stability. His fingers were knitted around the butt, except for his index fingers, which were wound around the trigger. They didn't have much room to move—I hoped he wouldn't sneeze. Each second that passed made me happy to be alive. He smiled.

"So, to finish the story," he went on. "I came across this woman who had written a check for her ironing board, and she told me: 'Oh yes, Sir, I did see this blonde woman, loitering in a yellow car. I even noticed that it was a yellow Mercedes, with a local license plate, and even that she was wearing sunglasses.' Well, I can tell you . . . it was a Sunday afternoon, not too late, and I went and sat down at a sidewalk café, thinking of you— thanking you very much for the help. I'm the grateful type, see. Cars like yours . . . there aren't a whole lot of them in these parts—in fact, there's only one."

I jolted ridiculously—the kind of jolt I'd file under Taking a Kick at the Great Wall of China. I tried to play coy. I shook my head.

"I don't understand," I said. "I've had that car stolen from me twenty times. . . ."

Henry got a big kick out of this. He grabbed me by the T-shirt and yanked me onto the table. I felt the tip of the silencer against my throat. I was putty in his hands. It might have made a difference if I had tried to defend myself, who knows—he was older than me and was starting to get pretty drunk. Maybe if I'd really gone nuts I could have turned things around—it's not impossible. But I knew that I didn't have it in me. I couldn't have gotten my motor to turn over. Try as I might, I couldn't get mad, I just couldn't. I was too tired—more tired than I'd ever been. I would have been right at home on the side of the road somewhere, a small lukewarm sunset for my nightlight, a few blades of grass, and *basta*.

The young one came back just as Henry was starting to say something. He threw me back in my chair so hard that I tipped

over backward and sprawled out on the tile. I was like a bump on
a log with my dead arm. I went down hard, like at the end of a
fifteen-rounder. I decided to stay down for the count. Nowhere
was it written that I had to stand up and go calmly toward the
torture chamber. I didn't budge, I didn't even move my leg,
which remained twisted in midair, my heel coming to perch on
a leg of the overturned chair.

I asked myself if the light bulb that hung from the ceiling
wasn't a 200-watter—if that wasn't why I found myself blinking,
or was it perhaps the satchel that the young one was holding in
his hands. He looked rather pale. He lifted it up slowly, though
it wasn't very heavy. It took quite a while for him to maneuver
it onto the corner of the table. We wondered what the hell was
wrong with him, Henry and I.

"I found this," he murmured.

Suddenly I felt sorry for him—he seemed to have lost his faith
in everything. He seemed sad. Henry didn't try to console him:
he grabbed the sack of bills and opened it up wide.

"Oh, Jesus . . . !" he said.

He shoved his hands into it. I heard the crinkling of bills, but
what he took out were my falsies and my wig. He held them up
to the light, like a river of diamonds.

"Oh my God in Heaven!" he wheezed.

I couldn't tell you why I'd kept those old things, or why I'd
decided to put them back in the satchel. I assume I'm not the only
one who does things he doesn't understand, for whom things
seem to organize themselves to their own ends, dizzying him,
pulling him by the hand and God knows what else. Had I been
able to dig myself a hole in the kitchen linoleum, I certainly would
have.

"It's Josephine . . ." the unhappy fellow sighed.

"No shit, Sherlock!" said Henry.

All at once the kitchen changed color—it turned all white. My
ears started ringing at full speed. Before I could get my leg out
of the way, Henry took aim at my big toe and fired. The pain went

up to my shoulder—I saw blood spurting from my shoe like a poison fountain. Oddly enough, it was then that the feeling came back into my arm. I grabbed the chair leg with both hands, pushing my forehead into the floor. Henry jumped on me and turned me back over. He was breathing heavily, sweat beading in his eyebrows and dripping onto my face. His eyes were two baby vultures with their beaks open wide. He grabbed my T-shirt.

"Come here, pretty boy, come here, baby. . . . I'm not finished with you yet!"

He picked me up and threw me onto a chair. He was smiling and grimacing at the same time. He was really into it, running his tongue over his lips and talking to the young man:

"Okay, now we're going to take him for a ride. Find me something to tie him up with. . . ."

The young one shoved his hands in his pockets, looking like a beaten dog.

"Listen, Henry, I think this has gone far enough. Let's just call the police. . . ."

Henry made an obscene noise with his mouth. I was looking at my foot—the eruption of Mount Vesuvius.

"You poor kid," he said. "You're really a little jerk. You don't know me very well. . . ."

"But Henry . . ."

"God damn it, you asked to come with me, now do what I say! I'm not about to give him over to the cops, so he'll be out in three months. Jesus Christ, after what he did to me . . . Jesus Christ! You must be kidding!"

"Yeah, but Henry, we're not authorized to . . ."

Henry went crazy—I thought he was going to start beating on him. They argued, but I couldn't understand all that they were saying—I had just noticed a small stream of lava spurting out of the west flank of my shoe. It burned so much that I couldn't get near it with my hand. I don't know what they decided, but when I lifted my head back up Henry was putting the falsies on me. He got a little worked up over the hooks in back. The other one was standing in front of me. We stared at each other. I sent him a silent message. Help me, I told him. I'm a doomed writer. Henry screwed the wig onto my head.

"So . . . now do you recognize him?" he shouted. "This the little whore, or what? Is this what you got all weak in the knees about? This?"

The young one bit his lip. I just stayed there, not moving. There was obviously nothing that could get me angry—I wondered if there ever would be again. Just then, though, I felt myself flowing toward the waves, sinking into the ocean. Henry looked like an oil well on fire. His fury had turned him red-orange. He grabbed my last-hope's arm and threw his head between my breasts, then started throttling the two of us.

"All right, God damn it!!" he screamed. "Is THAT what you want? Is that what you had in mind, you fucking little creep . . . ?"

The young guy tried to get away. His hair smelled of cheap cologne. He whined and cried in a smothered voice. I was afraid he was going to step on my wounded foot. Then Henry pulled him backward and flung him into the table. The chili almost went all over him. The kid was on the verge of tears, red splotches all over his face. Henry put his hands on his hips—a horrific smile on his face, and his stench permeating the room.

"So, asshole . . ." he said. "You going to go get me that rope now?"

Henry held his forearm up in front of his face. A bullet, however, goes easily through a forearm, then continues through the skull, and if there is nothing behind it except an open window, goes right on whistling over the rooftops, disappearing in the night on its way to Bullet Heaven. Henry slid to the floor. The young man put the gun back on the table and slumped into a chair. I've never seen hide nor hair of the kind of silence that came down on us then.

*   *   *

His elbow propped on the table, he looked at the floor. I took my wig off and tossed it in the corner. I popped the hook of the bra—it fell onto my lap. I was exhausted. I had to stop to catch my breath. The kitchen was a block of translucent resin, shot in the air and endlessly spinning. I never knew that I loved life so much—this is what I thought as I sat there rubbing my busted lip. It hurt a little. You really have to love it to keep on going against all the suffering—to have what it takes to reach out and grab a few aspirin tablets.

There was a bottle of them in the drawer. I always keep aspirin nearby—this shows that I've been around. I put three of the little white jobs on my tongue.

"Want some?" I asked.

He shook his head without looking at me. I knew what he was thinking. I didn't insist. I breathed out heavily, then bent over toward my shoe. The general sensation was one of having left my leg in a campfire, smoldering in the coals at dawn. I grabbed the rope sole and slipped my shoe off delicately, as if I were undressing a sleeping dragonfly. I had to admit that it was a miracle—I'd call it that—a bullet that goes right between two toes, leaving only a bit of torn skin, a little slice of destiny. I stood up, straddling Henry without feeling a thing, then went and drank a tall glass of water.

"I'll help you carry him downstairs," I said. "Take him as far away as you can."

He didn't move. I went around behind him and helped him stand up. He wasn't in good shape. He held onto the table without saying a word.

"You and I would both do well to forget this whole affair," I suggested.

I took a few handfuls of bills out of the satchel and stuffed them in his pocket. He had two or three hairs on his chest, tops. He didn't argue.

"You got to learn how to open the door when opportunity knocks," I said. "Take his legs."

We dragged him. It was like dragging a dead whale down the stairs. No one outside—minimal moon, small wind. Their car was parked right in front. We jammed Henry into the trunk. I went back upstairs as fast as I could, grabbed the gun with the bottom of my T-shirt, then limped back down. He was already sitting behind the wheel. I knocked on the glass.

"Open the window," I said.

I slipped him the gun.

"When you're done, go bury this at the North Pole," I said. He nodded, looking straight ahead.

"Drive smart," I told him. "Don't get noticed."

"Yes," he muttered.

I sniffled, both hands on the roof of the car. I looked up the street.

"Remember what Kerouac said," I sighed. "The jewel—the real center—is the eye within the eye."

I gave the fender a slap as he pulled away. I went back upstairs.

I took care of my foot. I cleaned the place up a little—the urgent things. To tell the truth, it was almost as if nothing had happened. I put the chili back in the saucepan over a low flame. I put the music back on. The cat came in through the window. The night was calm.

"I saw the lights on," he said. "Were you writing . . . ?"

"No," I said. "Just thinking."

THE TASTE OF A MAN

Slavenka Drakulić

One autumn in New York, a young Polish poet, studying literature, and a Brazilian anthropologist researching a new book, meet, fall in love and move into a tiny apartment together. Tereza has a lover waiting for her in Poland, Jose a wife and child in Sao Paulo, and it would seem this could only be the most temporary of affairs. Yet, as Tereza recounts the extraordinary substance of their lives together, there emerges the mesmerizingly explicit portrait of a relationship conducted at the extreme edge of sensuality, defying conventional definition. Jose and Tereza are needy, starving children in the land of plenty; with no common language, exiled from their culture, for each of them the body of the other becomes everything: spirituality, sustenance, almost unbearable pleasure.

Breathtakingly erotic, intensely physical, profoundly intelligent, *The Taste of a Man* pursues the path traced by a love based on pure appetite with shameless and unflinching candour, to its ecstatic and terrible conclusion.

'A disturbingly insightful novel of love gone wrong . . . gruesome and highly accomplished'
Time Out

Abacus
978-0-349-10866-7

SEX AND THE CITY

Candace Bushnell

'Wildly funny, unexpectedly poignant, wickedly observant, and now a major television series, *Sex and the City* blazes a glorious, drunken cocktail trail through New York as Candace Bushnell, columnist and social critic *par excellence,* trips on her Manolo Blahnik kitten heels from the Baby Doll Lounge to the Bowery Bar. An Armistead Maupin for the real world, she has the gift of assembling a huge and irresistible cast of freaks and wonders, while remaining faithful to her hard core of friends and fans: those glamorous, rebellious, crazy single women, who are trying hard not to turn from the Audrey Hepburn of *Breakfast at Tiffany's* into the Glenn Close of *Fatal Attraction,* and are – still – looking for love.

'Intriguing and highly entertaining' Helen Fielding, author of
Bridget Jones' Diary

'Irresistible, hilarious and horrific, stylishly written . . . Candace Bushnell has captured the big black truth'
Bret Easton Ellis

'Jane Austen with a martini, or perhaps Jonathan Swift on rollerblades' *Sunday Telegraph*

'Hilarious . . . a compulsively readable book, served up in bite-sized chunks of irrepressible irreverence'
Marie Claire

Abacus
978-0-349-13898-5

FOUR BLONDES

Candace Bushnell

With its uncensored observations of the mating rituals of
Manhattan's elite, Candace Bushnell's *Sex and the City* created a
sensation. Now, with *Four Blondes,* Bushnell triumphantly returns
to the playgrounds of the beautiful and powerful – once again
capturing the essence of our era, like no other writer.

Four Blondes charts the romantic intrigues, liaisons, betrayals and
victories of four modern women: a beautiful B-list model scams
rent-free summerhouses in the Hamptons from her lovers until she
discovers she can get a man but can't get what she wants; a high-
powered magazine columnist's floundering marriage to a literary
journalist is thrown into crisis when her husband's career fails to
live up to her expectations; a 'Cinderella' records her descent into
paranoia in her journal as she realises she wants anybody's life
except her own; an artist and aging 'It girl' – who fears that her
time for finding a man has run out – travels to London in search of
the kind of love and devotion she can't find in Manhattan . . .

Studded with her trademark wit and stiletto-heel-sharp insight,
Four Blondes is dark, true, and compulsively readable.

Abacus
978-0-349-11403-3